Michelle Douglas has been [writing] since 2007, and believes sh[e has the best job in the] world. She lives in a leafy su[burb of Newcastle,] Australia's east coast, with her own romantic hero, a house full of dust and books and an eclectic collection of sixties and seventies vinyl. She loves to hear from readers and can be contacted via her website: michelle-douglas.com.

Justine Lewis writes uplifting, heart-warming contemporary romances. She lives in Australia with her hero husband, two teenagers and an outgoing puppy. When she isn't writing she loves to walk her dog in the bush near her house, attempt to keep her garden alive and search for the perfect frock. She loves hearing from readers and you can visit her at justinelewis.com.

TEMPTED BY HER GREEK ISLAND BODYGUARD

MICHELLE DOUGLAS

THE BILLIONAIRE'S PLUS-ONE DEAL

JUSTINE LEWIS

MILLS & BOON

First published in Great Britain 2024
by Mills & Boon, an imprint of HarperCollins*Publishers* Ltd,
1 London Bridge Street, London, SE1 9GF

www.harpercollins.co.uk

HarperCollins*Publishers*, Macken House, 39/40 Mayor Street Upper,
Dublin 1, D01 C9W8, Ireland

Tempted by Her Greek Island Bodyguard © 2024 Michelle Douglas

The Billionaire's Plus-One Deal © 2024 Justine Lewis

ISBN: 978-0-263-32135-7

07/24

TEMPTED BY HER GREEK ISLAND BODYGUARD

MICHELLE DOUGLAS

MILLS & BOON

To my splendid book group: Gerda, Alex, Deb, Janet (Epi), Janet (Hemm), Trisha, Anne, Gwenda and Lucy (not to mention all of our past members).

A huge thank you for all of the books we've read together over the years, for the discussions and laughter…and the red wine.

Looking forward to our future reading lists, spirited opinions and laughter.

CHAPTER ONE

ZACH'S FINGERS TIGHTENED around his phone. 'What the hell, Sarge? *No!*'

'Too late, soldier.'

Gray, Zach's ex-sergeant from the elite squad he'd served with for eight years, actually used his sergeant's voice. *His sergeant's voice.* Even though when Zach, Gray and Logan had left the army they'd agreed they were equal partners in the business they'd formed—Sentry Protective Services.

His nostrils flared. 'You're not putting me out to grass yet.' He was still in his prime. He thrust out his jaw. Forty-four was still one's prime.

As long as he didn't dwell too much on how his knee ached after completing the army obstacle course he used for training. Or how his muscles ached for days and the bruises took longer to fade after a bout in the ring with Logan.

He could still run a mile in under seven minutes. He could do a hundred sit-ups followed by a hundred push-ups without breaking a sweat. He was a lean, mean fighting machine, thank you very much.

'I'm not ready to retire,' he barked into his phone.

'I'm not talking about retirement, Zach. I'm talking about you stepping up and taking on a more managerial role in the company.'

He gritted his teeth. 'I'm not ready to retire from *the field.* I'm not a darn pen-pusher.'

'Then it's about time you damn well became one!'

He blinked.

'Damn it, Zach, I'm not getting any younger.'

Two damns in as many sentences. Zach's senses went on high alert.

'We need a succession plan.'

What on earth...? 'You're not sixty yet!'

'And you need to loosen the reins and start letting Brett and Francine head up some of the assignments.'

Brett and Francine? They were kids!

He opened his mouth, but before he could speak Sarge barrelled on. 'Hell, Zach, you need to get a life soon or it'll be too late.'

Too late for what?

His back molars ground together. 'I have a life, thank you very much.'

'Work isn't a life—it's a poor substitute for one. Age is supposed to bring wisdom, but you keep burying your head in the sand. It's time to stop. And if you won't see sense on this then you and Logan can buy me out.'

His head rocked back, his mind racing. Sarge had been due a physical this week. Had he had bad news? Cold sweat bathed his neck. The man was the closest thing he had to a father. He moistened his lips. 'Look, Sarge—'

'I *need* you to take this assignment, it's important to the business. There's no one else who can do it. They're expecting you in thirty minutes.' He repeated the address. 'Be there.'

The line went dead.

Striding out into a crowded London street, Zach hailed a cab, gave the Knightsbridge address to the driver and immediately rang Logan, swearing when the call went to voicemail. He didn't leave a message, didn't know how to verbalise the fears chasing through his mind.

Twenty minutes later he found himself alone in a ground

floor room—a library—in one of Knightsbridge's mansions, waiting to speak to the client. His phone vibrated in his pocket. *Logan.*

Striding across to the window to stare out at the massive green square with its immaculate rose garden and towering maple trees, he lifted the phone to his ear. 'Logan.'

'What's up?'

'Did Sarge get a bad report on his physical?'

A heartbeat of silence sounded. 'Not that I know about. Why?'

'Because he's pulled me off the South American job for a domestic assignment—*a dolly assignment.*' He ground his teeth together so hard he started to shake. He was supposed to be shadowing a South American diplomat who a local militia group were targeting. It was the kind of job that demanded his all—every skill, every instinct, every nerve. The kind of job he loved.

Air whistled down the line. 'Pulled rank, huh? Interesting. And Zach, unclench your jaw. You're going to break a tooth.'

That was the problem when you worked with people who knew you so well. They *knew* you.

'Tell me what he said.'

He repeated the conversation.

'Look, you know he's been wanting you to bone up on other aspects of the business—'

'But—'

'And it makes sense. What if one of us gets sick or injured? The others are going to have to step up. You've avoided the management side of things for long enough. I'm with Sarge on this one.'

It took force of will not to clench his jaw again. 'We always knew where my skills lay. I made no secret of it.'

'Well, maybe it's time to upskill, buddy. Prove the old adage wrong, prove that you can teach an old dog new tricks.'

He wasn't *old*!

'How can you train others for what you call a dolly assignment when you never take one on? You know they're our bread and butter. They bring in the money.'

True, but—

'And you're going to have to do this for Sarge. You know that, right?'

That was the kicker. He *was* going to have to do this.

'Don't worry, I'm toeing the line. I'm about to meet with the client.'

'I'll find out what I can about the physical. What job has he put you on?'

His nose curled. 'Apparently I have to babysit some pampered little daddy's girl while she swans around some frivolous socialite scene spending a fortune on hats and shoes while throwing the odd penny to some unnecessary charity or other.' He had visions of endless garden parties and black-tie events and—

Oh, God. 'Just kill me now.'

Logan's laugh hooted down the line. 'You watch your back, mate. From all accounts those society madams can be deadly. Which daddy's little girl in particular?'

'Plain Jane.'

He used the press moniker without thinking. Because he was still incensed at being pulled from the South American job. And as a displacement activity, because beneath everything ran a deep fear that all was not well with Sarge, and if anything happened to the older man...

The delicate sound of a throat clearing in the doorway had him swinging around. He froze. He'd have cursed except his throat had seized up.

Jane Tierney stood in the doorway, one delicate eyebrow arched. And seeing her for the first time with his own eyes, rather than via random photographs splashed across the papers, *plain* wasn't the first word that came to Zach's mind.

She hip-swayed into the room. 'I'll wear the daddy's girl comment, and I'll own to many attempts at swanning—which I almost have down pat, thanks for asking—but I draw the line at *unnecessary* charities.' Turning to survey him once more, she sank to the sofa and crossed remarkably shapely legs. 'And, just so you know, I don't like hats.'

Logan swore at the other end of the line, clearly hearing her words too. 'You smooth this over and make it right, Zach. Her father has influence—a lot of influence. Don't mess this up for us.'

'Roger that.' He stuffed his phone in his pocket and tried to formulate an appropriate apology.

She leaned back, for all the world as composed as a queen. 'Mr Cartwright, I presume?' She had a voice like warm honey and sin, and soft caramel eyes that momentarily danced.

He swallowed and nodded, resisting the urge to run a finger around his collar. She deserved an apology and he needed to make it good.

The laughter melted from her eyes and while he hadn't thought a smile graced her lips, it melted from them as well. She folded her hands in her lap—the fingers long, the nails short and square. 'The Plain Jane comment, though, should've been beneath you.'

He dragged a hand down his face. It *really* should've been.

'I'm sorry, Ms Tierney. That was inexcusable. I was angry about something totally unrelated to you.'

'Except for the fact that you apparently now have to baby-sit me.'

Fighting a wince, he forged on. 'And worried about someone I care about.'

'Sarge?'

How long had she been standing there?

'I directed all of that at you, unfairly. Just…venting. But none of that changes the fact that I shouldn't have said it.'

She blinked.

'I'm truly sorry. I hope you'll accept my apology and let me start again.'

Sarge had said this job meant a lot to them—so it meant a lot to *him*. Zach couldn't mess it up. If he did, he'd never convince the older man that he hadn't sabotaged the assignment on purpose. His hands clenched. He might be as stubborn as his partners accused him of being, but he wasn't selfish. At least, he hoped he wasn't.

Jane Tierney stared at his clenched hands and a frown marred the smooth skin between her eyes.

'I'm appalled at my lack of professionalism. It won't happen again, I swear.'

She leaned back, her shoulders loosening. 'Oddly enough, I believe you.'

A pent-up breath eased out of him. Jane Tierney was the daughter of music legend Joey Walter and lauded actress Colleen Clements. Those two, while no longer married, were rarely out of the papers. To call this family high-profile was an understatement. Their daughter mightn't court the media but she had no hope of avoiding it, no matter how much of a low profile she tried to keep.

'Very well, you're forgiven.'

He almost collapsed at the relief and a devilish dimple appeared in one of her cheeks and it made him think she'd deliberately drawn out his punishment to make him suffer.

If that were the case, it was no more than he deserved. But things inside him sharpened. He'd now need to keep a close eye on her. Not everyone he worked with reconciled themselves to the need for a bodyguard. And if he was being thrust on her against her will, she might try and give him the slip at every available opportunity.

She might not be in any actual danger, hiring him might be a precautionary measure as it was in ninety-five percent of these cases, but he had every intention of treating the assignment as seriously as any other.

A low laugh hauled him back. 'Your face is very easy to read, Mr Cartwright.'

'I make no apology for that. Reading my face could save your life. And please, call me Zach.'

Those shapely brows lifted. 'Well, let me put your mind at rest and assure you I've no intention of being uncooperative. Please, take a seat.'

He took the seat she indicated.

'As you can imagine, this isn't the first time my life has been threatened.'

He detested men who used violence as a weapon against women. And children. Loathed them. Men like his father, who'd used his fists to get his own way, to punish the voicing of a different opinion, or just because he'd felt the need to blow off steam. Men who took pride in the bruises they placed on the bodies of their wives and children, who laughed for days afterwards when they saw the welts and discolouring and said things like 'Serves you right' and 'You'll think twice before you open your mouth next time'. He'd love to rid the world of all such men.

'Heavens! I expect that expression might keep me safe too.'

Her eyes had gone wide and he shook himself back into the present, buried the vicious memories.

'Ms Tierney, what's different about these particular threats? Why would you call in Sentry rather than have your own team deal with it?'

Her nose wrinkled. It definitely wasn't plain. It was kind of cute. And while the face it graced might not be considered conventionally beautiful, it was...

Sweet?

Full of character?

Sexy. The word whispered through him, making things inside him clench in unfamiliar ways. His blood heated and a pulse in his throat burst to life.

'What the hell are the press thinking?' he burst out. 'You—' he pointed a finger at her '—are *not* plain.'

He looked as startled by his words as she was, and Janie didn't know whether to laugh or not.

The way he looked at her had things inside her melting.

Oh, stop it!

She didn't have time for such nonsense. Or patience for it either. After Sebastian, melting over any man was well and truly off the agenda.

Thoughts of Sebastian had acid churning in her stomach. The man had played her for a fool. For two years she'd had no idea of his real agenda. Love had made her blind. When she'd found out the truth it had crushed her, had shattered her sense of self-worth and self-esteem. Her self-respect. It had left her feeling as broken and ugly as the thirteen-year-old she'd once been after she'd first heard the tabloids' reprehensible Plain Jane nickname.

She pulled in a breath. She wasn't making that mistake again. She'd learned her lesson. Never again would she give any man the chance to make her feel so small.

So, no melting!

All the self-talk in the world, though, couldn't stop the light in Zach Cartwright's eyes from making her heart hammer. She'd been shocked at the size of him—a tall, broad man mountain. He wasn't one of those loose-limbed big guys either, but bristling with... She bit back a sigh. Currently he was bristling with irritation.

Not fabulous.

'When placed beside my parents, Mr Cart—'

Blue eyes narrowed.

'Zach,' she hastily amended. She needed this man to stop

being irritated with her. She needed him to not make her job harder. 'The fact is, beside my parents most people look plain.'

He dipped his head. 'There's probably something in that.'

Of course there was. If there was anyone who was an expert on the subject, it was her. Not that she resented them for it.

'People are always surprised when they meet me in the flesh.'

He didn't move a muscle, but she felt his wince. She winced too. She hadn't meant him to take it personally.

'As one esteemed member of the press told me—' she affected a cockney accent '—you're not a dog's dinner, miss, but it's the angles, you see. The camera just doesn't love you.'

She watched, fascinated, as one large hand clenched. 'If I hear anyone speak to you like that, I'll deck them.'

'You most certainly will not!' She shot to her feet. 'As my undercover bodyguard, I need you to be low-key and blend into the background.'

He stood too. 'Undercover?'

She bit back a sigh. He didn't know?

'With your height, that's going to be hard to pull off, though, isn't it?'

His nostrils flared as if she'd wounded his professional pride. 'I'm very good at my job, Ms Tierney. If I need to blend in then that's exactly what I'll do. And I'll do it well.'

This man would always stand out in the crowd. *Always*. And she should probably tell him to call her Janie, but… She recalled the words he'd spat into his phone and had to stop her shoulders from inching up towards her ears. He didn't want to be here. He'd made that abundantly, if unintentionally, clear. She either had to get him onside or get rid of him.

She moved a step closer, peered up into his face. 'What does my father have on you?'

Those compelling eyes narrowed again. 'What do you mean?'

'My father is many things, Mr Cartwright.' He opened his

mouth, but she held up her hand. 'I know you prefer Zach, but Mr Cartwright just rolls off the tongue. I enjoy saying it. And it still feels friendly, while being more respectful than Zach.'

One side of his mouth kicked upwards. 'Whatever turns you on, Ms Tierney.'

If she'd been drinking anything she would've choked, but then noted the teasing light in his eyes and had to bite back a grin.

'Your father is many things?' he prompted.

'And where I'm concerned, one of those things is over-protective.'

'I'm reliably informed that's a fault of many fathers.'

She digested that in silence. His father hadn't been like that? 'If my father has a weak spot, it's me. The thought of me being harmed is his worst nightmare.'

'And again, I'd say—'

'Yes, yes, I know. But most fathers don't have the money, power or reach of Joey Walter "King of Crooners" Tierney.'

'Ah.' Big hands rested against lean hips and just for a moment Janie found herself bombarded with unbidden—*forbidden*—images.

Her mouth went dry. Recent events had proven to her how *wrong* she could be about a man, and that begged the question: What else in her life had she been wrong about? She needed to keep a clear head. She wasn't letting hormones get in the way of all she needed to achieve.

Not when she had so *much* to achieve.

Strolling away a few paces to put some much-needed distance between herself and Zach's overpowering physicality, she turned and spread her hands. 'When his baby chick is threatened...'

He didn't say anything. He didn't even move—not so much as a flicker of an eyelash.

Fine, she'd spell it out. 'Joey Walter will do whatever he

deems necessary to keep me safe—and happy,' she added because her father hadn't crossed that line yet. 'You clearly don't want to be here. So what I'm wondering is how has my father convinced you to take on this job?'

Those blue eyes shifted from the middle distance back to her. 'I've had no communication with your father so far.'

'So it's your boss then.'

'Business partner.'

'What does my father have on your business partner?'

'I've no idea. Hopefully, nothing. But if he does, I'm going to find out what it is.'

The way he said it had gooseflesh breaking out on her arms. 'You don't know much about this job yet, do you?'

'No.'

No explanation accompanied the single word. He was cagey. In other circumstances she'd consider that an asset.

'Well, you're about to find out as there's a strategy meeting starting in—' she glanced at her watch and swore '—two minutes. I was hoping to fill you in on most of it myself, but we were side-tracked. We'd better head up to the boardroom. And we'd better get a move on.'

'Your house has a boardroom?'

'Tut-tut, Mr Cartwright, this is a complex—an entity unto itself—not a house.'

She led him up the stairs and took the corridor to the left in the direction of her father's business centre. Halting several feet short of the door, she swung around. Before she'd thought better of it, she seized his forearms. 'Can I ask you a favour?'

His brow pleated. 'Of course.'

The corded flesh beneath her fingertips pulsed with heat and power, immediately sensitising her to the fact that this was a hot-blooded man—an *attractive* hot-blooded man—who she was currently manhandling. She snatched her hands away.

His frown deepened. He leaned close until his lips were

only a hair's breadth from her ear. 'Are you in danger here, Jane?'

'Janie,' she automatically corrected. Closing her eyes, she hauled in a breath and tried to control her runaway pulse. The man was simply doing his job. 'No,' she forced out from uncooperative lips. 'At least, nothing a bodyguard would consider a danger.' Or could help her with.

'The favour?'

Straightening her spine, she forced her shoulders back. 'The project I'm about to embark on is really important to me. I don't have time to explain what it is now, but you'll find out soon enough. It's just...' Her hands twisted together. 'If you hate the thought of it, and if you don't think you can do it justice, will you please bow out?'

He dragged a hand down his face. 'If your father is blackmailing my business partner...'

Her stomach churned. His loyalty lay there, not with her. And she couldn't blame him for it, but—

'I promise you, though, that I'll keep you safe.'

'I don't want to be kept safe,' she hissed. 'I want to win!'

Before he could respond, the door flew open and her father stood there, beaming at her. 'I thought I heard voices. You're just in time, just in time.'

She submitted when he pulled her into a bear hug.

'How is my princess this morning?'

'Hi, Dad.' She kissed his cheek and then gestured to the man beside her. 'This is Zach Cartwright.'

Her father's paternal affability fell away as he made a long study of her potential bodyguard, taking his time as he sized him up, noting all of Zach's...potential. Zach, unlike most of the men subjected to her father's scrutiny, stood there unmoving and stared back, not a single emotion crossing his impressive face.

And it hit her in that moment that Zach's face was indeed as impressive as his size. He had regular features—a firm mouth that had an intriguing fullness to the lower lip, a strong square jaw and a nose slightly bent as if it had once been broken, which saved that face from being too pretty, too perfect. Short chestnut hair completed the package. She found herself wondering what that hair would look like if he grew it out a little.

'Well, at least he looks big enough to take a bullet for you, pumpkin.' He didn't offer to shake Zach's hand, but turned and headed back into the boardroom.

Janie rolled her eyes. 'Zach also has a sense of humour, which I consider a necessity in a bodyguard,' she called after him.

Just for a moment, blue eyes flashed with humour and Janie thought Zach might actually grin, but it was all quickly contained, his face becoming impassive again. This man rarely smiled.

'You can come and sit up here with me, princess.'

Nuh-uh. She wasn't allowing her father to infantilise her in front of all the people gathered in this room. She wanted—needed—Zach to respect her. Instead, she took the next seat on the left at the bottom of the long oval table, gesturing for Zach to take the seat opposite.

Gathered around the table were her father, his two PAs, the head of their own security detail and her usual bodyguard. She didn't know the man beside her, but she caught the look Zach exchanged with him.

The man turned, held out his hand. 'I'm Gray Garrison, Zach's business partner.'

Sarge? She shook it.

'Gray will be coordinating everything from a home base, the location of which, of course, is yet to be decided,' Joey Walter said.

'Before we discuss that…' Janie folded her hands lightly on

the table. 'Can we have a sensible discussion about whether this level of security is actually necessary?'

'Pumpkin, if you insist on continuing with this hare-brained scheme, it's absolutely necessary. Non-negotiable.'

'Three things, Father.' Joey Walter's eyes narrowed. He hated it when she called him Father, considered it too formal. 'One, the scheme is not hare-brained. Two, in business meetings you will refer to me as Janie or Jane.'

'Now listen here, pump—'

'Joey Walter!' He hated it even more when she called him by his name. Their eyes clashed and she was aware of the man opposite taking in this silent battle of wills.

'And three?' her father grumbled.

'Security is not your area of expertise. Let Gray and Zach assess the information, and then we'll listen to their recommendations for the most appropriate action plan.'

Her father merely hmphed and gestured to one of his PAs, who rose and distributed copies of the three threatening letters Janie had so far received. Janie refused her set. She'd read them once. She didn't need to read them again.

She watched Zach as he scanned the letters, his face growing sterner and grimmer. 'These are ugly.'

Ugly and frankly terrifying. She managed to maintain a stiff upper lip. 'The writer has quite an imagination.' The things the author of those letters threatened to do to her were *vile*. Very carefully, she folded her hands on the table. 'And yet threats are made against my father, my mother and me all the time. Should we give these letters more credence than any of the others?'

'We can't ignore the fact that these might have a personal element,' Gray said beside her. 'They might not, but the threats are…unusually specific.'

'I wouldn't want to take that chance either,' Zach agreed.

Not what she wanted to hear. But after a glance at those letters she suppressed a shudder and nodded. 'Okay. As I said, you guys are the experts. So now to my next question.' Joey Walter opened his mouth, but her glare silenced him. She had Zach's and Gray's full attention. 'Is it necessary for someone to actually be on set with me?'

'What do you mean, on set?' Zach leaned towards her, everything about him going on high alert. He drew the eye like a neon-lit billboard. How on earth would they ever convince an audience he wasn't anything other than what he was—a bodyguard?

'My darling daughter,' Joey Walter drawled, 'has agreed to take part in a reality TV show where contestants vie for a million pounds in prize money.'

'To be donated to the charity of their choice,' she inserted.

Zach's jaw tightened. 'And what do you have to do to win this prize money?'

'For *charity*,' she stressed again. She didn't want him forgetting that. 'The show is called *Renovation Revamp: The Resort Brief.*' Which she thought pretty self-explanatory. 'It involves renovating and styling a rundown resort in a glamorous location.' Pulling in a breath, she did what she could to calm the nerves fluttering in her stomach. 'There are six teams, and six different locations.'

'Where's your resort located?'

'It hasn't been decided yet. That happens during the filming of episode one.'

He held the fistful of letters up. 'You're seriously going to go ahead with that after receiving these?'

'Absolutely.' She gestured to herself and her father. 'If we let every threatening letter we receive frighten us we'd never leave the house. I can't live my life that way, Mr Cartwright. I refuse to.'

And she had too much to prove to walk away from this opportunity now.

CHAPTER TWO

ZACH LISTENED IN silence as Aaron, Joey Walter's head of security, outlined the role Zach was expected to play. Across the table, Janie stared at her neatly folded hands, not saying a word.

An ice-cold fist reached inside his chest. Those letters were appalling. And even though he knew that in the majority of cases things rarely escalated into anything more, acid burned in his stomach.

When Aaron's explanation came to an end, he understood why Sarge had chosen him. And it didn't make him any happier about being here.

He glanced at Janie again and something in his chest solidified. 'The police have been informed about the letters?'

Aaron nodded. 'They're investigating.'

What he didn't say, but what they all knew, was that there was very little evidence to go on and until the perpetrator of those threats actually made a move there was zero chance of the police catching him. Or her.

'Why aren't you dealing with it internally?' He ignored Sarge's narrowed glare. 'Using your own team?'

'Our faces are known,' Aaron said. 'We could've hired someone new but...'

They'd have wanted someone they could trust, and working relationships took time to build.

'Sentry have a proven track record. We want the best on this job.'

He, Sarge and Logan had worked hard to gain that reputation. He ought to be proud of it. He *was* proud of it. It didn't stop him wishing himself away to the South American rainforest, though.

He met Sarge's gaze. 'I want Drew, Janie's usual bodyguard, as part of the team.'

Sarge nodded. 'Exactly what I was thinking.'

'Oh, but...' Crestfallen golden eyes lifted.

He raised an eyebrow. 'Problem?'

'It's just Drew and power tools are not friends.' She grimaced in Drew's direction. 'Sorry, but this role requires DIY expertise.'

'It's true. I can make excellent use of them as weapons, but when it comes to using them for the purpose they were designed for...' Drew shook his head. 'It's not just power tools. It's all tools. I'm strong, though. I can lift heavy things, hold them in place for a long time. But Janie is already giving up her builder and it doesn't seem fair to weaken her team even further.'

It hit him in that moment how much Aaron and Drew *liked* Janie. They respected her father, but they liked her. Interesting.

He pulled his mind back to the problem at hand. Zach was being swapped in for her qualified builder and Janie was trying to maintain a brave face, but the way the light in her eyes had dimmed told its own story.

'You want someone on our detail on the job. Someone the perpetrator will recognise?' Aaron said.

'Surely he's only a perpetrator once he's committed a crime.'

The sharp edge to Janie's words had Zach stiffening. She'd

continually stressed that the prize money was for charity... Did he have a bleeding heart on his hands?

He recalled the fire in her eyes when she'd said, *'I want to win!'* She might be a bleeding heart, but she was a fighter too.

He stabbed a finger to the letters in front of him. 'Sending threatening letters like this *is* a crime.'

Swallowing, she glanced away.

Damn it. He shouldn't have been so harsh.

'Will it ease your disappointment if I tell you that I worked in construction for a number of years when I was younger?' Not that he'd had any choice, his father had forced Zach to work part-time in his building company from the age of fourteen. At sixteen he'd been hauled out of school to work for him full-time. 'My father was a builder. I not only recognise the majority of power tools, but know how to use them. And I'm a pretty decent carpenter.'

The light in her eyes brightened a fraction. 'Okay, well, that's something.'

'Nick has some handyman skills,' Drew said. 'We could—'

'He's newly married.' Janie shook her head, her caramel blonde hair bouncing. 'His wife is expecting a baby. He won't want to be away on set for nearly three months.' She tapped a finger to her lips. 'Darren!' Her face cleared. 'He's been renovating his own home.'

Her father stared. 'How do you know all this?'

Her chin lifted. 'How do you not?'

Zach watched another silent battle between the pair. Joey Walter clearly adored his daughter, but a cord of steel ran through the man and Zach wondered what lengths he'd go to in the interests of keeping his daughter safe, what lines he'd cross.

Over the next twenty minutes the larger scale details were thrashed out and then everyone stood to leave. Joey Walter stared down the table at Janie. 'Let me take you to The Ivy for lunch, princess.'

'Sorry, Dad. I've already promised Zach lunch.'

Zach found himself on the receiving end of a stony glare, before Joey Walter swept from the meeting through a door at the far end of the room, his PAs and security team hot on his heels.

Janie turned to him. 'I am actually hoping you're free for lunch, Mr Cartwright.'

The way she said his name! It made him want to grin. Except he wasn't much of a smiler.

'Zach's free for lunch, Ms Tierney,' Sarge said.

Zach glared at his partner. 'Except I need a quick word with Gray first, if that's okay with you, Janie?'

'Of course.'

She noted his glance at the cameras on the opposite wall and hitched her head in the direction of the door. Silently, she led them down the corridor and his gaze caught on the way her hair shone a particular shade of burnished gold when the light caught it.

'If you'd like a private word...'

He nodded. That's exactly what he wanted.

'Then let me suggest the library.'

Perfect.

She halted at the top of the stairs. 'Do you remember the way or would you like me to—'

'I remember perfectly. We'll be fine.'

She glanced at her watch. 'Then shall I meet you down there in fifteen minutes? If you need longer...?'

'Fifteen will be perfect.'

She started up the stairs for the second floor then turned back. 'Might I make a suggestion...? Close the library door behind you.'

Her father had bribed his staff to listen in at doors? He didn't raise the hair of even one eyebrow. 'Thank you.'

'I'll see you in fifteen minutes.' She took the stairs two at a time. 'And I should warn you—' that honeyed voice floated down to curl around him '—that I'm hideously prompt.'

Excellent. So was he.

'Look,' Sarge started as soon as Zach had closed the library door behind them. 'If this is more of the same—you registering your dissatisfaction—'

'Why is this job so important to you?'

Neither man sat. Sarge frowned. 'You know I want to expand this side of the business. If we do a good job on this assignment…'

If *he* did a good job.

'Joey Walter has a lot of sway, a lot of connections. With a single word he can open previously closed doors for us.'

'We've plenty of work coming in from our current client base.'

'I know you don't want to face the thought of no longer taking part in fieldwork, that you love danger and think you're indestructible and can keep doing it for ever. But no matter how fit and healthy you keep yourself, Zach, in another decade your body is going to start betraying you. And that will put you *and* the client in danger.'

But that was another ten years away and—

'And if you and Logan want to be in control of a thriving business when I retire, and Zach, I do mean to retire, then we need to start diversifying now.'

The thought had him swallowing. He should've realised this sooner. Sarge had taken him and Logan—both lost boys back then—under his wing. He wouldn't want to leave them high and dry. He'd want to make sure their futures, and the future of the company they'd built from scratch, were taken care of and in good shape.

'Logan sees the sense in this and is willing to embrace it. Why are you being so pig-headed?'

Because when he was working in the field he felt alive—more alive than he felt anywhere else. When he was working in the field there was no time to think, no time to let the past intrude, no time for anything else. And the thought that he was going to spend this assignment *building*. That their damn set was going to be a *construction site…*

His stomach churned. *Don't think about that now.*

Sarge's face softened. 'You're going to need to find a sense of purpose in the real world eventually, son.'

Zach rolled his shoulders. In his experience, the real world sucked.

'Now, I trust you recognise why I thought you the right candidate. I have another meeting in an hour, so you'll have to excuse me.'

'Does Joey Walter have something on you?' Zach widened his stance. 'Is he forcing your hand to take this job?' He lifted his chin, aware he was crossing a line. 'Is he blackmailing you?'

Sarge froze. When he turned back, his face had gone full Arctic. Zach refused to show how much it rocked him.

'Even if he was, Private, that would be none of your business.'

He turned and left, his back ramrod straight.

Zach tapped a fist against his mouth. Right. That *hadn't* been a no. Sarge could be stiff-necked, but he usually shot from the hip. Which meant there was an issue. One he didn't want to share with his business partners.

He blinked when Janie appeared in his line of sight. She'd changed into a pair of jeans and a simple cotton top, all of that burnished gold hair caught up in a baseball cap, dark sunglasses perched on her nose and a huge tote hung from her shoulder. She fiddled with the shoulder strap. 'Did you find out what you needed to?'

'Not yet.'

She assessed him for a moment but didn't press, for which he was grateful. 'Ready?'

He wasn't sure what he was agreeing to, but what the heck. 'Sure.'

Janie scanned the interior of the Chelsea pub, noted Beck and Lena on the other side of the room, but the women, as prearranged, pretended not to notice one another.

'Is this your local?'

She selected a table. 'I don't have a local, Mr Cartwright. Apparently, that's not wise.'

His eyes met hers for the briefest of moments. 'It's the same advice I'd give if I was on the Tierney detail.'

Such a small thing, having a local pub, and nobody in her world seemed to think it a sacrifice. Oh, but she dreamed of being able to walk into a place where they knew you and said hello and made your favourite drink without you asking. Resting her chin on her hand, she let herself think about that for a moment, but then realised piercing blue eyes were scrutinising her.

She straightened. 'What can I get you to drink?'

'I'll get—'

'Nonsense. I asked you to lunch. It's my shout. Besides,' she added quickly, 'I want you to check out the people in the pub, while blending into the background.'

He eased back, folded his arms. 'Just a soda, thanks.'

She suppressed a grin. 'You can shout lunch tomorrow.'

His gaze narrowed and her grin broke free. 'Such an expressive face!' She couldn't help laughing. 'Never fear, Mr Cartwright, my purposes are far from nefarious.' And, of course, she'd be paying tomorrow too. This wasn't a date. He was working and she'd cover their expenses.

She didn't explain further, but went to grab their drinks,

returning with his soda, half a pint of bitter for herself and the menus.

He nodded to her glass. 'Your drink of choice?'

'Nope, I'm incognito. Or at least trying to be.'

He removed the straw from his soda and took a generous swig. 'Why?'

'You've scanned the room?'

'More comprehensively than you're aware. There are four exits, not including the two windows I could smash if I needed to. There are only half a dozen people here in the snug, but voices tell me there'd be at least another half a dozen in the main bar. There's only one barman, but I can hear kitchen staff, so I'd expect two to four additional staff that we can't see.' He nodded to her beer again. 'What is your drink of choice?'

What would it take to make this man laugh? 'I'm now tempted to sing "I Love Pina Coladas".' Not so much as a smile. Sigh. 'However, in my opinion, a glass of red can't be beaten. Though beer is good too.'

She set her glass down. 'You see the women sitting at the table near the door with the laptop?'

He didn't even glance across. 'Yep.'

On cue, her phone pinged with a message.

You get him for ten weeks? Am pea-green!

Janie typed back, grinning.

Twelve weeks!

The ten weeks of filming and the fortnight leading up to it.

And green looks good on you.

She stuffed her phone back into her tote. 'They're my bes-
ties. In a little while, Beck's going to snap a photo of us, so
please don't tackle her to the ground and wrest her phone
from her.'

'You want to tell me why?'

She pushed a menu at him. 'After we've ordered.'

She tried to guess what he'd choose, and blinked when he
opted for the steak and kidney pudding. Comfort food. A far
cry from the burger she'd thought he'd settle for.

'What are you having?'

'The grilled fish with a garden salad.'

His nose wrinkled. She ordered.

His lips twitched, though, when the food arrived and he
saw her generous side serving of chips. Popping one into her
mouth, she shrugged. 'I couldn't resist. But— Oh! Hot!'

She waved her hand in front of her partly open mouth, to
try and mitigate the burn. Reaching for her beer, she gulped
down a mouthful. When she glanced back up she found Zach's
gaze fixed on her mouth, an arrested expression in his eyes.
Her stomach coiled over and over on itself. Her toes and the
tips of her fingers tingled.

Oh, that wasn't good. She and Beck might joke about her
proximity to Mr Smokin' Hot, but she didn't actually want
that heat invading her body and she especially didn't want it
messing with her mind.

Clearing her throat, she hauled out the magazines she'd
stuffed in her bag and smacked them to the table.

He blinked, and she sent him what she hoped was an uncon-
cerned smile. Her pulse, however, refused to behave, doing a
weird unsyncopated dance which made her breath stop-start.

Oh, for pity's sake, Janie! Really?

She did what she could to pull herself back into straight
lines.

'Homework,' she explained, opening each magazine to the

pages she'd marked and fanning them out across the table. 'I've been researching potential options for renovating and styling different kinds of properties.'

'Tell me about the women by the door.'

'The blonde is Beck Seymour. We were at school together and then at design school. Her mother is in banking and her father sits in the House of Lords. They own an extraordinary estate in Surrey, and disapprove of my parents, though they never fail to attend one of Joey Walter's dinner parties when invited. Beck works in graphic design and is smart, talented and all round brilliant.' She decided to push her luck. 'She's also currently single if you'd like me to introduce you...'

As she spoke, he ate. He looked relaxed, but across the table she sensed the power and energy coiled inside him. 'The brunette is Lena, who comes from quite a different background, but does have a long-term boyfriend, so you're out of luck there, I'm afraid.'

An eyebrow rose and blue eyes turned wintry. 'Tell me about the logic behind the photo.'

Her face heated. He made her feel like a recalcitrant child. Glancing down, she stabbed a lettuce leaf. 'You don't laugh much, do you?'

'Not much call for it in my line of work. People don't hire me for my sparkling personality but to keep them safe. I'm very good at that.'

'But—'

'The photo.'

She heaved out a sigh. 'Once the TV programme airs there's going to be a lot of speculation about why I've chosen you as my partner on the show. Especially when I could've had...' *a qualified builder or architect, sob.* 'The media will try to find out who you are and how we know each other. They'll do Internet searches.'

'We'll set up fake social media profiles and a website that

has my name on it et cetera. The team will have that in hand. You'll be briefed on our cover story once it's been worked out.'

'Don't I get any say in it?'

He blinked as if the question surprised him. One shoulder—deliciously broad—lifted. 'As you pointed out in the meeting, we're the ones with the expertise.'

'Well, I figure a few photos of us together, leaked at strategic intervals, will add veracity to the fact that we know each other.'

'You want us to pretend I'm your boyfriend?'

'No!' Reaching for her beer, she took a careful sip. 'I really don't.'

Something an awful lot like amusement played through his eyes. 'Should I be offended?'

Fact of the matter was she didn't want her name linked romantically with any man's ever again. She wasn't giving any man the smallest opportunity to make her feel bad about herself.

'To feel offended, you'd need to have emotions, and I doubt you trouble yourself with those.'

Her words, snapped out with acid, made him laugh. She stared. Laughing transformed him. The stern lines around his mouth softened, those blue eyes became warm and vibrant, and that mouth...

Stop staring at the mouth.

Swallowing more beer, she strove to cool the heat rising through her, tried to regain the thread of the conversation. 'Except for professional pride. You have a lot of that.'

'I do.' Resting his forearms on the table, he leaned towards her. 'Tell me what story you'd like for our fictional history and I'll take it back to the team.'

Really? She set up straighter. 'That we're friends? That you work in construction and have a good eye for making over a property?'

'How did we meet?'

A little fizz of excitement shifted through her. She told herself it was the novelty of coming up with a story. 'Mutual friends.'

'And why would someone like you choose a construction worker over an architect or builder?'

'For his muscles,' she teased, but this time he didn't smile back. She shifted, forced herself to focus seriously on the question. 'Because builders are the boss on a job site and they have apprentices and other workers to do the hard labour for them—they're good at what they do but will they have the stamina for doing a lot of the hard work themselves? Besides, *I* want to be the boss.'

'Not bad.'

The praise gave her an odd sense of pride.

Don't be pathetic.

'And you know what? It doesn't seem in the spirit of the show to turn up with ridiculously overqualified people. I want the viewers to feel that maybe they could achieve a renovation like this themselves.'

'That's a load of rubbish.'

Her jaw dropped.

'I saw the expression on your face when you said you wanted to win.'

Yeah, she *really* wanted to win.

'You'd choose a qualified builder over me in a heartbeat if you could.'

Her shoulders drooped. 'Guilty as charged.' A moment later she forced herself to straighten. 'You're the brother of a friend and I owe her a favour. So I'm doing it to help your fledgling building business become better known.'

He finished his food and pushed his plate to one side. 'A version of that could work.'

'I'm expecting all of the contestants will be asked why they chose their partner.'

'Is there much lag time between when we're filmed and when the show airs?'

'Next to none. Welcome to the joys of reality TV.' She blew out a breath. 'And you know what these shows are like. The director will do their level best to dig up dirt to create drama.'

Easing back, Zach studied the golden face in front of him. 'Why would a person in your position put themselves through that?'

She spread her hands. 'What part of *million-pound prize money* didn't you hear?'

He rolled his eyes. 'For the charity of your choice. I know, I know.' Was she after the kudos? Was that it?

'That money could make a significant difference to some people's lives.'

What charity was she so passionate about that she'd—

'And seriously, Zach—' she leaned towards him '—what am I other than a useless waste of space?'

What the hell...?

'According to the papers, I'm a leech living off Daddy's money.'

'Who cares what other people think? Or—'

She stabbed a finger to the table. 'I have my own interior design business that no one knows about. I want that to change. Also, I'm in an incredibly privileged position. If I have the opportunity, I should be doing all I can to make the world a better place.'

'Which is admirable.' And a million pounds really could make a difference. 'But you're going to a lot of trouble—'

He broke off when one of Janie's best buds, the blonde one, started across to the ladies' room. Janie straightened.

'That's our signal. Beck will snap the photo on her way

back to her table. And I want it showing us poring over pictures like these ones—' she gestured to the magazines '—as if we're planning what to do once we're on the show.'

Setting her plate to one side, she fanned the magazines out between them. She'd hardly eaten any of her lunch. Reaching across, he plucked the bowl of chips off the plate and placed it in the centre of the magazines and ate one. 'Eat your chips, Janie.'

She ate one too and then pointed. 'Could you build cabinets like those ones?'

He pulled the magazine towards him. 'Yep.' Piece of cake.

They both noticed the moment Beck emerged from the ladies' room and started back towards her table. Janie tensed. He figured, though, that she'd want the photo to look natural. 'You ever knock a wall down with a sledgehammer?'

His question startled a laugh from her. 'No.'

'It's ridiculously satisfying. Do you want to practice that before we do it on national television?'

Her eyes sparkled. 'For real? Do you mean it?'

'Yep.' He leaned over to point to one of the other magazines. 'Which do you like best—that or that?'

She pointed. And then Beck was past and had taken several photos in quick succession and now she and Janie's other bestie packed up their bags and left.

'How many photos were you thinking we needed?'

'I don't know, maybe three or four in different locations. Tomorrow, I thought we could go to the library.'

'I have a better idea. Why don't we let Beck and Lena off photography duty and I'll get one of the team onto it?'

'Okay.'

They might as well do it right. 'You said the resort locations would be allocated during episode one.'

'Drawn out of a hat. Not a literal hat, but you know what I mean.'

'Do you know the potential locations yet?'

She seized her phone, clicked a few buttons. 'There are several tropical beach resorts, as you'd expect—an island in French Polynesia, one in Australia's Whitsunday Islands and one in Puerto Rico. There's also a Swiss chalet and a gorgeous villa on the Italian Lakes.' She ran a finger down the list and her nose wrinkled. 'Ah, yes, and we have the wild card.' She stuffed her phone back into her bag. 'A surprise location, just to keep us all on our toes.'

He swore silently. 'If you could opt out of one, which would it be?'

'The wild card, simply because I've no idea what to expect, which means I can't start making any plans for it. And after that probably the Italian villa. I mean it's beautiful, but the scale of the rooms...and the associated building regulations. There's less room to manoeuvre with a building like that. It has headache written all over it. I'm hoping for one of the beach resorts.' Leaning her chin in her hand, her eyes went dreamy. For no reason, his mouth went dry. 'So many options for styling. I could really make a mark there.'

Shaking herself, she glanced up, grimaced. 'I'm guessing the wild card will make it hard for your team.'

An absolute nightmare. 'Gray has all the information?'

She nodded.

Good. Sarge would be making contingency plans.

Her head tilted to one side. 'Where do *you* hope we end up?'

Somewhere remote where they'd be able to monitor who came and went. 'French Polynesia or the Whitsundays.'

'They look gorgeous.'

Except thoughts of strolling along the beach with Janie—

He snapped off the image. He needed to keep things professional. He'd never found that difficult before. And this assignment would be no different.

'Wherever we end up, we will keep you safe, Janie.'

'I don't doubt that for a moment.'

Her smile was too bright and he was seized with an unfamiliar desire to pull her into his arms and proffer what comfort he could. Except that wouldn't be professional.

Shooting to his feet, he said, 'We done here?'

'I…uh…sure.'

'Right then, I have work to do. I'll be in touch about arranging photos and knocking down that practice wall.'

She didn't say anything, but he felt the weight of her gaze as he turned and marched out of the door.

CHAPTER THREE

ZACH'S BROWS ROSE. 'You're nervous.'

With his legs stretched out and his shoulders loose, he looked completely at ease. Janie bit back a sigh. Why couldn't she feel like that?

The two of them were seated in one corner of the green room, waiting for the filming of the first episode of *Renovation Revamp* to start. The five other couples were dotted about the room. She'd tried to start up a conversation with Antoine Mackay, a celebrity chef she'd met a few times, but he'd held out one hand like a stop sign, had said, 'Let's not pretend we're friends.'

Zach hadn't shown it, but she'd felt him bristle. Taking his arm, she'd led him to the sofa in the far corner where he'd have a comprehensive view of the room.

'Charming,' he'd muttered.

'He can be. But not today.' Clearly the rivalry from that quarter wasn't going to be of the friendly variety.

She pulled her mind back. 'Why aren't you nervous?'

'I've done tours of duty in war-torn countries. Whatever else this TV show throws at us, there aren't going to be mines or missiles. So yeah, I'm thinking this will be a doddle.'

'A dolly assignment,' she murmured, recalling his words from a fortnight ago. The reminder that he considered this job nothing more than the overreaction of an overprotective father was oddly reassuring.

'You're not going to let me forget that, are you?'

'Actually, I found it rather comforting. I mean, it was rude too, but hey, you didn't know I was standing there and I think we're past that now.' She grinned. 'After all, we've smashed a wall down together with sledgehammers. We're practically best buds!'

He didn't crack so much as a smile.

Actually, smashing the wall down hadn't been as much fun as she'd hoped. Oh, the smashing itself had been but, rather than the quiet affair she'd hoped for, they'd been surrounded by members of his team, and while he'd been perfectly polite and his instructions clear and to the point, there'd been a distance she'd not been able to breach.

Photos had been taken in strategic locations—the design museum, an architect's office, a tile warehouse. Each of those meetings had lasted less than an hour.

What did you expect? That you'd start the show as best friends?

Well, not best friends, obviously. She already had two of those. But it'd help to have a sense of camaraderie with him. Renovating a resort was going to take all her ingenuity, all her reserves of strength, and being able to share a laugh and a joke with someone...

She straightened. With or without it, she *would* win this challenge. She'd do it for Lena. And all the other Lenas out there. The world was a ridiculously unfair place, and she was in the privileged position of being able to help.

And she'd do it for herself. She'd do it to silence Sebastian's sneers and slurs once and for all and prove she wasn't a failure. She *did* have talent. She *wasn't* wrong about that.

'The dolly assignment comment downplayed the level of danger for you?'

She sent him a swift smile. 'Especially when coupled with the babysitting comment.'

He held her gaze and an unfamiliar pulse ticked to life inside her. 'We're taking those threats seriously.'

'I know.'

She didn't just have a bodyguard; she had an entire team on the case. There'd be two team members at the location pretending to be tourists, as well as Sarge, who'd be setting up and monitoring remote cameras. And Darren. She had a lot of people watching her back.

But hearing Zach denigrate this assignment—the scorn in his voice when he'd spoken to his colleague on the phone—had eased the worst of her fears. Her family received threats all the time. These ones might be more graphic than most, but she shouldn't pay them any more heed than she had any of the others she'd received over the years.

'So why the nerves? You must be used to this kind of thing.'

Most people wouldn't believe her but... 'I don't like the limelight, don't like being the centre of attention.'

'Then why put yourself through this?'

She stared down her nose at him.

He rolled his eyes. 'For the million-pound prize money *for the charity of your choice*, which I've been meaning to ask—'

'I tried hiding when I was a teenager.' She kept her voice conversational, but his mockery stung. 'That didn't work out so well for me—I became awkward, started jumping at shadows. I learned then that facing my fears was more constructive.'

He blinked.

'Is that how you face your fears?' she asked. 'By running away from them?'

'I don't run away from danger.'

She gave a soft laugh. 'I don't think danger is something you're afraid of, Zach.'

They were interrupted by the production assistant clapping her hands in the doorway and asking for the couples—

Janie preferred to think of them as teams—to follow her out to the set.

It was a closed set, thankfully, but the lights were bright and the cameras rolling and her stomach tightened and her palms grew damp. Zach leaned down to whisper, 'You've got this, Ms Tierney.' She couldn't explain why, but it bolstered her nerves, had some of the tension bleeding from her shoulders.

The host introduced the couples and they each said a few words. She channelled charm, humour and self-deprecation, but without an audience it was hard to gauge if she'd succeeded.

'Perfect,' Zach murmured, so she chose to believe him. Anything to keep the nerves from showing.

It was then time to draw lots to decide in what order they'd draw their locations in an attempt to stretch this out and make it as painful—oops, suspenseful—as possible. They'd agreed beforehand that Zach would draw their number and she their location.

Zach drew out their number, three and five had already been taken, and wrinkled his nose. 'Number four.'

'Disappointed?' Mike, the host, asked.

He gave a lopsided grin and Janie found her heart thump-thumping. He really should do that more.

'I was hoping for number one.'

Everyone laughed.

Antoine, the celebrity chef, drew number two and whooped and cheered and jumped up and down, punching the air like a footballer who'd just scored a goal.

Isobel, an actor from a recent historical drama series, drew out number one. She glanced at the camera, all hauteur and entitlement, and gave an elegant shrug. 'And number one is where I'm going to be at the end of the series too.'

Janie bit back a grin. Clearly, Isobel meant to play the same catty character here as she did on the drama series. Fun!

'We'll see about that,' Antoine challenged.

And Antoine was going for full drama.

'Low-key, hard-working, self-deprecating,' she murmured to Zach.

'We are all over it. We're going to leave these patsies in the dust.'

Isobel got French Polynesia, because of course she did.

Antoine got the Whitsunday Island.

Contestant three drew the Swiss chalet.

And then it was her turn. With a heart that thumped, Janie made her way across to Mike and the huge electronic board with its six squares.

'Are you feeling lucky, Jane Tierney?' Mike hooted.

No, dammit. She was going to get that rotten Italian villa, wasn't she? Dragging in a deep breath, though, she beamed at him. 'I'm here and about to embark on an amazing adventure. How could I not feel lucky?'

A drumroll sounded. 'Behind which square is your dream location, Janie—the place you're going to spend the next ten weeks? Are you ready to change your life and decide your destiny?'

She resisted the urge to roll her eyes. '*So* ready.'

'Which square do you choose?'

She pointed to the middle square on the bottom row and crossed her fingers.

Please let it be Puerto Rico.

More drumrolls sounded, shredding her nerves further. 'And your *Renovation Revamp* destination is...'

Bells and whistles filled the air and streamers flew all around. *What on earth...?*

'Janie, you've chosen the wild card!'

Her smile froze. As soon as she realised, she turned it into a comical grimace. 'Oh, my goodness, I'm so nervous. Put me out of my misery. Where am I going?'

She was made to guess, of course. 'Hawaii? Or... Banff?' She gave what she hoped was a hopeful smile.

Please don't let it be some historic villa where she'd need to remain true to the character of the building to make the renovation shine. She wanted a blank slate, a place where she could go wild and where her talents would have jaws dropping.

She watched as a pre-recorded reel revealed the wild card location—an historic villa on the picturesque Greek island of Corfu.

'Excited?' the host demanded.

'*So* excited.' She clasped her hands beneath her chin and beamed up at the screen even as her heart sank. 'Look at it. It's beautiful! I can't believe I get to spend the next ten weeks in such a dream location. I told you I was feeling lucky, Mike.'

She moved back to her seat. Antoine smirked. 'Never mind, Janie. You were always toast.'

She ignored him.

Zach leant down and murmured, 'Not good,' in her ear.

'It's an island, though. That's what we want, right?'

'Not the right kind.'

She had no idea what that meant and there was no opportunity to ask as the last two contestants chose their locations, and then it was time for each team to say a few words about the charities they were supporting.

The charities were enough to break your heart. But a cynical part of her couldn't help thinking that the other contestants had chosen theirs for pathos rather than any real commitment to the cause. There was a fight against Third World hunger, and two separate cancer charities—breast cancer and skin cancer. Her two nemeses, which was how she'd started to think of Antoine and Isobel, represented critically ill children with rare diseases and pet rescue charities respectively. Sick kids, and kittens and puppies. She could already see the photo opportunities. And then it was her turn. She didn't doubt that the director had deliberately saved her for last.

Mike sent her a pitying smile. 'And what's your chosen charity, Janie?'

'It's a small charity in London that I've been associated with for over a decade now, and I hope that my time on *Renovation Revamp* will help raise its profile as more people learn about the good it does.'

'It's called Second Chances.' He made a funny face at the camera. 'And what is it, exactly?'

'A prisoner release assistance scheme.'

Mike cleared his throat. 'That seems an *odd* choice.'

Everyone tittered. It took a superhuman effort to keep a pleasant expression on her face. She spoke about the prisoner support programme and how it helped young offenders turn their lives around. 'Not everyone is born with the same advantages I've had. And—'

'As we've all seen in the other charities we've heard about this evening.'

She gritted her teeth at the interruption. She was used to people dismissing the charity. So what if it wasn't popular or pretty? Neither was she.

'Supporting this charity is my chance to do what I can to help make someone else's life a little bit easier.'

'Don't starving children and maltreated animals and cancer sufferers deserve your help too?'

Ordinarily, by this point Zach would've interrupted Mike. Zach had a way of speaking—with soft menace underlaid with steel—that made most men back off. Not Sarge and Logan, but then they weren't most men. The host's constant interruptions and not so subtle belittling of Janie and her charity were appalling. Except...

In this case, Zach happened to agree with him.

What the hell...? He was going to be helping convicted criminals? Over his dead body!

'What the client's politics are is no concern of yours.' Sarge's voice sounded through him. *'We've been hired to do a job, and we're going to do it whether we agree with their views or not.'*

He took a steadying breath. All valid. All true. He was a professional. He needed to let this go.

'And what do you think about this, Zach?'

Janie turned to glance at him and her eyes widened at whatever she saw in his face. *Damn.* He couldn't feed her to the wolves, no matter how much he might loathe her bleeding heart politics.

'I think, Mike, you ought to let Janie speak without constantly interrupting her.'

Mike's head rocked back and he gave an unsteady laugh. 'Oho, we have a white knight among our contestants.'

He did what he could to stop his lips from twisting. That moniker would probably stick now.

Mike gestured for Janie to continue speaking.

'I was just going to say that the charities you just mentioned, Mike, already have a lot of advocates. A lot of important people are already lobbying governments, the medical fraternity, and the public, to fund research. And they're doing a great job. I applaud each and every one of them. As for me, though, I just want to shine a light on a lesser-known problem. It's one...' she flashed a smile directly at the camera that made Zach's heart kick '...that means a lot to me.' She gave another of those self-deprecating laughs that were starting to set Zach's teeth on edge. 'But I guess everyone can now see that for themselves.'

Mike gave a good-natured laugh too. 'And as the series progresses we'll no doubt learn more about the reasons Janie has chosen this particular charity.'

He moved on, and Zach only had to work at keeping his face expressionless for another ten minutes before someone called, 'That's a wrap.'

The camera, sound and lighting crews started packing up their equipment, Mike strode off without speaking to anyone and the contestants started making their way back to the green room.

Janie was the last to slide from her stool and both Isobel and Antoine glared at her as they strode past.

She blew out a breath. 'If looks could kill.' She glanced up at him. 'Any idea why?'

'I'm guessing it's because you stole some of their thunder.'

She blinked at him.

'Well, clearly the actress is going to play the coldblooded ice queen—all chilly entitlement and win at all costs. While that celebrity chef will be throwing arms and temper tantrums all over the place, creating storms in teacups and blaming everyone else for his mistakes. The other three contestants are all low-key, hard-working and self-deprecating.'

'No, no.' She shook her head so hard all of that old-gold hair swished around her shoulders. 'That's us. That's me.'

'Not any more.' They'd stopped walking and stood at the edge of the set. He leaned down until they were eye to eye and pointed back the way they'd come. 'Not after your performance out there, you're not.'

For the briefest of moments her gaze fixed on his mouth. She moistened her lips, the gold flecks in her eyes briefly flaring. He shot upright, chest tight, fingers clenched so hard they ached.

Her throat bobbed. 'What do you mean?'

'Now you're the bleeding heart.'

'The *what*?'

'Naïve, earnest...*misguided*.'

Her eyes narrowed as he spat the last word.

'What the hell kind of charity is that?' He pressed a fist to his brow. 'A prisoner release assistance scheme?' He swore. 'You *can't* be serious.'

He'd never known that gold could turn to ice, but her eyes were rimed with an Arctic chill and she stood straight and tall. Unflinching.

'You're not being paid to have an opinion on the topic.'

Which was both true *and* infuriating.

He stabbed a finger ceilingward. 'Criminals deserve to go to jail.'

'And when they've done their time, they deserve a second chance. They deserve the opportunity to start again and make a new life for themselves. Everyone deserves a second chance, Mr Cartwright.'

Her *Mr Cartwright* didn't sound teasing or friendly or fun. And he couldn't explain why but it was a knife to the heart.

And then a sound came from his right and instinct took over and he immediately moved in front of Janie to block her from view.

The production assistant appeared. 'We wondered where you'd got to.'

She had a phone in one hand and a folder in the other. Things inside him drew tight. How long had she been hovering in the shadows? Why the hell hadn't he been paying more attention?

'Here are your plane tickets, along with all of the other information you need about the rules and the production schedule.'

Janie moved out from behind him to take the folder the assistant held out. 'Thank you.'

'You'll be flying out first thing in the morning. It's an early start, I'm afraid.'

'No problem.'

Janie's voice was all smooth urbanity—no anger, outrage or

agitation coloured it. If he hadn't witnessed any of it himself, he'd have been hard pressed to sense it now. Except perhaps in the deepening of the creases at the corners of her eyes as if she was fighting a headache, and the paleness of lips that had been pressed together too hard.

He bit back something between a groan and a growl. Her life was hard enough at the moment. He shouldn't be making it harder.

But... A prisoner assistance scheme? *Seriously?*

He'd witnessed the effects of violent crime—he and his mother had both been victims to it, and the memories of that time made him sick to his stomach. For Pete's sake, one of her father's crazed fans was threatening to do unspeakable things to her. How, for a single moment, could she believe supporting a charity like Second Chances was a good idea?

Pulling his phone from his pocket when they reached the car, he informed Sarge of the resort's location and took photographs of all the documents in the folder and sent them through too.

'Home?' he asked when he was done.

'Yes please.'

She didn't look at him when she spoke and he had to bite back an oath.

'Look, we don't have to agree on political or social issues. All we have to agree on is that I'll do my utmost to keep you safe and my best on set as your builder.'

She swung to him, her eyes flashing. 'I had no idea you were so judgemental, that your world was so black and white.'

He preferred the fire to the ice. 'You haven't seen what I've seen.'

'And you haven't seen what I've seen.' He blinked at her swift retort. 'Are you really so incapable of empathising with other people?'

What the hell...?

'Though I guess empathy isn't a requirement of your job. Maybe it's even an impediment.'

'I can empathise!' he hollered.

His teeth ground together. This woman was starting to get under his skin and that wouldn't do. It wouldn't do *at all*. He didn't allow women to get under his skin. And he was on assignment. Even if he didn't believe she was in any real danger, he still needed to keep a clear head.

'Well, that's good to know.' She folded her arms. 'Because on this particular social issue, plan to have your views challenged.'

Silently he said, *Yeah, good luck with that.*

As soon as the plane was in the air the next morning Janie handed Zach a copy of the documents that had been in the folder. She'd emailed copies to both him and Sarge as well. He had a printout in his suitcase but he didn't mention that, just let her be efficient.

He was hoping after her snit with him yesterday things between them could get back on an even keel. Somewhere in the back of his mind laughter sounded. *Even?* None of his dealings with this woman could be described as even.

For a brief moment he recalled the pub lunch they'd shared and…

And what? Was he hoping for more of that? *Seriously?* He swatted the thought away. All of Sarge's arguing with him about getting a life was making him soft in the head.

'Why is Corfu not the *right kind of island*? You said an island would be a good location.'

'Corfu is neither small nor remote. It's a big tourist destination. It'll be impossible to monitor everyone who comes and goes.'

He watched her mull that over.

'But we can work with it.' He didn't want her worrying

about her safety. He shuffled through the file until he came
to the photo of the villa. A three-storey stone building with a
semi-circular first-floor balcony. 'So this is what we're working with.'

She traced a finger over the photo. 'This wouldn't have
been my first choice.' Her scent rose up all around him—
something sweet and restful, a blend of cashmere and violets.
'But it's rather beautiful.'

If your taste ran to rundown and ramshackle.

She glanced up and their gazes locked. The air between
them shimmered. 'A Greek island.' She swallowed. 'You ever
been?'

Adrenaline flooded his every cell. 'Nope. What's it like?'

'I've never been either.'

She hadn't—

Her gaze snapped away. 'But it's a dream location. So romantic. We need to do it justice for the people watching the
show.'

'Why?'

Did she want to win the audience vote?

What was he thinking? *Of course* she wanted to win the
audience vote.

'What do you mean, *why*? Where we're going, what we're
about to do, that's some people's dream. It should be treated
with respect.'

It wasn't his damn dream. He'd give his right arm to be
heading to South America right now.

She shook the papers she held. 'Okay, to work. We've the
production schedule—the show will air on Sunday nights—
and a list of the rooms we'll be making over.'

'Bedroom, bathroom, dining room, reception room, reception foyer, outdoor area…and a mystery challenge tailored individually to each property,' he said, ticking them off.

'You've memorised it.'

'I like to be prepared, and when I'm undercover I take my role seriously. We get a week to renovate each room, but two weeks for the mystery challenge. At the end of each week the judges will inspect the rooms via a video call and give a score out of twenty.'

'And you can go to the top of the class.'

Internally, he smiled. There might now be an undeniable distance between them, but she still had a sense of humour.

She gestured between them. 'You and I can work all the hours we want, but we're only allowed to work our team a max of eight hours a day, as set out in their industrial award.'

'Are you going to work me sixteen hours a day?' He was up for it, but curious to see what she'd say.

'I expect so. After all—' she sent him the sweetest of smiles '—we're representing a very worthy charity.'

He grinned. He couldn't help it. 'Is that my punishment?'

For the briefest of moments her gaze lowered to his mouth, but she dragged it away and shrugged. His heart sounded loud in his ears.

'You said you'd do your best for me.'

'I meant it.'

Working sixteen-hour days sounded like a great idea. If he was working sixteen-hour days he'd be too tired to think about stupid things. Like what it'd be like to kiss Janie Tierney.

He didn't *feel* things for his clients. That was a road leading straight to hell, not to mention personal ruin and devastation. Cold and clinical, vigilant, those were his code words. Janie might be easy on the eye, but he couldn't let it mean anything.

He clenched his jaw. He *wouldn't* let it mean anything.

CHAPTER FOUR

JANIE STARED OUT of the window as their minibus travelled the hour north from Corfu city. The Ionian Sea sparkled sapphire in the morning light, the exact same colour as Zach's eyes. When the road dipped inland they were treated to golden fields, grazing goats and shady olive groves that looked as if they'd been there for centuries.

'It's unbelievably gorgeous,' she murmured.

Beside her, Zach said nothing. A man of few words. Though as she hadn't appreciated the ones he'd blasted at her yesterday, that was probably a blessing.

Despite the heaviness that wanted to settle on her shoulders, the voices whispering in her head that said she'd bitten off more than she could handle and the low-level dread that had weighed heavily in the pit of her stomach since she'd read that first threatening letter... The longer she stared at the view, the lighter she started to feel.

She could do this and she would. To prove her naysayers wrong, and to find herself again. For Lena and every other person who deserved a second chance. None of them were failures.

'The villa should be just up ahead,' Cullen, the head of their production crew, said, turning the minibus into an overgrown drive that she made a mental note to clear. Overgrown could be picturesque, but this was a jungle.

Her silent laugh had Zach glancing at her. She pretended

not to notice. She'd already been far too aware of him on the journey. His big body so close to hers, the intriguing flex and play of muscles when he moved, the way those blue eyes took everything in.

While she wanted him to be vigilant, she didn't want him sensing the ridiculous fantasies plaguing her where he was concerned. As if she was some schoolgirl with a stupid adolescent crush. Except the fantasies chasing through her mind were far from innocent.

And they weren't going to happen! She forced herself to remember how she'd felt when she'd learned the truth about Sebastian. She'd felt small. Stupid. Diminished. No way was she going through that again, or setting herself up for another fall. The only way to prove she wasn't a fool was to stop acting like one.

'Something funny?'

She waved a dismissive hand, eyes glued to the window. 'Just spending our budget already.'

She needed to be careful with the budget, though. If she overspent they'd be penalised and then everyone would think her a loser who couldn't—

Stop it!

As they broke through the trees she kept her attention on her surroundings rather than the man beside her. They emerged into a clearing and—

Her heart stopped for two-tenths of a second. The view... Oh, the view! *This* was why words like azure and cerulean had been invented because, no matter how hard it tried, the word blue couldn't capture that much beauty.

A sapphire sea spread before them in sun-sparkled splendour, framed by a rocky shoreline, date palms and cypress trees. How had she never known that Corfu and the Ionian Sea was this beautiful?

Only after she'd drunk in her fill did she follow the green

lawn up from the pebbly beach to the villa overlooking it. That was when reality hit her right between the eyes. She winced, commending herself for not grimacing, groaning and swearing. Or for bursting into tears.

At some point in its past the villa had been rendered in plaster and painted, but haphazard sections of dirty yellow render had fallen away to expose the stone beneath, leaving it pockmarked and disfigured. It looked decrepit, unloved and unlovely. The alternately weedy and stunted excuse for a garden reflected the same neglect as the building.

Zach stared from it to her and back again. Nobody spoke. Wordlessly, they piled out and stood there staring.

'Is this some kind of joke?'

Zach's demand snapped her out of her daze.

Cullen scratched his head. 'I, uh… It's more rundown than I expected.'

With a frown, she shook her head at Zach. This wasn't Cullen's fault. He hadn't chosen the location. He was just doing his job. Gritting her teeth, she pushed her shoulders back. And so would she.

She'd show *everyone* what she was made of.

'You need to film our arrival, right?'

He sent her a grateful smile, motioned for the crew to set up. 'We'll film the two of you in front of the villa to share your first impressions. Then we'll follow you inside. Today only you and Zach will appear on camera. I won't appear, but viewers will hear my voice when I ask a question or prompt you.'

She knew all of that already, but was grateful for the recap. It gave her a chance to gather her wits and recharge her game face.

'Ready?' At her nod, Cullen called, 'Action.'

Janie turned from viewing the villa to smile at the camera. 'Well, it's a little more rundown than I expected.' She held up their photograph of the villa. 'This looks like it was taken a decade ago, but I'm guessing all of the contestants are going to find themselves in the same boat.'

'Zach?' Cullen prompted.

Zach made a noncommittal noise.

Janie winked at the camera. 'You're going to find that Zach is a man of few words. He's the strong, silent type. I'm emphasising *strong* because we're going to need all your muscles on this job, Zach.'

'And yours.'

'It might not be looking its best at the moment but...' she nudged him '...tell me it has good bones.'

Planting his hands on his hips, he surveyed the villa. The sun glinted off chestnut hair, turning the colour rich and vibrant. The dance of light and shadow against his face—

She dragged her gaze back to the villa, her heart pounding.

'It has good proportions,' he allowed. 'In its heyday it would've been a handsome building.'

And it'd be handsome again. She *could* do this. An old fire ignited inside her.

'This is seriously exciting!' Grabbing Zach's arm, she dragged him in her wake until they were silhouetted against the view. 'Look at that.' She silently screamed at the camera. 'Isn't it beautiful? I know the next ten weeks are going to be challenging, we've a lot of hard work ahead of us, but being able to look at that every day... I can't believe how lucky we are.'

Zach stared as if afraid she'd had too much sun.

She clapped her hands. 'Come on, let's see inside.'

Gloom greeted them as the front door opened and they stepped into a large foyer. A generous staircase arced up to the first floor. Off to the right, a huge room opened out, thick with dust and must. She wrinkled her nose and moved across to the chinks of light showing through huge wooden shutters. Opening the window, she swung a shutter open.

'Let's see if we can let in some light and—' The hinges gave an ominous shriek, Janie jumped as first one hinge and then the other pulled away from the frame and the whole thing clattered to the garden below. With a hand clapped to her mouth, she turned back to the camera, shaking with laughter. 'Right, we'll be fixing the shutters then.'

Moving past her, Zach simply pulled the other shutter from the window frame and eased it to the ground. 'The wood's rotten, but that's an easy fix.' He did the same with the other two sets of shutters.

A light breeze floated through the windows, stirring the dust, making her sneeze. Old tables and chairs, discarded boxes of crockery and cutlery and other assorted odds and ends littered the room. They'd have to clear this, or pay someone else to do it.

'You're both quiet,' Cullen prompted.

'I'm just taking it all in.'

'Does the dirt and grime bother you?'

That had her grinning. No way was she being thrust into the role of pampered princess. 'It's going to get a whole lot dirtier before we're through with it.'

'This could be a great room.' Zach moved across to a wall and rapped his knuckles against it. 'High ceilings, a generous floor space. We've a ceiling rose that needs some work but…'

'The fireplace will be fabulous once we clean it up.' In her mind's eye she could see it crackling away, all cheerful and warm. 'And then there's that view…' She gestured out of the windows. 'We have to find a way to do it justice.'

'What are you seeing?' Cullen prompted.

'Two sofas facing each other here in front of the fireplace… a bookcase on the far wall with a couple of wingback chairs… A writing desk there…'

Zach crouched down, tapped the floor. 'Antique tiles.'

She pointed. 'And a decorative frieze along the top of the wall. This could look so grand!'

Before she was aware of it, she and Zach were throwing around ideas and making plans and she forgot about Cullen and the camera. She only came back to herself when Cullen seized on a brief silence while she and Zach regrouped.

'I think we might wrap it up there.'

Oops. She might've got a little carried away. But it was better than feeling overwhelmed and useless, and a poor ambassador for Second Chances and a failure in general.

'We'll unload your bags and head back to our digs.'

The production crew, along with the other two members of their renovation team, were staying in the nearby village. Only she and Zach would live onsite.

'Here's the building report.' Cullen fished the folder from his bag and handed it to Zach. 'Apparently, someone has given the bedrooms and bathroom set aside for your use a thorough clean. And here are the keys to your hire car, which should be parked around the back. I think that's it. We'll reconvene nine a.m. Monday.'

Today was Saturday.

Their bags and associated equipment were unloaded onto the lawn. No special VIP treatment for them.

Zach turned to her after they'd waved the others off. 'Where do you want to start?'

She folded her arms. 'How about with you telling me why you have such a set against my charity?' She ought to let it go, but it burned and chafed at her. A horrible thought occurred to her. 'Have you or someone you love been a victim of crime?'

His face tightened and he pointed a hard finger at her. 'That's not up for discussion.'

'Shut down, smacked down and stonewalled. Let that be a lesson to you, Plain Jane.'

'Stop calling yourself that!' He gestured to the house. 'Focus on that. *That's* why we're here.'

Biting back a sigh, she shouldered a bag and lifted two of the suitcases. 'Let's take these inside and do a full reconnaissance.'

'I'll carry those.'

Her answer was to stick her nose in the air and start towards the house. 'I am sledgehammer woman! I am strong and invincible.' Also, for the last month she'd been lifting weights—a training of sorts. And while it had made her stronger, it didn't stop the suitcases from being dead weights by the time she got them inside. Dumping them in the foyer with a sigh of relief, she moved down the corridor, glancing into a series of rooms, to eventually emerge into the kitchen at the back. The place looked as if it hadn't been cleaned in years.

'Generous but primitive,' Zach said behind her.

They retraced their steps and headed upstairs. On the first floor there were six bedrooms—none of which had en suite bathrooms. A shorter flight of stairs took them to two smaller bedrooms tucked in the eaves that looked out over an overgrown back garden. As these had their names pinned on the doors, clearly they were the ones put aside for their personal use.

She opened her door and stared. 'I thought Cullen said they'd been cleaned.'

'You can take my room.'

'I'm not afraid of a bit of dust. I know how to use a vacuum cleaner and mop. Besides—' moving past him, she pushed open his bedroom door '—your room isn't any better.'

'Nothing to do with cleanliness, Janie. That room had your name on it. Means someone will be expecting you to sleep in it.'

Fear flickered in her stomach. She did what she could to quash it. Those letters had been sent to scare her. Someone's idea of a sick joke. Nobody was out to get her.

'Probably innocent enough, but my job is to make it harder for anyone to find you where they expect to.'

Of course it was innocent. She refused to start seeing bogeymen behind every door. Hitching up her chin, she moved across to the window. 'They'd need a pretty tall ladder.'

Zach moved to stand beside her, scanned the back garden. 'No pool.'

'And we've neither the time nor the budget to put one in, but a pergola—grapevines hanging from it…a paved courtyard.'

One side of his mouth hooked up and it made her pulse dance. 'A pizza oven?'

'Yes!' She'd research how to build her own pizza oven tonight. 'Come on, let's get these rooms shipshape.'

'I'm going to do a recce outside. And I need to check in with Sarge.'

'Okey-doke. Let's get to it.'

It took her two hours, but eventually the two bedrooms and bathroom had been cleaned to a reasonable standard.

Zach halted when he crossed the threshold of his room. 'You didn't have to clean my room.'

'I saw what you were doing outside.' She shrugged. 'It only seemed fair.'

Zach had found a brush-cutter in one of the back sheds, along with a hedge-trimmer. He'd spent two hours laying waste to the jungle at the back of the house. Both he and Sarge thought the threats empty, didn't expect to see action on this assignment, but Joey Walter was paying a hefty amount to keep Janie safe and Zach was playing this one by the book. He planned to be ready for anything.

And limiting the places where any potential stalkers could hide was one of them. The pine grove out the back was now shady but clear. He'd be able to see anyone loitering out there.

'I can envision little café tables beneath the pines…carafes of something lovely and chilled…condensation forming on glasses.'

Her eyes went dreamy and Zach backed up a step, forced his gaze away.

'Happy chatter and laughter.'

A vivid picture formed in his mind. He could almost imagine himself, beer in hand and legs stretched out at one of those little tables she described, taking it easy.

He shook himself. *Relaxation?* Was he nuts? He loathed being still. And yet he couldn't shake the image.

Janie turned and headed downstairs. He stared after her and frowned, scrubbed a hand through his hair. The woman he'd met at the pub—playful, slightly mischievous—had gone. All of that *vividness* had been replaced with friendly efficiency. He'd thought, when they'd started riffing off each other downstairs, coming up with ideas for the reception room fast and furious, that they'd regained their previous footing.

But nope.

He tried telling himself that this professional distance was wiser. He gritted his teeth. *It was.* Except…

'If you hate the thought of it and don't think you can do it justice, will you please bow out?'

Her words from their first meeting rose in his mind to peck at him. He hadn't promised, not out loud. He'd promised to himself, to Sarge, to keep her safe, that was all, and yet…

Damn it all to hell.

This professional distance would be better for him, but some instinct told him it wouldn't be better for her. Some people needed to like the people they worked with. It helped them concentrate on the work rather than wasting time labouring over how to negotiate a difficult relationship—or what they saw as difficult. They used their energy rehearsing what to say and what not to say, guarding their thoughts and their tongues. He suspected Janie was one of their number.

If he was going to keep the promise he hadn't made, he was going to have to work out a way to win her trust and get her to like him again. How the hell was he supposed to do that? He wasn't good with people. He was good at sensing danger and being vigilant, keeping people safe and making sure the bad guys got their comeuppance.

'What are you doing up there, Zach?' Janie hollered up the stairs. 'We've got a lot to do before the team arrives on Monday.'

They did? He rolled his shoulders. If he did that well enough, maybe it'd earn him a gold star.

He found her in that front reception room. 'Private Cartwright reporting for duty, Captain.' He saluted and clicked his heels together.

Her brows lifted and the corners of that very mobile mouth twitched. It gave him a shot of adrenaline. Odd. Adrenaline usually came from facing danger and thwarting it. No matter how hard he tried, he couldn't view Janie as any kind of threat.

He shook out his arms and legs. 'What's the plan? What do you want done?'

'I want to clear this room and move everything into that smaller reception room off the kitchen. We're not throwing any of it yet—we might need it or use it for staging once the rooms are renovated.'

He glanced around. Something felt off about this room. It was too full of junk as if—

As if that was deliberate. The director's way of saying welcome to *Renovation Revamp*?

'And the kitchen needs a spit and polish because whether it's part of the renovation or not, it's going to be where we cook, where the team keeps their lunches and makes coffee…eats.'

The less time anyone had unsupervised access to his and Janie's sleeping quarters the better. As much as possible, he'd like to keep everyone where he could see them.

He needed locks for those bedrooms. Deadbolts.

'And then I want to go into town.'

'For?'

'Groceries, a late lunch, some additional cleaning products, and to touch base with local suppliers.'

At this rate they might be in bed by midnight.

Moving across to a window, he surveyed the view. 'There's a big tree out there, nice and shady. Looks like an oak.'

'Is this you making conversation?'

'I'm a man of few words, remember? I don't make conversation.'

She huffed out a laugh. Another surge of adrenaline sharpened his senses, made him aware of sun sparkling on sapphire water, the way her hair gleamed like tarnished gold even in the dust and grime of the room, the scent of salt in the air.

'I was thinking we could take this table and a few of the chairs out there. It'd make a nice place for the team to sit during break times.'

'That's a great idea!'

They cleared the room of all the big things that required two people to lift, and created a casual eating area outside under the big tree. He nodded when they were done. Everyone would much prefer to eat out here than the kitchen. Mission accomplished.

He turned back to Janie. 'Breakfast was a long time ago. I vote we go into town now and tackle the rest of this when we get back. We'll work better after some food and fun.'

'Fun?'

He might've made her smile once or twice, but he hadn't breached her guard. Not yet.

You could apologise.

But he wasn't sorry about what he had said.

Apologise for the way you said it then.

He widened his stance. 'When we get back we'll divide

and conquer. One can keep moving this stuff while the other tackles the kitchen.'

'And bathroom. It's filthy too. And as the team will need to use it...'

Right. 'Whoever finishes first will then help the other. And you can choose.'

'Me?'

'You're the boss.'

She folded her arms. 'You're happy to clean?'

'You learn to keep things shipshape when you're in the army.'

She glanced around. He waited, intrigued to find out which one she'd choose—cleaning or packing.

'It'd be safer if I took the kitchen.'

'You have a cleaning fetish or something? Surely your father employs an army of cleaners.'

Laughter lit those golden eyes. 'I don't *live* with my father, Mr—'

But the Cartwright never came and for some reason it made his heart sink. 'Why not?'

'That's one of those off-the-table topics.'

Interesting. 'Why would the kitchen be safer?'

She pointed to the boxes littering the room. 'I'm dying to see what's inside those, but now is not the time to get distracted.' She gestured towards the kitchen. 'But there's something dead in the oven and I really don't want to deal with it.'

'You go take first shower. I'll deal with the oven.'

'Thank you.'

After showers, they headed out the back to the tradesman's van they'd been allocated. She took one look at the manual gearbox and handed him the keys.

'I'll give you lessons.'

'We won't have time for that.'

'If something happens, you need to be able to drive this thing.'

Her head whipped around. 'If something happens... Like *what*?'

Hell, he'd alarmed her. He kept his voice casual as he started the van. 'Like I fall down the stairs and break a leg.'

Her shoulders loosened, but tensed again a moment later. She pointed at him. 'No falling down the stairs. No broken legs.'

'Roger that. Now, buckle your seatbelt.'

The village was only a five-minute drive away and they ate a hearty lunch of moussaka and bread in a courtyard with a large olive tree. They stuck with drinking water, but he made a note to buy a few bottles of the local wine to keep at the villa.

Sipping a glass of wine at that table under the shady tree, staring at what even he had to admit was an amazing view, might help loosen Janie up, because the food hadn't worked. She didn't make idle chitchat or tease him. She busied herself making a shopping list and researching local suppliers on her phone.

Rolling his shoulders, he shifted on his chair. 'Look, I'm sorry for the way I spoke to you at the end of filming yesterday, okay?'

She started as if she'd been a million miles away. 'Okay.' Eyes the colour of cognac narrowed. 'But you're not sorry for what you said.'

'I'm sorry I expressed myself so...'

'Rudely?'

'Forcefully.'

That infuriatingly mobile mouth pursed. 'And yet the reason why you're so opposed to my charity is off the table, not open for discussion.'

He had no intention of telling her the real reason he hated her charity. 'Criminals should be punished,' he ground out.

'And jail isn't punishment enough?'

'These are people who have made seriously bad choices. They need to understand there are ramifications for that.'

'I'd have thought jail was a pretty big ramification.'

He slammed a finger to the table. 'Violence should *not* be rewarded.'

Two beats of silence passed. 'Not all criminals are violent, Zach.'

She stared at him, her eyes going dark and troubled, her teeth gnawing on her bottom lip. He wanted to tell her to stop that, that she'd do herself an injury. But the longer he stared the greater the hunger that ballooned in his chest. It grew so big it blocked his throat.

'You were a victim of a violent crime,' she said quietly.

The soft words knocked it free with the force of a punch. *What the...?*

Her brow pleated. 'Heck, Zach! The person who'd get the better of you had to be a giant or—'

She broke off, her face falling and going sort of soft in a way that had things inside him melting and jerking and roiling.

'You were a child,' she whispered. 'Someone bad hurt you when you were a child. Oh, Zach...' Her hand lifted and for a moment he thought she meant to reach across the table and touch him. He told himself he was glad when she didn't. 'I'm sorry that happened to you.'

What the hell?

'I haven't said a damn thing!' But an old pain he'd never been able to extinguish burned and throbbed. 'How can you go from that Point A to that particular Point B on absolutely nothing?'

'Your face. I keep telling you it's expressive.'

It damn well wasn't. It was only expressive when he wanted it to be.

'Look, we're never going to agree on this charity of yours, so—'

'You're saying you refuse to even hear my reasons for supporting Second Chances?'

He didn't want to hear her reasons.

'I'm saying that despite our opposing views on that topic, I'm planning to do my best for you on this project. I promise to neither undermine nor sabotage you.'

'I never thought you would.'

'And now we're going to the hardware store.' He stood. This conversation was well and truly over.

CHAPTER FIVE

ON MONDAY THEY started work for real. Not that they'd done anything else since arriving. But this time the camera was rolling.

Their first assignment—to makeover a bedroom.

Janie chose the big double bedroom on the first floor with its French windows out onto the circular balcony and sweeping views of the sea. Breathtaking. Not only was it the largest of the bedrooms but it was also the one that needed the most work. But as far as she was concerned they might as well go big or go home. She had a reputation to establish.

Window and door frames needed replacing and the floorboards were in desperate need of sanding. Plaster needed fixing and the wood panelling on one wall had rotted. Pulling several boards off, though, and she saw the potential of the underlying stone as a feature wall. She bounced from foot to foot. This room could look fabulous!

One glance at the grim set of Zach's mouth, though, had her stomach plummeting. He didn't want to be here. He might've promised he'd do his best but it didn't change the fact that he loathed everything about this assignment. She needed to find a way to get him onboard.

Out on the lawn, circular saws cut through the air. Pulling the rotted wood from that wall, she went over her and Zach's previous conversations. She needed to find a way to help him not hate this job.

I'm a pretty decent carpenter.

She paused. The way he'd said that… Maybe—

'Everything okay?'

Zach measured the inside doorframe, a toolbelt fastened around his hips. A sigh rose through her. What was it about a man and a toolbelt?

Ha! Both Darren and Tian were wearing toolbelts but she hardly noticed them.

'Janie?'

She looked back at him.

I'm a pretty decent carpenter.

'Zach, could you build me a bed?'

'What kind of bed?'

Scizing her sketchbook, she made a sketch of a four-poster bed—a light, airy concoction she could swathe with delicate, floaty drapes. Darren and Tian, carrying in the freshly cut window frames, glanced over her shoulder as they passed. All three men shrugged.

She blew out a breath. Where was their enthusiasm? 'Okay, guys, look. You might not think aesthetics matter much to a lot of people.' Secretly, though, she thought they did. 'But I think when you have a beautiful space it makes you feel beautiful too, and deliciously spoiled. It can be a wonderful escape, a sanctuary from the real world.'

'You're right.' Tian set down his bundle of timber. 'It's not conscious, but it's win-win.'

'More often than not, real life isn't particularly romantic. But every now and again it's wonderful to indulge and feel like we're experiencing life and romance like it is in the movies.' She hugged her sketchpad to her chest. '*That's* what this room is about—it's dream-come-true material. A person who comes to stay here will cherish the memory forever. Gentlemen, we're now in the business of making dreams come true and giving people an experience they'll never forget.'

Their shoulders went back at her words. Zach reached for her sketchpad. 'This—' he slapped the back of his hand to her sketch '—is a piece of cake.'

She bounced on the spot. 'I *cannot* wait to see it once it's finished!'

Janie lugged wood and debris down to the skip, took a turn on the sander and inventoried the deliveries that arrived. She didn't stop. And yet even through the frenetic activity she couldn't shake her continuing and ever-growing awareness of Zach. Something inside him had lightened and she gave thanks for it.

Not that it made it any easier for her to understand the man. She didn't get him. At all. He acted all judgemental and inflexible one minute and then did something sweet the next. Like setting up a café table for her in the pine grove, and putting locks on the bedroom doors to keep her safe. This morning when the team had arrived he'd told them the third floor was off-limits.

That's not him being heroic. That's him doing his job.

The table wasn't. That was sweet.

'What are you thinking?' he asked on day two of the renovation.

She stood inside the small room behind the bedroom—a storeroom of some kind. There were a couple of them on this floor. This one had shelving on either side. For linen, maybe?

'You're thinking of an en suite bathroom, aren't you?'

She'd refused to turn around when he'd initially spoken because every single time her eyes connected with that big hard body her pulse did stupid things. It was infuriating!

She turned now and found him effortlessly balancing several thick planks of wood across one broad shoulder as if they weighed nothing. Tanned skin shone in the light pouring in at every window and her pulse predictably jostled and surged and her mouth went dry. She snapped back to the storeroom.

'It's big enough, if that's what you're worried about.'

His voice, low and gravelly, had goosebumps lifting on her arms. For the last eight months she'd been indifferent to men and she wanted it to stay that way.

Why now? And why Zach?

'But do we have the time?' she forced out.

'Hold on, let me take this timber through to Darren.'

Why did her stupid hormones have to come out of hibernation *now*? She rubbed a hand over her face. It *had* to be the location. This gorgeous old villa was the epitome of romance, and they were in Greece...on a Greek island. And the sun was shining and the view out of every window stole her breath. The romance of it all had gone to her head.

Zach came back with Tian and together they measured the cupboard and discussed water pipes, waterproofing, timeframes. He moved with a lean-hipped economy that held her spellbound.

So stop looking at him!

Wise advice. But hard to follow. One thing she knew for sure, though—she shouldn't be thinking about sexy times on a Greek island with her hot bodyguard. She shouldn't be contemplating sexy times with anyone! After Sebastian...

Bile burned her throat. This was probably a rebound thing. If she gave into it she might find herself making an even bigger mistake. She couldn't risk it. She couldn't face what that might say about her if she did.

'Janie?'

She came back to earth to find Zach and Tian watching her. She swallowed. 'Sorry, you were saying?'

Zach's eyes searched her face. 'Tian says that he can have it done by the end of the week.'

She straightened. 'Really?'

Tian explained that they'd need to keep things simple—a standard configuration with basic lighting, nothing too fussy when it came to tiles. 'Then we can remove the washbasin in the bedroom.'

All of the bedrooms on the first floor had antiquated washbasins. They were rather sweet, but they didn't scream *luxury resort*.

'That's wonderful. I'll research tiles tonight and we'll talk tomorrow.'

'Okay?' Zach checked when Tian got back to work.

'Very okay.'

'We'll get to work knocking down these shelves, knocking through here into the bedroom, and we'll board up this corridor doorway.' He picked up a sledgehammer and held it out to her. 'Want to do the honours?'

'Yes, please!'

She knocked down shelves, fetched and carried and was general dogsbody. All the while reminding herself that fantasising about Zach was pointless. She wasn't his type. She was a pampered little daddy's girl. Plain Jane.

He said you're not plain.

He was being nice!

He's just being nice, she reminded herself that evening when he brought her out a glass of wine where she sat at the table under the big tree, admiring the sunset. The sea was a wash of pale blues and pinks and so still it made an ache open up inside her.

Lifting his glass of water in a silent toast, he set up a portable barbecue and cooked two steaks to go with the salad he'd tossed and the crusty bread rolls arranged in a basket. They'd agreed to take it in turn about cooking and tonight was his first night. The food looked good, smelled great, and she realised she was ravenous.

He set a plate in front of her before planting himself in the seat opposite. 'It's not fancy, but—'

'I don't need fancy. I need hearty.'

They ate in silence until the worst of their hunger had been slaked. And as long as she didn't let her gaze shift to him too often, safeguarding her pulse from unnecessary jumping and jostling, it was weirdly comfortable.

'Are you disappointed?'

She glanced up. 'About?'

He gestured to the villa.

Oh, that.

'I was initially, but now...' She surveyed the villa's shabby façade, let her eyes roam across the surrounding gardens and then back to the water, which had turned a deeper blue. 'I love this place.'

She frowned. When had that happened? 'Don't you?' she blurted out. 'The villa mightn't be pretty on the outside, but inside it is. And yes, if we're going to do it justice it does lock us into a particular ethos of styling. But what the heck, let's embrace that and go all-in.' She leaned back. 'I find myself...'

Blue eyes flared in the dusk. 'What?'

'Eager to bring the villa back to life.' After his initial lack of enthusiasm, Zach had knuckled down, his dissatisfaction and restlessness melting away. 'Aren't you even a little bit interested in how it's all going to look once we're done?'

He shrugged.

'You know what?' She folded her arms. 'I don't think you hate this job as much as you thought you would.'

Sometimes he was incredibly difficult to read, but now wasn't one of those times. She could practically see the words *Janie has rocks in her head* suspended above him in neon.

She sipped her wine, a luscious red. 'You were humming while you grilled those steaks.'

He scowled. 'Was not.'

'"Sittin' on the Dock of the Bay". Michael Bolton.'

'What the hell…? Otis Redding is the *only* version worth its salt.'

She grinned. That was her favourite version too.

He rolled his shoulders, thrust out his jaw. 'So what if I was?'

'It would indicate a certain level of relaxation and contentment.'

His frown turned inward. Resting her chin on her hand, she allowed herself the momentary pleasure of simply gazing at him while she had the chance.

He stiffened when he realised, his blue eyes spearing to hers. 'What?'

She forced her gaze away. She ought not drink any more wine. It had barriers that should remain steadfast weakening. 'You've been oddly nice to me these last couple of days.'

'Why wouldn't I be nice to you?'

'It's not part of your job description.'

'It's not part of my job description to not be nice to you either. And nice how?' he demanded. 'Because I cooked dinner? It was my turn to cook. Nice because I check all the details of the renovation with you? Well, as you're the boss and the one who needs to approve everything that—'

'You put a café table in the pine grove for me.'

'Just an experiment,' he muttered. 'I wanted to see if you were right. You had coffee there this morning. Did you enjoy it?'

'I did. Why didn't you join me?'

He glanced away. 'Thought you might want to be alone.' He reached for the bottle to top up her wine, but she covered her glass with her hand and shook her head. 'You're surrounded by men on this job, Janie. Seemed important to give you a place to retreat to if you needed it.'

'See? Nice. You didn't have to do that. And you didn't have to buy red wine for dinner either, especially when you don't appear to be drinking it.'

'That's just common courtesy. You're working hard. You need quality downtime.'

And yet that wasn't the impression she had of how he lived his life. He worked hard, but she had a feeling he didn't play hard.

'Can I ask you a question?'

He eyed her warily from behind his glass of water. 'Only if I can ask you something in return.'

Her heart started to pound. What would he ask? What the real Joey Walter was like? Or maybe he'd ask how much plastic surgery her mother had really had done, or which of her stepfathers she most liked now that Mum had married for the fifth time.

'What do you want to ask, Janie?'

'Why you were really so reluctant to take on this job.' She moistened her lips. 'What did you want to ask?'

He stared at her for two beats and then lifted something that rested on the ground at his feet and placed it on the table. A wrench.

She stiffened. *Her* wrench. 'You've been sneaking into my bedroom.'

'I do a thorough sweep morning and night. Just making sure all is as it should be. *Not* snooping.'

She shouldn't be surprised. And she wasn't really.

'For the last two mornings I've seen this poking out from beneath your pillow. Want to tell me why?'

She hated what it revealed about her. Hitching up her chin, she glared, though he didn't really deserve it. The person who'd sent those awful letters did.

'I figured it wouldn't hurt to have something handy to use as a weapon if the need arose.'

He remained silent. It took an effort of will not to roll her shoulders, fidget…curl up into a tiny ball beneath the table. *Don't be pathetic.*

'In case of an intruder... Or something.'

'Or something?'

He wanted her to spell it out?

'You've read those letters. We both know they're probably a hoax, but if they're not that means there's someone out there who wishes to hurt me, who wants to see me suffer. And before you say anything, I know I have a lot of people on my side protecting me and looking out for me, but if this person manages to sneak past everyone then I'm not going down without a fight. So I figure I'm better off with a wrench than without.'

'To give you a chance to knock the assailant out and get away?'

'Exactly.'

'You know the chances of this person getting through are extremely slim.'

'Yes.' She nodded at the wrench. 'But having that helps me sleep better at night.'

'In which case, let's replace the wrench with this.' He handed her a heavy-duty cylindrical torch. 'Army issue. It has a good grip, won't slip, and you can use it as a baton. Once you've knocked the sucker out, you can switch it on to find your way out if it happens to be dark.'

Perfect.

He went to say something else, but both his phone and watch buzzed. He spoke into his watch. 'Sarge?'

'Car just turned into the drive. Headlights off.'

'Roger that. Muting you now.'

She swallowed. 'Do we need to worry?'

'Probably not, but we're going to take precautions anyway. Get behind the tree, Janie.'

She did as he said without argument, taking the torch with her.

'See that branch up there?' He pointed. 'That's where you're going.'

He hoisted her up and one part of her couldn't help but purr at this evidence of his strength and power—those muscles could make a grown woman swoon. Reaching up, he wrapped a warm hand around her ankle as she steadied herself on the branch—standing on it and pressing herself against the trunk.

'I'm not going to let anything happen to you.'

'I trust you.' And oddly enough, she did. Having him near had helped chase away her nightmares too.

'Whatever happens…' They watched the dark shape of a car quietly crunch down the drive and halt. 'Don't move. And don't make a sound.'

Glancing down at him, she mimed zipping her mouth shut. 'Be careful, Zach.'

The car halted, the driver's door opened and someone dressed in dark clothes crept out and tiptoed towards the villa. Her heart picked up speed when Zach left his post beneath her to move out silently and circle behind the man with a stealth that she'd ordinarily admire, except… What if that man was armed?

Damn it! Where the hell with Sarge and the other two operatives? Why weren't they storming the gates and—

Oh, God. Oh, God. Oh, God.

Zach was closing in on the man and…

With one swift stride, Zach grabbed the intruder from behind, kicked his legs out from beneath him and had him eating dirt as he pulled one arm up in a painful hold and ground an unsympathetic knee into the small of his back.

'Want to explain what you're doing, pal?'

The man wheezed and coughed and swore. 'Jesus! It's me, Zach.'

Zach frowned.

'Cullen. It's Cullen. *My shoulder!*'

Zach eased off a fraction. Damn. The team had done a

thorough search on the production crew. Nobody had raised any red flags.

'Jeez, what did you jump me for?' Cullen's voice was muffled by the ground. He wheezed some more. 'Let me up.'

'Not until you explain yourself. Creeping around in the dark isn't making me feel real friendly towards you, Cullen.' He tightened his hold again, making the man groan.

'Okay, okay, I didn't want to blow my cover so soon, but I have to deliver bits of film to you and Janie over the course of the next ten weeks. They're supposed to come from an anonymous source.'

Say what?

'Look, over there.' With an effort that cost him, Cullen nodded towards something on the ground. 'It's an envelope with a cryptic note and a thumb drive. Footage of what's been going on with the other contestants.'

Just to be on the safe side, Zach did a thorough frisk to make sure Cullen wasn't carrying any weapons. Finally letting the man up, he reached for the envelope.

Cullen dusted himself off, eyeing Zach warily. 'What the hell...? Was that necessary?'

Zach shrugged. 'Didn't know it was you. And if we're being brutally honest, I'd have expected better from you. Let me make a suggestion. Don't do that again. We've been working our butts off, we're tired, and I don't take kindly to suspicious intruders creeping around in the dark. They usually mean trouble.'

'And we've all heard tall tales of sabotage on set,' Janie said, ambling up behind them.

What the hell...? He'd told her to stay put!

She ignored Zach to raise an eyebrow at Cullen. 'Why don't you leave the next lot in the letterbox at the top of the drive? Or hand them over in person and have a glass of wine and a chat before heading home again?'

Cullen had the grace to look shamefaced. 'I didn't mean to frighten you.'

The image of that wrench rose in Zach's mind and his hands fisted. Janie lived in enough fear as it was without having to deal with stupid games like this.

A laugh gurgled from her throat. 'As you can see, we were shaking in our shoes. What on earth possessed you to do something so silly, Cullen? Wine?'

Zach shook his head as she led Cullen down to the table, but she turned and mouthed *laptop* to Zach behind Cullen's back. He nodded.

He returned a few minutes later with Janie's laptop. She'd lit three fat yellow candles and they flickered in the night in the same way the stars flickered on the still water. For the briefest of moments he glimpsed the paradise Janie had spoken about earlier. She was right. There was something about this place.

Setting the laptop in front of her and pointing a warning finger at Cullen when he made as if to leave, he and Janie watched the footage captured on the thumb drive.

Janie stiffened... And then stiffened even more as the footage played. When it finished, she played it again. Antoine, Isobel and several of the other contestants all mocked Janie's charity—and Janie herself. He planted himself on the chair beside hers, fought the urge to reach for her hand and to squeeze it, his insides raging at the unfairness of such a pile on—one deliberately created to make Janie look as bad as possible.

When it had finished playing for the second time, Janie snapped the lid of her laptop shut and glared at Cullen.

He rubbed a hand over his face. 'Look, I don't make any of the creative decisions or... Or any decisions at all really. I'm told what to film, what questions to ask... And you do know the producers aren't your friends, don't you? All they care about are the ratings and attracting big-name advertisers. And...'

'And?' Janie's voice was hard.

Cullen shrugged. 'Drama sells.'

'That's not drama.' Zach must've said it more grimly than he'd meant to, though, as Janie stared up at him with big, startled eyes. He shrugged. 'It's spite and malice.'

'Don't shoot the messenger.' Cullen held up his hands. 'I already have enough bruises in the service of this so-called drama.' He turned to Janie. 'I'm sorry. I know it's awful. If it's any consolation, I expect everyone will get their turn. You can get your own back then.'

'Sorry to disappoint you, Cullen, but we won't be dissing on anyone.'

Cullen sent them both a weak smile. 'In some ways you could view my drop-off as a public service.'

Zach leant back to stop himself from grabbing Cullen by the collar and shaking the living daylights out of him. 'And you figure that how?'

'We'll be filming your reactions to all of this when the show goes live on Sunday night. At least now you can prepare yourselves.'

Zach was minutely attuned to Janie's every movement. She chafed her arms as if she were cold and it disturbed the nearby air, sent it brushing against his skin like a breeze. The night was balmy, though, so he knew it wasn't the temperature that chilled her. He'd worked with enough clients who'd felt hunted and vulnerable to know that was how she felt now.

'Have you shown us the worst footage?' he demanded.

'I hope so.' Cullen lifted his hands, let them drop. 'That's the only footage I've been sent.'

After Cullen left, Janie turned to Zach. 'Everyone on the show, the audience at home, they're all going to hate me.'

'Not true. If you were sitting at home watching that, who would you actually be rooting for—Antoine and Isobel?'

'I *never* cheer for the mean boys and girls.'

A whisper of a laugh fluttered through him. 'Janie, I don't believe truer words were ever spoken.' This woman was kindness personified.

She stared at him with wide eyes. Eyes he could fall into. Her scent, all cashmere and violets, made his head swim... the candlelight flickered—

With a squeak, she leapt up, strode around the table and paced for a bit before planting herself in the seat opposite. His heart drummed in his chest. For a moment there he'd been tempted to lean forward, press his lips to hers and—

His gut churned.

She gestured heavenward. 'Why start with me as public enemy number one?'

Because she was the easiest target. He didn't say that out loud.

'Neither Antoine nor Isobel was exactly warm to you on episode one. I guess the director is building on that. If I wanted to maximise the programme's potential drama, I'd be giving Antoine and Isobel enough rope to hang themselves and filming their comeuppance later in the series. It'd make their downfall all the sweeter for the viewer when it comes.'

'Which is ugly in and of itself. And despite what you say, while the audience might detest Antoine and Isobel for being mean, they're probably also going to secretly agree with them. I'm now going to go through the rest of the series with a big black mark against my name.'

'Or because you're the first target and there are another eight episodes to go it gives everyone time to forget what was said during this second week.'

Her laugh lacked mirth. 'You don't believe that for a moment. That's not how these shows work.'

The despair in the depths of those amber eyes chafed at him. Moving, he straddled the chair beside hers, stared out at the water. 'Do you remember what you said earlier about us needing to fully embrace the Greek ethos and styling to do the villa justice?'

'What's that got to do with anything?'

Confusion was better than despair. 'What if you were to wholly embrace the role they're trying to thrust you into?'

Her mouth opened and closed. She cleared her throat. 'You know, that might be worth thinking about.' She drew shapes on the table with her finger. 'Why are you being so Pollyanna all of a sudden?'

Because the haunted expression in her eyes gutted him and he couldn't explain why. Except she'd worked so damn hard for the past couple of days, had been sleeping with a wrench under her pillow, and now he'd witnessed for himself how much she truly loathed being in spotlight. Yet she was still putting herself through all of this for charity. He might not like the charity she'd chosen to support, but he had to admire her dedication.

'Don't know what you're talking about.' He might not be able to change what had happened but he could take her mind off it. 'We were interrupted before I could answer your question.'

'What question?'

'The one about why I didn't want to take this job.'

Cognac eyes immediately lifted to his. Under the glare of her full attention, his nape prickled.

'Water?' she asked when he remained silent.

At his nod, she filled his water glass before filling her wineglass with water too and shifting in her seat to gaze out at the moonlit water. As if aware it might be easier for him to speak if she didn't watch him while he spoke.

Damn it, the woman was thoughtful. But even if she wasn't, after what she'd overheard him say the day they'd met she deserved an honest explanation. Even if it didn't paint him in a particularly edifying light.

'When Sarge, Logan and I left the army we started Sentry.'
She nodded.

'Sarge was always going to be the brains of the outfit while
Logan and I were the brawn. Meaning, Sarge would administer and direct operations while Logan and I worked in the
field. Obviously, we've a team of people, it's not just the three
of us. As we've grown more successful the number of staff
we employ has grown too.'

'Makes sense.'

'I've always worked the more dangerous jobs while Logan
has worked the ones requiring diplomacy. Each of us playing
to our skill set. I'm fit and strong and was one of the army's
best hand-to-hand combat fighters in my time there. I can
keep someone alive in a jungle or on top of a snowy mountain or in a desert.'

'No way! Really?'

He shrugged. 'Logan is interested in politics, trained in
diplomacy and negotiation skills.'

'The three of you make a formidable team.'

'Except Sarge is now talking about retirement and making a succession plan.'

'And you don't want to be stuck behind a desk.'

He really, *really* didn't.

'You *enjoy* dangerous jobs?'

Her incredulity made him smile.

'*Why?*'

'Thwarting danger and bad guys…there's no better feeling." He shrugged again. "I can't say I like the real world all
that much.'

The moon lit a golden path across the sea and a small
breeze had blown up, making the reflections dance. Pine and
salt scented the air.

She was quiet for a long moment. 'So, you don't actually
have a home base or anything like that?'

'I've an apartment in London.' Not that he spent much time there.

'But you spend most of your time travelling from assignment to assignment?'

'Yep.'

'What about your birthday and the holidays? Don't you want to celebrate those with family and friends?'

Things inside him tightened. 'I've always been a loner.'

She turned to face him fully. 'There are a lot of good things to be enjoyed in the real world too, Zach.'

Not from where he was sitting, there weren't.

'You didn't look as if you were chafing too much today or wishing yourself elsewhere. There were times when you looked as if you were enjoying the work.'

He'd expected to hate the work, had expected the associations with his past to plague him. But once he'd found a rhythm all of that had fallen away. He was even looking forward to making that bed she wanted. He scowled, rubbed a hand through his hair. It didn't mean he was going soft or anything.

'Though it's early days and you've been working so hard you probably haven't had time to chafe yet.'

True. Though he couldn't deny there was a certain sense of satisfaction in seeing the bedroom take shape. He hadn't expected that.

'And although this is a *dolly* assignment…' he winced at her words '… I've seen how thorough and vigilant you've been.'

'I'm taking this assignment seriously.'

'I know. I also know what the stats are on the author of those poison pen letters being a crank. But seeing you in action this evening…' She shook her head. 'Cullen had no idea what hit him.'

Which was how he liked it.

'You were amazing, tough guy.'

Her words caught him off-guard. She thought him...

Their gazes caught and clung. Her eyes darkened as they roved across his face, her lips parted, and his heart pounded loud in his ears. She wanted him with the same urgent hunger roaring through him. Heat and elation speared to his groin, the world shrinking to this moment and this woman. Would she taste as golden as she looked—all sunshine and champagne and laughter?

One of her hands lifted as if to reach out and touch his chest, as if to slide up behind his neck to pull it down for a kiss...

The breath jammed in his throat.

Blinking, she snapped away, breaking the spell. Both of them breathed hard.

Before he could say anything, she scrambled to her feet. 'Time for me to head for bed. Goodnight, Zach.'

He stood too.

Janie started for the house. Stuttering to a halt, she turned on her heel, came back and reached for the torch, but her eyes drifted up to his as if they couldn't help it and time stopped.

CHAPTER SIX

AIR SLAMMED OUT of Janie's lungs, leaving her strangely and helplessly immobile. She hadn't meant to come back but she'd wanted the darn torch. Intellectually, she knew she wasn't in danger from the author of those letters, but having a weapon helped her sleep better, helped her feel less pathetic.

Her mistake had been in glancing at Zach…and getting caught up in the turbulent blue fire of his eyes. She'd told herself that she wasn't his type—that he thought her a plain Jane—but that was a lie. She'd known after their first meeting that he hadn't thought her plain.

His stunned *'What the hell are the press thinking?'* had informed her of that. Stupidly, foolishly, it had buoyed her spirits, had fed her vanity. Had made her teasing and flirtatious during their pub lunch.

Pathetic.

She'd told herself the lie because she didn't trust her judgement any more. She'd told herself the lie because of the hunger that stretched through her when she gazed at him. She'd wanted to create a barrier. She had a job to do and things to prove to herself. She didn't want hormones interfering with that.

But all of that fled when she met his gaze, the air between them sparking with heat.

'Janie.'

Her name sounded like a plea on his lips. And when he stared at her like that...

She reached for him and his mouth landed on hers—a sensual assault that had her standing on tiptoe and begging for more. He wrapped her in a heated tenderness that had a moan gathering in the back of her throat. Winding her arms around his neck, she pulled him closer and his groan of approval weakened her knees. She'd have fallen, but his arms held her firmly against him, refusing to let her fall.

He kissed her with a slow and thorough precision as if memorising every line of her lips, as if committing them to memory—unhurried and with a quiet relish that curled her toes...and had a crick starting up in her neck. The man was so tall!

Without breaking the kiss, she pushed him into a chair and straddled his lap. Bracketing his face with her hands, she held him still while she explored his lips with the same slow candour he had hers. The hands at her waist tightened, the fingers digging into her flesh as if it took all his strength to hold still for her.

When she nibbled his bottom lip with her teeth, though, that passion unleashed and he dipped her over his arm, his mouth fierce and possessive, and one hand slid beneath her thigh to pull her hard against the bulge in his jeans and all she could do was hold on as heat and need swamped her and she found herself trying to crawl into his body.

Long moments later his lips lifted from hers and he straightened, breathing hard. She wanted to protest, but the expression in his eyes wasn't horror or regret and it eased the fear that had flared in her chest. Lifting trembling fingers, she touched them to her mouth, unsure if her lips would ever feel the same again.

Drawing her to him, he wrapped her in his arms, her cheek pressed against his shoulder, his chin resting on her head.

'What are you doing?' She was incapable of speaking in anything above a whisper.

Their chests rose and fell in unison. 'Hugging you.'

She closed her eyes. 'Can I ask why?'

She felt his nod and had to swallow.

'Because I don't think my legs will work just yet, which makes me think yours might feel a tad shaky too.'

Understatement much? But...he wanted to stand?

'And not ready to not touch you,' he added.

Okay, cue relief.

'But I think we both need a chance to let oxygen hit our brains again.'

She nestled closer, staring at the water, twinkling with the reflections of a thousand stars. One large hand roved softly across her back in hypnotic arcs.

'I never mindlessly fall into bed with a woman. And Janie, we both know that's where this was heading. I thought you might like a breather before things went that far.'

Wise. And oddly gallant. Smothering a sigh, she straightened, briefly cupped his cheek before forcing herself off his lap.

Piercing eyes searched hers. 'Is this you making a decision?' His gaze never wavered.

She shook her head. 'If you want me to be sensible...well, I can't do that when I'm in your arms. Even if the touch is innocent.'

His nostrils flared as if her words excited him and she had to swing away before she threw sensible to the gutter and devoured him whole. Forcing her legs down to the water's edge, she planted her butt on a large rock, rested her elbows on her knees and her chin in her hands. He sat beside her on the grass. Not too close. 'Want to tell me what you're thinking?'

'I'm trying to remind myself of all the reasons that sleeping with you would be a bad idea.'

'Wanna hit me with them?' He turned his head to meet her gaze. No pressure. No hurt male pride. Beneath his gruffness, Zach had a kind heart.

She let out a slow breath. 'First on my list is that I don't want any distractions. I want to be fully focused on this project.'

'I can understand that.'

And generous. Kind *and* generous.

'But the thing is, whether we sleep together or not, you're already a distraction. I look at you and I want you. I can't help it.'

'I didn't mean to be a complication, Janie.'

She stiffened. 'I'm not *blaming* you. We have…chemistry. It happens sometimes.' Apparently.

'You've felt this before?'

Biting her lip, she shook her head, amazed at her own honesty. Yet it felt right to be honest with him. It felt safe to be honest with him. 'Not like this. This is intense.' All-encompassing. 'You?'

'Not like this,' he agreed.

Her heart pounded. She swallowed and breathed through it. *Remember what's important.*

'Zach, I don't feel as if I've achieved much of any note in my life, on my own merit. Take this TV show. I was given it because Joey Walter is my father. But it *is* a chance to show the world what I can do. And I can do it for the betterment of a cause that means a lot to me. That's where I should be focusing my energies.'

His eyes glowed almost midnight in the moonlight.

'And that's why I wish I didn't feel this—' she gestured between them '—thing.'

Reaching for her hand, he pressed a kiss to her knuckles before releasing it again. 'Which is why we shouldn't do this.'

He started to rise.

'And yet…'

He sat again, eyed her warily. 'And yet…?'

'I've been wondering if I shouldn't sleep with you to get you out of my system.'

He stiffened.

'I know. Appalling, right? How cold-blooded does that sound? I've thought a lot of things about myself over the years, but cold-blooded?' She gave an unsteady laugh.

He rubbed a hand over his face. 'Janie, I think you'll find you're hot-blooded.'

'Your turn. Why did you need to stop and think about it? What are your reasons for hesitating?'

Narrowed eyes stared into the darkness. 'I'm supposed to be working. You're a client. My brief here is to keep you safe. I shouldn't let anything get in the way of that.'

She huffed out a laugh. He looked as perturbed as she felt. 'Never had a dalliance with a client before?'

'Nope.'

'We both know that you being here is an over-the-top measure and that my father is being ridiculously overprotective. Your being here is a reassurance to him, nothing more. But it's like calling in a surgeon to put a plaster on a papercut.'

His lips twitched. 'Have you been listening in to my phone calls with Sarge?'

'That said, I know you're taking the job seriously.' Tonight had proven that, to Cullen's regret. 'But your level of expertise isn't necessary.' She chewed on her lip as another thought occurred to her.

'Out with it,' he ordered.

'I don't want you to feel coerced because I'm a paying client.'

He actually grinned at that. 'Not feeling coerced, Janie. There's no boss-employee dynamic here.'

She let out a breath. 'Good.'

'The other thing…'

She raised an eyebrow.

'I don't know where you stand on relationships,' he said with a shrug. 'Do you want one? Is that what you're looking for? Because I don't do relationships. There's no time for them in my line of work. And I wouldn't want you thinking—'

He broke off when she laughed. 'What part of *"I don't like the real world"* do you think I didn't hear? Relationships belong squarely in the real world, Zach.' Leaning down, she caught his eye. 'But in this instance I feel the same.' After Sebastian... She shuddered. 'I'm definitely not looking for anything long-term.'

His gaze lowered to her mouth and her pulse pounded with a reckless surge. Oh, she could—

'If you lean any closer to me, Janie, I'm going to kiss you again.'

She let herself consider tumbling into his arms. She had the Ionian Sea gently lapping at her feet and it was a balmy moonlit night, the air flooded with the scent of jasmine... Talk about an adventure she'd remember forever.

For the first time since Sebastian, it occurred to her that avoiding romantic entanglements didn't mean she had to sacrifice sex. She liked sex. Why deprive herself of it? She'd just need to choose her partners wisely if she didn't want her personal life splashed across the pages of the gossip rags.

Her heart started to pound. Could it be that simple? After Sebastian—

The edges of her vision darkened and a chill chased down her spine. Sebastian had fooled her for two years. *Two years.* She'd thought she'd known him.

Choose a partner wisely?

Ha! How was she supposed to do that when wisdom and discrimination were two traits she clearly currently lacked? And to think she'd thought that she'd had them mastered! It was enough to make a grown woman weep.

Her throat tightened. She had wept. Too much.

But no more.

And no sex for the foreseeable future either. Pulling in a breath, she let it out slowly. She had a goal. It was time to focus on that. When she'd achieved it, maybe then she'd be ready to…consider other things.

'The expression on your face is telling me you've made your decision and that the answer is a firm no.'

Couldn't he try to look a little more disappointed about that?

She shook herself. What the hell? The fact that even *bothered* her told her more eloquently than anything else that keeping her distance from Zach was a wise move.

She made herself smile, but it felt thin and insubstantial. 'You wanted me to be sensible. This is me being sensible. Sleeping with someone isn't the way to make me feel good about myself. Doing the job I came here to do will. *That's* what I need to focus on.'

He didn't say anything. Just nodded.

'And now I'm really going to bed. Goodnight, Zach.'

His 'Goodnight' followed her on the breeze and, no matter how hard she told herself otherwise, it sounded like a promise.

When episode two of *Renovation Revamp* aired, Zach didn't have to jockey for position to sit next to Janie like he'd expected to. Cullen ordered them to sit side by side.

While the team respected him, they *liked* Janie. As they worked, she'd chatter away like one of the woodlarks that visited the pine grove. She'd start silly philosophical discussions like, 'If you were boss of the world what's one fun rule you'd put in place?'

She'd chosen a TV and Internet blackout for Wednesday nights, decreeing that everyone had to join a music group of some sort or play board games. 'How much fun, huh?' she'd demanded.

Everyone had agreed. Except him. He was the strong, silent type, remember?

And then a discussion would start up about what musical instrument you'd play if you had a choice. Or they would go off on a tangent. It was how he knew she could play the guitar.

She knew the names of the team members' families and asked after them, knew who followed what football or basketball team and asked who they were playing at the weekend and what the odds were like. She made them feel like a team. Hell, yesterday he'd checked the scores to see if Darren's and Tian's teams had won. He'd then checked how the team he'd followed in secondary school—Leeds FC—were doing.

He'd snapped his phone shut when he'd realised, his lips twisting. If he wasn't careful, he'd find himself yearning for a white picket fence next!

Ha! Like that was going to happen.

Cullen, however, declared that, for the purposes of filming, he needed Zach and Janie sitting side by side on the sofa, meaning Zach didn't have to fight the other men for the privilege. He'd made sure Darren and Tian knew about the *surprises* this episode had in store, though.

In the upstairs room of the local tavern that Cullen had organised for their private use, Janie, Darren and Tian fidgeted and shifted. When the theme music for *Renovation Revamp* started, Zach's stomach clenched.

The episode was every bit as bad as expected. Between every snippet of renovation they showed of the individual teams, the negative comments directed at Janie and Second Chances mounted up relentlessly. Zach wrapped his hand around Janie's and squeezed, glad when she squeezed back.

'What do you make about all of that, Janie?' Mike asked with his inane grin.

Cullen's cameraman had his camera balanced on his shoulder and pointing at them, but before Janie could speak Tian leaned forward. 'Janie is a very nice woman. She works hard. Why didn't the cameras show her lugging piles of rotten wood down to the skip or sanding the floor?'

Darren leaned into the camera's view too. 'Tian's right. Seriously uneven footage and—'

'Team, team…' Janie started to laugh, but a light had fired to life in her eyes and Zach couldn't work out if that was a good thing or not. He guessed they were about to find out. No denying, though, that it made her look alive, as if someone had just plugged her into the electricity mains.

Which then had him thinking about that firecracker of a kiss. His skin stretched tight.

Don't think about the kiss.

It should never have happened.

'As you can see—' Janie gestured '—I have the best team. These guys have been great. They've worked their tails off all week, but we've had a lot of fun too. Now, Mike, you asked for my thoughts… I'm pleased with the score the judges gave our bedroom renovation. Team Puerto Rico did an amazing job and deserve to be top of the ladder at the moment, but equal second is a nice position to be in.'

'And what about all of the negative comments directed at you and your charity, Janie? That has to hurt.'

'In the interests of full disclosure—' she pressed her hands together and stared at the camera, her chin high '—someone leaked part of that footage to me earlier in the week. I think I was expected to retaliate with some mean girl comments of my own in an attempt to smack down my detractors.'

She was magnificent.

'But I'm not going to do that. Nobody here has yet heard why I'm such an advocate for Second Chances or the good work the charity does. That footage was filmed prior to being on location, so I know it'll appear in an upcoming episode. Second Chances is an easy target because it's not a *pretty* charity, and to be honest all of that bad sentiment simply feels like a cheap attempt to create fake drama.'

'Hear, hear,' Zach murmured.

Darren and Tian both nodded.

'What I would like to say, though, Mike, is that I'm dedicated enough to Second Chances that I'll be donating my appearance fee to the charity. I sincerely hope the other contestants are doing the same for their chosen charities. Perhaps they can let us know next week?'

'Cut!' Cullen called.

When the episode ended Zach turned to her. 'That was pitch-perfect.'

Her eyes lightened at his words, but then her gaze snagged on his mouth and her nostrils flared. 'Thanks.'

They shot to their feet at the same time, moved apart. What the hell was wrong with him? She'd said she didn't want anything to develop between them. He had to respect that and stop the mooning and ogling. Pining like some pathetic teenager. His hands clenched. Unlike his father, he *could* control his baser instincts.

The rest of the team gathered around Janie to offer their support and Zach moved across to the window to scan the street outside with a professional eye. While waiting for the wholly unprofessional ache in his groin to subside.

This was what happened when he wasn't on some high-powered assignment. It left him adrift and all at sea with nowhere to direct his pent-up energy or—

You know exactly where you want to direct that energy.

Displacement, that was all this was.

He had to rid himself of any thought of making love with Janie. Tian was right. She was a nice woman. She worked hard. He didn't want to make her job here harder than it already was. Despite his body's protestations, the decision she'd made was the right one.

In his world, women like Janie had always been off-limits. The Janies of the world always eventually wanted more. He didn't have *more* to give. He didn't stay in one place long because he didn't want emotional attachments, especially not of the romantic kind. As far as he was concerned, love was emotional suicide. Only a fool or masochist would put themselves through it, and he was neither.

His childhood had been defined by fear. And helplessness. Never knowing what would trigger his father's violence—his sheer defencelessness against it when it did erupt. The helpless fury that he could do nothing to protect his mother.

An ache stretched through his chest. Love and commitment had led his mother to heartbreak and misery. He wasn't making the same mistake. It had taken him a long time to feel secure, to find his place in the world. He would never hand anyone the power to make him feel that scared and helpless again.

They made the trip back to the villa in silence.

He glanced from the road to her and back again. 'You stressed about what Antoine, Isobel and the others said about you?'

Golden eyes sparked with surprise. 'Hell, no! I couldn't give two hoots what Antoine and the rest of them think. I don't know them. They don't mean anything to me. They're not my family or friends. Water off a duck's back.'

'Not entirely sure I believe you,' he said, but that only made her laugh.

'Look at who my parents are. I've been surrounded by exaggeration and drama and hyperbole my entire life. People saying mean things about them, and me, all because...'

'They're famous. And in an attempt to grab a little of the spotlight for themselves,' he finished for her.

She tapped a hand to her chest. '*I'm* the party-pooper who's always the voice of reason. Whenever Mum or Dad fly into a tizz over a bad review and it's all "This is the end of the world, I'm so untalented, my life is over" drama, I'm the person who makes the tea and talks them down.'

Yeah, he could see that.

She snorted. 'Antoine is an amateur when it comes to insults, while Isobel insinuates a lot but there's no substance behind it.'

He frowned. Something didn't add up. 'You were gutted when you first saw that footage.'

'Gutted for Second Chances, not because someone said something mean about *me*. I'm here to lift Second Chances' profile, not damage it. But I couldn't change what they planned to air tonight so I had to suck it up.'

He pulled the van to a halt in its spot behind the villa. There was something he wasn't getting. And he planned to find out what it was, but first he had an online meeting scheduled with Sarge.

When the meeting was done, he grabbed a can of soda and started down to the table under the big tree where Janie sat with a glass of wine. Halting, he swung back, searched the kitchen cupboards for snacks—olives, cheese and crackers—and took them down to her.

At her raised eyebrow, he shrugged. 'Dinner seems a long time ago.' They'd eaten early due to the show. She'd eaten next to nothing. 'Thought you might be hungry.'

'I'm good.' She sipped her wine. 'You tuck in, though.'

Something was wrong. And if it wasn't Antoine and Isobel...

Popping an olive into his mouth, he chewed and swallowed before chasing it down with a mouthful of soda. 'You must be pleased. The judges loved what you did with the bedroom.'

Her head swung around, her eyes widening. *'Seriously?'* She gaped at him.

Whoa!

'They loved what you and the team did. Tian's en suite was pitch-perfect, the treatment of the stone wall inspired, and the bed you built a masterpiece of craftsmanship, whereas I—'

She what?

Shooting to her feet, she marched down to the edge of the lawn and stared out to sea. He scratched a hand through his hair. What the hell was he missing? 'Janie?'

'I let you all down. *I'm* the weak link.'

He was on his feet and in front of her in a millisecond. 'What the hell are you talking about?' He had to step down to the pebbly beach to face her and it put them nearly at the same height. He tried to ignore the shape of her mouth. 'What part of second place didn't you hear? You—'

'And what part of *I played it safe and didn't take risks* didn't you hear?' She jabbed a finger at his chest. '*That's* what one of the judges said.'

'She also said your use of colour was incomparable and that the overall harmony was superb. And she acknowledged you needed to make decisions between balance and budget. The other judge said it was a bedroom he'd love to sleep in. Why are you focusing on that one quibble?'

Her glare didn't lessen.

'Janie, I didn't know you were going to go full drama queen on me. There weren't any notes in your file to warn me about this.'

'I'm not...*a drama queen*!'

'Well, where on earth is that voice of reason you boasted about earlier? Where's the water off a duck's back? Because I hate to tell you this, but you're doing the whole over-the-top exaggerated thing you just accused your parents of doing whenever they receive a bad review.'

Her mouth worked but not a single sound emerged. Her eyes sparked and her chin thrust out. But as he watched, it all slowly bled out of her. Her shoulders drooped and with a funny little hiccup she stumbled back to the table and fell down into the nearest seat—his. He hesitated for a moment before heading around to her seat and switching their drinks. She looked as if she needed something stronger than wine.

'They say pride comes before a fall, don't they?' Her voice was shaky, and it pierced through the usual protective armour around his heart, making it ache. 'I feel as if there's some Greek chorus above my head pointing a finger and laughing itself silly at me right now.'

He didn't know what to say. He should've brought chocolate rather than cheese and crackers. He sliced off a piece of cheese, stuck it on a cracker and handed it across to her. She demolished it, a martial light in her eye. He made her another one, and then another.

'It's just that's what I always thought I was good at—not getting swept up in the nonsense, seeing the bigger picture and maintaining my equilibrium, keeping perspective... Cutting through all the noise to see to the truth. My dad is great at singing, my mother is great at acting, and I'm good at...'

'Wading through all the hype. Seeing the facts.'

She stared at her hands. 'All my life I've seen my parents swing between the highs and the lows that comes from living their lives in the spotlight. Similarly, they've always been totally over the top in their praise of me. That kind of upbringing can go to your head.'

She'd had such a different childhood from his. And he was glad of it. Didn't mean it hadn't had its challenges, though.

'I was lucky enough to have had a very wise nanny. Nanny Earp, who taught me to look beyond all of the noise and nonsense and to see it for what it was. She taught me to question everything, because everyone has an agenda—reviewers, theatre critics, producers, fans...one's peers. And while some people are genuine, others are pushing their own agendas.

She taught me to recognise hyperbole and exaggeration and to understand how they distort reality. She taught me to come to my own conclusions about what was true and false, and to not simply believe either the good or bad press.'

Which explained why she hadn't thrown a temper tantrum when she'd overheard him grumbling on the phone to Logan that first day.

'Nanny Earp sounds like quite a woman. Where is she now?'

'She retired to a little house in Suffolk that my parents bought for her. I see her regularly. She's unofficial family.'

He sliced more cheese and handed it across. She ate as if on autopilot, but he was glad. She needed to keep her strength up.

'So what happened, Janie? What made you overreact to one little comment a judge made tonight?'

Her lips twisted. She gulped wine. 'Sebastian happened.'

CHAPTER SEVEN

'SEBASTIAN. YOUR EX-BOYFRIEND.'

Of course Sebastian would be in whatever file they'd compiled on her.

'Then while we're speaking of agendas—' Zach eyed her steadily '—let me push mine for a moment.'

'You want to know if I think Sebastian could've written those letters.'

His eyes gave the tiniest of flickers—a minute narrowing and release—as if he knew it was an awful question, but it was his job to keep her safe and he'd do it regardless. She fought an entirely inappropriate desire to reach across and lay a hand against his cheek.

No touching!

'Well, they did arrive after we broke up. And the breakup wasn't amicable.'

'Go on.'

'And he'd take great delight if I were publicly humiliated or if my business failed. But those letters...' She shook her head. 'I just can't see it.' Though she'd been spectacularly wrong about Sebastian in other ways. 'Never say never, I suppose.'

'But you'd be surprised if he was the culprit?'

'Really surprised. They just don't sound like him. And while he might like to do me a bad turn, he wouldn't risk his own neck to do it.'

'The man sounds like a toad.'

'Total toad.'

Something in his face gentled. 'What did he do, Janie? How did such a toad manage to shake your confidence so badly?'

She reached for another slice of cheese and slammed it onto a cracker.

'Did he cheat on you?'

'Not that I know of. Though I suspect that would've been easier to deal with. Some men are incapable of fidelity—the grass is always greener, the thrill of the chase and whatever other nonsense they tell themselves. It has nothing to do with the attractiveness or worth of their girlfriend. And before you say anything, I know some women are like that too. But while that would've hurt me, I'd have managed to maintain a degree of objectivity. I'd have kicked his sorry butt to the kerb and moved on, older and wiser.'

She crunched her cheese and cracker with a savage satisfaction. Zach ate an olive and remained silent—not hurrying her, just waiting.

'All my life I've had people befriend me to try and get close to my parents. Sometimes they're after money, sometimes they want an introduction to a recording studio executive or a film producer. Sometimes they want the kudos of moving in what they see as exalted circles.'

'According to your file, you don't move in exalted circles.'

'I don't usually, but most people wouldn't believe that. For me a great night out is getting together with Beck and Lena, ordering in pizza, drinking cocktails and watching a romcom.'

Zach nodded. 'Few things can beat watching *Match of the Day* with Sarge and Logan, cold beer in hand.'

'And see? If you stopped hurdy-gurdying all over the world, you'd get to do more of that.'

That amazing mouth stretched into a rare smile. 'Hurdy-gurdying?'

Her heart pitter-pattered, her pulse did a samba and her

chest billowed like a parachute filled with air. She stuck her nose in the air, hoping none of that showed. Because *nothing* was going to happen between them. She *was* going to be sensible. 'You know what I mean.'

She couldn't hide the breathlessness of her voice, though, and it had his gaze lowering to her mouth.

Swallowing, he pushed the dish of olives away to seize his soda and ease back in his chair. 'Back to Sebastian.'

She dragged her gaze from the powerful lines of his shoulders to fix it on the villa behind him. The villa she'd fallen in love with. Taking two steadying breaths, she prayed the breathlessness would ease. She and Zach might be attracted to each other, but there were good reasons for not following through on it.

She sipped her wine. 'Right, so... I learned pretty early on to work out if people had an ulterior motive when it came to befriending me. I've had a lot of practice at it over the years and I've learned to read the signs, recognise the red flags.'

'But it sucks.'

She shrugged. 'It is what it is. And some people would consider it a small price to pay for the privileged life I lead.' He opened his mouth as if to argue, but she shook her head. 'Everyone has challenges in their lives, Zach—things they need to overcome. In the general scheme of things, mine are small.'

'Janie—'

'Anyway—Sebastian,' she cut in. 'We met at a nightclub. I hardly ever go to those places, but it was Beck's birthday and it's what she wanted to do.'

'Had you been drinking?'

She had to laugh at his less than subtle suggestion that she'd need to be drunk to go out with Sebastian.

'We were both being the sober friend who'd get the others home safely. He was fun, easy to talk to, and when he suggested we meet for coffee some time I didn't see any harm in it.'

Blue eyes flashed in the semi-dark. 'He was too smooth by half.'

'That's the thing, though. He wasn't.' At least he hadn't acted like it. 'He was a bit bumbling and awkward, which made him oddly endearing.' She bit her lip. He'd played her so well. 'He didn't pretend not to know who I was, but he didn't ask a single question about my parents.'

'But it was all a façade?'

She ran a finger around the rim of her wineglass. 'As it turns out. But at the time nothing he did or said made me suspicious. And I'm not the kind of person who's forever falling in and out of love.'

'Me either.'

That didn't surprise her.

'I led him a merry dance, and yet he kept bumbling along and not giving up.'

'Until he wore you down.'

'Until I trusted him. And then I let him into my inner circle.'

'Beck and Lena?'

'They liked him too.'

'Your parents?'

'Mum liked him. Dad will never like any of my boyfriends.'

Those lips curved into another toe-curling smile. 'Nobody will ever be good enough for Daddy's little girl?'

'I could sing the chorus to the song,' she agreed, which made him laugh, and had the heavy things inside her lifting. 'We were together for two years before I found out Seb was only dating me to get access to Joey Walter and the music industry movers and shakers among my father's cohort.' She stared at her hands. 'I didn't even know he wanted to be a singer.'

He'd sing in the shower, and she'd tell him she loved the

sound of his voice, and he'd beam at her whenever she said it. That had been it.

'I'm sorry.'

'I didn't know until he threw a massive temper tantrum about my father refusing to back him and urging me to intervene on his behalf. I hadn't even known he'd raised the topic with my father or requested a meeting. That's when I knew.' She paused, collected herself. 'I gave him a chance to prove me wrong. I told him I never interfered in any music or business decisions my father made, and that I wasn't about to start now.'

'What happened?'

'He told me I owed him. That he'd spent the last two years making me happy on the unspoken proviso he'd be rewarded with Joey Walter as his mentor. I asked him why he hadn't told me he wanted a career in the industry, and he said because he knew it would've made me suspicious. And you know what he said? He said, *"I will marry you and make you happy if you make this happen for me."'* She shook her head. 'Talk about delusional.'

'Weren't you the slightest bit tempted?'

'What the hell, Zach?' She reared back. 'No way! Why would you even ask such a thing?'

One shoulder lifted in a seemingly casual shrug, but she sensed the tension behind it. 'I knew someone once who made compromises like that.'

Her stomach churned. Someone he'd loved? When he didn't add anything, didn't explain, she didn't dig. The expression on his face forbade it.

'I showed Sebastian the door.' Blowing out a breath, she stared up into the branches of the tree. 'It wasn't a pretty scene.'

'Did he try to hurt you? *Physically?'* The words barked out of him like bullets.

'Nothing like that. Just said a lot of vile things about me

being a bad girlfriend, boring, and a crap interior designer. And that I'd only got where I was because of my parents.'

A scowl darkened his face. 'And you're letting his opinion now cloud your judgement and have you doubting yourself?'

'Don't be daft. I couldn't give two hoots what Sebastian thinks or doesn't think about me. Not any more. What do you take me for—some delicate little petal?'

He blinked.

'What's thrown me is that for two years I had no idea of Sebastian's true colours. *For two years*. I believed in him; I trusted him. I… I thought he loved me. But all that time he was using me. I was nothing more than a pawn. And I never sensed it. I didn't see it until the bitter end.'

All of the cheese she'd eaten churned in her stomach. 'I thought I could read people. I thought it was my superpower. From the age of twelve I've done my best to keep my parents from their wildest flights of either despair or euphoria by reminding them that a particular reviewer might have been less than complimentary because of an incident that happened three years ago, and that another singer or actor might have been super complimentary because they're hoping for a good sound-bite for an upcoming album or film they have coming out.'

Pity she hadn't been able to do that for herself.

'For most of my life I've reminded them that they're super talented and super successful, and not to pay too much attention to the hype either way, to stand firm in their own worth.'

'Keeping them grounded.'

And trying to keep herself grounded too.

'But if that really was my superpower I'd have seen Sebastian for what he was. Two years, Zach. He fooled me for *two years*! And if I was so wrong about Sebastian, what else have I been wrong about?' That was what really chipped away at her self-confidence—what else was she wrong about? How could she ever trust herself again?

'Janie, what he did to you was unforgivable.'

'Can't you see this isn't about him? It's about me.' She slapped a hand to her chest. 'I thought I could read people, but Sebastian proved me wrong.' And it had shattered her world and left her reeling. She'd been ready to build a life with a man who'd lied and tricked her, and been ready to keep up that lie forever. Had there ever been a poorer lack of judgement?

Of course there has been, the sensible part of her snapped.

She wasn't the only person who'd been taken in by a liar and a cheat, but…

She'd been so totally and incomprehensibly wrong about Sebastian, and now she couldn't trust in anything. Perspective had flown out of the window. The fear of being that wrong again—about anything—crippled her.

'You made one mistake in one person. We all make mistakes. You need to stop beating yourself up about it.'

She huffed out a laugh. 'Beck and Lena tell me the same thing. It's why they urged me to do the show. They thought it'd boost my confidence.'

'I like these friends of yours.'

'They tell me to stop beating myself up and move on, chalk it up to experience. But the fact is I don't feel as if I am beating myself up.'

Those blue eyes pierced into hers and she wanted to blow the candles out and drench them in darkness in the hope that it would lessen the intensity.

'How do you feel?'

Though maybe it *wasn't* intensity and she was *mistaken* and simply imagining it.

'That I can never trust my judgement again.'

He sucked in a breath that sounded loud against the water lapping on the shore and the crickets cheeping in the garden.

'I always thought I was a pretty good interior designer. I studied hard, my teachers were complimentary, and I work hard now. I love transforming a room—or a house or apartment—and making it look wonderful in a way that delights its owner and makes them happy.' Achieving that brightened both her and her clients' worlds.

'I know I gained some of my early jobs due to who I am. It's inevitable and I have no way to combat that. But I thought, now I was established, that I was being sought on my own merits, that it was my own reputation that had started to precede me, rather than my parents'.' She met those peculiarly intense eyes again. 'But what if all of that *is* wishful thinking?' How would she bear it if she discovered she'd been wrong about all of that too?

Zach reached across the table, seized her hands in his and squeezed them hard. 'You're a brilliant interior designer, Janie. What you did with the bedroom over this last week has been breathtaking.'

She wanted to believe him, but…

'And the judges recognised that. We came second, Janie. We're only a whisker behind Team Puerto Rico.' His grip tightened. 'You want some advice?'

'I only want good advice.' And these days she wasn't sure how to tell the difference between good advice and bad. So what was the point?

He shook her hands as if reading that thought in her face. 'My advice is the best.'

She rolled her eyes. 'Of course it is.'

'Focus on the entirety of what the judges say—don't take one tiny piece of it and worry at it with the kind of focus your parents have always done and blow it out of proportion. It's probably your default setting because that's what you saw growing up, but Nanny Earp taught you better than that.'

Zach had the most ridiculous desire to hold his breath as a range of emotions raced across Janie's face. She pulled her hands free from his and it left him oddly bereft. He swiped his palms down the sides of his cargo shorts, tried to rub the feel of her away. It didn't work.

She ran her hands over her face. Eventually she pulled them away and nodded. 'You're right. Nanny Earp did teach me better and I should be doing her proud rather than making a mockery of all that she taught me.'

This woman put too much pressure on herself.

She dragged in a breath that made her entire frame shudder. 'Right, back to basics.'

'Back to basics,' he echoed. What were the basics?

'She said I had to be my own compass. Don't fixate on just the one line that stung in a review, or half a paragraph in the paper, or phrase in an entire conversation. Take it as a whole. Only then could I make an informed judgement.'

He opened his mouth, but she held up a finger. Silhouetted by the light of the moon and with the Ionian Sea as her backdrop, she looked like a Greek goddess. Need rose through him, hard and fast. His mouth went dry. His groin went tight. He wanted this woman with a raw hunger he'd not experienced since he was a teenager. It took everything he had to remain in his seat and not to act on it.

She'd said no. He *would* respect that.

'She'd tell me to take into account who made the comments and why they might be making them.'

Ignoring the throb and burn of his body, he nodded. 'Sometimes what's being said is more a reflection of the speaker than who or what they're talking about.'

'Nanny Earp had a saying—it's a quote from Robert J Hanlon. *"Never attribute to malice that which is adequately explained by stupidity."*'

Nanny Earp's philosophy had his full approval.

That cute nose wrinkled. 'Of course, that's not the kind of motto that'd work in your line of work.'

Which was a shame. Maybe—

He blinked, straightened, shook himself.

What the hell...?

He refused to mourn the lack of stupid people in his life. The life he'd chosen was the *right* life. He didn't belong in Janie's world. He didn't *want* to belong in Janie's world.

Pulling in a breath, he folded his arms. 'So what did that judge say *in its entirety*? And why might she have said it?' Seizing her laptop, he found the replay of tonight's episode and fast-forwarded to the judges' comments, hit play. When it finished, he spread his hands. 'Well?'

She sucked her bottom lip into her mouth and it was all he could do not to groan. 'I have a good grasp of colour and proportion,' she started slowly. 'And our bedroom complemented its surroundings.'

'What else?' he urged when she paused. He pointed to the laptop. 'They said you handled the budget really well.'

A finger tapped against her lips. 'That was a deliberate decision. I'm trying to save the bulk of the budget for the big reception room and the outside space.'

The colour had returned to her cheeks and he let out a careful breath. 'Do you wish you'd blown the budget to avoid the *playing it safe* comment?'

'The criticism would've then inevitably been that I'd spent too much money,' she said slowly. She dragged in a breath. 'And that judge is known for her innovation, her playfulness with form—that's her *thing*. That's how she'll be judging everything on the show.' She slumped as if some great tension had drained out of her. 'Every team received at least one positive comment and one "room for improvement" comment.'

She sagged in her seat, glancing across at him. 'And as far as criticisms went, ours was pretty mild. Oh, God! I don't know if I should laugh or cry, but you're right. I panicked and blew all of that out of proportion. Just call me Joey Walter or Colleen Clements.'

'Okay, Joey or Colleen or whatever your name is, you should definitely laugh.'

Her shaky laugh threatened to split him in two.

'Not that I'm not good with crying damsels,' he found himself babbling. *Shut up, idiot.* 'But you're no damsel, Janie. You're smart and capable and you're talented.' And damn Sebastian to hell for making her doubt herself. If he ever got his hands on that slimeball—

'And good with panicking drama queens ready to throw themselves off cliffs too. Thanks for talking me down, Zach.'

His heart beat hard and he willed it to slow.

'Nanny Earp did most of the heavy lifting.'

She stared at him for a long moment, folded her arms. 'You seem strangely reluctant to take any credit. Keeping someone alive in the jungle or on top of a snowy mountain isn't the only way to be a hero, Zach.'

She thought him a hero? The expression in her eyes caught him in a web of longing. He should look away, but he didn't want to.

'If you hadn't pulled me out of that negative spiral...'

Her lips shone in the candlelight. 'I've seen both of my parents descend into the pit of despair. It's awful. It takes so much energy for them to climb out again. If that had happened to me here, I'd have started second-guessing myself, constantly changing my mind, stressing everyone on the team out and—'

She broke off. 'It would've been awful. I'd have ruined everything. But you helped me gain perspective before that could happen.'

She made him feel like a superhero.

'I know you're here first and foremost as my bodyguard, but tonight you've been the voice of reason and I can't tell you how much it has helped. Or what it's meant to me.'

She moistened her lips. Hunger roared through him.

'I know that being here is making you chafe.'

Except he wasn't chafing. And that ought to worry him. Being stuck here, grounded, should have him tearing his hair out. Yet when he stared into that golden-eyed gaze, he couldn't be bothered with any of it—couldn't be bothered working out what it meant either.

'I really am grateful, Zach, thank you.'

He wanted to seize her in his arms and kiss her until—

He cut the image dead. He didn't force himself on women. He *wasn't* his father.

'You ought to go to bed, Janie.'

She swallowed. Her nostrils flared as if she could read the battle raging through him. Temptation crept across her face, making her eyes glow.

'Bad idea,' he ground out. 'You don't need or want distractions, remember? I'm here to help, not hinder. I promised.'

He could say something ugly to create distance between them, something that would send her marching stiff-backed to the house. Something like him not being sure she could keep her emotions from becoming embroiled if they did embark on a steamy affair—suggesting he knew her better than she knew herself like some patronising prat. Utter tosh, but it'd do the job.

But he couldn't do it. Janie had enough ugliness in her life. He wouldn't add to it. 'Goodnight, Janie.'

With a nod, she stood and made her way back to the house. It took all his strength not to call her back.

They started working on the dining room the following day.

The team trailed after Janie as she moved into the large room that opened to the left of the wide entrance hall. 'This is our dining room. There's a paved patio out of the side doors there for alfresco dining, and the same big windows at the front looking down to the sea as the other reception room. It could be a beautiful room.'

The team started inspecting walls and floors, door and window frames, and the state of the ceiling. Zach planted his hands on his hips when they were done. 'Repair-wise, there's not much to do in here.' Like all the other rooms, the door and window frames needed replacing and new shutters fitted. 'Hit us with your vision for the room.'

'Right, I want this room to be full of colour to reflect the sun and the sea. This is a room to live in, a place to enjoy good food and good company. I want it to be stimulating without being overwhelming.'

She listened to the suggestions the team made and made adjustments as needed. She was, quite frankly, amazing. She might've said she wouldn't have the scope to experiment here like she would at a beach resort, but from what he could tell she wasn't letting that hold her back.

'I don't want it to look too formal or uniform so I'll be using an assortment of tables that were already here. They'll need some mending and painting, but we might need a couple of extras. Do we buy or build them?'

'Build them,' they all said at once.

'I don't want to skive off, but at some stage I need to do some shopping. I'd like to showcase some local wares to thank the town for being so helpful.'

The villagers had been delighted to have them here filming. Nothing had been too much trouble.

He couldn't let Janie venture out alone, but… 'How about we put in a full day today and then see how we're travelling tomorrow?' He glanced at Darren and Tian. 'We could start earlier and finish earlier.' It'd give Janie time to browse the shops before they closed.

Darren glanced up as if realising where Zach was going with this. 'There's a market in the village tomorrow afternoon.'

Janie's eyes lit up. It made something inside him lift too. He tried to stay cool, look unfazed. 'And there's that little mezze place across from the waterfront if anyone is up for dinner afterwards. Who's in?'

Everyone sounded their agreement—even Cullen's production crew.

Seven days later they trooped back into that upstairs tavern room to watch the next episode of the show—all surreptitiously girded for battle—but things went as smooth as butter for Team Greece. Janie's styling and vision were unanimously celebrated, and the local arts and crafts she'd seamlessly incorporated into the room—beautifully handcrafted bowls, a spectacular wall hanging and embroidered tablecloths—admired. At the end of the episode Team Greece found themselves in equal first place with Team Whitsunday, while Team French Polynesia trailed one point behind.

Janie's smile, the way her eyes sparkled, her *delight,* knocked the breath from Zach's lungs, made his heart race. Retreating outside, he did two laps around the tavern before leaning against a tree on the other side of the road to keep watch.

He needed to get a grip. Janie wasn't the first woman he'd ever wanted and she wouldn't be the last. He dragged a hand down his face. Maybe Sarge was right. Maybe he needed to make the time to focus on things other than work once in a blue moon.

And that didn't mean he was going soft! It was just… He couldn't recall craving any woman with the intensity he craved Janie.

Clenching his jaw, he dragged in a breath. It'd be easier to resist her if he didn't like her so much, but he refused to get hung up on her. He wasn't becoming emotionally engaged with any woman. He didn't *do* emotional vulnerability. He wasn't repeating his mother's mistakes. He'd lived that nightmare once. Never again. He'd worked too hard to make himself strong and unassailable to throw it away now.

Seven days later they once again assembled in the tavern. They hadn't received any further *secret* footage, and he'd started to breathe easier.

The first half of the show went smoothly—for Team Greece at least. Team French Polynesia had a shocker and he could see Isobel gritting her teeth. The judges were again complimentary about Janie's styling of the family bathroom that had been this week's challenge. They'd praised her use of local tiles while her colour scheme again drew admiration.

'I'm afraid, though, Janie—' Mike, the host, gave a smarmy smile '—that it has come to our attention that you've broken the rules.'

She leaned forward, staring intently at the TV. 'Broken them how?'

Zach leaned forward to whisper, 'Cullen is filming,' so she'd know to be on her guard. The brief touch of her hand on his knee acknowledged that she'd heard him, and had the blood surging in his veins.

'You worked the team longer than the prescribed eight hours.'

She straightened. 'I did not.'

Footage of the team at the village market last Tuesday afternoon played on screen.

She gaped. 'That wasn't work! We were socialising, having fun. We went out for dinner afterwards.'

Darren and Tian muttered their agreement. It made no difference. They'd apparently *'discussed plans for the villa'* and that counted as work. They were deducted five points and Darren and Tian banned from working on Monday. They dropped from first place to third.

'We have someone here who says you often don't play by the rules, Janie. Your ex-boyfriend, Sebastian Thomas.'

What the...?

He curled his hand around hers. This now felt personal. Did someone within the network have an axe to grind? Were they out to get Janie, or Joey Walter via Janie? Was this the same person who'd written those threatening letters?

Fury built as Janie gripped his hand tighter and tighter as Sebastian—the scheming, lying, snake in the grass—droned on about how Janie's good girl, clean-cut image mattered more to her than the people in her life. He claimed that she'd used and abused him, and had then tossed him aside like a dirty rag.

'And we're now going to a live feed in Greece... What do you say to that, Janie?' Mike threw at her.

Zach stabbed a finger at the camera. 'I'm saying you're scraping the bottom of the barrel if you're now bringing people's exes onto the show. And if you think that smarmy toad is a defender of truth you're dumber than you look, Mike.'

'Oho, and I see you're still playing knight in shining armour, Zach. It looks good on you!'

'If Janie cared about her image,' Tian growled, 'like this Sebastian claims, she'd be supporting one of those pretty, feel-good charities. But she's not. He lies.'

Go, Tian.

'It appears that you're surrounded by knights, Janie. You don't have anything to say in your own defence?'

Janie straightened. 'I'm torn between saying *No comment*, which is the classy thing to do, and what I've always said in the past...'

She paused. Zach glanced at her.

Folding her arms, she lifted her chin. 'Except have you noticed it's always women who are told to be classy and remain silent—less said soonest mended and all that don't rock the boat nonsense?' Her eyes narrowed, the gold in them flashing. 'Ladies, we need to stop putting up with that garbage. The fact of the matter is Sebastian used me—pretended to be in love with me to gain access to my father.'

On screen, Sebastian's jaw dropped, his shock palpable.

Go, Janie.

'When Joey Walter refused be Sebastian's mentor or endorse an album for him, and I refused to intervene on his behalf… Well, let's just say the truth came out. As you'd expect, and as any sensible woman would've done, I kicked his sorry butt to the kerb.'

Both the building team and production crew cheered.

'Was your father's assessment of Sebastian's talent correct, or was it coloured by your opinion?'

'Look, Mike, Sebastian has a YouTube channel. If you're so inclined, you can go and listen and decide for yourself whether he has talent, or if Joey Walter was right when he said that Sebastian has a monopoly on mediocrity.'

'What's your opinion on the matter?'

'That's my father's area of expertise, not mine.' She pushed her shoulders back. 'What I can tell you is that Sebastian is a liar and a cheat and I'll be happy if I never hear his voice again.'

CHAPTER EIGHT

JANIE FELL DOWN into one of the armchairs they'd placed in the kitchen and stared across the room. Had she just made a fool of herself on national television, and in the process blackened the reputation of the charity she was supposed to be supporting?

She closed her eyes and dragged in a breath, but Sebastian's face rose in her mind—his smirk, his lies—and she found her hands clenching so hard her entire body shook, her mind going over and over what she'd said in retaliation, making her wince again and again. *Oh, God, she shouldn't have—*

'Come on.'

She snapped to when a big warm hand curved around hers and pulled her to her feet. The warmth and understanding reflected in Zach's incredible blue eyes had a lump forming it her throat. And it had her swallowing against the want that heated her veins, despite the agitation roiling through her.

He led her outside and down towards the table beneath the big tree. He urged her to sit, and she watched as he unpacked the bag he'd had slung over one shoulder. But all the while she couldn't stop Sebastian's words from going around in her head, couldn't stop thinking what a terrible ambassador she was for Second Chances.

He produced a bottle of dessert wine. 'Name five things you can see.'

She blinked.

'Go on, humour me.'

Him. She saw him.

Don't say that.

Swallowing, she forced her gaze to their surroundings. 'I can see the silhouette of the big tree against the sky. And the sky is a shade lighter than navy because the moon is so big tonight there's a lot of light. We almost don't need the candles.'

He lit them anyway and produced a container of baklava.

'I see a bottle of Sauterne and a dish of baklava and…' She stared at the water and a slow breath left her. 'And the shoreline where those little waves are rolling up onto the rocks looks edged in silver.'

'And in your usual fashion you've excelled. The tree, the sky, the moon, candles, Sauterne, baklava and the shoreline. That's seven.'

She blinked. 'How did you do that?' Her agitation, while not gone, had receded enough for her to draw oxygen into her lungs.

'It's an old army technique for battling anxiety.' He sat. 'What can you hear?'

'The crickets, the water splashing, the call of a night bird I don't know the name of…your voice.' She let out what she hoped was a quiet breath. 'You have a good voice, Zach, deep and low, unrushed. You could be a radio DJ if you wanted.' She frowned, things inside her clenching. 'Do you sing?'

'I can hold a tune well enough, but I'm no singer. The life your father leads…' He shook his head. 'It's not for me.'

Of course it wasn't. The tight things unclenched again.

He set a piece of baklava in front of her, poured a generous slug of wine in one glass and a splash in another. 'You were brilliant tonight.'

She grimaced. 'No, I—'

'I'd like to propose a toast.' He lifted his glass.

Frowning, she lifted her glass too.

'Tonight you stood up for women who've spent too much of their lives being belittled and bullied by men. I don't think I've ever been prouder to be associated with anyone than I was tonight.'

Her jaw dropped.

'To you, Janie, for leading by example and refusing to let bad behaviour and slander go unchallenged.' He touched his glass to hers, but when she didn't raise it to her lips he frowned. 'Do you regret what you said?'

She had been, but…

'I don't regret sticking up for myself and setting the record straight.' She wrinkled her nose. 'I shouldn't have said that bit about him having a monopoly on mediocrity.'

'Best smackdown I've heard in ages.'

'It was mean, and I don't like being mean.'

'You were put on the spot. You had next to no time to compose yourself, let alone prepare something pretty to say. You showed grace under fire and you should be proud of yourself. Also, Janie, Sebastian should never have gone on national television and said the things he did. So he can't complain if he doesn't like the outcome. He had it coming.'

When put like that…

He touched his glass to hers again, raised an eyebrow.

She took a sip. 'Thanks, Zach.' He'd talked her down off a ledge *again*.

'I don't think you recognise the value of what you did tonight.'

That had her shaking her head. 'I'm not the only woman to ever call a man out.'

'There can't be too many voices.' His fingers drummed against the table. 'I happen to feel strongly about this.'

She could see that.

'I've had first-hand experience of what happens when a

woman is too frightened to take a stand and stick up for her-self.'

Her gaze lifted and her heart stopped. The expression in his eyes…

It took all her strength to remain in her seat rather than move around the table to put her arms around him. She had to swallow before she could speak. 'Who?'

Shadowed eyes met hers. His nostrils flared. 'My mother.'

The breath punched from her body. She wanted to hit some-thing.

Reaching across, he removed the wineglass from her grasp. 'Cheap glass. Wouldn't take much to break. And the last thing you need is stitches in your hand when we have a room to renovate next week.'

Even now he was looking after her. But who'd ever looked after him? She moved around the table to sit beside him, peered up into his face. She didn't take his hand, although she wanted to.

'Your father?'

A tic started up in the side of his jaw. 'My father was a vi-olent man. He abused my mother with words *and* his fists.'

She pressed a hand to her mouth to hold back a gasp…and a far from ladylike curse. But as Zach had just toasted her for what some would consider unladylike behaviour, he probably wouldn't mind her cursing.

'I'm sorry.' She swallowed carefully, forced her hands not to clench. 'Did he hit you too?'

He didn't answer. He didn't have to. She saw it in his eyes. Everything inside her drew as tight as a bow. Puzzle pieces fell into place.

'I worked in construction for a number of years when I was younger.'

'He made you leave school to work for him,' she said slowly. *What a weasel.*

His laugh was bitter. 'I shot up when I was fourteen, filled out. That's when he realised he had a use for me and I started working for him part-time. At sixteen, he hauled me out of school altogether.' His eyes narrowed, his mouth settling in a cruel line. 'But working in construction means you develop muscles, and I'd had enough of him by then and started fighting back with hard fists of my own.'

Everything she had ached for him. He shouldn't have had to suffer that. No one should.

'At sixteen I could physically defend myself, give as good as I got, but I could still be emotionally manipulated.'

Cold dread spread through the pit of her stomach.

'When I wasn't home, he started giving my mother the beatings he wanted to give to me.'

She covered her face with her hands.

'Hey.' He pulled her hands away. 'It was a long time ago.'

'That stuff stays with you forever.' She dragged in an unsteady breath. 'Tell me she left him.'

He dropped her hands. Reaching for his baklava, he bit into it as if needing the sweetness. Her heart sank, but she did the same with hers. The flaky pastry, the honey and nuts followed by a sip of the sweet wine helped to ground her in the present.

'How did you end up in the army?'

'When I was eighteen I was done—I left home. I refused to be manipulated by my father any more. I wanted my mother to leave him, promised her I'd look after her. I started working for someone else, found a house to rent, but she refused to leave.'

A lump lodged in her throat. 'Why?'

'She said she loved him.'

He looked so suddenly lost that she wrapped a hand around one huge bicep and rested her head against his shoulder, her eyes burning.

'Here's something they don't tell you about abusive men, Janie. They can be Jekyll and Hyde.'

'Meaning?'

'Meaning they can be charming and charismatic, until the switch is flicked.'

She couldn't imagine staying with someone who hurt her... Even if she loved them.

'Her mother was timid, as were all my aunts. My grandfather died when I was small, but from all accounts he was a domineering man. She had no one to show her how to stick up for herself. Or to tell her she deserved better.'

Her hand found his and she squeezed it tight.

'That's why what you did tonight, and what you said, matters.' He pressed her hand between both of his own. 'You showed other women—and men too—anyone who watched the show, an example of how to stand up for themselves, how to call out bad behaviour, and that it's okay not to settle for less.'

He'd made her see this evening's events in such a different light.

They sipped their wine in silence. 'Do you see your mother any more?'

He shook his head. 'When I was eighteen and still trying to get her to leave my father, I turned up one day to find her black and blue. I lost my temper and when my father got home we came to blows. The police were called.'

Her stomach churned.

'My mother refused to press charges against him. He threatened to have me charged with assault unless I stayed away and didn't see either him or my mother again. My mother said that's what she wanted. She begged me to stay away.'

Her heart caught. 'Oh, Zach, I'm so sorry.'

'One of the policemen took me aside and talked to me about the cycle of abuse. He told me that until my mother made the decision herself, there was nothing I could do. He also told me it wasn't uncommon for the son of a violent man to become violent himself, and that I was displaying the early signs.'

'What the hell?'

He laid a hand on her arm. 'He was right. I'd have never hit a woman, but another man…' He shrugged. 'He advised me to get a change of scenery, gave me a brochure about joining the army.'

'And you took his advice.'

'I didn't know what else to do. And the army kept me busy, gave me a purpose, gave me a place to channel my anger while giving me something to work towards. I ring my mother every year on her birthday and at Christmas and leave a message, but so far she's never returned my calls. I've an aunt I talk to a few times a year. She tells me how the family is getting on—keeps me up to date with my mother's phone number and where she's living…' He trailed off with a shrug.

'Wow, Zach. I…'

He smiled as if he knew all the things she wanted to say. 'The army was good to me. I got a degree, developed skills, made lifelong friends.'

'So why did you leave?'

'Sarge, Logan and I decided we wanted to be our own bosses, and that's worked out great.'

'You're amazing,' she breathed. 'If anyone here should be proud of themselves it's you.'

His brows shot up.

'After everything you've been through, you're a good man. You didn't go off the rails. Instead, you became a living, breathing crusader for those weaker than you. You're…a superhero.'

'Not true.' He rolled his shoulders. 'I just do what I can. Do what's needed.'

'I'm sorry I pulled you away from working on important

things. No wonder you hate Second Chances. Your father is a criminal who should be locked up and the key thrown away.'

She'd bet that black and white world view of his had kept him alive more often than not, and kept alive the people he protected.

'Do you want to hear a real confession?'

The expression in his eyes held her spellbound. She nodded.

'I'm not the least bit sorry to be here. I'm *glad* to be here.'

She couldn't help herself then. She reached up and kissed him.

Janie's lips on his threatened Zach's every semblance of control, whipping him into a frenzy of need and heat. His tongue tangled with hers, his fingers diving into her hair to curl around her scalp and pull her closer. He wanted to bury himself in her, take everything she offered. He wanted that oblivion with a greed so all-consuming he had to pull back and drag air into starved lungs.

He stared down at her glazed eyes and swollen lips. She— *What the hell?*

Putting her away from him, he shot to his feet and backed up two steps, the taste of panic bitter on his tongue. 'I *won't* take advantage of you.'

She blinked. 'I beg your pardon?'

He backed up another step. 'You said you didn't want distractions.' No matter how hard he tried, his heart refused to slow. 'You said you didn't want this to happen.' He *would* heed her wishes.

'But—'

'I've had to use all of my resources over the past few weeks to stop myself from kissing you, touching you.' He jabbed a finger skywards. 'And I'm not asking for applause or a pat on the back, but I'm *not* going to ruin all of that hard work now by taking advantage of you when you're feeling fragile and grateful and—'

'Hold on a minute—'

'I am not my father!'

Silence followed his bellowed words and it had his nape prickling.

Behind the soft caramel of her eyes, he sensed her mind spinning and whirling. Very slowly, she stood too. 'You're *nothing* like your father, Zach.'

Because he held himself on a tight rein, kept himself in check and refused to be ruled by his emotions.

'Your father was all about control and coercion. You've been nothing but protective and kind.'

Because he worked hard at it. 'But if I let things between us go any further...'

'That still wouldn't make you like your father.'

He *wanted* to believe that.

'You've helped me feel empowered. You listened to me and let me help to come up with our cover story. When you found the wrench you gave me a better weapon instead of patronising me and laughing at me.'

'You're smart and proactive—that doesn't deserve to be laughed at.'

'See? Definitely not like your father.'

Her words lightened something inside him.

'And I think you're forgetting something. *I* kissed *you*.'

Yeah, but he'd kissed her back.

'You've done nothing wrong. If someone should be blasting themselves it should be me.'

He shook his head. 'It's been an emotional evening—'

'And maybe I would be if I regretted it, but I don't.'

For a moment everything—the wind, the waves, the twinkling of the stars—froze. What was she saying?

'I like kissing you, Zach. I want to do a whole lot more of it.'

But... 'You said...'

'I know what I said.' Her eyes never dropped from his. 'Back then it seemed the right thing to do. The sensible thing. Back then I couldn't decide if falling into bed with you would be a mistake that'd distract my focus. Or an inspired move that would send my creativity soaring and...'

The pulse at the base of his throat pounded. 'And?'

'Be the best adventure of my life.'

The best... Something frozen at the centre of him started to thaw. He bent until they were eye to eye, needing to make sure he'd heard her correctly. 'You want to kiss me?'

'Madly.'

'You want to do a whole lot more than kiss me?'

'I want to make love with you.'

His breath quickened. Violets and cashmere flooded his senses.

She lifted her chin. 'Interested?'

'Yes.' The word left him without hesitation. She shouldn't be the only one here putting herself on the line. 'I want you so much I'm shaking with it. That's the problem. I've wanted you too much. It shouldn't have been so damn hard to remember what *you* wanted.'

She reached up and touched his face. 'You haven't done anything to make me feel pressured, Zach. You're not that kind of man.'

He could no sooner stop from kissing her than he could stop the tide. She tasted like honey and wine, summer and warm breezes. He fell down onto a chair and pulled her onto his lap and drank her in. Winding her arms around his neck, she melted against him. Nothing in his life had ever felt more real. Nothing had ever felt this good.

Slipping a hand beneath her blouse to touch warm skin, he

lost himself in the feel of her. Janie arched into his touch when he cupped her breast, her nipple beading to a flatteringly hard nub as he brushed his thumb across it. The little sounds she made in the back of her throat incited him to push the blouse up, pull her bra to one side and draw the nipple into the hot warmth of his mouth.

Her cry pierced the air and in a flash the summer breeze became a thunderstorm. Fingers dug into his arms, the short nails raking and urging him on, not that he needed urging. He'd gone rock-hard and needy. She tasted like sin and salvation and he was starving for both.

Pulling back a fraction, he dragged air into starving lungs. They stared at each other, both breathing hard, eyes glittering.

Lifting herself higher on his lap, she caught his face in her hands. 'Neither of us is the other's true north. I'm not looking for anyone to be my compass, but you make me feel...'

He raised an eyebrow.

'Better.' The breath left her on a whoosh. 'I was feeling like crap and you've made me feel better, calmer, more at ease with myself...happier.' She shook her head as if it was a miracle. 'You've made me like myself more.'

A lump lodged in his throat.

'You're a great big gorgeous, squishy stress ball, Zach Cartwright.'

Her words surprised a bark of laughter from him. She had him hot and bothered *and laughing*. The combination was shockingly seductive.

'I know you said you didn't want to be a distraction, but I'm thinking distraction is exactly what I need.' She bit her lip, looking oddly vulnerable, and it occurred to him how much she hid that side of herself from the rest of the world. To see it, to be allowed to see it, left him moved, humbled. Honoured.

'And just so you know, I'm well aware that what happens on a Greek island stays on a Greek island.'

A hot summer fling with this extraordinary woman…? His pulse spiked. A better man might pull back, but he wasn't a better man.

'I take exception to squishy.'

She glanced down—cheeky, flirtatious, those lovely lips curving up. 'I see your point.'

'But we're not doing this outdoors.' He lifted her off his lap. 'We've cameras monitoring the perimeter of the property, but…'

Her gaze lifted to the first-floor balcony. 'There's a romantic bedroom up there that I think we've earned the right to.'

Without another word, they moved back to the house. On the landing at the top of the stairs Janie turned and swallowed. 'I feel I ought to go and put on something seductive and—'

He swooped down and claimed her mouth in a hungry kiss, backing her up against the nearest wall, running his hands down the sides of her body, making her tremble and moan. He kissed her like a warrior intent on subduing a rival—not giving her time to think or react, bombarding her instead with sensation as he made short work of the buttons on her blouse and dropped it to their feet. Her jeans followed.

'Mission accomplished,' he rasped, lifting his head, his mouth tingling from the intensity of their kisses, his bottom lip burning from the way she'd sunk her teeth into it in mindless passion, before laving it with her tongue.

She wore nothing now but a pair of simple cotton knickers. They were a shocking red against the pale honey of her skin and stars burst behind his eyelids.

'*That's* what I call seductive.'

She pushed a finger into his chest, breathing hard. 'Where did you learn to kiss like that?'

He crowded her against the wall again. 'Is that a complaint?' He didn't wait for an answer, but rubbed his chest against hers. Her breath hitched. 'Undo the buttons on my shirt, Janie.'

Dazed eyes lifted at his command, excitement glittering in their depths. 'Are you trying to scare me, tough guy, with the bad boy act?'

She wasn't scared and they both knew it.

Lowering his head, he gently bit her earlobe. 'You've been boss for over three weeks now and I think it's time someone else took the reins so you don't have to make any decisions or do any of the thinking. I'm in charge now.'

Her fingers fumbled on his buttons and he smiled against her neck as he pressed a series of kisses there. 'Push the shirt off my shoulders, sweetheart.'

She did. As if his words hypnotised her.

Insinuating a thigh between her legs, he pressed against the sensitive core of her. Her head dropped back and her breathing grew ragged.

'You want a stress release? Then I plan to give you one. You won't be thinking, you won't be making plans, the future doesn't exist here. All you'll be doing is focusing on the now and sensation.' He eased his thigh away and then pressed it back again, and her eyes glazed and she caught her bottom lip between her teeth.

'When I'm done, Janie, you're going to be limp and satisfied. *Very* satisfied.'

A tremor shook through her.

'So I suggest you hold on tight.' He lifted her into his arms. Golden eyes gazed into his. 'If that's okay with you,' he murmured.

'It's very okay,' she whispered, running her fingers through his hair, and he realised how much it had grown since he'd been here, and how much he liked the sensation of her fingers against his scalp.

The moon glittered through the glass of the French windows. He laid her on the bed and stared. Bathed in moonlight, she looked like some Greek goddess—all silver and gold and achingly beautiful. But when he lowered himself down beside her she was all warm womanly flesh and he took his time exploring every inch of it with lazy hands and tongue and mouth.

She arched into his touch, her hands tugging at him mindlessly, her moans and sighs urging him on, begging him for release. He built her to a fever-pitch of excitement—never had his own need been so…secondary. He made her come with his mouth, and then he built her to a fever-pitch level again and only then did he kick off his cargo pants, roll on a condom and sink into her silken flesh.

Her eyes flew open and found his in the moonlight. Her lips parted as if on a revelation, and then she smiled and he found himself lost in it as they moved together, setting a rhythm. With each stroke, though, he fell deeper, felt more, moved beyond anything he'd ever experienced.

Gritting his teeth, he tried to focus on nothing but increasing her pleasure… But her hands on his back… The way her legs wrapped around his waist… The sharp bite of her teeth at his shoulder. It dragged him under until all he could think, feel and want was Janie.

Her body bowed, her muscles tightened and she cried out—exhilarated, exuberant. Moving with a will beyond his own, he too flung over the edge. Pleasure spiralling through him, a hoarse cry dragged from the depths of him. The intensity, the pleasure, lasted…spread out…gentled.

As he floated back down, he rolled onto his back and gathered her against him, feeling remade.

He woke early. Unlike the bedrooms on the second floor beneath the eaves, this room faced east and sunshine flooded the room, gilding it in a warm glow—a magical Greek island benediction.

Janie lay on her stomach, arms flung out, her eyelashes making dark half-moons against the creaminess of her cheeks. Last night had been—

He had no words for it. Maybe it was the result of all the banked heat that had built between them. Maybe it was the magic of the island or the hothouse atmosphere of the show. Or maybe it was simply the woman herself. Janie might consider herself ordinary, but she was wrong.

He let her sleep. It was Monday. Darren and Tian were grounded. It'd do her good to rest, to catch up on some sleep. To take some time off.

Dragging on a pair of shorts and T-shirt, he headed downstairs. He'd bet she'd enjoy breakfast on that balcony with its amazing view. Poached eggs, sourdough toast and peaches. He started gathering breakfast things when his phone buzzed.

Logan. Pressing it to his ear, he said, 'What's up?'

'Found out Sarge went to school with Joey Walter.'

The air whistled between his teeth. 'No way. Old friends?'

'Looks like it.'

'And on the health front?'

'His cholesterol is up and he's showing signs of being pre-diabetic.'

'He keeps himself fit.'

'But he likes a beer and a burger a little too much, apparently. It can all be reversed by a healthier eating plan.'

'Sarge has to go on a diet?'

'Yep.'

Hell, no wonder he'd been in such a foul mood.

'Neither of our lives will be worth living if you let him know that we know this, Zach.'

'Roger that. And thanks, mate.'

No sooner had he rung off than Sarge called. 'Found out something interesting. Janie's ex has started dating again and you'll never guess who it is.'

His lip curled. 'Whoever it is has seriously bad taste.'

'Isobel Jamison.'

'Of Team French Polynesia fame? You have to be kidding.' At his side his hand clenched and unclenched. 'Are the threatening letters linked?'

'Sabotage rather than a personal threat? Distinct possibility. Isobel clearly has an axe to grind where Janie's concerned, but whether that's because of her relationship with Sebastian or because Janie's design skills are streets ahead of anyone else's on the show is anyone's guess.'

Zach nodded. 'Those skills have surprised a few people.' Because Janie really was exceptionally talented. 'But if Isobel already had that intel from Sebastian, maybe the letters were an attempt to persuade Janie to pull out of the show.' His finger tapped against the phone. 'Do we know why she might want to win the show so badly that she'd go to those lengths?'

'I've Jo and Tully on the case.'

Good call. They were both exceptional agents.

'There are rumours that Isobel's character in the drama series could be written out. If that happens, she'll be out of work.'

He mulled that over. 'She needs to lift her profile to either keep her current job or find another.'

'That's the theory. We're going to keep digging, see what we can find, but it's looking more and more likely that Janie isn't in any physical danger.'

A hard knot inside him loosened. They'd never really thought she was. But it was good to have their suspicions confirmed.

'Zach, I know I came down hard on you, son, but it was important to me that we gave this job everything. I want to thank you. I know it's not the kind of job you enjoy. And…' he hesitated '… I shouldn't have snapped your head off when you asked if Joey Walter was blackmailing me. The thing is, I know Joey from back in the old days.'

So Logan was right.

'You serious?' He feigned surprise.

'He's a good guy.'

'Well, if we're doing confessions… This job hasn't been as bad as I thought it'd be.'

Sarge chuckled. 'I don't believe that for a moment.'

'I haven't enjoyed the fake drama and the cameras, but the building…'

Sarge was quiet for a moment. 'I thought you'd hate it because of your father.'

'Me too. But I don't.' He rolled his shoulders. 'Just thought you'd like to know. Didn't want you worrying about it. Now, next question,' he forged on. 'Janie's like her dad—she's a nice woman. Last night's episode shook her up.'

'What are you thinking?'

'That a day away from this place might do her good. Thought we could go play tourist in Corfu town.'

In the background he heard Sarge tapping away on his keyboard. 'It's busy, lots of people—you'll blend into the crowd—Yeah, I don't see the harm. Me and the crew will keep an eye on the villa.'

They rang off, and Zach made breakfast. When he walked into the bedroom, Janie was stirring. Opening her eyes, she blinked up at him and her slow smile smacked into him like a big warm hug.

He tried to keep his voice even. 'I have a suggestion.'

'Whatever it is, I say yes.'

CHAPTER NINE

JANIE'S PULSE GALLOPED at the sight of Zach wearing nothing but a pair of soft cotton sleep shorts and white T-shirt, holding a tray of something that smelled delicious and smiling as if all was right with the world. She wanted to hug herself.

'But first, madam might enjoy breakfast on the balcony.'

With a grin, he nudged through the curtains at the French windows. Ooh! The way the cotton of his shorts hugged the muscles of his thighs and backside...

Deep breaths, Janie. Deep breaths.

Last night had been amazing, but it was probably a good idea—necessary—to let the poor man get some sustenance before dragging him back to bed.

Actually, last night had been better than amazing. It had...

Thought stopped as images played through her mind. She doubted words could capture precisely how amazing the previous evening had been.

Zach poked his head through the French windows. 'Coming?'

She might feel fabulous—reinvigorated and restored—but she was also stark naked and she wasn't sitting out there wearing nothing but—

Then she saw her silk wrap sitting at the bottom of the bed, and Zach's thoughtfulness had her stomach softening.

'Yes,' she said, unable to hide her breathlessness—or eagerness. Actually, with Zach, she didn't feel as if she had to hide anything.

When he disappeared back behind the curtain, she scrambled out of bed and pulled the wrap around her and nipped into the bathroom to roughly finger brush her hair and splash cool water onto hot cheeks, before padding out to the balcony.

The view should've stolen her breath—a green lawn sloping down to water that was millpond smooth, the only sound the morning chorus of birds and the lapping of water. But when blue eyes speared to her as she hovered in the doorway, darkening in appreciation, all she saw was him. For one heart-stopping moment she thought he might leap to his feet, haul her into his arms and kiss her.

Instead, he poured her a mug of coffee and gestured for her to take a seat, his hand not quite steady.

Perching on a chair, she lifted her mug and inhaled the steam. 'This looks wonderful.' It was as if he'd not only heard her words during the renovation of the bedroom but had memorised them, intent on making her vision of romance a reality.

Something in his shoulders eased. 'Eat, Janie.'

She took a piece of toast, grabbed a peach, glanced out at the view and then back at him. He raised an eyebrow. She bit into a corner of her toast.

'Something on your mind?'

Come on, you stood up for all of womankind yesterday. Don't let yourself down now.

'Last night was…'

Both of those eyebrows rose.

'It was wonderful, Zach.'

His shoulders, his spine, the muscles of his forearms all relaxed as if her words had melted him like wax. 'Couldn't agree more.'

'Really?'

He'd started to cut into his egg on toast, but halted. 'You doubt it?'

Her cheeks heated. 'I sort of got swept away and…'

'And?'

'Well, I'd hate for it to have been one-sided and— Well, I just want you to have enjoyed it as much as I did,' she finished in a rush.

He leaned towards her. 'Last night was extraordinary. All of it.' He placed a hand on his heart. 'I'm looking forward to doing it again if that's what you want too.'

'Again and again,' she said, a grin rising through her.

They ate their breakfast, casting surreptitious glances at one another, appreciative and admiring…hungry and lusty.

When they'd finished Zach cleared his throat. 'I thought it might be fun to go into Corfu town today.'

She blinked.

'We deserve a day off. We've been working hard and I suspect you're going to say we need to get to work on the reception room. But we've done a lot in there in our downtime during the last few weeks and even taking into account that we won't have Darren and Tian today we're ahead of schedule. Also, who knows what other inspiration we'll find if we get out and about a bit and learn more about the island?'

She opened her mouth, but he held up a hand. 'Neither one of us has been to Corfu before. I'm curious to see more, aren't you? And,' he added before she could speak, 'if you remember, you already said yes to my suggestion.'

She started to laugh. He wanted to spend the day with her? It was all she could do not to hug herself. Perhaps it was irresponsible, but they were ahead of schedule. And to have a whole day with Zach away from here? Talk about dream-come-true stuff and making memories.

'I think that's an excellent idea.'

Something in his face lightened. 'You do?'

'Can I suggest an amendment to the plan, though? The shower in the en suite is big enough for two…'

Before she was even aware of it, he was on his feet and she was in his arms and they were naked and warm water was pouring down over them in a delicious stream, but hot water wasn't the only thing that steamed up the bathroom mirror.

The town of Corfu was larger than Janie had expected—they'd barely seen any of it on the drive from the airport. They wound through quaintly cobbled alleyways with colourful shopfronts painted a variety of pastel pinks, greens, blues and yellows, the strip of bright blue sky above an invigorating contrast. She bought gifts for Beck and Lena—colourful bead necklaces and olive oil soaps—and a Greek fisherman's cap for Zach that he promptly placed on his head. He surprised her with a gift of a pretty dish she'd admired.

'What's your favourite thing to eat?' she asked as they walked along the waterfront with its row of tantalising restaurants.

'Seafood. We didn't have it much when I was growing up.'

Because his father hadn't liked it? She didn't ask. She didn't want thoughts of his father marring their day.

'And you?'

'Pizza.' She smiled. 'For much the same reason.'

They chose a restaurant with a forecourt right on the water, a large awning providing shade, the splash of pink bougainvillea cascading over the restaurant's whitewashed façade utter perfection. They ate seafood pizza and shared a carafe of local white wine with bold notes of summer fruits and spring flowers. After lunch he captured her hand in his and followed a set of directions on his phone.

'There's something I think you'll like.'

Winding along several streets, they eventually turned and squeezed down an alley no wider than her arm span, merging into a beautiful courtyard. A fountain stood at its centre, the path surrounding it bordered with cypress trees. Beneath the trees sat wooden benches. The surrounding buildings were all of honeyed brick. Water cascaded from the mouth of a dolphin on one wall. Resting against the other walls were troughs and hanging baskets overflowing with pansies, petunias, geraniums. Moving to the fountain, she turned on the spot. 'It's magic.'

'Apparently it's a closely guarded local secret.'

Trust him to have found it then.

With his hands on her shoulders, Zach urged her down to one of the benches. 'What's your favourite gelato flavour?'

'Strawberry.'

He disappeared down an alley, returning soon after with two gelatos. They ate them soaking up the atmosphere and throwing around ideas about how to create something like this on a smaller scale back at the villa.

Afterwards, she took him to a museum of Roman artefacts where an ancient village had been recreated. While he marvelled at the craftsmanship of the old masons, she marvelled at him.

They bought lovely things from a deli—bread, feta and a slab of hard yellow local cheese, spiced olives, cured meats, locally made ginger beer—and took them home to have a picnic supper at the table beneath the big tree. Which they did, sitting side by side as the sun went down.

Janie rested her chin in her hand and drank it all in. 'What an absolutely magical day.'

His gaze roved over her face and he sent her one of his rare smiles. 'Exactly what the doctor ordered.'

'For me or you?'

'Both. We've been working our tails off. It was good to have some R&R.'

She blinked.

'What?'

'That's not something you'd have said a month ago. A month ago R&R was the last thing on your mind.'

Two lines appeared on his brow. He rolled his shoulders and her stomach clenched. Had her words made him think she was trying to change him? Had they made him think that the lovemaking and the fun they'd had today meant more to her than it should?

She swallowed. Had it?

Don't be ridiculous.

She knew this fling would end as soon as their Greek adventure was over. And she was totally okay with that. She flipped her hair over her shoulders. As she'd told Zach, she wasn't looking for anything long-term. She wasn't ready to have her heart broken again. Doing a great job on the villa was her first priority, but where was the harm in having some fun along the way?

Reaching for an olive, she popped it in her mouth, gave a careful shrug. 'I'm glad it hasn't been as awful as you expected. For all I know you could be an amazing actor, but—'

'I hope I'm an excellent actor when the situation requires it, but you're right.' His frown deepened but it was in consternation rather than annoyance. 'I expected to be bored, constantly chafing…restless, but I haven't been. I've enjoyed the work and watching the villa transform. And I like our team. Darren and Tian have been great to work with.'

His words made her pulse race, but she didn't know why. 'Ditto to all of that.'

'And you—' he pointed a finger at her '—are an interesting woman and good company. This job has proved anything but boring.'

She knew she must be grinning stupidly, but she couldn't help it. Didn't want to help it.

'I'm sad we've only a few more weeks left.' Well, they still had a whole month and a half, but the time seemed suddenly precious. 'I suggest we make the most of it before we have to return to our not so ordinary worlds. Starting right now.'

'Excellent plan.'

They gathered up the debris of their meal, left the dishes in the sink and, taking Zach's hand, Janie led him upstairs and had her wicked way with him. She wanted to learn the shape of his body, the sound of his breath quickening when she did something he liked, the way his body tightened and jerked.

'Janie, you're killing me,' he finally groaned. 'If you—'

He didn't get any further as she sheathed him with a condom and lowered herself down onto him. His fingers dug into the flesh of her hips, the air whistling between his teeth. She loved watching him like this—unguarded—a compelling combination of fierce and vulnerable. She could stare at him all night long and not grow tired of it.

Heavy-lidded eyes opened, spearing into hers, and a lazy thumb lowered to circle the most sensitive part of her, making her gasp. Before she knew it, she was moving with a new urgency that shut out everything else. Their cries of release echoed around the room when they climaxed. It should be illegal to feel this good.

Afterwards he pulled her against him and she rested her head against his chest. When their breathing had returned to normal she pressed a kiss to the firm, warm skin beneath her. 'Let's play a game of hypotheticals.'

'After what you just did to me, we can do whatever you want.'

She grinned and kissed him again. He tasted of salt and something darker, like cloves or rum. It was a taste she could become addicted to. Resting her chin on her hand, she stared up at him. 'I think you've fallen into the habit of only seeing yourself according to your role with Sentry.'

He raised an eyebrow.

'I think you're so much more than a hotshot bodyguard, Mr I-Don't-Like-the-Real-World Cartwright. For one thing you're seriously skilled with your hands.' She laughed when he ran his hands down her body, all teasing temptation. 'You're a natural leader, but a team member too—smart enough to take advice and let everyone play to their strengths. And you're a good friend.'

The teasing light in his eyes disappeared. Her mouth went dry. 'I know that I've been a job to you, but I also feel like we've become friends.'

Janie's words speared into Zach with a sting he didn't understand.

'And I hope that when this is all over, we can remain friends,' she continued. 'Maybe catch up for the odd meal or drink when you're in London.' She traced patterns on his abdomen. 'I know a lot of people, Zach, but I don't have many friends. I like to keep the ones I do have.'

Had all of this meant more to Janie than he wanted it to?

Yet a part of him yearned for what she offered. To catch up with Janie once in a blue moon for a drink or a bite to eat, to make sure she was safe and happy... Where was the harm in that?

'So that's hypothetical number one: if we're friends, can we catch up in the real world every now and again when this adventure is over?' Before he could answer she rolled onto her tummy to stare fully into his face. 'Because here's the thing, Zach.'

He sat up against the pillows. What thing? She wasn't going to say she'd started to fall for him or—

'Eventually you will have to retire from your high intensity fieldwork.'

What the hell...?

She ignored his glare. 'One day you'll be eighty and while you'll probably be an insanely fit eighty-year-old, you won't have the lung capacity you once did, and you'll probably need a knee replacement from that old injury you have and—'

'How do you know I had a knee injury?'

She shrugged. 'Lucky guess. Sometimes when you've been crouching down for a while, you stand up and flex it and give it a rub.'

He did?

'So…' she continued. 'While retirement might not be imminent, I think we can agree that eventually it's inevitable.'

Her words made him feel like an idiot. Because *of course* it was inevitable. That was all Sarge and Logan had wanted him to admit and come to terms with. Instead of agreeing with them he'd bitten their heads off.

He moistened his lips. 'So what's the hypothetical question there?'

'Well, when you're no longer playing superhero, what do you want to do if you don't want to be stuck behind a desk?'

He frowned.

She nudged him with a soft laugh. 'We're playing a game. You don't have to be so serious about it.'

Except eventually he was going to have to be serious about it, wasn't he? And while she might not know it, she'd made him see that being prepared and having a plan would make the transition easier.

On second thoughts, scrap that. She knew *exactly* what she was doing.

'Okay, play genie and tell me what you see in your crystal ball.'

Sitting up against the pillows too, she feigned staring into a crystal ball. 'Ooh, Mr Cartwright, your future is full of promise and adventure. I see travel to far-flung places—snorkelling in Australia's Great Barrier Reef, jet skiing in Jamaica, skiing in Banff… I see prawns on barbecues and cocktails on the beach and hot chocolate in ski lodges. Oh, and wait, there's something else…poker tournaments in Vegas as well as—'

'I can't spend my entire life on holiday, Genie Janie.'

She gave an offended sniff, but her eyes danced. 'You wouldn't be doing those holidays one after the other like some playboy gadabout.'

He tried to rein in a smile. 'No?'

'Of course not. They'd be your reward for taking a run-down French château—or Greek villa—and bringing it back to life and turning it into your dream home.'

Like they were doing now?

'While training Sentry's new recruits on some nearby piece of land that you've bought that has an insane obstacle course and—' her fingers wriggled in the air as if searching for other things new recruits might need training for '—electronic communication facilities.'

He stilled. That idea had legs.

'Or—' she tapped a finger against her lips '—you decide to part company with Sentry and flip houses for a living instead.'

Working on the villa had been fun, and doing up a place of his own appealed, but he didn't want to make a career out of it.

'You get your pilot's licence and start flying freight planes to Africa or Asia, learn a new language…play basketball.' She gave a wicked giggle. 'Or you could have a midlife crisis and buy an outrageously expensive status symbol of a sports car and take up with a twenty-year-old showgirl.'

With a growl, he lunged and pinned her beneath him. 'I'll skip the midlife crisis if it's all the same to you.'

'Very wise.'

Her hands smoothed down his back and flanks as if she loved the feel of him, as if she couldn't help but touch him. It was all he could do not to purr.

'Turnabout—tell me what features in your hypothetical future.'

'The fantasy one? The one I'd wish for if I had a genie to grant me wishes?'

He nodded and she grinned and it snagged at something inside him.

'Well, first of all I'd drop out of the media spotlight entirely. However, my interior design business would take off and all the people *in the know* would pay outrageous sums to have me designing their home and office spaces. I'll be so in demand I'll get to pick and choose what jobs I do.' Her eyes twinkled. 'Even The Palace will call me in.'

He chuckled. 'You like to dream big.'

'It's the only way to do it.'

It hit him then that he'd never dreamed big. Ever. He hadn't actually dreamed at all, beyond wanting to get away from his father and wanting his mother to do the same. He'd worked for his father's building company because he'd been forced into it; he'd joined the army as it had been the easiest option open to him; he'd left the army with Sarge and Logan to start a business because it had seemed like the next logical step. But he'd never asked himself what, given the chance, he'd *like* to do.

She cocked her head to one side. 'And I'll continue to support Second Chances, and the charity will gain nationwide prominence and go from strength to strength.'

'Sounds like you're going to be busy.'

'But not too busy to holiday in my Greek island villa whenever I can, because, of course, I'll have made enough money to buy this place.'

'Of course,' he agreed gravely.

Actually, it wouldn't be a hardship to spend more time in this place. He loved what she'd done—what *they'd* done. He had more than enough money in the bank to buy the villa too. Sentry was ludicrously successful. He worked hard but rarely spent the fruits of his labour. He could—

What the hell...?

He shook the thought away. That wasn't *his* fantasy.

'Kids? A family of your own?' he forced himself to ask.

'Maybe not. I've never been particularly maternal. I keep waiting for that ticking clock everyone talks about to start counting down, but so far...' She shook her head. 'And I'm not having kids unless I *really* want them.'

'I feel the same.'

'As for getting married...'

A shadow passed over her face and he knew that she was thinking about Sebastian.

'This is your fantasy guy, remember?' Not some lying, cheating scumbag.

'Okay, then he's someone who isn't the least interested in what my parents do for a living, he's kind—'

'How is he kind?'

'He feeds stray dogs, stands up to bullies, and because he's my dream man he brings me chocolate whenever I'm feeling down. Also, he's really good in bed.' Her eyes danced. 'If I find a guy like that I might be tempted to keep him, although a husband doesn't *have* to feature in my future. I could instead take a series of beautiful men as my lovers.'

He grinned. 'So you're going to embrace your midlife crisis with gusto then.'

And then she was laughing beneath him, and they were kissing... And it was a long time before either one of them spoke again.

They spent the rest of the week renovating the reception room. In the evenings, when everyone left, the villa became their cocoon—a cocoon where fantasies played out, where he found himself laughing more readily and enjoying everything more.

He savoured the food they made rather than ticking it off as fuel for his body, savoured the buoyancy of the sea when they swam, savoured the touch of skin on skin when they made love.

It became a cocoon where he found himself playing a series of fantasy games with Janie—silly nonsense games like, 'If you could only visit one place on earth where would you go?' Or, 'Who would you most like to look like? Sing like? Be an expert like?'

Something odd happened as he played these games. It was as if the world opened up to him in ways it never had before. Even though he didn't actually want to have the Beatles around for dinner or look like one of the Hemsworth brothers, or sing like Elvis or paint like Picasso, the parameters around him seemed to expand.

And their makeover of the reception room was a triumph. They'd restored the ceiling rose and ornate cornices, while those extraordinary floor tiles gleamed. The fireplace sported a beautiful stone mantelpiece, and Janie had recycled pieces of furniture that had been in the house when they'd first arrived. Sofas and armchairs were recovered in a beautiful woven fabric she'd sourced locally. Coffee and side tables, a desk and an antique dresser were all sanded and oiled. He custom built a bookcase while Darren and Tian fixed table legs and chair arms.

The pastel colour scheme—powder blues, mint greens and salmon pinks—picked up highlights in the floor tiles and ornamental frieze. There were sociable areas as well as cosy nooks. The light pouring in at those big windows, framed with new shutters, had the room dancing with holiday promise. The room was grand and homely and he loved every inch of it.

Their achievement was rewarded the following week when Team Greece were the runaway winners. They were first again the week after as well with their entrance foyer. The desk that Zach built as a centrepiece—a stylistic rendition of a Greek temple—won the judges' plaudits. He'd been working on it since completing Janie's dream bed. Her eyes when she'd seen it had been worth all the hard work.

That was also the episode that aired Janie talking about Second Chances. He still didn't approve of her chosen charity, but he kept his expression stoic.

On screen, Janie introduced the woman who helped administer the charity—Lena.

Hold on, bestie Lena?

'When I was seventeen, I was home alone when an intruder broke into my mother's house in Camden,' Janie said. 'I was doing homework in my bedroom on the first floor when I heard the kitchen window smash.'

What the hell?

'I crept up to the attic and called 999.'

Smart.

'I was terrified, and it felt like forever, but the police came really quickly and the intruder was caught with a bag full of stolen electronic equipment and some of my mother's jewellery that had been lying around downstairs.'

He listened, equal parts horrified and spellbound.

'The thing is, the reason the intruder was caught was because they were so hungry they stopped to eat the leftovers from dinner. The intruder was only nineteen years old.'

'The intruder was me,' Lena said, taking up the story. She explained how she'd been thrown out of home, how her father had refused to hand over any of her ID or ATM cards or her phone. 'I know now that I should've gone to the police, but my father was a Presbyterian minister and I didn't think anyone would believe me. We'd only recently moved to London so I had no contacts. I could've gone to one of the many church charities, but my experience with my father made me… sceptical about those.'

His heart pounded so loud he was sure everyone must hear it.

'I didn't know anyone was home that night. I didn't know

I'd scared Janie so badly.' She rubbed a hand across her heart. 'I was sentenced to fifteen months in jail. Two months into my custodial sentence, I couldn't believe that this is what my life had become and I tried to take my own life.'

His gut churned. If he'd had a sister, one living in the same house as him…

Janie took up the thread of the story again. 'When I heard about that, I visited Lena in prison. I couldn't get the thought out of my head that she'd been so hungry she'd stopped to eat leftovers. It didn't fit my idea of a hardened criminal.'

It didn't fit his either.

'And when I met her I realised she wasn't that different from me. We'd just been born into very different families. I'd received all of the advantages while Lena had received none.' Janie paused. 'Sure, Lena had other options; she didn't have to break and enter. But she was young, desperate and scared. Given the same set of circumstances, I don't know if I could've done any better.'

In that moment everything he'd thought about Janie's charity turned on its head. The two women explained how their friendship had transformed them both and how Second Chances had helped Lena get back on her feet. They were engaging, articulate…and the evidence of their strong personal friendship had his throat thickening.

Janie was doing good work and, whether she won the prize money or not, she'd accomplished what she'd set out to do, which was raise the profile of what he now had to admit was a worthwhile charity. There would be industry professionals lining up to work with Second Chances, offering those in need employment and support. And people like Lena, those in desperate need of a second chance, would now get one.

'I misread everything,' he told Janie when they were back at the villa that night. 'I'm sorry. I've been every bit as blinkered as you accused me of being. You're doing great work, Janie. Necessary work. You should be proud of yourself.'

She didn't gloat or say *I told you so*. Her eyes glowed. 'Thanks, Zach, coming from you, that means a lot.'

It was the sound of a motorboat engine that woke him. A glance at his watch told him it was two a.m. Janie's slow, regular breaths told him she was fast asleep. Slipping out of bed, he padded across to the balcony and saw the lights of a little runabout bouncing out on the water. Probably tourists fishing. He started to turn back when he caught the scent of smoke.

It jerked him into instant action. Shouting, 'Fire!' into his watch to Sarge, he gathered Janie into his arms and headed down the stairs, getting her to safety the only thing on his mind.

She blinked up at him in a daze, but startled into full alertness when she smelled the smoke. And saw the direction of the flames. 'Oh, God, it's our beautiful reception room! Quick, Zach, there's a fire extinguisher and blanket in the kitchen.'

The fire hadn't had time to gather much momentum and they had it quickly under control, but if they'd been sleeping in the second-floor bedrooms at the back of the house... His lips thinned.

Janie stared at the scorched wall and ceiling, the burned-out armchair, and her bottom lip wobbled. 'We haven't lit any of the candles in here. The electricals were all checked.'

Sarge appeared, a silent shadow in the doorway, and held up a jerrycan. 'I don't know how the hell they slipped under our guard, but—'

'By boat. I saw it on the bay. They must've been leaving.'

Janie gaped at both of them. 'You're saying this is deliberate?' Her eyes narrowed and her hands slammed to her hips. 'Who the hell is trying to sabotage us?'

CHAPTER TEN

ZACH AND SARGE shared a glance.

Janie tapped a foot. 'Come on, out with it.'

Zach rubbed a hand over his hair. 'This may not mean anything, but we've reason to believe that Sebastian is now dating…'

His hesitation cut her to the quick. 'I don't care if he's dating again. I'm just glad he's not dating me.'

'Isobel.'

It took a moment to connect the dots.

Oh! Sebastian and Isobel?

'You're saying…' Her stomach plummeted. 'Sebastian would love to avenge himself on me because, you know, apparently I cost him two years of his life.'

They all rolled their eyes.

'And clearly Isobel wants to win. But deliberately setting fire to a competitor's property seems a bit of a stretch.'

Sarge showed his phone to Zach, and while Zach's expression remained the same she felt the change in him. He took it and showed her the picture on the screen. Her heart sank. 'Sebastian is on the island?'

Sarge reclaimed his phone. 'That footage came through late last night.'

'It doesn't feel like a coincidence, does it?'

'It does not,' Sarge agreed.

Her mind raced. 'I'm not afraid of Sebastian physically.

He's a dweeb, never been in a fight in his life. Which is a good thing. As a rule, I don't condone violence.' But if Sebastian was in this room right now, she'd kick him in the shins.

As if reading her mind, Zach's lips tightened.

'If you shaped up to him, Zach, he'd be a quivering, cowering mess.'

'No offence, Janie.' Sarge flashed her a grin. 'But most men would be a cowering mess if Zach shaped up to them.'

She laughed and something in Zach's posture eased. 'He's big,' she agreed. 'And he can look menacing when he wants to. But the fact is Sebastian would be the same if I slapped him. He wouldn't know what to do.'

'He wouldn't hit you back?'

'I'm ninety-nine percent sure he wouldn't. But this—' She gestured at the scorched wall. 'This I can see him doing.' Her hands clenched. 'Zach, if you hadn't heard that motorboat...' They could've died.

Dragging in a breath, she pushed that thought away. They hadn't died. She wouldn't panic. 'We've no solid evidence against him.'

'But we'll be keeping an eye on him.' Sarge turned to Zach. 'I'm calling in Lee and Ahmed as reinforcements. They can tail him.'

Zach gave a single nod. 'Good plan.'

'There's nothing else that can be done here tonight. I suggest the two of you turn in and try to get some sleep.' The older man hesitated.

'Sarge?'

'I know what's going on here.'

He gestured between her and Zach and Janie found herself swallowing. 'Are you about to say you disapprove?'

'You're both adults, and it's none of my business. I just want you to keep your wits about you. Keep your eyes and ears open. It looks like somebody wants to win that prize money and they're prepared to go to extreme lengths to do so.' He smiled at her briefly. 'You're in their sights because you're doing such an amazing job here, Janie. We *are* going to keep you safe, but it'll help if you remain alert.'

His praise warmed her. 'Roger that.' She imitated the words she'd heard Zach use. ''Night, Sarge.'

With a casual salute he was gone. Turning, she threw herself into Zach's arms. 'Thank you, tough guy, for saving the day.'

His arms wrapped around her, firm and strong. 'Wish I could've caught the rotter before he started the fire.'

'I'll take a scorched wall and a ruined armchair over what could've happened. Come on. Bed. We've another big day tomorrow.'

The team were horrified when they arrived in the morning and saw the damage. A grey-faced Cullen had the cameraman film it. The authorities were called in to investigate. It all took time they didn't want to spare, but Janie was ridiculously relieved they were working outside, away from the smell of charred wood and smoke. Darren and Tian doubled down, working extra hard as if wanting to somehow make amends. It had her fighting back tears.

Maybe it was that sense of camaraderie—of pulling together—that gave the outdoor space an extra sparkle, but between them all they laid pavers and built a simple pergola that ran the length of the villa on the dining room side. They planted ornamental grapevines that would eventually twine around the wooden beams and supports and turn it into a green oasis. Planter boxes and barrels of petunias, begonias and geraniums in bright colours were added and café tables dotted its length.

The *pièce de résistance* would be the tiny alcove created at the far end between the wall of the villa and the garden shed.

A sunny three-walled nook that would be surrounded by lattice trailing with jasmine, and with a small fountain splashing merrily at its centre.

'Ooh, look, the final touches have arrived.' Janie gestured to a newly delivered crate. Seizing a crowbar, she pushed it under the lid and levered it free—an action she'd become adept at. Pushing the lid to one side, she reached inside but pulled her arm back with a muffled shout.

Zach was at her side in seconds, Darren and Tian hot on his heels.

'Bitten,' she gasped, pressing her hand to the painful site on her forearm.

Tian knocked the lid completely off the box and peered inside the crate. Darren blew out a breath. 'I don't know what kind of spider that is…'

Zach had started to bind the bite with a bandage he'd magicked out of thin air. Janie peered into the box and swayed. *Oh, God, it was huge. And hairy.*

Lifting her, Zach carried her to a seat in the shade and made her sit while he finished binding her arm.

'It's a tarantula,' Tian said. 'Tarantula venom isn't normally lethal, but can be painful. Worst case scenario is you might feel unwell for a day or two.' His forehead wrinkled. 'This spider isn't native to the island.' His expression grew grim. 'There's three of them in the crate.'

Three!

'You have to go to hospital and get checked out,' Cullen ordered. 'Rules of the show. Health and safety.'

She wanted to argue, but Zach was already agreeing with him. 'Can we turn the camera off now?' she said weakly. 'I really don't want to throw up on national TV.'

Cullen made a cutting action and Zach carried her to the bathroom and held the hair off her face while she vomited. He flushed the toilet, supported her while she rinsed her mouth.

Closing the lid of the toilet, he sat on it and drew her down to his lap. 'The vomiting will be due to the shock. I was bitten by one of those a couple of years ago. No ill effects.'

She nodded, taking comfort in his strength. 'Three spiders, Zach. That's not a coincidence.'

'Sarge will start an investigation immediately. And from now on, only I open any deliveries.'

She nodded and tried to pull herself together, but her arm hurt like the blazes and the thought that someone had done this deliberately...

Don't think about that now.

'Okay, you stay and oversee things here.' There was still so much to do! 'Cullen can take me to the clinic and—'

'I'm not leaving your side.'

Damn.

'That's right. Bodyguard. Where I go you go.'

A gentle finger under her chin lifted her gaze to his. 'Because I'm your friend and I know you're scared, although you're hiding it well, and I'm not letting you face that alone because I care about you. Darren and Tian know what to do. We can trust them to do it.'

She wept a few quiet tears into his shoulder then, but eventually stood. 'Okay, let's go do this.'

Janie was allowed home later that afternoon, after the medical staff were satisfied that she wouldn't have an allergic reaction, but on the proviso she took it easy for the next couple of days.

When it became clear to the rest of the team that she had no intention of resting indoors, they placed an armchair in a shady spot where she could direct operations. She appreciated being part of things. And she appreciated the distraction from her father's overdramatic phone calls and emails, even though she'd assured him ten times now that she was fine.

Zach unearthed a footstool from somewhere and literally

made her put her feet up, setting a table to her right and placing her tablet there. Tian brewed her pots of healthful tea from a recipe his mother sent—nettle, lemongrass and liquorice root—and after the first cup she developed a taste for it. Darren brought her sun-warmed figs and a broad-brimmed hat. It meant she was able to watch as their beautiful courtyard came to life even if they wouldn't let her lift a finger.

'I want to take you all home with me when this is done and work with you forever,' she said, blinking hard at the tears blurring her vision.

The network hired a night-time security guard to patrol the grounds in case of further sabotage. And when the team went home in the evenings, nothing was too much trouble for Zach. He cooked and cleaned, refusing to let her help even a little bit. He brought her baklava and chocolate and chilled glasses of ginger beer. He watched her like a hawk.

At night he wrapped her in his arms until she fell asleep. She still burned for him, but when she'd turned in his arms to kiss him, he'd kissed her back gently but then tucked her head beneath his chin. 'Rest, Janie.'

So she had. She couldn't remember the last time she'd felt so taken care of. If she wasn't careful, she could become addicted to this.

A chill chased through her. She couldn't let that happen. This fling was temporary. She wasn't in the market, remember? And even if she changed her mind about that, Zach sure as heck wasn't interested in extending their affair beyond their time here in Corfu. And she was good with that. She swallowed and nodded. She really was.

The realisation that in another month they'd be leaving this heavenly island for good, though, had her heart twisting over on itself.

Stop it!

She was just feeling fragile from the spider bite and the

fire. But the bite no longer throbbed, and she'd noticed that whenever the team had a spare moment they worked hard to fix the fire damage. She suspected that in another week all evidence of the fire would be erased.

But every time she thought of leaving, of kissing Zach for the very last time, it sent a hot rush of panic through her. And during the night Zach turned to her whenever that happened, as if some part of him was minutely attuned to her.

He said he didn't do relationships. To hope he'd change his mind would be the height of foolishness.

You didn't think you wanted a relationship either.

She hadn't counted on Zach, though. Meeting him had turned her world upside down.

Once her two-day rest period was up, the team let her carry out the finishing touches. She hung lanterns on the pergola, placed candles on the tables. A mouthwatering platter of cheese and carafe of wine was strategically placed on one table, a bowl of fresh fruit on another, and a throw rug and book draped on one of the benches in their tiny courtyard. She wasn't sure she'd ever been prouder of a project.

When the show aired, anticipation threaded the air in the upstairs room at the tavern. As they watched, it became clear that while some of the other outdoor areas were beautifully finished, their makeover was outstanding. They couldn't keep the smiles from their faces.

'Except there's a serpent in Janie's Garden of Eden,' Mike, the host, said, turning to the camera.

What an earth...? They'd already covered Team Greece's fire and spider incidents. Had the team been keeping something back from her? Before she could ask, the screen cut away to the network studio, zeroing in on Zach's furious face.

'What the hell kind of charity is that?' he bellowed.

Oh, God.

Beside her, Zach stiffened as their fight after the filming of the first episode played out on the screen.

Mike's face appeared. 'Janie and Zach, do you have any comment to make?'

Her brain seized up. 'Well, Mike…' She moistened her lips. 'I…'

'As you can see,' Zach broke in quietly, but all the more authoritative for it, 'I was as blind and narrowminded as Janie's and Second Chances' very vocal detractors were in episode two. I think we all now know what a great job Second Chances is doing and I'm proud to be associated with the organisation.'

'Well, that is the knight in shining armour line we expect of you, Zach, but—'

'If I'm a knight—' Zach pushed his shoulders back '—it's because I have first-hand experience of violence, especially the kind directed at women. My mother has been a victim of domestic violence all her married life—my father has terrorised her—but she refuses to press charges. Probably because she's afraid for her life if she did.'

Everyone went so silent she could hear the water lapping in the bay.

'My father belongs in jail. He's a criminal. In my mind I've conflated all criminals with the kind of person my father is— the kind of person who believes they have the right to hurt and dominate others. But as we've learned from Janie and Lena, that's not the case. Some people don't have the support networks or opportunities the rest of us are lucky enough to get. They deserve a chance to turn their lives around. I'm grateful people like Janie recognise that and are doing something about it. I'm glad I've had my eyes opened and my prejudices challenged. And if there's anything I can do in the future to help Second Chances, I'll be doing it. And that's a promise.'

The room broke into applause—her, Darren and Tian, as well as the production crew, all on their feet and cheering.

'You can't say fairer than that, Zach,' Mike agreed.

Afterwards, Janie and Zach leaned against the car, watching the boats bobbing in the tiny harbour.

He glanced at her with shadowed eyes. 'I'm sorry that was caught on camera.'

'You were brilliant, Zach. Perfect!' She wanted to throw her arms about him and dance them around the car.

She opened her mouth to tell him how much she admired him and all he stood for, when her heart pounded in her throat and unbidden words threatened to spill from her tongue. Very slowly, she closed her mouth, a wave of heat washing over her. She'd been about to say, *I love you*.

She couldn't love him.

She *didn't*.

Her heart gave a giant kick but then slowed and the heat leached out of her, leaving a new knowledge behind in its place. She nodded. She loved Zach. Of course she did. But what, if anything, was she going to do about it?

Zach dragged a hand down his face. Janie had been through enough. He still worried that she suffered after-effects from that spider bite. And for him to have made things worse for her by having that stupid temper tantrum broadcast…

He deserved to be shot!

'Tell me what you need me to do to fix this.' He'd do anything.

'Zach, you absolutely and utterly just saved the day in there.' She pointed to the tavern. 'We couldn't have scripted this better if we'd tried. You just described the same emotional arc that a lot of viewers have gone on, but with a more personal element. I—'

He pushed away from the car to stand in front of her. 'You what?'

'You told the world a personal story—a *painful* personal

story—to save the day for me and Second Chances. That had to have been incredibly difficult. You didn't have to do that.'

'I wanted to make things right.' He'd had to make them right. Janie and the rest of the team had worked so hard over the last six weeks, and last week Lena had spoken so eloquently about what had led her to commit a crime at the age of nineteen, and how meeting Janie had changed her life. She'd laid herself bare. She'd cried, Janie had cried, and he expected there hadn't been a dry eye in the house.

It hadn't mattered what kind of sacrifice he'd had to make; he'd needed to make things right.

'Thank you.' Taking a step forward, Janie wrapped her arms around his waist and hugged him. His arms went around her as if that was what they'd been designed for. Resting his chin on the top of her head, he breathed in the scent of her shampoo and some hardness inside him melted.

Eventually she eased away. 'Come on, take me home.'

Home? Was that how she saw the villa?

He mulled that over as he drove. The villa felt more like a home than his apartment in London did. That was just a stopping-off place between assignments.

Things inside him quickened. Could he buy it? During the final episode, the resorts went to auction. He could buy it and start taking holidays, like Sarge and Logan nagged him to. Maybe Janie would like to join him and—

He cut that thought dead. This thing between them would end when they left the island, never to be repeated. If he bought the villa, and came out here for the odd holiday—a few days here, a week there—he could remember all that had happened here, recall the happy memories and…relax.

He might be ready to consider retirement…in a decade maybe. And he might be ready to take the odd holiday. But a relationship? That was *never* going to happen.

Arriving back at the villa, Zach grabbed a bottle of wine

from the fridge. 'Glass of wine down by the waterfront?' It had become the norm.

Her answer was to kick the door shut behind her and advance on him. 'For the last four nights you've played the perfect gentleman, ordering me to rest, but I've recovered from the spider bite and tonight I'm having my wicked way with you.'

She took the wine bottle and set it on the bench. Winding her arms around his neck, she drew his head down to hers and kissed him with a needy hunger that flooded his senses with her heat, her scent, and the shape of her. Growling, he lifted her into his arms and strode up the stairs to the master bedroom they'd made their own.

They made love with an oddly fierce tenderness that left him shaken to the core though he didn't know why. The intensity of their lovemaking shocked him and yet he revelled in it too.

'Oh, man,' she breathed afterwards, her head resting against his shoulder. 'That was…'

He nodded. 'Yep.'

They lay like that, not speaking until their breathing became quiet again. 'Can I ask you something, Zach?'

'Sure.'

'It's personal.'

He raised an eyebrow, which made her chuckle.

'Yeah, I know what we just did was pretty personal, but this might be off-limits personal. It's just… You said you don't do relationships. You said it wasn't conducive to your line of work, but lots of people make long-distance romances work. Haven't you ever been tempted?'

He understood her curiosity. He felt the same way— couldn't help wondering how long it would be before she met someone who'd chase Sebastian's betrayal from her mind and have her ready to settle down.

He wanted that for her. His molars ground together. *He did.* She deserved to be happy. It was just… He couldn't imagine any man good enough for her—who would deserve her.

'Ooh, looking really grim now. I'm sorry. I shouldn't have asked.'

He shifted up against the headboard. 'I don't mind you asking.'

She sat up too until they were shoulder to shoulder, pulling the sheet up to tuck beneath her armpits.

He grinned. 'Protecting your modesty?'

She grinned back. 'Just trying not to distract you.' Which made him laugh. He'd never met a woman so easy to be with.

Slowly, though, he sobered. 'I saw what so-called love did to my mother. According to books and films, love is supposed to make your knees weak, but in my experience it's your mind that love makes weak.' He fought back the long-ago darkness that threatened to close around him now, his chest growing tight. 'When you fall in love with someone, you give them the power to walk all over you.'

'Not every love affair is like that, though. In the best relationships the couple are each other's true partner—helping each other, supporting each other, laughing together and having fun, holding onto each other during the tough times and comforting each other. A relationship like that is beautiful, and something to aspire to.'

'Uh-huh, like the kind of relationship your parents had?' It was an ugly thing to say. The world knew the acrimony of that particular split. 'Like the relationship you had with Sebastian?' He couldn't stop the ugly words spilling from his mouth. Her words had burned through him, making him yearn for something he'd never had, and something he was determined to keep at arm's length.

He didn't *want* the kind of life she described.

He rubbed a hand over his face. 'I'm sorry—'

'So I finally see what the tough guy is afraid of—he's afraid of falling in love and being vulnerable.'

His head rocked back.

She slid out of bed and pushed her arms through the sleeves of her robe. 'I'm going to grab a camomile tea. Want something?'

But she didn't move. Her hands slammed to her hips. 'I didn't have you pegged as a coward, Zach. But here's the thing about being vulnerable—it doesn't have to make you stupid. As soon as my parents' marriage became toxic, they ended it. That was smart. As soon as I found out Sebastian had been using me, I ended it. Unlike your mother, we demanded more for ourselves. I'm sorry that was the example of love you were given as a child, and I'm sorry that's the message you took away from it. But being in love doesn't rob you of choice, free will or brain cells.'

'Yeah, well, I don't see the point in taking the risk.'

'That's what I meant when I called you a coward.' She tied the sash of her robe with a short sharp movement. 'I thought you were the kind of man who'd face his fears, not run away from them.'

Closing her eyes, she dragged in a breath. 'You've been enjoying our interlude here, haven't you?'

'Because it's an interlude!' he shot back. 'Temporary by definition.'

'Can you honestly say you don't want more of this in your life?'

'Hand on heart,' he shot back, slapping his hand to his chest.

She paled. 'Well, I do.'

An icy fist wrapped around him, squeezing the breath from his body. This wasn't a hypothetical. This had become personal for her. Throwing the covers back, he stalked across to her. 'We agreed this was temporary.'

She folded her arms. 'We did.'

'You said this wouldn't mean anything to you.'

Her gaze slid away.

'Has this thing—' he gestured between them '—started to mean something more to you?'

He wanted her to deny it. He didn't want to hurt her, but he'd warned her relationships weren't on his agenda and he wasn't changing his mind.

Her chin lifted. 'What if it has?'

He wheeled away. 'This ends now!'

'Is that you attempting to protect me?' She advanced on him, pushing a finger in his chest. 'Because you think you know what's best for me? Well, you know diddly-squat, Zach Cartwright. You're not trying to protect me. You're trying to protect yourself.'

'We're moving out of this bedroom and back to the bedrooms on the second floor. *Now.*'

'Fine with me!' She gathered up her things from the side table. 'One day, when you're no longer working your high-stakes assignments, you're going to look at your life and see all you've sacrificed, see all you missed out on, and you're going to regret it.' She pressed a hand to her heart, her eyes shadowed. 'I fear for you, Zach. I hope something happens to help you see the world differently.'

With that she left and he heard her move up the stairs to her bedroom beneath the eaves. She hadn't made her camomile tea.

Heading downstairs, he made the tea, but when he reached her door it was firmly shut and he didn't have the heart to knock on it. Taking the tea to his room, he set it on the bedside table. He tried sipping it.

But it didn't help. It didn't help at all.

CHAPTER ELEVEN

JANIE WOKE MUCH as she'd fallen asleep the previous night, much as she'd slept—poorly, in fits and starts, and with an ache in her chest that felt as if it would smother her. An ache that threatened her entire life and happiness.

Stop exaggerating. Where's your perspective? Think of Nanny Earp.

Yet it didn't feel like an exaggeration. And Nanny Earp had never denied pain and sadness. They existed alongside life and love and being human.

She loved Zach, but he didn't love her back. It sucked. It hurt. But she wasn't the only person who'd faced this same situation. While it might feel as if the sky was falling, it wasn't. It'd pass. Eventually. Broken hearts healed. *Eventually.*

She rubbed her hands over her face. *What was I thinking?* Not the falling in love thing. She couldn't help that part. Zach might be a big tough guy on the outside, but he had a marshmallow centre. He'd listened to her, cared what she thought, and had tried to make things easier for her. He hadn't bellyached about being stranded in Corfu when he'd have preferred to be somewhere else, doing something else.

Zach might be self-contained, but he was also kind. She didn't blame herself for falling in love with him at all. What she blamed herself for was letting him know.

He'd made it clear he wasn't interested in anything long-term. They could've had two more weeks of hot sex and friendship, if only she'd kept her mouth shut.

'No use crying over spilled milk.' Nanny Earp's voice sounded through her. *'What's done is done.'*

Pulling in a breath, she let it out slowly. Worrying about it, going over and over it…obsessing wouldn't help. And if it weren't for Zach, she might never have remembered that. She might have a broken heart and plenty of regrets, but it wouldn't stop her from doing the job she'd come here to do—to prove what she was capable of, to both herself and the world.

Forcing herself out of bed, she showered and dressed. Girding her loins, she headed down to breakfast. Zach had his back to her when she entered the kitchen, but he froze all the same. The rigid lines of his body had her heart throbbing.

'Right, let's say a few things, clear the air, and draw a line under this forever.'

He set toast onto a plate before turning and planting his feet. As if getting ready for her to take a swing at him or something. A part of her wanted to weep for him then because *that* was the experience of love he'd had growing up. No wonder he didn't want to take a risk on it now.

'We both know that what's happened here has meant more to me than it has to you. And now you're feeling guilty about that, and probably worried I'm going to make a scene.' She gripped her hands in front of her. That *wasn't* going to happen. 'All of that is a waste of time and energy. So stop with the guilt trips already and I won't throw any temper tantrums, agreed?'

Easing past him, she placed bread in the toaster, stared out of the window towards the pine grove. 'We're both adults. We've a job to do. Let's focus on that.'

'And that's it?'

He wanted more? Her toast popped up. Dropping it onto a plate, she took a seat at the table and reached for the butter and marmalade.

'Unless you have something to say?'

He shifted his weight from one foot to the other, his frown deepening.

'Very articulate.' She rolled her eyes. 'I didn't mean to fall in love with you, Zach. You didn't know it was going to happen. Nobody's to blame.'

He sat with a thump.

'And I'm not going to argue with you or try to change your mind. You're an adult, you know your own mind.' She bit into her toast, relishing the tart sweetness of the marmalade. 'I mean, clearly you have appalling taste turning someone like me down when I'm such a prize.'

He stabbed a finger at her. 'Don't put yourself down!'

She raised her hands. 'It was a joke.' She huffed out a laugh. 'I could have so much sport with you, but I'll refrain.' She ate more toast. 'I'm sorry you're cutting love from your life, Zach. I think it's a mistake.' She was sad for him. She swallowed the lump in her throat, sadder for him than she was for herself. 'But it's your mistake to make.'

A frown etched hard lines on his brow. 'You sound so… *together.*'

'I feel together.' And it was true. 'The thing is…' she met his gaze, refusing to flinch '…broken hearts mend. This isn't the end of the world and I refuse to turn it into the tragedy of the century.'

She'd cry buckets over this man when she returned home, but she'd also get up each morning and go to work, meet up with Beck and Lena, have dinner with her parents. Nothing much would change. Eventually she'd start to date again.

'You've found your internal compass.'

It seemed she had. And she was glad of it.

She dusted off her hands. 'Okay, with that out of the way, can we now talk about the mystery challenge?' This would be their final challenge. Each team would be given a task individually tailored to their property's needs, and two weeks to complete it. 'It's going to be the kitchen, isn't it? They're going to want us to transform this room into a commercial kitchen.'

'Is that bad?'

'Stainless steel benchtops…a brand spanking-new commercial oven…' Her nose wrinkled.

'Blow the budget?'

'More a case of spoiling the charm of the room.' She'd hate to transform it into something so soulless.

One broad shoulder lifted. 'They could ask us to turn the bedrooms under the eaves into a honeymoon suite.'

'Ooh!' Images fired through her. 'That would be so much fun. Hurry up, finish your breakfast and let's get up there and make some plans.'

She needed to keep busy and she'd work with whatever she had to hand.

'And here is your mystery renovation challenge, Team Greece.' Mike's face flashed onto her laptop's screen.

Janie crossed her fingers and toes.

'We want you to makeover your villa's façade—just the front—and turn it into something that would make people want to stay. You have transformed the interior and we now want to see that reflected in the front of the building. First impressions count and I think we can all agree that at the moment it's shabby and unloved. Good luck!' And with that, Mike's face vanished.

'How do you feel about the challenge?' Cullen asked, the camera and sound men in position. She and Zach sat at the table under the tree; Darren and Tian stood behind them.

She hadn't seen this challenge coming, not for a moment.

'Nervous,' she admitted. 'This is totally out of my wheelhouse.' She pushed her shoulders back. 'But I have a great team, we still have a decent amount left in the kitty, and we'll give it our best shot.'

Gathering around her laptop, they made a plan.

'We need to get rid of the plaster render and take it back to the original stone,' Zach said.

'It'll make all the difference,' Darren agreed. 'Backbreaking work, but once it's done...'

She glanced at them. 'Amazing?'

'Totally,' Tian said.

Pulling out her phone to make a shopping list, she said, 'Tell me what we need.'

Scaffolding,' Zach said.

'Wire brushes,' Darren said. 'Lots of them. And lime mortar.'

'Plants,' Tian said. 'And pavers.'

The suggestions came thick and fast. She ordered the scaffolding, to be delivered in the morning.

Zach took her phone and glanced down the list. 'It'll be quicker if you and I go and grab this now.'

'Darren and I will begin pulling out the garden,' Tian said. 'We need to make it beautiful.'

'You worried?' Zach asked as they drove to the town of Kassiopi. Their little local village wasn't equipped with all they'd need.

'A bit, but we have a plan, and if we can pull this off...'

If they pulled this off, she might just win a million pounds for Second Chances.

Two hours later, Janie checked their list. 'All that's left are the wire brushes.' This was their third hardware store. All three of them had been out of wire brushes. As if someone had bought them all up, knowing how necessary they'd be to Janie's renovation.

Stop being paranoid.

Zach did a search on his phone. 'There're another two hardware stores within a thirty-minute drive. We'll give them a go.'

'Okay, but I'm parched.' She gestured to the convenience store across the road. 'I'm going to grab a drink. Want one?'

His phone rang. He pressed it to his ear, but nodded at her. 'Sarge, what's up?'

Janie didn't wait to hear what Sarge had to say, but jogged across the road, dodging traffic, needing to take a moment for herself. She might've spoken adult words this morning at breakfast, but too many times today she'd wanted to hurl them to the wind and beg Zach to give them a chance. Her stomach churned. She couldn't do that. It'd be awful for both of them. Not to mention pointless. She needed to remain strong.

Striding past a van, she gave a startled yelp when a hand snaked out and grabbed her and started to haul her inside. She shouted out for Zach, saw the expression on his face as he swung to her before the door slammed shut. A hood was thrown over her head and strong arms banded around her as the van sped away.

Her heart hammered so hard that beneath the smothering darkness of the hood she thought she might faint.

Oh, God. Oh, God. Oh, God.

'Don't panic, Janie.'

The voice that sounded in her mind was Zach's. And the thought that he'd be in hot pursuit helped to steady her.

But Zach had been on the other side of the road. He'd have to turn their van around on a busy road. The kidnappers had a head start. And the number of streets they twisted and turned down had her fighting for air again. Whoever had her captive knew their way, knew where they were going, and they were doing their best to shake Zach from their tail.

The man who held her eventually eased his grip. Dragging in a slow breath, she steadied herself for a moment, before ramming her elbows back into his ribs and trying to smash the back of her head against his nose. He grunted, evaded her head, and the arms around her became steel bands once again.

'Who are you?' she shouted.

Nobody answered her.

Oh, God. Oh, God. Oh, God.

What if it was the person who'd written those vile letters? She lost her mind then in wild panic as she recalled the threats they contained. She fought—tried to bite and scratch and send her head crashing back into her assailant's face again and again. But he evaded all her efforts with an ease that made her feel sick. Finally, she made herself go limp. She couldn't beat him. It would be better to conserve her strength.

At some stage the van finally slowed to bounce down an unsealed road, and finally stopped. She couldn't tell if they'd been driving for twenty minutes or two hours. She was lifted out and carried up steps. A door closed behind her and a lock thrown. She was eased down into an armchair and the hood removed.

Blinking, she stared up at the man standing in front of her. Her jaw dropped. '*You?*'

Zach pulled the car over to the side of the road, slamming his palms to the steering wheel. 'I've lost them!' he shouted with a string of curses. 'I've lost them!' If whoever had Janie hurt her, he'd—

'Calm down, soldier!' Sarge barked from Zach's phone. 'I need you cold and focused. *Janie* needs you cold and focused.'

His knuckles turned white on the steering wheel. Sarge was right. His panic and fear wouldn't help Janie.

'We're going to get your girl back.'

Except she wasn't his girl. Because he'd been a stupid idiot and hadn't realised what she meant to him—had been hiding from his emotions like the coward she'd called him. It wasn't until he'd seen her bundled into that van and driven away that he'd understood all that she meant to him.

Everything.

In that moment he'd realised that he'd settle into quiet domesticity for her—a white picket fence and eight kids, or cats, if that was what she wanted. His high-powered, high-octane life meant nothing to him if she wasn't a part of it.

'Right.' Sarge's voice hauled him back. 'You tracked them to…' He called out the coordinates. 'There's a couple of different directions they could take from there, west or north, but neither lead out of town.'

'If I get my hands on the men who've done this—'

'When, not if,' Sarge hollered. 'And I'll be there to help you tear them limb from limb.'

'*When*,' he growled, holding onto that promise.

'When,' Sarge repeated. 'Because whoever's done this won't have our special forces training. They're toast.'

He wasn't sure he'd ever heard Sarge sound grimmer or more determined. It helped him focus. He and Sarge made a formidable team. They *would* save Janie.

Because any other outcome was unthinkable.

'The smart money is they'll take her somewhere remote, but according to the map it's not going to be too remote.'

Sarge gave him a road name and a set of coordinates. 'Go west until you reach the end and start working your way back. Keep your eyes peeled for the vehicle or anything suspicious. Tully is liaising with the local police and they're tracing the numberplate you called in. I'm sending Lee and Ahmed to search the road to the north. Don't turn your phone off. I want to know your every move—keep talking.'

For the next thirty minutes that was what he did. But with every passing minute the icy hand around his heart squeezed tighter and tighter. *Please give him the chance to tell Janie he loved her. Please give him the chance to grovel and beg her to build a life with him. Let him have the chance to tell her he was sorry, to tell her what an amazing woman she was.*

Halfway through the next thirty minutes he started making different bargains. He'd give up everything—thoughts of building a life with her, his job, his life—if she was returned safe.

'I have an address. The entire team is on its way.' Sarge called out an address. 'I'll call out directions—I can see you on the map.' They shared a tracking device. 'I need you to stay within the speed limit, Zach. The city is teeming with police. The last thing Janie needs right now is you delayed by getting a speeding ticket.'

He wasn't stopping for anyone, not even the police.

'Or shot,' Sarge added as if he could read Zach's mind.

That cooled his impatience. For Janie's sake he needed to play this smart. He'd curb his impatience, his panic. He'd give into both when they had Janie back safe and sound.

He arrived at the location—a remote but remarkably glamorous-looking farmhouse on the north-western reaches of town. If Janie could see it, she'd approve of the pink stone, the rustic wooden barn and the orange grove. It looked idyllic—as if nothing bad could ever happen here.

He drove into a secondary driveway that Sarge directed him to. It wound behind the barn to the far side of the house where their cars could be hidden behind a grove of trees. Sarge was already there. Zach's nostrils flared when four police cars turned in at the top of the long main drive.

He glared. 'This would've been quicker and easier if the two of us could've gone in there unnoticed and taken the villains out.'

'Agreed, but the mutual exchange of information made that impossible. We'll let them start negotiations, but you and I are getting in there now. Here's the plan...'

But before they could implement the plan, the front door opened and Janie marched out. Unhurt. Unharmed. And he was out from behind the shelter of the trees in seconds.

She stopped dead when she saw the police cars. Glancing in the other direction, she saw him. He kept moving towards her and then she was moving towards him. She started to run. In the back of his mind he wondered when he'd started running too, and then she was in his arms, her arms wrapping around his neck, and he swore he'd never let her go.

CHAPTER TWELVE

ZACH CARRIED JANIE back to the shelter of the trees. 'Are you hurt? Did they hurt you?'

He put her down and started checking her for cuts and bruises.

'Nobody hurt me,' she managed through chattering teeth. 'Zach, I don't want to stay here. I want to go back to the villa. *Please*. I don't want to stay here.'

'But—'

'Nobody hurt me. They had no intention of hurting me. I'll explain when we're home.'

He and Sarge exchanged glances.

'They scared the hell out of me, and I'm *so* angry and I… just want to sit at the table beneath the big tree and have a glass of ginger beer and—'

She burst into tears. He pulled her against his chest.

'Take her home.' Sarge clapped a hand to Zach's shoulder. 'I'll take care of things here.'

An hour later they all sat at the table beneath the big tree—Janie, Zach and the building team, Sarge and the security team, and the production crew. Janie had eaten and showered and her colour had returned to normal, though her eyes had turned stormy. Which was better than them being cloudy with fear.

She pointed a finger at the production crew. 'If you film or record any of this I'll hit you over the head with the camera.'

The crew rose and packed the equipment in their car, handing their phones across to Sarge for safekeeping.

She turned to Darren. 'Did you know?'

'That you were abducted?' He nodded, his face pinched. 'As soon as it was called in I went on high alert, contacted your father. My instincts were to wait here in case a ransom demand arrived.' This incident had blown both Zach's and Darren's cover.

Something inside her seemed to unbend then. 'So you didn't know Joey Walter planned to kidnap me?'

'He *what*?' Zach bellowed.

She winced and touched a hand to her ear.

'Sorry.' He did his best to moderate his volume, but nothing on God's green could have him unclenching his fists.

They listened in stunned silence as Janie told them how her father had totally freaked out at the twin incidents of the fire and spider bite. He'd been convinced the writer of those letters was behind the sabotage.

'He let those letters get inside his head, and they messed with him.'

They were the kind of letters that could mess with anyone's head, but to kidnap his own daughter...'

Sarge briefly described the letters for those who didn't know about them. When he was finished, Cullen stared at him, horrified.

'When reports informed him that Sebastian had been seen on the island...' Janie trailed off, her lips twisting.

'The idiot panicked,' Sarge bit out.

'He sent Aaron to, quote, *"get me somewhere safe"*. They knew I wouldn't go quietly. Hence the reason for their subterfuge.'

Subterfuge? They'd snatched her—terrified her! Zach's hands clenched so hard his whole frame shook. If Joey Walter had been sitting at this table right now he'd punch him into the middle of next week.

Janie wouldn't like that.

He rolled his shoulders. Okay, he wouldn't. But he'd want to.

'As soon as I saw Aaron I put two and two together, and was on the phone to my father so fast his head must've spun. He'll still be smarting from the blasting I gave him. I made it clear that this time he'd gone too far. I said that if he didn't tell Aaron I was free to go that I'd disown him. And that I'd make that public.'

Good for her.

'He blustered and spluttered until I told him he had until the count of ten to make up his mind. He gave in when I reached eight.' She shrugged. 'Aaron handed the van keys over and I walked out of the farmhouse ready to ring you when police came hurtling down the drive.'

And he'd shepherded her away.

'Joey Walter was amazed we'd traced Janie so quickly.' Sarge looked grim, and Zach bet Joey Walter's ears were burning with whatever well-chosen words Sarge had directed at him too. 'He's agreed to make a generous donation to the local police's swear jar in reparation.'

That almost made him laugh. It shouldn't but... Janie was safe. And that was all that mattered.

She turned to the production team. 'You could make a lot of money if you went public with this story.'

'Not going to happen.' Cullen glanced at his sound and camera men, who nodded their agreement. 'Janie, during filming you've given us all a lesson in integrity, and it's one I'm personally never going to forget. As soon as this show has been put to bed I'm leaving the network.'

She frowned. 'That's a big step.'

'Reality TV isn't for me.' He raked a hand through his hair.

'I don't like this network's ethics. And I might, um...have some information that's of interest to your security team.'

Zach straightened. 'Like?'

'Antoine is secretly dating one of the executive producers on the show.'

'He's married!' Janie gasped.

'Not for much longer. And his old network will drop him like a hot potato once the scandal breaks.'

Zach glanced around. 'Why?' People broke up and got divorced all the time.

'Because he's married to the network head's son,' Janie said, pursing her lips. 'And with a whole new generation of TV chefs snapping at his heels, he might find it harder to pick up a plum job.'

What a piece of work. Zach raised an eyebrow at Cullen, noticing the way he fidgeted. 'And?'

'One of the writers on a daytime soap told me an odd story recently about being asked to write an ugly threatening letter to be used in an upcoming episode. But the brief was not... on point. And it never did appear in any upcoming episodes.'

The security team all straightened.

'I don't know if it's linked. And I'd have mentioned it earlier if I'd known Janie's situation. I mean, it could be a coincidence, a storyline that was dropped, but it's stuck with me, and when you mentioned the letters Janie received...'

'We don't believe in coincidences,' Sarge said. 'I'll get the writer's details from you before you go.'

Janie stared. 'Those letters were a scare tactic to keep me from joining the show?'

'Could be,' Zach said. 'But until we're sure we'll be remaining vigilant during the rest of the filming. That is, if you want to remain.'

'Of course I'm staying.' She folded her arms. 'I vote we take the rest of the day off, though, and start afresh tomorrow.' Her jaw tightened. 'And we still don't have those damn wire brushes!'

'I have some in the minibus.' Cullen scuffed the ground with the toe of his shoe, not looking at anyone. 'A…uh…contact told me that we might find all of the local hardware stores' supplies non-existent. I grabbed a few before that could happen, just in case.'

Janie beamed at him. 'Cullen, you're a star.'

He winced. 'Just don't tell anyone.'

The production crew left with Darren and Tian. And then the security team left. Janie glanced at Zach, returning from the villa with a tray of fresh ginger beer on ice and some bread and cheese. She recalled the way she'd run to him when she'd emerged from the farmhouse, the way she'd clung to him. She hadn't been able to help herself. She'd thought she'd never see him again.

Being in his arms had helped. It had made her heart rate slow, had meant she could finally let her guard down, trust she was safe. It didn't mean anything had changed between them, though.

With a superhuman effort, she dragged her gaze from the broad lines of that powerful body.

Chin up.

She *wasn't* going to fall apart now. It'd be poor form to reward all of his hard work and chivalry with tears and begging.

No matter how much she might want to. Even if it felt like it was killing her not to.

It's not going to kill you!

Dragging in a breath, she thought about all the movies she'd watched, the books she'd read, the girlfriends she'd comforted through broken hearts. She'd be depressed for a while, would find it hard to have fun or muster enthusiasm for anything, but she'd be fine. Eventually she'd come out the other side. It wouldn't be fun, but she'd survive.

Blowing out a breath, she nodded. Inside she might feel like she was dying, but that wasn't the case.

'What are you nodding about?' Zach slid the tray onto the table, taking the seat beside her rather than the one opposite like he normally did. Maybe he wanted to stare at the view too.

Maybe he just didn't want to look at her.

He poured them both glasses of ginger beer, sliced generous slabs of cheese. She focused on what she could hear—water lapping, the distinctive call of a reed warbler, the rustling in the undergrowth as a gecko searched for insects. It helped keep her agitation in check.

Reaching for a napkin and a piece of sourdough, she nibbled on the bread, focusing on the texture and trying to appreciate it. She could feel the weight of Zach's gaze on her, but she didn't turn to meet it.

'I let you down today, Janie.' The words were softly spoken and all the more powerful for that. 'I'm sorry.'

What the heck...?

She spun to him. 'What are you talking about?'

'I let my guard down. I was hired as your bodyguard and yet you were snatched on my watch and—'

'Yeah, well, as you, Sarge and everyone else *other* than my father knew, the letters were a hoax.'

'We're ninety-five percent sure, not a hundred percent,' he argued.

'And seriously, who could've predicted that my father would do *that*?' She slapped both hands to the table. 'And you did save me. You found me in under two hours. That was amazing.'

He dragged a hand down his face.

'Stop beating yourself up for something you had no control over. Talk to Sarge. He'll tell you the same. Also,' she added before he could argue, 'what would you say to Sarge if your positions were reversed? Examine *all* the evidence—don't exaggerate, don't panic, avoid hyperbole.'

A smile played at the edges of his lips. 'You really have found your mojo again, haven't you?'

She had. Thanks in large part to him.

'The thing is—' he rubbed a hand across his jaw '—I have no objectivity when it comes to you. When you were snatched—'

He broke off, his face haggard, and it made her chest clench. When his gaze lifted, the expression in those blue eyes had the breath catching in her throat.

'It was one of the worst experiences of my life.'

His expression...

She couldn't get air into her lungs.

'I could barely function. All my training... Poof!' He snapped his fingers. 'Gone. The only thing on my mind was following that van and getting you back. Sarge had to bark orders at me to get me focused again, to stop me doing something stupid that would've endangered civilians or had the police on my tail.'

The tortured twist of his lips, the helpless way his hand pushed through his hair, had her fighting the urge to reach for him. He looked... She had to be mistaken. Her heart started to thud.

'What are you trying to say, Zach?'

He shot to his feet, walked down to the shoreline. 'I don't know how to say it.'

She stared at the hard lines of his back, the spasms that passed across it, and ached for him. Moving to stand beside him, she nudged his arm. 'We've become friends over the last few weeks. Good friends. I'd be worried sick if anything like that had happened to you. But seeing me snatched would've reminded you of all the times you couldn't protect your mother, would've raised a lot of bad memories—'

'I wasn't thinking of my mother, Janie.' He glanced down. 'I was thinking how desolate my life would be without you in it. A world without you...' His jaw clenched. 'I couldn't bear it.'

Was he saying...? She had to plant her feet to remain upright.

'I'm struggling, at a loss how to say three little words. Three words I've never said to any woman other than my mother.'

In that moment it felt as if even the tide held its breath.

'Are those three little words *I love you*?' She held her breath too.

He nodded.

She let her breath out on a careful whoosh. 'Why are you afraid to say them? Do you think once you've said them that you'll have to give up your exciting high-powered life?'

He thrust out his jaw. 'I didn't say I was afraid.'

'I'm just working with the evidence at hand.' She wanted to kiss him. 'Do you think if you say those words to me that I'll treat you like your father did your mother?'

His face gentled. Reaching out, he trailed a finger down her cheek. 'You're the opposite of my father. You're a giver, Janie, not a taker. You treat people with respect and kindness. I'm not afraid you'd ever use and abuse me. And for another thing,' he added, 'I'm not scared about changing my lifestyle or my role at Sentry. You've made me see that real life has a lot to offer. Hell, you make me want to join a football team, take up woodworking and find a pub I can call my local.'

Her jaw dropped, hope unfurling in her chest. Zach wasn't talking about them dating between his far-flung assignments and seeing where this might take them, he was talking about something so much more.

She willed her heart to slow. If he was wholly committed to making a relationship with her work…

'Are you afraid I'll throw those three little words back in your face?'

'It's what I deserve.'

'And maybe I don't agree with that, tough guy.'

His chest rose and fell. The pulse in his throat pounded.

She backed up to lean against the table. 'So if you know I'm not going to take advantage of you, and I'm not going to demand you give up your job, or that I'll be unkind or unreasonable, and you know I'm not going to fling the words back in your face and…?' The pulse in her throat pounded like a wild thing too.

'And?'

'And if you really do love me…'

'Don't doubt that for a moment.'

The expression in his eyes told her more eloquently than words ever could the depth of his feeling. She wanted to fling her arms out and dance, wrap them around his neck and kiss him until nothing else on earth existed except the two of them.

Zach loved her!

She had to swallow before she could speak.

'Well, if you know all of that and really feel that way, and I told you it was important for me to hear those three little words… What's holding you back?'

'Important?' His gaze sharpened and he was in front of her in two strides, his hands cupping her face. 'I love you, Janie Tierney. If you need to hear them, I'll say them over and over. It's just that the words aren't big enough to cover everything I feel for you, everything I want with you. I love you with every molecule of my being. I never want to be without you.' His hands tightened on her face. 'A man like me doesn't deserve a woman like you, but I promise, if you'll let me, I'll work hard every day to be worthy.'

He dragged in a breath that made his entire frame shudder. 'I love you, Janie. I love you. And I want you to be my wife, even though I know it's too soon to say that. I want the right to look after you forever—white picket fences, the lot, I'm all in. I'm going to love you to the end of my days and I want you with me until the end of days.' He swallowed. 'If that's not what you want, then tell me what will make you happy and I'll do that instead.'

He stared at her with such naked vulnerability her heart turned over and over and her eyes filled.

'Oh, Zach, that's the best *I love you* speech I've ever heard. I love you too—every bit as much. I want to make you happy. I want to show you how wonderful the real world can be. I want to marry you and build a life with you too—' she gave a shaky laugh '—but I should warn you I'm not all that fond of white picket.'

He stared as if her words were the sweetest music he'd ever heard. 'Janie…'

'Kiss me,' she whispered.

Later, much later, as the sun sank on the western horizon and a pale golden light fluttered behind the sheer white curtains moving in the soft breeze from the French windows of that beautiful master bedroom she'd started to consider theirs, Janie nestled against Zach's side and let out a long slow breath.

'Okay?' Zach asked, his muscles tensing beneath her cheek.

'Everything is perfect,' she told him. 'I never knew I could be this happy.'

'Or that life could be this good,' he agreed, pressing a kiss to the top of her head.

She rested her chin on her hand so she could look up at him. 'What now?'

'We renovate the façade of the villa—brilliantly—and hopefully win Second Chances a million pounds. We return to London, where you'll be inundated with the kind of projects that make your mouth water, while I start a conversation with Sarge and Logan about a new role in the company. When we were playing your hypothetical games and you were throwing around wild ideas for me, one of the things you mentioned was a training facility. I'd like to do that—set one up and run it.'

She sat up. 'You'd be great at that.'

'I never wanted to be stuck behind a desk but that…' He nodded. 'I think I'd enjoy it.'

She beamed at him.

'I won't enjoy it as much as coming home to you every day, though.'

She snuggled down against his shoulder again.

'Your father and I are going to have a blunt conversation when we get back to London, because he's never pulling another stunt like the one he did today. Then…eventually, you and I will move in together. Maybe buy a little place in the country.'

She happy sighed. That sounded wonderful. 'And one day we'll find a pretty little church and get married there when we decide the time is right,' she said.

Placing a finger beneath her chin, he lifted her face to his, his eyes solemn and shining with love. 'I do,' he murmured.

'I do,' she whispered back.

They sealed the promise with a kiss that had their toes curling and a future full of hope and love unfurling before them.

EPILOGUE

Ten months later...

Breaking News!

Renovation Revamp *winners Janie Tierney and Zach Cartwright were wed today in a private ceremony at a stone church in Suffolk.*

Viewers of the reality TV show will remember Janie and Zach not only for their extraordinary renovation of a villa on Corfu, but the remarkable events that occurred during the filming of the show, when two separate sets of contestants attempted to sabotage them.

Unsurprisingly, the guest list didn't include either Isobel Jamison or Sebastian I-Have-a-Monopoly-on-Mediocrity Thomas.

In a surprising twist worthy of a soap opera, however, Antoine Mackay, who did several months' community service at the charity Second Chances for his role in said sabotage, was in attendance. Sources close to the celebrity chef claim he's become dedicated to the charity.

Other guests included members of Team Greece, Tian Tengku and Darren Baker, along with the production crew who were with them in Corfu, including Cullen Brax, who is now the producer of a series of hard-hitting documentaries.

It's reported that the bride wore a designer gown of

cream silk and lace, while the bridegroom wore a smile as broad as the Atlantic.

When asked for a comment, father of the bride Joey Walter said, 'I'm delighted to welcome Zach into the family. He's a king among men.'

The couple have embarked on a honeymoon to an undisclosed location. We wish them well.

JANIE GAVE AN excited wriggle as the car passed through a shaded grove of olive trees. 'We're spending our honeymoon at the villa, aren't we?'

'What gave it away?'

Zach flashed her a grin. He did a lot of that these days—grinning, smiling...looking happy. It made her toes curl. Every single time.

'Ooh, the fact we landed at Corfu Airport this morning, perhaps?'

He laughed and her heart expanded until it felt too big for her chest.

Her husband. She still couldn't believe her good fortune that this man was *her husband.*

'But...how?' The villa had sold at auction to an anonymous buyer for a price that had sent the network into ecstasies. Not even the tabloids had been able to unmask them.

He touched a finger to the side of his nose and winked.

Grinning, she shook her head. Of course he, Sarge and Logan had tracked the unknown buyer down. And knowing Zach, he'd have made an offer the new buyer couldn't refuse.

A whole week at their villa... She happy sighed, but it was threaded through with bittersweetness too that it was only for a week.

She pushed the thought away. The next week would be wonderful. A week to make memories they'd never forget. They'd visit the village where people knew them and said hello, asked how they were but didn't take photos of them or invade their privacy. They could go into the tavern where a glass of red wine would be poured for her and a beer set in front of Zach. Or they could head down to the little restaurant on the water and be given a table on the terrace without even asking for it. She couldn't think of a better way to spend a week.

Except spending hot, steamy Greek island nights with *her new husband*.

And speaking of hot… 'Beck and Logan were looking awfully cosy at the reception last night.'

He glanced at her. 'I noticed that too. Worried?'

'I think they're perfect for each other.' She bit her lip. 'Are you worried?' Did she need to warn Beck?

'Never seen him look happier.'

She folded her arms and grinned at the world. 'And Sarge was all puffed up with pride at the pair of you.'

Sarge and Logan had been Zach's groomsmen, while Beck and Lena had been her bridesmaids. As the newspapers had reported, the wedding had been a small affair. But perfect.

'Ready?'

Zach halted the car at the top of the long drive that led to the villa. Her heart pounded. Would it be as wonderful as she remembered?

At her nod, he started down the drive—the lush, well-kept drive—and she gave thanks that the person who'd bought the place made the effort to maintain it. They emerged from the cover of the trees…

Her heart caught. 'Oh, Zach,' she breathed.

'It really is something.' His voice was as reverent as hers.

'Back then, this is the moment I fell in love with the place.' When she'd seen that view. A cerulean sea sparkling in the sun, a rocky shoreline and a pebbly beach. And not a soul in sight.

'And then you saw the villa…'

'And had an immediate reality check.'

Holding her breath, she followed the lush lawn up to the villa, and the tension in her chest released on a puff of warm appreciation. 'It's beautiful.'

He nodded.

During their final challenge they'd removed the pock-marked, discoloured render to expose the golden stone beneath. They'd scrubbed and re-mortared until the façade had emerged, grand in its understated simplicity. The gardens they'd planted ten months ago were now a riot of colour. Scarlet geraniums, pink and white petunias and deep purple violets spilled from the two hanging pots either side of the door.

'It's even *more* beautiful than when we left.' She stared her fill. 'It shows what a difference a bit of hard work and attention to detail can make.'

'And vision. This is all due to your vision, Janie. You put a lot of yourself into this project, a lot of love. And I can speak from experience about the miracles your love can work.'

'Stop it,' she whispered, her eyes filling. 'You'll make me cry.'

Reaching across, he took her hand and lifted it to his lips, pressing a kiss to her palm. 'I love you, Janie.'

She would *never* tire of hearing him say that. 'And I love you. More even than I love Corfu and this villa,' she teased.

Laughing, he pulled her from the car, gave her a kiss that had her blood fizzing, and then gestured at the villa. 'Wanna look inside?'

'Yes, please!' She couldn't wait to see what changes the new owner had wrought.

They walked through the large rooms hand in hand—the ground floor, the first floor, and then up to the bedrooms beneath the eaves. She couldn't utter a single syllable.

Back in the kitchen, her mind whirled. Zach took a bottle of champagne from the refrigerator, along with a platter of delicious nibbles. She followed as he led the way back outside to the table beneath the big tree.

'Nothing has changed.' She eased down into a chair, glancing at the tree, the water, the villa. 'It's as if it was sealed up when we left.' As if it had been waiting for them to return to finish the job.

He handed her a glass of champagne, eyeing her carefully. 'Disappointed?'

Slowly, she shook her head. 'I don't want to see someone else's stamp on our villa.' She wrinkled her nose. 'Silly, right?' Because it wasn't their villa, despite the current fantasies playing through her mind.

'I'd like to propose a toast.'

He sounded so serious and formal she rose to her feet. 'And Zach, how could I be disappointed? I'm here with you. It's *you* that makes this special. We just promised to spend the rest of our lives together. Life couldn't be more perfect.'

The blue of his eyes darkened and it made her breathless in the most delicious way. She waited for his lips to seize hers in a spine-tingling kiss, but he held back.

'I don't know how I got so lucky, because I believe you mean that.'

'Of course I mean it!' How could he doubt her?

Those stern lips softened into a smile. 'So if I were to tell you that the villa is in fact ours—that I was the mystery buyer—and that I had the deeds transferred into your name, that wouldn't impress you in the slightest?'

He was...? He had...? They owned...? Her mind fogged.

Reaching into his pocket, he pulled out a document and handed it to her. Setting her champagne down, she took it, her fingers shaking as she unfolded it. She had to read the words twice.

'We own the villa?' She glanced up, searching his face. 'It's *ours*?'

'Well, technically it's yours. You always did call this place home.'

And he'd bought it for her?

'You wonderful man!'

She started towards him, but he held up a hand. 'Stop.'

She stopped.

'Because the moment you kiss me, I suspect we're not going to stop for a very long time.'

Sounded great to her.

'And we haven't had our toast yet.'

She reached for her glass, feeling as if she had sunbeams pouring out of her.

'Who knows what life will throw at us, Janie.' The expression in his eyes had tears filling hers. 'But here's to a life filled with as much love and sunshine and laughter as we can jam into it.'

She touched her glass to his. 'To a life filled with love.'

They sipped their champagne. He set his glass down. She set hers down too. 'Can I kiss you yet?'

'Please.'

Stepping into his arms, she kissed him with all of the delight and exuberance in her heart. When they eased away long moments later, she held his gaze. 'I love the villa, Zach. But I love you more.'

'I know.' His eyes danced. 'But it's still the best present ever, right?'

She grinned and then laughed for the sheer joy of it. 'Best present ever,' she agreed, throwing her arms around his neck.

As he whirled her around, she swore that somewhere above their heads she heard a Greek chorus singing with unrivalled glee.

* * * * *

THE
BILLIONAIRE'S
PLUS-ONE DEAL

JUSTINE LEWIS

MILLS & BOON

For The Usual Suspects

xxx

PROLOGUE

WILL WATSON SLID off his tie and threw it on his desk. It was hot, early evening, and sixteen storeys below him the peak hour traffic hummed, but Will still had a few hours of work to do.

He scrolled through his emails searching for the deed he needed. The sun hit his screen and bounced right back into his eyes. He should bring the blinds down. Before he could, there was a knock at his door. His assistant, Belinda, always called through with visitors, so this would be either her or one of his parents. His father, David, had established and still headed up the company, Watson Enterprises, and his mother was a board member. The pair made a formidable duo. Once upon a time he'd wanted a partnership just like theirs. Despite years of wishing otherwise, his chest still ached with the thought that it wasn't to be, but he pushed the feeling to one side, as always.

The visitor was his mother, Diane Watson. She walked around his desk and kissed him on the cheek.

'Hello, darling.' She ruffled his hair. The only person in the world who'd do such a thing. He smoothed it back down again.

'Are you heading home soon?' she asked.

'Not yet. What's up?'

Diane sat across the desk from him. After a pause long enough to let him know what she was about to say was serious, she said, 'Will, we're worried about you.'

'I'm completely fine.' And he was. As long as he could be left alone to finish his work.

'Since Georgia left…'

Not again. This was not the first time Diane had voiced these concerns. It wasn't even the first time this year and it was only January.

'We talked about this.' Yes, his ex-fiancée, Georgia, had broken his heart. But that was years ago. And he was grateful for the lesson she'd taught him. He was stronger and more sensible because of it. He was *fine*.

'Have you thought about hiring a professional?'

'A *what*?'

'Calm down. Someone to talk to. A psychologist.'

Will didn't need a psychologist, or any type of professional. He was perfectly fine. Not wanting a relationship didn't mean he needed help. Being single was a perfectly valid state of being.

'I'm worried you're using work as an excuse not to have a life. It seems as though you're using work to distract yourself from the pain she caused you—'

'My work—our work—is important. You believe in it as much as I do.'

'I know you have a hard time trusting people. What if I introduced you to some women?'

'No! I really don't need that kind of help.'

The thought of meeting a woman on a date arranged by his mother was mortifying.

'When was the last time you went on a date?'

'Mum, no.'

He had to get back to work or he'd never get home. But his mother looked so concerned. She wasn't going to let this drop.

'Look, Mum, I'm okay. I wasn't going to say anything because it's still early days.'

Diane leant forward. 'You're seeing someone?'

It was late, he was tired and wanted this to end. He nodded.

Diane's face opened into a smile that could have lit up the CBD.

'Who is she? What's her name?'

Will looked out over the city, felt the sweat on his skin from the heat outside. 'Summer,' he said.

'Summer who?'

Through the window the sun still streamed in, hitting his screen. 'Summer Bright. That's her name.'

An image popped into his mind from nowhere. A beautiful woman, surrounded by a halo of hair, golden and fiery. But it was strange this woman had a face; she was a fiction. He'd just invented her and with a name like that she couldn't possibly be real.

'Oh, she sounds lovely,' gushed Diane.

Will stared at his mother.

She sounds made up.

'When can we meet her?'

'It's early days.'

'Sure.'

'And meeting the Watsons isn't a small thing.'

'We're not scary.'

But they were intimidating. David had built a multi-million-dollar plastics company from nothing. His mother sat on half a dozen boards, including companies and charities.

'We can be. *Dad* can be.'

Diane nodded, conceding that David Watson was not always an easy man.

'Well, when she's ready.'

Will nodded and smiled back at his mother. Relaxing back into his chair a sense of relief rolled over him. It was that easy. Make up a girlfriend who his mother would never meet and she'd get off his case once and for all. He was now free to get on with his life just how he liked it.

Alone.

CHAPTER ONE

Two years later...

SUMMER BRIGHT ADJUSTED the straight blond wig. Platinum blonde was definitely not her colour. She had asked to be Frida tonight, her own auburn locks were much closer to Frida's dark curls, but Stacey had arrived first and snagged the brown wig. Summer would be singing Agnetha, the blonde member of ABBA on stage tonight.

They were doing a show in one of Adelaide's largest hotels. It was a fundraiser, but the audience was going to consist of corporate types, drinking bottomless glasses of cheap sparkling wine. They wouldn't be as enthusiastic as a roomful of fans who had only come to hear Summer and her crew perform some classic hits, but once they had a few drinks under their collective belt, they'd get into the spirit of things; alcohol, nostalgia and familiar songs were always a good cocktail for a party. Summer had sung in enough tribute shows to know that, regardless of what someone might say about their musical taste sober and in the daylight, if you started singing a few songs from their childhood, most people would start to sing along.

She had been performing tribute shows for a few years now. The manager, John, started a Beatles tribute show and when that proved successful, he branched out to others: Fleetwood Mac, Elton John. Summer had joined when he was looking for women to perform in an ABBA line-up. Since then, she'd branched out to Stevie Nicks and Christine McVie and one weekend, when they were short one singer, played a very popular Ringo Starr.

They toured around Australia occasionally, but were now back in her hometown of Adelaide, for which she was glad. She loved travelling, but with her mother's health deteriorating Summer no longer wanted to be far away for long. This job paid well and since she'd lost her guitar her other income stream, busking, had totally dried up.

Summer knew the songs by heart and sang them without thinking. On nights like this it was the choreography and the unfamiliar layout of the stage she had to pay attention to.

They were in the ballroom of the hotel, the sort of room that had probably hosted a seminar on the insurance industry earlier that day, so it was not a purpose-built stage. She wanted to stomp her feet hard to 'Knowing Me, Knowing You', but worried her white boots would go right through it. She noticed him first during her solo of 'The Winner Takes It All'.

He was looking right at her. She turned, did a lap of the stage and he was still looking at her. When their eyes met, he looked down.

Did she know him? She didn't know many people well and certainly no one she could think of would be at a gig like this. Corporate fundraiser? The only people she knew here tonight were backstage, serving or performing. No one she knew could pay one thousand dollars a ticket, no matter how noble the cause.

But he looked at her like he knew her. In the half-light, she couldn't make out the colour of his eyes, but there was no hiding his careful, intense stare. His hair was dark, she guessed, and he would also be tall, she guessed, comparing him to the figures sitting around him. Each time she turned, she vowed not to seek him out again, but her eyes kept coming back to him. Did she know him? She was sure she'd remember someone with that sort of presence. Someone who made her tummy flip with simply his gaze.

She turned from him. As she sang the conclusion of the song, the swelling crescendo, the poignant lulls, the song lyrics pushed the handsome man from her thoughts and with each new line about heartbreak and betrayal she thought of the men she'd known over the years. As usual, she was addressing the words to this song to every man she'd ever known.

Brett.

Jason.

Michael.

And her father.

There was a blonde one and a brunette, just like the real ABBA but it was the blonde who caught his eye. There was something familiar about her, but he couldn't place her. It was highly unlikely he knew her; he didn't cross paths with many cabaret singers. Lawyers, bankers, yes. Singers, no.

The evening was billed as 'an immersive dining experience'. It wasn't his first. Dinner shows were part of his job, an occupational hazard, but this was the first ABBA tribute show he'd suffered through.

He didn't hate ABBA, just to be clear, but he did not love ABBA as much as the group of women a few tables down who were singing along and waving their hands in the air.

Attending fundraising dinners, such as this one, organised by his mother, was part of his job as CEO of Watson Enterprises. This evening was for a cause close to his mother's heart: research into ocean preservation. Since Watson Enterprises' main business was now recycling plastics and keeping them out of said oceans, it was good corporate practice to attend events like this. With a big cheque.

The blonde was singing again. The brunette and the two men had stepped to one side, in their white jumpsuits, and the spotlight was on the pretty blonde. Not many people could carry off a white satin jumpsuit, but she definitely could, with just the perfect amount of curves to be interesting.

And she was interesting, her voice strong and full of emotion, undoubtedly. Dark eyebrows framed her bright eyes. Green, he thought. Her pretty cheeks were round, like two half-moons. But something was off. She didn't look like a blonde. No, it was definitely a wig.

He kept watching her because she kept turning to him. Each time she'd turn back to his side of the room her eyes would land on his. With a question. Causing a tightness in his chest.

Did they know one another? Should he recognise her? Will hadn't known so many women so well he'd forget one. Especially not one as captivating as the one on the stage now.

She was singing a breakup song. Unlike with the other songs, the crowd were reasonably subdued, they were watching her, captivated. Listening carefully. This woman could sing. Not only was she hitting the musical notes, but she was also hitting the emotional ones. She sang as though she understood the lyrics. Like she might have written them.

Not angry, but resigned, putting on a brave face.

'The Winner Takes It All.'

Even though he'd heard the song many times before, he'd never really listened. The way she sang the words made him feel the emotion behind the song. The singer was upset, but not bitter.

How did someone reach that level of magnanimity?

His thoughts naturally fell to his ex, Georgia.

He hated Georgia.

He hated what she'd done to his company. What she'd done to his reputation. He hated that he'd trusted her and that because of her, he'd never trust anyone again.

Hate wasn't too strong a word, it was completely appropriate for someone who had seduced him, got him to promise himself to her entirely and then stolen his business plans and sold them to the highest bidder.

As the blonde woman sang he felt a strange sensation in his head. Like she understood.

'Why ABBA?' Will groaned to his mother as they stood in the hotel foyer, looking back into the ballroom where the party was still in full swing. The tribute band had departed the stage, but a DJ was now playing other retro hits.

'It's fun! It gets people in and it gets them relaxed and donating. It could be our most successful fundraiser yet.'

Will couldn't argue with that and it was a very important cause. He was glad it had been a successful night, but he wanted to get home to bed as soon as he could. He had a full day of meetings tomorrow and didn't fancy falling asleep in any of them.

'Besides, I thought you'd like an opportunity to see this particular band.'

Will was lost. 'Why?'

'Oh, I wonder why?' Diane looked at the ceiling as if avoiding his eye, but she was smiling.

In an effort to figure out what on earth his mother was referring to, he looked around the foyer, wondering if the tribute band had left already. Sure, the blonde singer had caught his eye, but surely Diane hadn't noticed. Will was careful to keep his eyes to himself when out in a professional setting and certainly when he was out with his mother. As far as Diane was concerned, Will had been dating a woman named Summer for the past couple of years. Summer was an invention, but served the very important purpose of making his mother believe he was in a stable relationship so she wouldn't worry that he needed fixing. Or worse, needed setting up with some eligible woman his mother knew. Instead of the blonde singer, he spotted his mother's boyfriend, Gus.

Boyfriend. Gus was in his midforties and his mother was sixty, but Will couldn't quite bring himself to use the word *lover*. Which was what Gus was.

Will's father had passed away suddenly just over a year ago following a stroke. He was glad that his mother was coping well following her husband's death, and Gus was a good man, but Will couldn't help feeling that it was all going a little fast.

His parents had been married for close to forty years. They had been childhood sweethearts and life partners. Within six months of David's passing, Diane had hooked up with Gus. Gus joined them now and kissed Diane on the cheek then held out his hand to Will. The men shook. Diane picked up Gus's hand and squeezed it.

'Darling,' Diane said, turning to her son. 'We have something to tell you.'

Will knew his jaw had dropped, a tell he'd never let himself do in a business setting. He shut his mouth and changed his look to impassive, sensing that he wasn't going to like what his mother was about to tell him.

'We're getting married.'

Diane and Gus smiled at one another like giddy teenagers.

'Why?' Will blurted before he could think better of it.

'I know it may be a shock, but we love one another. It's as simple as that.'

'But…' This was the twenty-first century; people didn't *have* to marry. Particularly not strong, independent women like Diane. The money didn't worry him; Gus and Diane came to the relationship as financial equals. Gus was younger than Diane and not by a little, by over a decade. Still, that wasn't it either.

Gus adored Diane, and Diane adored him. They got along very well.

Will took even breaths.

You should be happy for her.

But his question was a completely legitimate one. Her husband of forty years, the man who was meant to be the love of her life, had recently passed away.

David Watson had been ambitious, single-minded, and talented. A gifted businessman and a driver of change. He had been Will's father, mentor and then business partner. Will missed him every day.

Gus angled his body so he was partly standing in front of Diane. Will resisted the urge to roll his eyes at the protective gesture. His mother could take care of herself.

'Because we love one another, we want to spend our lives together and we want the world to know.'

Will nodded, resigned. It was shock, that was all. He didn't really disapprove; he was simply surprised.

'But you're not going to rush things, are you?'

The couple shared a look and Will's stomach dropped.

'We've booked a date in Bali for three weeks' time. Look, darling, I know it's a surprise, but once the shock wears off, I know you'll be happy for us. We love one another. We're soulmates.'

Like you were with Dad, Will wanted to snap, feeling fourteen years old and a petulant teenager again.

He had the good sense not to give voice to that thought.

He distracted himself by glancing around at the crowded ballroom. Looking for a blond wig.

Which was silly because he didn't know her. He was sure of it. Besides, he had a 'girlfriend'. Summer had a very busy career, just like Will, so couldn't make many family events.

He was proud of himself for inventing a name that was so unlikely, no one he knew would ever come across her.

He never intended to lie to his mother, but in a weak, frustrated moment it had just happened. Miraculously, the notion of a fictional girlfriend with the name of Summer Bright had stopped all his mother's attempts to 'fix' him. After everything that had happened with Georgia, falling in love was the last thing he was going to do.

There had been a few hiccoughs along the way. Like when Will realised Diane hadn't kept Summer's existence to herself, but had told several of their friends and colleagues, and the fact that he was dating Summer Bright had made its way to the board who had wanted to know all about her. After the mess with Georgia, he couldn't blame them. When David died and Will was taking over the CEO role, they had sought assurances that Summer had no conflicts of interest that would affect the business.

With some shame and a fair bit of regret, Will had signed a document on her behalf, attesting to this. He reasoned that he wasn't *actually* making a false statement, since Summer didn't exist, and they were not in a relationship, but he didn't want to consider too closely whether a judge would agree.

Requests by Diane to meet Summer were also becoming more and more frequent. Will wasn't sure how much longer he'd be able to last before he parted ways with the improbable Summer. Which was a shame since Summer was the easiest and most convenient girlfriend he'd ever had.

As though his mother had read his mind, she now said, 'I know Summer's busy with work, but it would mean the world to us if she could come.'

'I'll ask her,' Will said, offhandedly. He already knew Summer had some urgent business to attend to. Probably overseas. It was unlikely she'd be able to come at short notice. But why?

Summer had a vague occupation in sales, but it took her all over the world. She also had her own family responsibilities, something Diane didn't dare argue with. But he'd have to think up something pretty good to get Summer out of the wedding. Family emergency? Dead parent? She'd been 'caught overseas' when his father had died and Diane had been suspicious then. He didn't know how he was going to get Summer out of attending. The thought made him a little sad; his mother and the board were happy with how things were. He was happy with how things were. Breaking up with his fake girlfriend was a last resort.

It wasn't Diane he was worried about, although if she found out he'd lied her campaign to fix him would step up its pace. Will's main worry was the company board. The longstanding board members were his parents' good friends. A few of them were even here tonight. Daniel Jorgensen, the non-executive director, was standing just behind Diane's shoulder, talking to the CFO.

No one must ever find out that he'd made Summer Bright up. The board were already nervy about him taking over as CEO after his father's death. If they found out that he'd lied about this, on top of everything that had happened with Georgia, he could wave his good reputation goodbye. Professionally, he'd be toast. And burnt toast at that.

Summer changed into a long floral skirt and a flowing white blouse to go out to the pub around the corner with her cast mates, an after-show ritual. She'd stay for one drink, then head home to her mother, who, if she was feeling well, would be waiting up. Penny Bright suffered from rheumatoid arthritis and had recently been forced to retire from her job managing a day care centre. Penny coped on her own with most things, but Summer liked being around in case she was needed.

She was making her way across the foyer when she heard her name being called. 'Summer!' yelled her manager, John. 'Summer Bright! Hang on a moment.'

Her shoulders sagged and she walked back across the lobby to where John stood, looking down at his phone. He didn't even look up to say, 'They've cancelled next Saturday's show.'

Summer groaned silently. She depended on these regular gigs to make rent. Busking brought in a little money, but ever since Michael ran off with her beloved guitar, that wasn't an option. There was a real chance she wouldn't make this month's rent. Let alone have enough money to put towards her savings to buy the guitar back. It wasn't just any guitar; it was the guitar her grandfather had owned. The one she'd learnt to play on. The one he'd gifted her. When she played it, she felt closer to him.

And it wasn't just the guitar, it was her busking rig as well. And her car. Michael had taken all three things and skipped town. As far as she knew, he still had the car, but shortly afterwards he'd sold the guitar and rig onto a local man, Brayden from Bowden Park, who had offered to sell both back to her for seven thousand, seven hundred dollars.

Summer never thought there was much chance she'd actually be able to come up with the money, but now there appeared to be none.

'Is there anything else coming up?' Summer asked.

John pulled a face. 'We're doing a show in the hills next week, but I already gave it to the others. If one of them pull out I'll let you know.'

Everyone else was as skint as she was, it wasn't likely anyone would pull out.

With her mother no longer working, Summer would have to try to pick up some more shifts at the second-hand clothes shop she worked at casually, though that didn't pay nearly as well as a night dressed in a retro outfit belting out nostalgia.

As she made her way back across the lobby to the exit a middle-aged woman with a sleek silver bob stood into her path and grabbed her arm. 'Summer? Are you Summer Bright?'

A man rushed up behind the woman and Summer froze. It was the man from the audience and he stared at her intently again now, but this time his eyes were flashing with panic. And silent pleading. Summer looked from one to the other searching for some recognition. But she came up with none. She didn't recognise the woman and her relationship with the man only went back as far as 'The Winner Takes It All'.

'Are you Summer Bright?' she woman asked again.

Who was this woman? Should Summer know who she was? Summer thought she had a good memory for faces, but this woman wasn't ringing a bell. Afraid of what her answer would mean, but also curious to know who the man with her was, Summer nodded slowly.

'I'm so glad we bumped into you. Will is so secretive.'

The woman glanced over to the handsome man who looked at Summer and mouthed something unintelligible to her.

She shook her head once and he repeated the movement. This time she understood. *Play along.*

'Hi!' Summer said, hoping that would suffice.

The woman threw her arms wide around Summer. Surprised by the affection and now doubly embarrassed that she couldn't remember this woman, Summer hugged her back.

When the woman released her from the hug she still held on to Summer's upper arms. Her eyes were bright, even a little misty. 'You don't know how glad I am to finally meet you.'

She was about to open her mouth to ask the woman what on earth she was taking about when she felt another hand on her forearm.

It was a peculiarly intimate touch for a man she'd only just met, but as the warmth spread up her arm and into her shoulder she relaxed somehow. His touch was just right, pressure perfect. She felt some things uncoil inside her and others tighten.

'Summer, may I speak to you a moment?' he said and she heard his voice for the first time. Low and smooth, it hit all the sweet spots in her chest. But instead of the faraway, dreamy look he'd given her during the show, now the look in his eyes was one of pure terror. When he was ten metres away from her, in the shadows of the audience he had looked gorgeous. But shadows could hide all sorts of things so she didn't think much of it, but now, in the well-lit lobby, she saw that this man was stunning in a stomach-flipping, heart-stopping kind of way. His dark hair was cut close, his strong jaw freshly shaven. He had ridiculously symmetrical cheekbones and deep, deep blue eyes.

He's probably embarrassed that his mother has accosted a stranger with hugs.

'Please,' Summer said, but didn't add, *and tell me what the heck is going on.*

'Always hiding her away. I've met her now, so you no longer have an excuse,' said the woman with the silver bob, still not releasing Summer from her grip. The handsome man's hand was still on her arm, gently but persistently, trying to steer her away from the woman.

Summer was being tugged in two directions. Her mind warned against following a stranger away from a crowd, but her body wanted to go with the man. To somewhere private. To feel his hand slide up her arm. To feel his fingers on the rest of her. To taste him.

Down, girl!

'Excuse?' Summer asked, trying to grasp a thread of the conversation and to decide whether to stay or to disappear into the shadows with this man.

'To come to our wedding! Gus and I are getting married.'

'Congratulations?' Summer looked from the woman to the other man. Also handsome, but older than the first. Wasn't the first man her son? Maybe the woman was unwell. That would make sense. Dementia. Memory loss. The woman wasn't old, but she wasn't young either. Summer knew from caring for her late grandfather that arguing with someone with dementia was pointless and sometimes cruel. She wouldn't help this woman by trying to set her straight.

The woman touched Summer's hand. 'Please come to the wedding. We're nice people. You'll see. There's no need to be frightened. Will you come?'

'Of course,' Summer said. 'I'd love to.'

'Can I speak to you please,' the man said again in a gravelly whisper that Summer felt in her gut. He smelt good too. Like freshly cut wood. Expensive sheets.

Yes, you can speak to me anytime.

'Make sure you bring her back,' the mystery woman said to the man who was still holding on to Summer's elbow.

Summer wasn't frightened any more, but she was concerned.

'I promise,' Summer said, nodding to the woman but finally giving in to the gentle tugs from the man. Like she'd ever had any choice. She was going to follow him and find out what his hands wanted with her. And how they both knew her name.

'It's so good to meet you!' the woman yelled after them.

The man steered her to a nearby column and he stepped behind it.

Summer was damn well sure she was the only Summer Bright in the world. No one else's parents would give their child such a distinctive name. People often laughed at it, but she thought it was pretty, and it was not easily forgotten. And if she was going to make a name for herself as a songwriter it helped to be memorable. So, what on earth was going on?

Summer looked at the handsome man and then back across the lobby to where the woman was still looking after them. She waved and the other man, the one with the light hair gently turned the woman away. Summer joined the mystery man behind the column and out of view.

'Is she all right?'

'She's fine.'

'She doesn't seem fine. She seems confused. Is it dementia?'

'There's nothing wrong with her. She's sharper than I am,' grumbled the man.

'Then what's going on? Who are you?'

The man still had his hand on her elbow. Summer wasn't about to run away, at least not until she'd heard the explanation. But she didn't tell him that in case he removed his hand.

'Are you Summer Bright? Is your name really Summer Bright?'

'Yes.' Summer crossed her arms, and the man released his grip. 'Who are you?'

'My name is Will Watson.'

Summer shook her head. Nope. She'd never heard of him.

'Your real name is Summer Bright?'

This was ridiculous. She'd been mocked for her name before, but she'd never come across someone so incredulous. She pulled her driver's licence out of her phone case and shoved it at him.

He studied it.

Summer Angel Bright. Thirty-one years old. And her address. Was he memorising her address? She shivered and snatched her licence back.

'Were you in the show?' he asked.

She nodded.

'The blonde one?'

'Agnetha, yes.' Summer briefly understood how poor Frida

and Agnetha must have felt all their lives being labelled the blonde one or the dark one. With light auburn locks, Summer was neither. She was the ginger.

Then he put his face in his hands and groaned. The groan turned into a chuckle and when he finally removed his face from his hands, he looked pained.

'I'm sorry, but should I know you? Who was that woman?'

'That woman is my mother. Diane Watson.'

The name didn't ring any bells either.

'Do I know you? Am I meant to know her?'

'No,' he answered.

'Then why on earth does she think I'm coming to her wedding?'

'Well,' he said, running his hand through his hair. 'It's a funny story. At least, I hope you'll think so.'

'Why does she think I'm coming to her wedding?' she repeated slowly.

'I don't suppose there's any chance you'd like to. As my date?'

CHAPTER TWO

'YOUR DATE? You've completely lost me. Do we know one another?'

He shook his head.

'Is this some kind of prank?'

Will looked down and shook his head. 'No, I'm afraid it's all my fault.' Then he looked up and his blue eyes hit her with enough force to freeze her feet exactly where they were.

'I have a proposition for you. A business proposition.'

This man, Will, had been at the front of the audience. Probably at one of the expensive tables. If he was at this event, he either had money or knew someone who did.

'I'm a businessman. I can get people to vouch for me, if necessary,' he went on.

She wasn't in any business. Except show business.

'You want me to sing?'

'No. Not exactly.'

Alarm bells started to ring in her head. Loudly. Urgently. 'Nothing about the last five minutes is making any sense to me. I need to get going, it's late.'

'I know it's strange. I was wondering if you would like to come to my mother's wedding. And *pretend* to be my date.'

Summer laughed and turned, but he was after her. Touching her arm again. Not forcefully. Just gently. Sweetly.

'Please, please hear me out, Summer.'

Something about the way he said her name held her back. Familiar. Knowing.

'I'll pay you.'

'That's sounds worse!'

'No, please, it's not that kind of proposal. No funny business. I just need you to come to my mother's wedding and pretend to be my date. And I'll pay you.'

The man clenched his jaw tightly. In fact, it wasn't just his jaw that was clenched tightly. She now could see his shoulders, his neck, everything, stiffen. Wow, this man needed a massage. Or something else.

Not ten minutes ago next weekend's gig had been cancelled. She needed money. Even if the arrangement was unconventional, she should hear him out.

And the sensation of his hand on her elbow did all sorts of strange things to her.

'Why? Why me?' And why does someone as handsome and breathtaking and warm and sexy as you have to pretend to have a date?

'Now, this is very awkward. I'm sorry in advance for what I'm about to say.' He closed his eyes but didn't look any closer to telling her what was on his mind. He drew a deep breath. 'Do you have a mother?' he asked.

Summer thought of her own mother, probably waiting up back at their flat. 'Yes.'

'And do you love her?'

'Very much.'

'Does she, even though you are an adult, still worry about you? Still want what she thinks is best for you?'

'Yes. But what's your point?'

'This is very embarrassing.'

'So far all you've admitted to is loving your mother. In no world is that embarrassing.'

He opened his eyes. Blue. Bright. Brilliant.

'I told her something I shouldn't have.'

Ah. The puzzle pieces were clicking to place. 'You told her we're dating?'

He nodded. 'I'm afraid so.'

'But you just said we don't know one another.'

'We don't.'

'Then why did you tell her that we're dating?'

The crowd was filing out of the ballroom and the staff were packing the tables up.

'She was putting pressure on me to find a girlfriend.'

It was all weirdly starting to make sense. Except it also wasn't.

'So, I told her I had a girlfriend.'

'You told her *I* was your girlfriend?'

'Not you exactly, I thought I made you up.'

'But I'm a real person. You stole my name!'

'I know that now, and I'm sorry.'

'So, you told your mother you had a girlfriend and you used my name. Why?'

'I can't explain it. I made it up. Or thought I did.'

'You made it up?'

'It sounded...improbable.'

She took a deep breath and let the insult wash over her, but it still stung. It felt like she was back at primary school with kids sniggering about her name behind her back.

'And you want me to go to her wedding?'

He nodded.

The man standing before her had made up a pretend girl-friend and used her name because he thought it was so im-probable no real person could have her name. But on the other hand, he'd done it in a bizarre attempt to protect his mother. He was also gorgeous. He was at an expensive fundraiser for the oceans so he was probably a good person. And not the sort of man to steal her guitar and leave the state. But what was in it for her? A free meal? A night out. That wasn't nothing.

And is he part of the deal?

'When's the wedding?'

'Three weeks. But it's in Bali.'

'Bali!' She laughed now. 'I can't get to Bali.'

'I'll pay,' he added quickly. 'I told you.'

'For my flights?'

'Of course, for everything. And I'll pay you for your time. Like a job.'

She'd had some interesting jobs in her time. Tonight, she'd worn a white satin jumpsuit, a long blond wig and sung fifty-year-old songs to a room full of people in business suits.

This would be just like any other job, wouldn't it?

'I can get some references to vouch for me. I'm the CEO of Watson Enterprises. It's a plastic manufacturing company.'

The name meant nothing to her. 'Why don't you just tell her the truth?'

He nodded and then smiled. 'I suppose I could. But I like this idea too.'

She thought she caught a sparkle in his eyes and it did strange things to her belly.

'Besides, you just told her you'd come.'

'Because you told me to play along!'

'Please, think about it. Name your price.'

'Excuse me?' Was he out of his mind?

He might be crazy, but he's offering to pay you. And you need money. Seven thousand, seven hundred dollars to be precise.

'How many nights?'

'Four, maybe five. Whatever you can manage.'

'Seven thousand, seven hundred,' she said, without hesitation. 'Plus, flights and accommodation.' She stood up straight.

She'd learnt long ago that no one else was going to look after her, if she needed something she had to get it herself.

'Seven-seven. Are you sure?'

'Is that too much?'

'I've never paid a woman to pretend to date me before. I have absolutely no idea what the going rate is.'

Summer couldn't help but laugh. Despite everything telling her this was all ridiculous, at that moment she trusted Will Watson. He wasn't trying to trick her or do anything underhanded; he was just trying to protect his mother.

But the deal was still…unorthodox.

'What about sex?' she asked.

'What about it?'

'Are you thinking it's part of the deal?'

'I'm not going to pay you to have sex with me.' Colour rose high in his cheeks. 'That's not what this about. I would never.'

'Yes, good.' Heat rose in her own cheeks. 'I thought we should just get that clear.'

'We're not going to sleep together,' he repeated. 'Oh, God, that's not what I'm proposing at all.' His face was now the colour of her lipstick.

'Okay, right, good. But you can't blame me for checking.'

'I don't think we should sleep together. I have a rule about business and pleasure. A very strict rule.'

'I understand.' She nodded.

The feeling in her gut was nerves, not disappointment. She didn't want to sleep with this man. He was gorgeous, built, tall. And he smelt so good.

But she couldn't want to sleep with him. He was clearly uptight. A businessman who ran a plastic manufacturing company! He was nothing like her.

There would be no sex with this beautiful man who had now let go of her arm, but was standing so close to her, and whose urgent whispers were doing strange things to her chest.

'I'll write it in the contract if it makes you feel better.'

'Yes, it would.'

She sensed that Will Watson was not a man to breach a contract. Which was probably for the best. For many, many reasons.

An all-expenses trip to Bali. She would get her guitar back and all she had to do was pretend to date Will Watson. Every other hesitation melted away.

'Where do I sign?'

'Your next meeting is here,' announced Belinda.

Will stood and smoothed down his suit. It was immaculate and didn't need the attention, but he needed something to do with his hands and with his palms, which were suddenly slightly sweaty.

Was this the silliest thing he'd ever done?

No. *This* wasn't the silliest thing he'd ever done; the silliest thing he'd ever done was not checking whether Summer Bright actually existed before inventing her. Because Summer Bright did exist and now he knew what the twinkle in his mother's eye had been about when she'd hired the ABBA tribute band. His mother had done a search for Summer Bright and had found her. Summer also lived, against all odds and common sense, in Adelaide. Summer's social media showed that she was a singer, songwriter, and performer. And it had only taken a few inquiries for Diane to discover the tribute band Summer performed for and book them for her gala dinner.

Diane had admitted this to Will but said, 'But she's coming to the wedding. You must be happy about that?'

How could Will argue?

If his mother had found the real Summer Bright then anyone could. Including anyone on his board. Since piecing this all together Will knew he was enormously exposed. It was one thing lying about a fictional person, but he'd been lying about a real person. He'd signed a document on behalf of a real person. The thought of his mother and the board members finding out that he'd been lying to them for the past couple of years made him draw a deep breath. He didn't have any choice but to go through with this plan.

Summer strode in and through the floor-to-ceiling windows the sunlight hit her hair. Dark auburn curls framed her face, bouncier than last night. She was wearing brown boots and a long, loose cotton dress. She looked like she'd walked out of a country town, not an office block in the Adelaide CBD.

How had it come to this?

How was he supposed to know that some parents out there were so weird as to give their kid a name like that?

No, it's your fault for coming up with such an extravagant lie.

He could blame his bad luck on Summer happening to walk right past them in the hotel foyer at that time, but one rule his father had instilled in him from a very early age was there was no such thing as bad luck. Only bad planning.

And he had planned the ruse against his mother appallingly.

There were other options. The easiest would have been to whisk Summer away, explain everything and then tell his mother they, sadly, had broken up. But the look on Diane's face when Summer told her she'd come to her wedding had meant that Will had not considered that option until later that night when he was alone and thinking straight for the first time since setting eyes on Summer Bright. Standing next to Summer, in that hotel lobby, his only thought had been to convince her to come to Bali with him. Her eyes sparkled with amusement and incredulity. Her smile had made her cheeks do that half-moon thing that he'd noticed on the stage and every sensible thought in the world had deserted him.

Summer looked around his office. He'd given himself home ground advantage, but only because Summer held all the cards in this game. If she couldn't convince his family that they were a couple—and had been for about two years—then his lie would be exposed. And his lack of credibility with it.

'Hello and welcome,' he said as happily as he could.

He pointed to the sofas and armchairs. Belinda had put a tray with drinks and pastries on the table for them, but Summer went straight over to the floor-to-ceiling windows and took in the view.

'I can see why you didn't just want to meet in a cafe. Is this actually the tallest building in Adelaide?'

'No, I believe that's Frome Central.'

'Then I guess this is the best view.'

She wasn't wrong. On the horizon to the left was the ocean, to the right the Adelaide Hills. Straight below them were some of Adelaide's famous parks, the Adelaide Oval, and the Botanic Garden.

He had to approach this situation the only way he knew how, like a business deal. And if he were negotiating a deal now, he'd start with hospitality.

'Tea? Coffee?'

'Tea please. Black.'

He poured it for her and hoped his hand wasn't shaking. This was just like any other business meeting. Except that he rarely met with business associates as gorgeous as Summer. Or ones who smelt quite so nice. It wasn't an expensive perfume that she was wearing. Something simple. Natural. He couldn't place it, mixed as it was with the simple smell of Summer.

She took a pastry eagerly and picked the pieces off with her fingers as she ate it.

'Before we start, I just have to ask.' She looked around his office, taking in not just the view but the thick carpet.

Taking in the wealth.

He'd already sussed out that Summer was not materialistic or motivated by money. She was helping him because of his mother, and the amount she'd asked for was preposterous. She must have known that he would have paid much more than eight thousand dollars.

Except she didn't even ask for eight, but seven-seven.

'Why do you have to make up a girlfriend?'

This was not the question he was expecting. 'Like I told you last night, my mother was eager to see me with someone. But my job is my life and my mother doesn't understand that. She wants me to find someone, but I don't want a relationship.'

Please don't ask why not.

'Why not just come clean? Your mother seemed lovely. Wouldn't she understand?'

Summer's question was a good one.

Because if he came clean now, after telling Diane that Summer was coming to the wedding, it would be worse— Diane would *know* he needed help. The pressure to fix him would be even more intense.

'It isn't just my mother. She's on the board of the company. She's told many of the other members I'm in a long-term relationship.'

'How is being in a relationship relevant to your job?'

'It isn't directly, but if it got out that I'd lied, even about this, my professional reputation would be destroyed.'

Summer nodded and chewed on her pastry, thinking it all over.

'What if we just broke up? Why do you need me to go to the wedding?'

Summer made an excellent point. One that a supposedly intelligent person would have realised the night before.

'For starters, you told my mother you would.'

Summer narrowed her eyes.

'And then I told her you were.'

Summer was right, he couldn't pin any of this on her.

'It suits me to not have my mother worry about me. Are you having second thoughts?'

'I'm just trying to figure this all out.'

'You're happy to go ahead?'

'It's an adventure. You're paying me and I've never been to Bali. And I've looked you up. You don't seem like a serial killer.'

'High praise indeed.'

She shrugged and smiled.

'I've looked you up too.' Something he really ought to have done before declaring to his parents that he was dating her. His own research hadn't revealed any red flags. She worked as a singer, she had a diverse group of friends in Adelaide, no one he knew. They moved in very different circles, which was a good thing. There would be little chance of their social lives overlapping. And, importantly, there was nothing in her online presence to indicate she was some kind of corporate spy.

After Georgia he had to be careful about this sort of thing, but in Summer's case, even Will, who was careful to the point of paranoia, had to admit that the chances Summer was trying to trick him were low. This whole thing was a mess of his own creation.

'And?'

'And you don't seem like a serial killer either.'

'Great, we're just regular miscreants then,' she said.

Will's shoulders relaxed. Summer was nice, she seemed like a good person.

He shouldn't be as surprised as he was, but in Will's experience people usually wanted something from him.

'It is a bit ridiculous, isn't it?' he said.

'It's a lot ridiculous, but I'm thinking of it as an adventure.'

She smiled at him and her cheeks turned into small moons again. He felt something snag in his chest. The truth was, there may have been other options. But he liked this one best.

He wanted Summer to come to Bali with him.

'I've taken the liberty of writing up a deed of agreement. I'd rather not get anyone else involved. I trust my lawyer implicitly, but this is different. Personal. Unless you'd feel more comfortable with a more detailed contract.'

He slid the papers across the glass table to her.

'More detailed? This is four pages long!'

'Take the time to read it. If you want to get your own advice on it, that's okay.'

She looked at him like he had two heads.

'What sort of advice?'

'Legal advice.'

She laughed. 'I don't have a lawyer. Do you think I'd agree to be paid to be someone's girlfriend if I had enough money to afford a lawyer?'

'Would you like me to pay for you to get one?'

Summer continued to stare at him like he was from another planet.

'I can read this, and if I have any questions, I'll just ask you.'

'It has the same force as any other contract.'

She nodded, but was only half listening as she read the document he'd put in her hands.

'What's this?' she pointed to the clauses on the second page.

'The times we will meet. The times you will be required on the trip to Bali, obviously. And a preliminary meeting.'

'To get our stories straight?'

'Well, yes, to plan how we're going to do that.'

'You want a meeting to plan the plan?'

He nodded.

'You're joking, right?'

'Of course not.'

'You want a two-hour meeting to plan how we're going to plan?'

'It's one of the first principles of project planning.'

She pressed her lips together like she was trying not to laugh. 'And what are the other principles?'

'Well first, you decide how you're going to plan. And then you plan to assign the tasks and responsibilities, you decide on your outcomes and your KPIs and finally once it's all over you do a post-mortem.'

'A post-mortem? How badly do you think this is going to go?'

'I meant that we debrief.'

'What are our KPIs?'

'There's only one. To make my family believe we're in love.'

He felt her gaze on him again, and his skin warmed. Her eyes were like an X-ray and he was exposed.

Exposed, but not necessarily uncomfortable.

'I do things on the spur of the moment, but I'm sensing you're not the sort of person who does,' she said.

'Why do you say that?'

She picked up his carefully drafted contract. 'Exhibit A, Your Honour.'

'Look, we need to plan how we're going to do this,' he said. 'They think we've been dating for two years.'

'Two years? Two years!' Summer looked like she might stand up and leave.

'Saying it twice isn't going to make it any less real.'

'Why so long? Didn't they get suspicious?'

'Yes, many times. Especially when you didn't come to my father's funeral.'

'I didn't go to your father's funeral? They must think I'm awful.' Summer looked panic-stricken. 'I'm not awful. I would've gone. If we'd actually been dating.'

'I know. But you were overseas. You couldn't make it back.'

'Really, that seems a little callous. Have we had a rocky relationship? On and off?'

'You're away a lot for work,' he admitted.

'Oh, I see.'

'It is what it is, we can't change it now. I understood you couldn't make my father's funeral.'

Summer laughed loudly then caught herself. 'I'm sorry.'

'You don't need to be sorry.'

'No. I'm sorry about your father. If we had been dating, I would've flown back from wherever I was to be with you.'

Will's breath caught in his throat, which was suddenly as narrow as a needle and burning. Even though she was describing a hypothetical scenario, he was in no doubt of her sincerity.

She reached for another pastry, but instead of sitting to eat it, she started walking around his office. She paused at the large canvas behind Will's desk.

'That's amazing,' Summer said.

'It's my brother's. He painted it.' Will felt proud and guilty as he said it. The canvas was nearly two arm spans wide and its intense colours stood out in the otherwise neutral tones of his office.

'It's a beach, isn't it?'

'You can tell?'

'Of course, it might be abstract, but it's clearly the ocean and a beach. It's beautiful. I love the colours; I can almost taste the sea air.'

Will tasted something as well, but it was bitter. Jealously. 'You don't have to flatter him.'

'I wasn't. I was actually flattering you for having such good taste. Is he coming to the wedding?'

'I'm not sure. I assume so.'

'You're not sure if your brother is coming to your mother's wedding? Don't you talk?'

'Not often,' Will said. Sensing Summer was just the sort of person to want to fix a non-existent problem, he added, 'It's not as though we're not on speaking terms, we just don't talk. We don't have a reason to. We haven't fallen out.'

'He's your brother and you don't talk, but you haven't fallen out?'

'It's complicated,' Will said. He joined her by the painting.

Summer put her hands on her hips. 'Try me. Isn't a complicated relationship with one's brother something a girlfriend of two years might know about?'

'He's an artist.'

'And a good one, I guess. Does he live here?'

'No. He lives in London. I guess that's why we don't speak that often.'

'How long has he lived there?'

'Couple of years. I don't know. Four or five. Before that he was in LA and New York.'

The last time Will had spent any significant time with his brother had been when they were teenagers. Before Will decided to follow his father into Watson Enterprises. Before Ben decided he didn't want any part of it. Ben and their father had argued, seemingly nonstop from that point. Will didn't want to choose sides, he loved them both. But the simple fact that he had chosen the company annoyed Ben and created a rift between them.

'Have you ever visited him?'

'Nope.'

'If I had a family member living in London or New York or LA, and your kind of funds I'd go and visit them.'

But Summer wasn't him. She was spontaneous. Adventurous.

And Will most definitely was not.

'I have responsibilities here.'

'So do I. But he's your brother.'

Great, Summer might be happy to go along with this little charade, but he sensed that her wish to try to 'fix' him might rival Diane's. Maybe she was right, maybe they should 'break up' now instead.

'Look, Summer, are you sure about this?'

'I'm more certain than ever.'

'Do you want me to pay for a lawyer?'

'Lawyers never helped my mother in any of her divorces.'

'Is that a yes or a no?' he asked.

'If one of us breaks the bargain, then what does it matter? We'll both lose. How will a lawyer stop that?'

She was probably right. If his family found out the truth, a lawyer could only clean up the subsequent mess.

'Do you have a pen?' she asked.

He took one from the pocket inside his jacket.

Summer spun him around and shoved the paper against his back.

'There are several tables in this room you know,' he said even as he felt the pen press her signature into his back. Like a branding. Sparks shot through his back, into his chest. She spun him back around and handed him the paper.

They were doing this.

'I'll get you a copy,' he said.

'Great.'

'And I'll book our flights and next week I will take you out to discuss the plan.'

'To plan the plan.' She smiled.

'Yes.'

Summer laughed as she left the office.

What had he just done?

CHAPTER THREE

SUMMER READ THE contract on the way home. Four pages of numbered clauses, with subclauses.

She probably should've read it more carefully before she'd been so daring as to sign it across his back, but she'd read the only line she cared about. The one that said he would pay her seven thousand, seven hundred dollars to go with him to Bali for six nights.

The clause that said they wouldn't sleep together was also notable, but reassuring. This was a business deal, nothing more. She'd be required to make his family believe they were in love, but that was all.

The arrangement was not that far removed from an acting gig, which was not too far removed from performing other people's songs. Just like when she performed on stage.

She knew she'd have to tell her mother. She had to explain her absence for a week, but she hadn't quite decided if she'd tell her mother the whole story. Like the getting paid to pretend to be a girlfriend detail. Like everything else in her life, Summer decided it was something she'd make up as she went along.

Spontaneity hadn't worked out particularly well for her but she doubted that careful planning, such as the type Will Watson specialised in, would have put her in any better position. Sure, she didn't have any money. Sure, she lived with her mother, but that would have happened regardless of careful planning.

Planning would not have changed anything in her life. Planning would not have stopped her mother getting sick. Planning would not have stopped Michael stealing her car and guitar. The only way to have prevented that would have been not to have got involved with him in the first place.

Summer's mother, Penelope, was nothing if not open-minded. She was open-minded to the point of vulnerability, which is why the pair of them were now sharing a tiny rented two-bedroom flat.

Her mother had had three husbands and each had left her worse off than the last. Neither Summer nor her mother were any good at protecting their hearts from untrustworthy men. Summer, thinking she'd learnt from her mother's mistakes had been careful with Michael. She'd kept their finances separate, split everything down the middle. Got to know him before they moved in with one another. But despite being careful, he'd still managed to run off with her car and her grandfather's Gibson guitar.

The police were no help, telling her to get a family lawyer. Who would cost more than the cost of the car and the guitar combined. She had to begrudgingly admire Will's attention to detail, but who would have thought there would be four pages of things to put in the deal?

In one week's time, they would meet at Adelaide Airport to board a flight to Denpasar. Business class, the deed said. She would stay at a five-star villa on the island of Nusa Lembongan, all expenses paid by Mr Watson.

Ms Bright, as she was called in the contract, was required to 'maintain the charade that she and Mr Watson had been in a romantic relationship for two years'. Clause five point one.

Ms Bright was not required to have a physical relationship

with Mr Watson, 'beyond the occasional gestures in public necessary to maintain that charade'. Clause five point two.

Summer shivered, despite the heat on the stuffy bus. What did the 'occasional gesture in public' involve, exactly? Hand-holding, probably. A hug? A kiss on the cheek? Hopefully. Standing close enough to him that she could smell him? Seeing the humidity on his cleanly shaven chin?

A soft, tender kiss on the lips? All for show, of course.

No. This was a contractual arrangement only. She didn't know much about Will, but one thing she did know was that business was very important to him. The man was intense. She didn't dislike intensity but thought it would be much better directed at something else. Something fun.

She'd googled Will Watson before going to his office. Will was rich. The internet didn't know exactly how rich he was but he was rich enough to make her kick herself for not adding an extra zero to the amount she'd requested.

Will was the CEO and largest shareholder in Watson Enterprises, one of the country's largest plastic manufacturers. He'd taken over the management of the company after his father, David Watson, had passed away.

Plastic manufacturing didn't sound very ethical to her, which was probably why he was at the ocean health fundraiser. She had to keep remembering this about Will each time she felt a quiver in her stomach and a wish to kiss him: he was a planner, he was uptight, he made money from making plastic! And he wasn't from her world. This was a business deal only. And that was a good thing. In a few weeks she'd have her guitar back and would not have to deal with Will Watson again.

When Summer pushed open the door to her flat her mother was on the couch. Penny made a move to get up, but Summer waved her down. Her arthritis was crippling. Rheumatoid, the worst, most insidious kind that had plagued Penny for much of her adult life but had become particularly worse in the past few years.

'How are you?'

'Fine,' Penny said, though Penny's definition of *fine* was slightly different to Summer's.

'Can I get you a cuppa?'

'Only if you're having one.'

Summer could still taste the one she'd drunk with Will on her lips. She could still smell the expensive office on her cardigan. She boiled the kettle anyway and put bags into two cups.

'I have some news.'

'Bad news?'

'No, good. I think.'

'Then why did you say it like it's bad?' her mother asked.

Had she? No, she was just uncertain about exactly how she was going to explain her weeklong absence to her mother.

'So, a funny thing happened last night after the show. One of the attendees, the organiser in fact, has invited me to Bali for a week.'

'Oh.'

'To go to her wedding.' This wasn't a lie, exactly, Diane had been the first person to extend the invitation. And *technically*, if she was going to be like Will Watson about it, *technically*, she had accepted Diane's invitation.

'And do what? Perform?'

Summer exhaled. 'Yes, perform.' Exactly! 'And they're paying me.'

'Paying your flights?'

'Flights, accommodation, everything. And nearly eight thousand dollars.'

Her mother squinted at her, not believing her. And Penelope was right not to, Summer wasn't telling her the full story. Just a little white lie. So white it was practically translucent.

Penny opened her eyes wide and smiled. 'Eight thousand dollars! That's wonderful. You can get a new car.'

'I was going to buy back Grandpa's guitar.'

'Oh, yes, maybe both.'

Maybe both. Summer kicked herself again for not requesting more money, but it wasn't her way. It was strange enough getting paid to pretend to be Will's girlfriend. Asking for more felt…wrong.

'Bali! You've never been to Bali. It's lovely. Brian took me there once.'

Brian had been husband number two. Unlike Summer's father, who had just been lazy, Brian had actively gambled all of Penny's money away.

'Oh, Summer, are you sure?'

'Mum, it's the best gig I've been offered in ages.'

'Yes, but Summer, think about it. It's not going great, is it?'

'What?'

'You know I've always encouraged to follow your dreams but…'

Summer looked around the flat. It was clean and neat and comfortable. But it was small. She didn't mind living with her mother, but one day Penny was going to need more help than Summer could give her while still supporting both of them.

'I just want more for you than this. Dimity says they're hiring. They need a full-time receptionist. It's steady reliable work. You could still perform on the weekends.'

Summer had tried full-time work once, but it hadn't gone well. She wasn't available to tour so that greatly limited her income. She'd be exhausted by a long week of work and would have to find the energy to perform on the weekend. Most of all, she had no time to write songs. Her main love and passion.

'I do too, but music is my world. I don't want a life without it. That's why I need the guitar and rig. I don't want a job that will suck my soul away. We're doing fine. Especially now. With this trip.'

After Bali, things would be back on track. Her mother would see.

Will had chosen a French restaurant that Summer hadn't heard of, much less dined at. It overlooked one of Adelaide's leafy green parks and the river.

The waiter took her over to a table at the window where Will was already seated. He stood when she approached, flattening his already perfectly ironed suit again. Nervous.

She was getting to know some of his tells, but if they'd been dating for two years, she should probably know a lot more about him than the way he smoothed his suit down when he was nervous. One dinner was not going to be long enough for that.

'Thank you for coming. Would you like something to drink? Champagne?' he said before she'd even had a chance to sit.

She nodded. 'Thank you.'

'Can I take your jacket?' he asked.

She shook her head.

She wore a long pink silky dress. Not actual silk, of course, just silk-like. Nothing she wore had ever seen the inside of a designer store. The straps of the dress were a little tatty and worse for wear but she'd paired it with a silver jacket she'd found at the op shop where she worked. The dress only looked respectable if she wore it with the jacket. She wasn't usually conscious of her clothing, but she was acutely aware of Will's crisp blue suit and smart tie.

As she sat, she took in their opulent surroundings again.

'Do I look okay?' she whispered.

He gave her a confused squint. 'You look beautiful.'

Heat rose in Summer's cheeks and she looked down.

'Thank you. What I really meant was is my clothing appropriate? I don't dress like you, or your mother.'

Will nodded slowly. 'I think you look lovely.' His tone was honest.

'This is how I'm going to dress in Bali, you know.'

'You look great. How you dress is fine. We're pretending to be a couple—I think that's enough. I don't want you to pretend to be someone that you're not.'

Despite his reassurances, worry started to creep in on her. There were so many things she wasn't sure of. While he was no doubt sincere when he told her to be herself, he didn't know her. He had no idea how different they were from one another.

A waiter delivered a bottle of champagne and two glasses to their table. They sat in silence as she uncorked the bottle and poured them both glasses.

'What else have you told them about me? I mean we've been dating for two years you must've told them something more than I'm away a lot for work. What did you tell them I do?'

Will grinned sheepishly. 'I told them you're in sales.'

'Yes, but what does that even mean?'

'It's vague and non-specific, that's why I said it.'

'You do realise I sing in a tribute band? I busk. I work part-time in an op shop. I suppose that could be sales?'

'Yes, I do realise that. And my mother knows too. She looked you up. I think she booked your band for the charity dinner on purpose.'

'Oh.' Summer had thought their first meeting had just been a wild coincidence, but a meddling mother made more sense.

'She really wanted to meet you.'

'How did you explain never introducing me before this?'

'I told my mother that I didn't want my father to know I

was dating a singer. She believed that. And after that, I told her you were busy.'

Summer tried not to be offended at the idea that he felt he'd have to lie to his father about her various jobs.

'I read about your father. I'm sorry,' she said.

'Thank you.'

'He wouldn't have approved of me, then?' Summer took a big swig of champagne. Of course the Watsons wouldn't approve of her. She was a penniless musician. A busker who didn't even own her own busking rig. The Watsons were not her type of people.

'My father was…difficult.'

A ruthless businessman was how her internet search had described him. Will didn't seem to be ruthless. He was uptight, but she'd never got the impression that he was mean. Right now, he was telling her to order anything from the menu she wanted. Three courses. Summer's stomach churned at the prices written in very small font next to the description of the over-the-top-sounding dishes.

'Dad could be critical of things that didn't fit with his plans, Mum isn't.'

Summer bristled again at his use of the word *critical*. There was nothing wrong with her and if he or his family thought there was, then she should just leave now.

'Look, if you have to lie to your family, I'm not sure this is the best idea. If they aren't going to accept the idea of you dating someone like me then shouldn't we just call it quits?' Summer pulled her napkin from her nap and began to re-fold it.

'Please don't leave. Like I said, the only lie I expect you to tell is that we're dating. I don't have a problem with your career. I think it's interesting. Far more interesting than plastic manufacturing.'

She nodded and re-laid her napkin. For now.

'Yes, yes, it is. Plastic manufacturing? Really? I can't think of anything more dull.'

Her mouth fell at her gall in saying those last words but Will thankfully laughed. 'I agree, it sounds awful. That's what I thought when I was a kid. It's certainly what my brother thinks. But it is more interesting. Really.'

Will then went on to explain that when his father first established the company nearly forty years ago, they made disposable cutlery, cups, and plates, but since Will joined his father over a decade ago, they had pivoted to plastic recycling and making all sorts of products from recycled soft plastics, making Watson Enterprises the largest and most important soft plastic recycler in the country, and awarding his father a posthumous Australia Day Honour for services to the environment.

Before she knew it, they'd finished their entrees. Things had been going smoothly and she'd found herself relaxing. *That's just the wine*, she thought and shook herself back to reality. She shouldn't be trusting him so easily.

'I've talked for long enough. Tell me more about you, tell me about your parents.'

Summer bristled. 'Is this part of the planning?'

'No, it's just part of the getting to know you.'

Her parents were a touchy subject; people always found something to judge, whether it was her missing father or the former two stepfathers who had followed and also disappeared from her life.

'I'm guessing they were alternative types.'

Her hackles were definitely raised now. 'Again why?'

'Well, your name. It's not conventional. I'm sorry, have I said something wrong?'

'There's nothing wrong with my name. If we're going to talk about my name, why did you choose it for your fake girlfriend? Clearly you thought you could date someone with my name?'

'Touché,' he said.

'What made you think of it?'

'I honestly don't know. It was summer. A hot day. You know how hot and bright Adelaide gets in January.'

She nodded.

Will leaned in slightly across the table, his blue eyes drawing her gaze in to his and a gentle smile softening his face. Her stomach twisted. Will was gorgeous and being the subject of his attention was strangely exhilarating.

Wrong. But still exhilarating.

He'll find out all about you eventually.

'My mother worked as a childcare worker, but she's had to give up work as she suffers from rheumatoid arthritis.'

'I'm sorry, that can be an awful condition.'

It was probably because he seemed so understanding at the moment that she added. 'I've no idea where my father is. He left my mum and I when I was three.'

Summer didn't remember her father, but she did remember all the years that followed his departure. He'd left Penny and Summer with nothing but broken promises. Worse than nothing; in the first ecstasy of love he'd convinced Penny to give up her teaching degree, promising to support her. When he left, four years and one child later, Penny had nothing to fall back on and no means to support herself and Summer.

The main thing her father had given her was a life lesson: you cannot rely on other people, the only person you can depend on is yourself.

'I'm sorry.'

'Mum called me Summer because I was born on the first of December. Nothing more eccentric than that. I like my name. It's memorable.'

Summer might have seemed carefree, even unpredictable, but she knew she had a core of steel when she needed it.

Their main dishes were placed in front of them; fish for her and beef for him. Once they'd nearly finished their mains, he said, 'So, down to business. I suggest we use this time to agree on a list of topics and questions and we will go away and write out the answers. We can study each other's material and quiz one another on the flight over.'

Quiz one another? Was he for real? She didn't say that out loud, but was sure it was written across her face.

'It will give us the best chance of getting to know one another so we don't make a mistake in front of my family,' he added.

Surely the best chance of getting to know one another would be to talk, she thought, but she simply said, 'Of course.' She had to keep remembering he was paying her. This was a job. This was for her guitar.

'But like I said, the only lie we will tell is that we've been dating for two years. I don't want you to pretend to be anyone you're not.'

She nodded but still thought the idea of anyone believing they were a couple was so unlikely it was going to take an Oscar-winning performance to convince his family of that fact.

'So let's agree on some questions then we can go away and write down the answers.'

'Why not just talk about the answers now?'

'If we write them down, we can study them and we're more likely to remember.'

She was going to be earning every cent of this money. Summer took her notebook from her handbag. It was the one she used for writing songs. Will looked at it like it was the first time he'd ever seen paper.

He took out a thin tablet with a keyboard attached, like a mini computer.

'The sorts of things we'd probably know about one another would be things like date of birth, place of birth, who are parents are. Siblings' names and ages.'

Summer dutifully wrote down everything he said.

'And you should also write what you love about your siblings,' she said.

'Why would I do that?' Will asked.

'That's important. I don't have any siblings, but I imagine they'd be important to me.'

Will grunted and typed something into his tablet.

'First memory,' she said. He looked at her through narrow eyes, but he typed that into his tablet as well.

'School attended,' he said. 'Best subjects at school.'

'Best friends at school and favourite thing to have for lunch,' she added, mostly to spite him.

With a deep, deep sigh Will wrote that in as well.

'Sports played. Final marks achieved.'

Summer resisted the urge to roll her eyes. Who remembered that? People like Will, that's who.

'First crush, family pets,' she said.

'First job.' Will looked at Summer.

'First kiss,' she said, mostly curious about what his response would be. But he nodded.

'Other firsts?' he asked slowly and raised an eyebrow. Muscles she hadn't felt in ages quivered.

'First sexual encounter?' she guessed.

'Only if you're comfortable. Scratch that,' he said. 'No one's going to ask us about that.'

'Yes, yes, of course.' He was right. That was just information she was curious about. 'But we should probably know about any significant relationships the other has had.'

'I suppose so,' he said.

For the first time she was actually enjoying this, but that was probably because it was making him uncomfortable. He thought he had all the answers and all the questions, but there were some things Will Watson couldn't predict.

'Favourite song.' Will said.

'Just one? What about top five ballads, top five dance tunes?'

Will scratched his head. 'How about we just write down as many as we want?'

The man was serious! Write down as many favourite songs as she wanted? 'Favourite movie.' Will said.

'How about top five?' Summer added.

'Of every genre?' Will raised an eyebrow, but she could tell he was kidding. Something inside her chest uncoiled. This may not be as painful as she first thought.

'How about as many as you want to list,' she said with a smile.

'Books?' Will said.

'Same. And ones you've hated.'

She expected that to annoy him but he said, 'Good idea. And same for music and television too.'

This could be a long, messy list. It also had the potential to result in many arguments.

'Favourite food,' Summer said.

'Yes, and allergies and dislikes. Favourite drinks.'

'Worst moment of your life,' she said. 'And the best.'

Will didn't say anything about that suggestion but typed something down.

'Favourite bird,' she said.

'Now you're being silly,' he said.

'No, I'm not. Don't you have a favourite bird?' she asked.

'I can't say I've ever thought about it. What's yours?'

'Magpie,' she said without hesitation.

'Magpie? The stealth bombers of the suburbs?'

'They only do that in spring to protect their babies, but they're highly intelligent and they sing beautifully.'

Will sighed but typed it into his tablet.

With a growing list of things to write about, Will appeared to relax.

'We're going to need a story about how we met. It will be the first thing that anyone asks,' Summer said. 'Or have you already told your mother that?'

Will pressed his lips together. 'I don't…think so.'

She laughed. 'Well think. Because hands-down it's the most important question to have an answer to.'

'How do you know all this?'

'Because when I was in a relationship, a real one, it was what people asked. People are going to assume it's a real relationship until we give them a reason to think otherwise. When was your last relationship?' she asked.

'A while ago. I've been focused on work.'

Summer finished off the last of her lemon tart and spied his tarte tatin. Still half-finished.

'Do you want it?' he asked, picking up on her desire.

'Only if you don't.'

He pushed it over to her.

She could get used to Will and his restaurants and wine.

But she wouldn't. This was a temporary thing only.

'So?' she asked through mouthfuls of caramelised apple. 'How did we meet?'

'A bar?'

'Nope. We don't go to the same places,' she said.

'Through work?'

'That's even more unlikely, isn't it?'

He nodded. 'Then where would we have met? The beach?'

'I rarely go.' It's not that she didn't like swimming, but if she went down to Glenelg or Henley, it was to busk.

'Where do you go, when you're not at work?'

He shrugged.

'Of course. You're always at work.'

'Online?' he suggested.

'Maybe. But honestly, if you'd seen my profile online, which way would you have swiped?'

Will looked down, but when he looked up his eyes were earnest. 'If I saw a photo of you, I would have definitely swiped right.'

'And when you read my profile, you would have undone the match,' she said.

He shook his head.

With an uncomfortable feeling in her stomach she said, 'How about the truth? How about you saw me perform in a show? Not the one this week. Obviously.'

'A show? At some dinner?'

'Or you saw me busk. You loved my singing, took my card, and called me up.'

'That'll have to be it.'

She nodded. But even as she did, she knew it was something that Will would never do, even if he lived to be a million years old.

CHAPTER FOUR

AFTER LEAVING DINNER with Summer, Will tried to put their week in Bali out of his mind. He had several things to finish before he went on leave and didn't like the way Summer Bright kept popping into his thoughts at random moments. Like when he was eating his breakfast and thinking about what he would write down for the entry on his favourite foods. Or when he was choosing the playlist for his morning run and wondering what Summer's favourite bands were. What sort of music did she like? Probably old stuff if her ABBA job was anything to go by.

He finished off his answers to the questions they had agreed on the following night. It took him longer than he anticipated, needing to get everything right and ordered, and to give her as much information as possible. The more time he spent on these questions, the less likely anyone would be to guess that they had not been a couple for the past two years.

Still, it was going to be more difficult than he'd anticipated. Would his family really believe he was dating a singer in an ABBA tribute band? Summer had seen the problem from the very beginning—they were polar opposites. They had an uphill battle ahead of them if this was going to work.

He had the most to lose, his professional reputation. She was just in it for a bit of cash. But despite his resolution to put her out of his mind, he checked his inbox for her response more often than he would like to admit.

Three days out from their trip he was cursing. What was taking her so long? He had to study up on her. He thought about chasing her up, but decided against it.

She held all the cards. Was she not taking this seriously? He couldn't risk Summer revealing the truth. Should he send her a reminder? The little he knew about her made him think that she wouldn't appreciate the nudge.

Should he have offered to pay her more? He'd have paid her whatever she asked. The fact that she'd asked such a paltry sum made him worry. Finally, two days before they were due to leave, Belinda came into the office with a thick white envelope. 'She just dropped it off. Said it was personal.'

'Will Watson' was written across the front in a cursive that looked like it belonged to someone from another time.

She hadn't typed it up like he had, but written by hand. There were at least ten pages, in a beautiful cursive script, telling him about herself.

She'd given away a lot of herself, but he'd just given facts and figures.

Facts and figures are important, he said to himself, but it sounded like his father's voice. When he read the handwritten words, it was only Summer's voice in his head:

My name is Summer Bright. But you know that. Just like you know that I'm thirty-one years old and that my middle name is Angel because you've seen my driving licence. I had to prove to you that I am indeed who I claim to be.

I know you think it's ridiculous, but I've grown to love my name. It's memorable—people always remember me and that's usually a good thing.

Despite my name, my favourite colours are the colours of autumn leaves. Yes, I know I'm cheating—that's yellow and orange and crimson and brown and

all the colours in between. Autumn is also my favourite time of year. Unpopular opinion, I know. I can't explain it except that I love the leaves, I love when the air
turns crisp. I love wearing lots of clothes, being inside
and soups. And because I love dahlias and they mostly
bloom in autumn.

I love my job. I love to sing. But more than that, I
love to write songs. I'm still trying to make a living
from it even though my mother believes I should take
a receptionist job with a friend of hers. I tried the full-
time work thing a few times and it never really worked.
I don't care about the money; in my experience money
only complicates things. I only want enough to pay the
rent.

Who was this woman? *I only want enough to pay the rent.*
What about all the other things money could buy? Comfort?
Luxury? Power? Influence? Not to mention food. Concert
tickets? Surely those were things she wanted as well.

Boyfriends? Well, that's a story as short as it is pathetic.
My last boyfriend, Michael, and I dated for nearly two
years. He wanted me to move in with him, but I was
worried about leaving my mum. We were trying to find
her a new flatmate until I woke up at Michael's one
morning. He was gone. And so was my guitar, my busking rig, and my car. To set your mind at ease—as I'm
sure you are worried about this—I have no intention of
falling in love with you or anyone. I've finally learnt
that the only person I can rely on is myself.

Another thing I should tell you is that my relationship
with Michael overlapped with 'ours'. I've never cheated
on anyone, but in the unlikely event anyone puts two
and two together, you should be prepared to know that

you were cuckolded. I didn't post much about our relationship, but if anyone asks, Michael was a jerk and we're both glad he's gone.

Damn. He should have thought about this and the fact that the real Summer Bright had been living her life, dating, having relationships for the past two years. Her assurances assuaged his concerns. Besides, it wouldn't be the first time he'd been made to look like a fool in a relationship. He, too, was glad that Michael was gone, he sounded like the bigger fool.

Then followed some pages with her likes and dislikes, in no particular order, just in a stream of consciousness. Likes: soup, bees, magpies. Music of all kinds. Except those with misogynistic lyrics. Fair enough, thought Will.

Dislikes: anchovies, people who are rude and ignorant at the same time.

My dream is to support myself writing my own songs. I love singing but vocal cords age. As do bodies. There will come a day when I won't be able to sing and dance to 'Waterloo' on a shaky stage any longer.

Will touched the page with his index and middle fingers. He was learning so much about Summer from this narrative, some more than his spreadsheet would've taught her. After reading this he felt he knew something about Summer. He didn't understand her but reluctantly admired her. They had very little in common, but Will knew that you didn't need to have a lot in common with someone to be able to do business together.

Summer sat on her bed, legs straight out in front of her, with her laptop resting on them. She clicked on the attachment and waited for it to load. She hadn't opened her laptop in ages, and avoided it whenever she could. All her recordings were on it, but since Michael had bolted with her gear and her livelihood, it was just a reminder of how her life remained frozen. Will, unhelpfully had decided to use a spreadsheet, a type of document she was definitely allergic to. One she couldn't just read on her phone. And this one was a whopper; there were a dozen tabs with titles such as 'Life Story', 'Likes and Dislikes', and 'Relationship History'.

Naturally, she clicked on 'Relationship History' first.

His first kiss had been when he was thirteen with a girl at a school dance. There was a long dry spell, with conscientious Will no doubt focusing on his studies, until university.

She scanned the list, such as it was. First names only and no one for longer than a few months. There were even phone numbers next to a few of them. She laughed. Was he putting them forward as references?

The list of short relationships also told him he was a commitment-phobe. This wasn't a surprise; he'd confessed to her when they'd first met that he didn't do relationships. She shook her head and clicked on 'Likes and Dislikes'.

His favourite food was chicken burgers and chips. His favourite drink was red wine. His favourite colour was aquamarine. That was more specific than blue or green or red or pink and strangely gave her a glimpse into his mind.

She clicked on 'Life Story' next, but that was nothing much more than a résumé. Where he was born, where he went to school and his work history. His work history was odd: a few casual jobs while he was at school including the usual fast-food outlets, some bar work at university and then straight on to Watson Enterprises, except his time at Watson Enterprises was punctuated by a six-month gap about seven years ago. He probably went travelling or something, but it caught her eye. Where did he go? What did he do? That sounded more interesting than the rest of the 'Life Story' tab. Trust Will to leave the most interesting bits out and focus on the boring parts.

The tab marked 'Entertainment' was the longest of all.

Music, books, movies, all carefully rated out of five. This would've taken him hours.

Was she expected to remember that he gave *The Godfather* three stars? But *The Godfather Part II* five? He liked crime novels, mostly, but read a smattering of sci-fi and a frankly disturbing number of management books.

His favourite movie was *The Princess Bride*. His favourite television show was *The Golden Girls*. Odd, she thought. But she could work with it. His favourite band was U2, which showed a distinct lack of imagination.

She expected the last tab to be something like 'Balance Sheet', but it was blank. Had he created it and changed his mind? What was he going to write?

Will Watson was something else. She just wasn't sure what.

Will paced the departures hall at the airport looking, in vain, for Summer. She'd insisted on meeting him here rather than driving together, which he hadn't thought much of to begin with, but now it seemed like a mistake.

Where was she?

He was a fool, he was relying on her entirely, but she could back out of this deal at any moment. What had he told himself time and time again: Don't rely on anybody else. Don't trust anyone.

Finally, he spotted her red curls, bobbing up and down outside with the taxis. She was pulling a suitcase out of the boot of a car and waving away help from the elderly taxi driver.

'We're late,' Will grumbled. 'We'd better get going.'

'It's only five past. You said to be here at eleven. Besides the plane doesn't leave for another four hours. We've got heaps of time.'

'Check-In, Security, Customs. They can take hours,' he said.

To Will's great annoyance, they sailed right through all three, barely even slowing down to queue at any stage. Within twenty minutes of Summer's arrival at the airport, they were safely settled inside the business lounge, glasses of French champagne on the table in front of them.

Summer looked lovely. She was wearing soft blue jeans, a white tank top and a loose floral shirt over the top. Her wild hair was loose, but tamed by a small braid holding the front locks away from her face.

Her clothes were always happy and colourful. A lot like Summer. Did she seem nervous? He didn't know her well enough to be able to tell.

The only nervous person here is you.

He took another sip of champagne and felt his head becoming lighter, which didn't usually happen after only a sip or two. It was too late to back out now; they were at the airport. But now he was finally here, the doubts began to creep in. Would anyone believe they were a couple? He could believe that he might fall for someone like Summer; he could imagine asking her out, taking her on a date. Leaning in to kiss her soft dewy cheek…

No. Clause five point two. They would not have a physical relationship. This was a business deal. He was paying her, for crying out loud.

But would anyone believe Summer would fall for him? He knew what people thought of him. Women liked him enough; they flirted with him, asked him out all the time. His mother told him often enough that he was a catch. Why wouldn't Summer fall for him?

He put his champagne glass down. No one was actually going to fall for anyone. They simply had to convince his mother that they had already fallen for one another.

Diane probably knew him better than anyone in the world.

She would be able to tell right away that he and Summer had little in common. She'd be able to tell that they hardly knew one another.

They had to get to work.

'Have you been studying?' he said.

'Quiz me,' she said confidently. 'You like swimming in the ocean, but not indoor pools. You say *The Golden Girls* is your favourite show, but you gave every season of *The Good Place* five stars. What's that about?'

'Impressive.' And it was. Even he didn't remember the ratings he'd given to most shows, but they sounded about right.

'I have one question for you though,' he said.

She nodded.

'Why seventy-seven hundred dollars?'

'Excuse me?'

'Why did you ask for seven thousand, seven hundred dollars and not a round eight?'

'Because seven-seven is what I need.'

'What you *need*?'

'Yes. For my guitar.'

'You're going to buy a guitar with the money?'

'Yes, and a busking rig.'

He must have looked as confused as he felt because she added, 'An amp, microphone, you know?'

Will didn't really know. 'A guitar? That's all?' *Must be an expensive guitar*, he thought. Though admittedly he had no idea how much they cost.

'That's what I need. If you'd read my letter you'd know what happened to my last one.'

That was right, Michael the douche of an ex-boyfriend who took her grandfather's guitar, PA system. And her car! She'd told him their relationships had overlapped, but not by how much.

'When did that happen?'

'Three months ago.'

Three months wasn't long, the breakup would still be raw. He wasn't even back at work three months after Georgia left him. He wasn't even thinking straight until a good six months later, and here Summer was, three months later, getting on a plane with a stranger.

She's not with you. This is a job for her. You need to start thinking of it the same way. If the board find out you've lied, this could be the end of you. Your reputation will be destroyed.

'I'm sorry,' he said. 'I didn't realise it was so recent. How are you doing?'

'I'm okay. I've reached the angry stage. Acceptance will come eventually, but right now I'm just furious.'

He couldn't help but smile. 'Did you get another car?'

'No. It's the guitar I need.'

'Shouldn't you buy a car first?'

She groaned. 'You'd get on well with my mother.'

Summer's mother wanted her to get a full-time job, but Summer thought a job would interfere with her music. Even though he'd memorised her letter, he didn't understand her at all.

They sipped their champagne in silence until Summer said, 'That's all? Just one question? I have dozens for you.'

'Like what?'

'Like everything that isn't on your spreadsheet. You answered the questions, but you didn't tell me *why.*'

Why was a big thing for Summer.

'Why what?'

'Why is *The Golden Girls* your favourite TV show? Why is aquamarine your favourite colour?'

'Why couldn't it be?'

'It's very specific. Neither blue, nor green. What's that about?'

'I don't know. It just is.'

Summer sighed deeply.

Will could pass a test on Summer after reading her ten pages, but she might find it hard to talk about him. She'd given him feelings, he'd given her facts, he acknowledged, with a hint of regret.

No. Fact and figures were important. They had to know certain things about one another. They weren't meant to have feelings for one another; they only needed to convince his family that he was not a liar.

'Anything else?' Will crossed his arms.

'Yes. You haven't told me about your mother and Gus. We're about to go to their wedding. What are they like? How long have they known one another?'

'Just over a year I think.'

Summer tilted her head. 'I suppose that's long enough to get to know someone. What do you think?'

'I think no way is one year long enough.' He'd known Georgia for two years. They'd been engaged. And it still hadn't been long enough to really know her.

'Are you worried he's younger than your mother?'

'Why do you think I'm worried about something?'

'Because you're so on edge. You're either gripping that champagne glass like you want to break it or you're gripping the edge of your seat. Are you always this uptight?'

His current mood was more to do with the gorgeous red-head sitting across from him who held his professional reputation in her hands but was treating it like it was a frisbee.

She was distracting. Her hair, her eyes. The sound of her voice. And they needed to be concentrating on facts!

'Do you think he's a gold digger?' she asked.

'Yes, I mean no. I did wonder when they first started dating, but he's actually very wealthy. I don't think he's very materialistic.'

'I agree. He looks like a bit of a hippy.'

Will laughed.

'Is *that* what bothers you? That he's *not* materialistic?'

'Why on earth would that bother me?'

'Because...' She waved her hand in his direction. 'You're so serious, focused on your job.'

'That's not because I need the money.'

She glared at him and for a horrible second he thought she might stand up and leave. He felt his face burn. His last comment was only one that someone who didn't have to worry about money could afford to make.

'I'm serious about my job because recycling plastics and keeping them out of the oceans or landfill is not just important, but critical. And it is a very risky, marginal business. Plenty of companies that have tried to do what we do have failed and ended up in administration.'

'But you're successful—the company is doing well, isn't it?'

Will nodded.

'So surely you can relax?'

He shook his head. She didn't understand. 'You can never relax in business. You always need to keep an eye out. Stay alert for threats.'

She laughed. 'It's a business, not a hunting trip, surely?'

He gritted his teeth. 'I don't think I'm about to get shot, no. But things are always changing, there are always opportunities to take, or miss. If you don't trust the right people, make the right decisions then things can quickly fall apart.'

He didn't want to say any more, he certainly didn't want to tell her about Georgia and how he'd nearly lost his place in the company entirely. He didn't want to tell her how since his father had passed away and he'd taken on the role of CEO he'd felt like he needed to be on guard, on his best behaviour at all times. If the board lost their trust in him, if the share-holders did, then they could lose everything.

'So, no. I don't think Gus is a gold digger,' he said.

'Then what? You're worried about something.' Summer reached over and touched his arm. Electricity shot up it and into his chest. It wasn't unpleasant. It was warm. Exciting.

Summer whispered. 'Tell me more about your father. Not what I can read online, but what he meant to you.'

Who did this woman think she was, his counsellor?

No, she'd just trying to get to know you. She's trying to understand you. And you have to let her.

'Ah…he was amazing. Driven, inspiring and such a natural businessman.'

'You miss him?'

'Every day.' Losing his father had been a double blow, not just losing a parent so young and so suddenly, but losing his business partner and mentor as well. Even now, especially now, he longed to knock on his father's door and discuss something with him. They didn't always agree on everything and his father could be stubborn and set in his ways, but Will never stopped valuing his opinion. Even if it was to disregard it. But his father's office door was now his own office door, and there was no one he had to go to to ask for advice from anything about the volatility of the stock market to what on earth he was going to do about Summer.

'Don't get me wrong, I'm glad Mum has found someone. It's just very soon.'

'People grieve at different rates. He might have been an amazing father and businessman, but it doesn't follow that he was a good husband.'

Will straightened his back. 'My parents were happy.'

'I'm not saying they weren't…but maybe your mother wants to make the most of the time she has left.'

'She's only sixty, she's not on death's door.'

Summer sighed, 'I didn't mean that. Only that people re-assess their lives after a death.'

He studied her. She was remarkably composed for someone who had agreed to travel overseas with a stranger and pre-tend to date them. Like she did this kind of thing every day.

'How did you get to be so wise?'

She shook her head. 'I'm not wise. I want my guitar before a car, remember?' She smiled and his insides uncoiled a little.

And for the first time in days, he dared to think that maybe it would all be all right.

The flight was almost too short, a sentence he never thought he'd hear himself say.

They caught a ferry from Denpasar over to the island of Nusa Lembongan and a small open truck to their villa. If he'd been hoping to have a shower and a stiff drink before facing his family, Will would have been disappointed. Diane was waiting at the villa door for them.

'Here are your keys. Your place is just like Ben and Char-lotte's, down the road. Did you really need two bedrooms?'

'I snore. It disturbs Summer's sleep.' Will had already thought of this excuse.

Summer walked over and she slipped her hand in his. He flinched. Her hand was soft and smooth and took him com-pletely by surprise. Diane's eyebrow shot up.

He shouldn't have reacted like that; he should have been happy she was holding his hand. And the thing was, he was happy. He just hadn't expected to like it so much. He hadn't expected the sparks and the pleasure that rolled through him. To show his mother he was utterly at ease with Summer's touch, he slid his arm around her and pulled her close. Her body pressed against his and he was aware for the first time of how wonderful her soft, luscious curves felt against him, how her amazing hair smelt of roses and honey.

'And you know what he's like, he works all hours. I don't want him tapping away on his computer or making international phone calls while I'm trying to get some sleep,' she said.

Diane nodded, but frowned. 'You aren't meant to be working. This is meant to be a holiday for you, you know.'

'I know,' Will said. 'But the world doesn't stop just because you're getting married. It should, mind you, but it doesn't.'

Diane seemed placated and pulled them both into an extra tight embrace. Will was pressed even closer to Summer and he tried not to let his body tense.

Diane released them from her hug but her hands remained resting on their shoulders. She looked from him to Summer and back again, studying them.

She knows something's up.

A huge smile broke across her face.

'You two are both so beautiful. I'm so glad you're here,' she said and finally let them go.

'Dinner in an hour!' Diane called as she left.

'That was close,' Summer said, letting go of his hand. 'Thanks for arranging two bedrooms.'

'Of course. It was in the contract.' Clause seven.

'Do you think she's suspicious?'

'No, she knows I snore.'

Summer smiled. He liked it when she did. It made something lighten inside him.

'We can't make her doubt that we're physical with one another.' She reached for his hand again and took it in hers. 'You're going to have to get used to me doing that. We don't have to be big on PDAs but you probably shouldn't flinch if I take your hand.'

Will looked into her eyes. They were warm and kind and he nodded. She let go of his hand and he wanted to grab it back.

Summer looked around their villa and let out a long sigh. 'It's spectacular.'

She wasn't wrong. The main room, with a sofa and dining table opened up onto a spacious deck, also with a daybed, and other chairs. The deck overlapped a crystal-clear infinity pool, its sheen of water appearing to slide off the edge of the pool to the ocean below.

Even though she was distracted by the beautiful view, Summer hadn't forgotten what they'd been talking about moments before. 'How will I know about the snoring if you're in another room? How will I know if you talk in your sleep? How will I know what you wear to bed? Aren't those things a girlfriend should know?'

It had been so long since he'd had a proper relationship, he hardly knew any more.

'Nothing. I wear nothing.'

'Okay, that is good to know.' She coughed and he thought he saw colour rise in her cheeks.

'You?' It was wrong, but he wanted to know. A nightshirt. PJs. Or…like him?

'Just a T-shirt.'

He imagined her in an oversized tee, hair mussed, legs long, lean, and bare and he bit back a smile.

'No one is going to ask you what I wear to bed. Or how long I brush my teeth. Or what I say in my sleep,' he said.

'You speak in your sleep?'

'I've no idea. But it doesn't matter because no one's going to ask.'

As he spoke, he wondered if he was reassuring her or himself.

CHAPTER FIVE

IT WAS WITH no small amount of trepidation that Summer slipped on her bracelets, tied up her sandals and followed Will out into the warm Bali evening to meet his family. She was equipped with nothing more than the facts she'd crammed from an Excel spreadsheet and a deep sense of doubt. She and Will were opposites. He was a planner; she was spontaneous. He cared about money; she cared about music and passion. There was no way his family would believe they were a couple.

She could pretend to be attracted to him, that was not a leap. In Bali, finally out of his suit and tie, Will was different. He'd always been gorgeous. He'd always made a pulse throb in her throat. But in Bali, he was something else. He hadn't shaved, giving his face a slightly more rugged appearance. The moisture in the air gave his hair volume and he hadn't tried to tame it with a comb. Tonight, he wore a linen shirt. It was still buttoned high, but the sleeves were rolled up so she could see his beautiful forearms. Strong, with his muscles and veins for once on view. Acting as though she was physically attracted to Will wouldn't be a hardship. She would barely be pretending.

Pretending to be romantically involved? That was something else.

Watching him walk alongside her, their strides in unison, a strong sense of defensiveness kicked in inside her.

Why couldn't they be together? What was wrong with her? Precisely nothing! She was a successful singer. Maybe successful was a stretch, but she made part of her living entertaining people. That was important. Making people happy was a completely noble vocation.

Will *needed* someone exactly like her. Someone fun, someone to encourage him not to take everything in life so seriously. Besides anything else, she was a performer. She had this. She could pretend to be the type of woman Will would fall in love with.

What sort of woman would he fall in love with? Probably someone smart, ambitious, super successful like he was. Corporate, definitely. The spreadsheet had listed half a dozen women, but none of the relationships had lasted more than a few months. Was that long enough to fall in love?

I don't want you to pretend to be anyone you aren't.

But that was just the problem, would anyone believe that Will would love her?

They were about to find out.

The dinner was at a restaurant a short walk up the coast from their ocean front villa. The island of Nusa Lembongan was just to the south of the main island of Bali, a short ferry ride away. There were very few cars on the island, just small open trucks that acted as taxis for the tourists and made the bulkier deliveries. Otherwise, people got around on bicycles and motor scooters. Or they walked, as Will and Summer did now.

Luckily the dress code in Bali was relaxed and casual, perfectly suited to her own wardrobe. She wore a long floral dress and sandals and luxuriated in the tropical warmth.

The restaurant was open and overlooked the ocean, wrapped around by a long wooden deck. Will stopped at the entrance. 'Are you ready?'

She wasn't, but admitting it probably wouldn't help, when

she could see that Will was even more nervous than he'd been at the airport. He was pressing his palms down his shirt and shorts. In his button-down shirt, he still managed to look a little too formal. If only she could get him into a T-shirt. Or even a singlet. Or better yet, nothing.

She was about to shake the inappropriate thought away but then realised the sight of her drooling over Will wouldn't hurt the charade. She took his shoulders, spun him towards her and unbuttoned the top three buttons on his shirt. Then she spread her hands across his collarbone, and spread the shirt slightly apart, feeling the strength of his chest under her fingertips. She breathed in deeply. Oh, he was handsome.

'Do you work out?' she asked.

He coughed. 'Only when I have time.'

She raised an eyebrow.

'I swim. Or jog. Most mornings.'

She nodded. 'That would explain it. There's no need to be nervous, it's a completely normal part of going on stage and that's sort of what this is. Once we get out there, it'll be fine.'

Summer reached over and took his hand. Partly for their stage personas, but it felt natural to reassure him. And herself. They *could* be a couple.

She spotted Diane and Gus and they made their way over to them, still holding hands. They all greeted one another with kisses on the cheeks.

'Congratulations again,' Summer said. 'It's so lovely to be here. I'm so excited for you both.'

'No, we're glad that you're here,' Diane said.

Will leant towards her and said, 'Can I get you a drink?'

'Thank you, honey,' she said. So he was going to be a 'honey'. That surprised her; she'd thought he might be going to be a *darling* or a *sweetheart*, but *honey* just came to her tongue out of nowhere.

Will's eyes widened for just a second. 'Rosé?'

'You know it.'

Diane introduced her to her sister who was almost as excited as Diane that Summer was there.

'Oh, Summer, it's so lovely to finally meet you. We were beginning to wonder if Will had made you up!'

Summer feigned a laugh. 'Oh, no. I'm real. And here. And in love with Will.'

The words felt strange crossing her lips.

'We'd almost given up hope of him finding someone.'

Why was everyone so damned happy that Will had a girlfriend? Why were they so obsessed with his relationship status? There was clearly nothing wrong with Will, objectively speaking. He was rich, handsome, intelligent. Maybe a little uptight, but you couldn't have everything. Surely there were many women who would be able to see past Will's quirks to the kind man behind them?

But Will doesn't have a girlfriend, remember? That's why you're here.

'There you go, sweet pea.'

Summer took the wine and tried not to laugh. Sweet pea?

'Summer, I understand we had the pleasure of seeing you on stage the other week,' Gus spoke. 'But Will told us you work in sales.'

Don't pretend to be anyone you're not.

'Yes, I think he thought his family might not approve of him dating a busker. I'm a singer, and sometime songwriter. I sing in tribute bands and travel a little with that. I busk when I can.' *When I had a guitar.* 'But he didn't fib entirely—I do work part time in an op shop.'

Gus and Diane exchanged a look that made Summer's nerves tighten. It said it all. You're dating a billionaire and you work in an op shop. Pull the other one.

But to Summer's great surprise, Gus said, 'That's fabulous.

Second-hand shops are so important. Reusing and repurposing things is so important, don't you think?'

'Yes, of course. I know it seems like Will and I don't have much in common, but love's funny like that.'

'I'm sure you have plenty of things in common. I'm actually impressed that Will found someone like you. It makes me think Will has untapped depths.'

Both Summer and Will reddened. Were there compliments for both of them buried in that remark or insults?

'What do you mean?' Will said.

'Just that I didn't think you were so…imaginative.'

'Imaginative?' Will coughed.

'Yes, I figured Summer would be an ambitious corporate type, a mirror image of yourself. I'm glad to see she isn't. I think you probably complement one another.'

'Summer and I…' Will began and Summer leant in, desperate to hear him finish the sentence, but Gus cut him off.

'On paper, Diane and I don't have much in common. Many people are confused by the age difference. She's recently widowed. We've had very different lives. We come from different backgrounds. But we have the same values, we can talk about anything and we talk for hours. She's my favourite person in the world.'

Will picked up Summer's hand and squeezed it. They both exhaled in unison.

A couple entered the restaurant. The woman had long dark hair and was amazingly pretty. Summer blinked when she saw the man with her. He was a slightly less handsome version of Will. His hair was lighter. They were about the same height, but the other man was leaner. This must be the brother that Will was so reluctant to talk about, Ben.

'Ben! Charlotte!' Diane greeted them with kisses on both cheeks.

Introductions were made and both Ben and Charlotte

greeted Summer warmly with kisses on the cheeks as well. Diane explained that the pair had flown in from London a few days earlier, where Ben was a painter and Charlotte ran an art gallery. They were not, however, a couple, as Summer had initially thought, just good friends.

Charlotte pointed to Summer's jangling bracelets. 'They're so pretty. Where did you get them?'

'Back in Adelaide, but I'm hoping to go shopping for similar things here. I hear they have fantastic markets in Ubud.'

'Yes!' Charlotte exclaimed. 'Ben and I were planning on going tomorrow or the next day. You guys should come with us.'

'That'd be wonderful,' Summer replied. Will glared at her, but Summer straightened her back. Did he want his family to believe they were a couple or not? Besides, Ben and Charlotte seemed like an easier audience than Diane and Gus.

'You have to tell me all about Will,' Charlotte said to Summer. 'Ben is so secretive about his older brother.'

'Likewise!' Summer said, warming to Charlotte instantly. 'I have to drag every detail out of him.'

The guests took their seats and to Summer's horror, Will ended up a few people away from her, sitting with Charlotte. Ben was also nowhere to be found and Summer found herself seated next to Diane. While Diane was lovely, this was going to feel like a quiz show round.

No, Summer thought. She had this. She would turn the tables on Diane. Ask her about Will! Mothers loved to talk about their children. She would hit Diane with so many questions she wouldn't have time to ask any. Summer took a big gulp of wine and went for it.

'I wish I could see some photos of Will as a kid.'

'When we're back, I promise I'll show you.'

'It's so nice to finally meet you all.' Summer looked around the table. 'He's been so secretive about his family.'

'That's probably because of Georgia.'

'Georgia? What happened in Georgia?'

The look Diane gave her filled Summer with dread.

'Not the place. His ex.'

Summer had studied the spreadsheet. She knew his exes. She'd even contemplated texting one of the numbers Will had written down. There had been no Georgia.

'Of course, silly me. He doesn't talk about her much.'

'But he has told you about her?'

'Of course he has. And Prue and Rachel.' Luckily, she could name some of his other ex-girlfriends.

'Yes, well unlike the others, Georgia really hurt him. And then there was the business with the company.'

Summer nodded as if agreeing but she had no idea. 'Of course, yes.'

'I've never seen him so upset as the day he cancelled the wedding.'

Summer nearly choked on her wine. Engagement! She shot Will a look at the other end of the table, but he was laughing with Charlotte. She could have strangled him.

Diane continued. 'I offered to make all the phone calls but he insisted on doing it himself. It's bad enough to find out your fiancée has betrayed you, but to insist on calling the caterer, the celebrant and everything, that wasn't necessary. It was like he wanted to punish himself.'

'But he'd done nothing wrong.' Summer, who had no idea what had even gone down knew in her heart that Will wasn't to blame.

'No, but he still blames himself. He nearly lost his job. It was only his previous record and yes, nepotism, that allowed him to keep it.'

Will almost lost his job. The CEO of Watson Enterprises almost lost his position?

What on earth had happened?

The question would have to wait and Summer would have to deal with this the best she could, but she suspected that whatever happened with Georgia had something to do with why Will was so anxious for his lie about dating Summer not to be exposed now.

'He's very hard on himself,' Summer said, looking at Will. *But not as hard as I'm going to be on him later for neglecting to tell me about his fiancée.*

Diane touched Summer's hand. 'Yes, he is very hard on himself. Too hard. I'm glad you can see that in him. I'm sorry he felt he had to keep you a secret from us for so long. I'm sure he's told you about his father.'

Summer nodded. 'I understand he could be uncompromising.'

'He would have liked you once he got to know you. But David had...views.'

'And I'm a singer. A busker. Not the corporate type he envisaged for his son.'

'No, and thank goodness you're not. Will already had that with Georgia and look how that turned out.'

So, Georgia had been a corporate type. The type of woman that Summer had pictured for Will. The complete opposite of who Summer was.

A strange feeling came over Summer as she sat there, watching the man, his mother's hand warm but gentle on top of hers. The anger she'd felt moments ago was replaced with something else. Empathy. He might be annoyingly uptight, but his outward persona was masking a deep hurt.

Though she was still furious at him for not telling her about Georgia and leaving them both exposed like this. How was she meant to help him if he wasn't honest with her?

Once the plates had been cleared, Summer excused herself from the table and went out to the deck by the dining room for some fresh air and space to think. Behind her, she could hear chattering and excitement. It was such a happy family occasion. It would hurt them to know the truth.

This morning Summer had been in this for the money, but now she was here it was also very important to her to protect this lovely welcoming family from hurt, especially this week. When the wedding was over, then she and Will would quietly break up and go their separate ways, but Summer did not want to be responsible for ruining what should be the happiest of weeks for Diane and Gus.

Will joined her on the deck and he reached for her hand. She shook his away and hurt flashed across his eyes.

She wasn't sorry.

'You missed a few things on the spreadsheet,' she hissed.

'Like what?'

'Like one fiancée for starters! Like the fact that you were about to be married! Your mother totally sideswiped me with that one. Thanks for letting her ambush me!' Summer turned and walked along the deck, away from him.

Will followed her. 'We can't look like we're fighting.'

'Why not? It's what real couples do, isn't it?' Summer bit out.

Maybe it was, maybe not. She was too annoyed at him right now.

Will looked out across the water and ran his hand through his hair, scraping it back off his high, intelligent forehead.

Gorgeous.

But she was still annoyed.

'Okay, if we are fighting, then we need to make up. That's also what couples do, isn't it?' he said.

'I don't know.' Summer crossed her arms tight. 'I'm not sure I forgive you. You know how much is at risk here.' As an afterthought she added, 'For you.'

He leant in and whispered, 'You do know it isn't real?'

'A sexual relationship might not be, but we do have something.'

It wasn't quite friendship, though it could be. 'We have a business relationship, at the very least. We have to be able to trust one another.'

She crossed her arms even tighter. She was annoyed he hadn't told the truth, but a part of her was also hurt. Which was silly because they weren't even friends. Not really. She'd have to care for him for him to be able to hurt her.

'If you want me to be able to convince them that we're together, you're going to have to start sharing things about yourself. And not just in tabs marked "Entertainment". I'm going to need to know personal things. Like why *The Golden Girls* is your favourite show. Why aquamarine is your favourite colour. And how many ex-fiancées you have!'

She turned away from him and stared out over the ocean, dark except for the lights on the island reflecting on the surface.

'There was only one,' he said softly. 'I'm sorry for not telling you.'

Summer looked from the water and to Will. He looked down at her, earnestly, reached for her hand again and this time she let him take it.

'You should be.'

'I told you about the others.'

He had. But with Georgia it had been different. She had really hurt him. And some implications had followed for the business. Had they worked together? Was that it?

Will turned her hand over in his and studied it, flooding her with happy hormones. His hands were well cared for, and large. One of his could easily hide one of hers. He turned her hand over in his like it was a precious object.

'If they've seen us fight, maybe they should see us kiss and make up,' he said.

He looked at her and her stomach flipped. It would be so easy to lean forward and lift her toes.

But she was afraid of what would happen if she did. And she was still confused by what had happened at dinner.

'I don't know, would it fall within "appropriate physical affection"? I wouldn't want to breach the contract.'

Her hesitation was defensive only. She wanted, she realised with a jolt, to kiss him. But what if she couldn't stop?

Will coughed. 'Yes, I agree. I'm sure a hug will be sufficient.' He dropped her hand but pulled her into an embrace; she pressed her face against his chest and wasn't prepared for the sensations that swept over her. The hug was no less risky than a quick kiss would have been, maybe more so; Will was strong and solid and she couldn't help burying herself against him. She slid her arms around his back and then up, noticing each muscle in his back; her cheek came to rest on the smooth skin just above the lowest button undone on his shirt. If she moved her lips, she would taste him. If he tasted even half as good as he smelt then she wanted to eat the entire banquet.

He peeled himself gently away and she cursed herself silently for forgetting herself.

Luckily though when she turned to walk back in, she saw Diane watching them both, beaming.

Telling everyone they were tired from their trip, Summer and Will left shortly afterwards and made the short walk back to their villa.

'All things considered, I think that was a pass. It certainly could have gone worse,' he said as he let her into the villa.

'Due to good luck, rather than good management,' Summer said. Will could have taken a pop quiz on Michael and what he'd done to her, but Summer didn't even know of Georgia's existence. Let alone why they had broken up or what the fallout had been.

'Your mother might be more convinced than ever that we're together because she's seen us break up after a fight.'

'We can't mess up again.'

'No, we can't. Which is why you have to be honest with me, Will. You have to tell me about Georgia.'

She said this firmly, though a part of her didn't want to know about the woman who had so clearly broken Will's heart.

'You don't have to tell me everything, but it would help me get to know you. It might also just help.'

Will drew in a deep, resigned breath. 'Do you want another drink?'

'Are you going to talk?'

He nodded.

'Then yes.'

'Is red wine okay?'

'Red is great.'

Summer moved out to the deck overlooking the pool, which in turn overlooked the sea, which was crashing below them against a small cliff.

She sat on one of the deck chairs and Will joined her, passing her a large glass of wine. So, this would be a long story.

He sat in the lounge chair next to her.

'Her name was Georgia. Obviously.'

He was stalling and Summer wished she could make him more comfortable to get his story out.

'I met her through some mutual friends. She was a lawyer, working for a large private firm, and I thought that was great, because she was ambitious, and we moved in the same circles but not too close, if you know what I mean.'

Summer nodded, but she didn't really understand what it was like to be in this world he spoke of.

'She was fantastic, smart, sharp, clever.'

'She was intelligent,' Summer said, teeth grinding together.

Will laughed. 'Yes, and okay, yes, she was gorgeous. Beautiful. Tall, thin, straight long blond hair. She was a knockout.'

Summer's hand went reflexively to her unruly curls, even more unwieldy in the humidity.

Tell me you're not attracted to me without telling me you aren't attracted to me.

'After we'd been dating for about a year, I proposed. I knew she was the woman I wanted to spend my life with. I thought I couldn't have invented a better life partner for me if I tried. She accepted and I thought everything was perfect.'

Will took a big gulp of his wine.

'It's okay, we've all been there,' she whispered, hoping this would make it easier for him to open up.

'I don't know why she did it. I didn't then and I still don't really understand now. Things changed when we negotiated a prenup. It wasn't my idea, but everyone else insisted, including the board. I don't know if she spied a bigger prize elsewhere, if she fell out of love with me. Or if she ever loved me at all.

'She knew about the plan for the new product we were working on. It was a new type of fabric made of recycled plastics, but which can in turn be recycled. She knew enough about all the deals we were setting up with suppliers and buyers. She took the plans to a company overseas. Sold them to the highest bidder and made that other company a fortune in the process, leaving our future plans floundering.'

'I'm hardly an expert, but isn't there some sort of law against that?'

'It's complicated, but any prosecution of her would have also focused on me and the information I'd given to her or allowed her to access, even unintentionally. I'm lucky no one decided to prosecute as it would have made things even worse for me. Even though it meant she got away with it.'

'Oh, Will. I'm so sorry.'

'The board were upset. Actually, that's an understatement, they wanted me fired. It was only thanks to Dad's influence that they calmed down and let me return after I took a few months off. It's taken years to rebuild their trust.'

'You fell in love with her, and then she stole from you.'

Will swung his legs round to stand up. 'When you say it like that, it sounds trite.'

'Sorry, I didn't mean that at all. It's just like what Michael did to me. I was trying to tell you that I understand.'

'The ex who stole your guitar?' Will relaxed back into his chair.

'It wasn't just a guitar—it was my livelihood and my passion. And it was the only thing I had left from my grandfather. You keep saying just a guitar, but to me, it was as significant as what Georgia took from you.'

Will put his face in his hands and was silent for a long beat before he said, 'It wasn't even just the money. It was the shame. The embarrassment, the damage to my professional standing on top of the heartbreak, which wasn't insignificant.'

'I'm so sorry.'

He suddenly looked up from his hands and she felt as though he was seeing her for the first time. 'I'm sorry too. This thing with Georgia was years ago. Michael only left a few months ago.'

She shrugged. She was doing okay, emotionally. 'At this point I'm far more upset about the guitar.'

Will smiled. 'Really?'

'I was hurt, don't get me wrong. But part of me is glad to now know what a jerk he was.'

'That's very sensible. And philosophical. How do you move past the betrayal? You invested so much in him and he left you with nothing?'

They were strange words to use in respect to a relationship, she thought. 'Love isn't an investment or a business transaction.'

'No, but it still involves give and take. And trust.' Will leant forward and studied her. Under his gaze she felt her body start to sway.

He smiled again and heavens he looked good when he did, his entire aura was transformed from serious businessman to smoking-hot man she'd like to kiss.

She shook herself. No. Love may not be a business transaction, but this was.

'Why do you keep talking about the board, why do they hold so much power? I thought you owned the company?'

'Watson Enterprises is a public corporation. Mum and I own the controlling shares; we own the majority, but we still answer to a board. That's why if it gets out that I lied—even about something like who I'm dating—I'm not sure they'd trust me again. Given what happened with Georgia.'

The enormity of what he was saying hit her. Summer hadn't just come to Bali to protect his mother; she'd come to prevent any risk to Will's professional reputation.

'Then, Will Watson, we'd really better get to know one another.'

He looked up and when their eyes met, his blue bright and brilliant, her tummy did a summersault. They talked and talked. Will poured them both more wine and they sat by the pool. They talked and talked until they lost track of time.

CHAPTER SIX

WILL WOKE TO a gentle knocking at his bedroom door and a slightly heavy head. He had no idea what time it had been when he'd finally stumbled into bed, but knew it had been even later when his thoughts finally slowed enough to allow him sleep.

'Will,' Summer said through the door. 'You've got to get up. We're meeting Ben and Charlotte soon.'

Will groaned and rolled over. They were spending the whole day with his grumpy brother. He wished they could just stay at the villa, relax. And not feel the pressure to pretend.

After last night's long talk, he and Summer were probably new friends. They had talked until after midnight about their lives and he'd told her all about Georgia. It was the first time in years he'd said her name, let alone opened up so honestly about how he'd felt. Summer was a good, calm listener and he was surprised how easy she was to be around.

'Will, do you really want me to come in? I know what you wear to bed, remember?'

He smiled but pulled himself up. Summer liked to take charge, adjusting his clothing. Taking his hand at each opportunity last night. He could hardly complain, these were all normal things a woman might do to a man she was intimate with.

He remembered the way her hands felt on him as she spun him around to sign the contract across his back. How they felt unbuttoning his shirt and smoothing his collar. He felt the muscles tingle across his chest.

He wouldn't put it past her to come barging into his room if she thought they were late.

'I'm up,' he yelled as he swung his legs out of bed.

Will showered and dressed and came out to an enormous fruit platter and thankfully, a large pot of coffee, but Summer only gave him time to gulp down a few mouthfuls before she started hurrying him along again.

'We're late.'

Summer was wearing a short floral dress with thin straps. Her hair was tied up into a loose bun on her head, exposing the pink skin on her neck and shoulders. It would be smooth to touch. Warm to his lips.

But not for you. You made a deal, remember?

'So?' Will said. 'We'll just tell them we slept in.'

'But we'll miss the ferry.'

'You don't understand—we tell them that we *slept* in. It's perfect really. We have an excuse for being late that helps us.'

Summer sighed. 'I suppose so.'

They half ran up the road to the ferry port and saw Charlotte looking at her phone and Ben pacing.

As soon as he caught his breath Will said, 'Sorry we're late,' but Ben frowned.

The two women greeted one another with a kiss on the cheeks.

'We slept in,' Summer said, sheepishly and they exchanged furtive glances. The absurdity of the situation made him crack a smile and then she did too. And next she was giggling.

Ben rolled his eyes. 'Come on then, lovebirds. Try and keep your hands off one another.'

Will's stress levels began to dip, and he felt even more content when Summer reached over and picked up his hand. He squeezed hers. Mostly out of security. As long as they were holding hands no one was going to question their relationship. He liked the way her hand felt in his, not just the security of it but the promise it made. The promise to be by his side. The promise to help. The promise to stand by him.

She's pretending, that's all. None of this is real.

It wasn't real. Because he was paying her, an arrangement that had seemed natural that night in the hotel foyer, but now felt odd.

'Love isn't a business transaction,' she had said last night.

But this wasn't love.

This *was* a business transaction and he took comfort in that. He knew how business worked. It was love he had a problem with.

She's like any other of your employees. Off limits.

Ubud was pretty, but Will didn't enjoy it as much as Ben and the women seemed to, ducking in and out of shops and art galleries. The three of them were definitely in their element. Summer had, he realised with a sad gulp, more in common with his artistic, free-spirited brother than she did with him.

It was all right for Ben to gallivant over the world following his dreams, but Will had responsibilities. To his family. To his shareholders. To the world.

Focusing back on the mission at hand, at least for now, Will was confident that Ben and Charlotte were convinced that he and Summer were, indeed, a couple.

While the women lingered in a craft shop, Ben scuffed his feet outside it. Out of nowhere he turned to Will and said, 'Summer seems lovely. Don't take this the wrong way, but she's not the sort of woman I imagined you with.'

Will's shoulders tensed. 'What's that supposed to mean?'

Ben took a step back, 'Nothing, really. I guess I imagined you with someone more corporate. But it's good really.'

The day was warming up and Will suggested they grab a

beer together while they waited. The brothers took a seat on the deck of a small bar overlooking the bustling street.

Over the beers, they chatted about Gus. And their mother. And caught each other up on the goings on of other family members, aunts, uncles and cousins, some of whom would be flying in for the wedding as well. Then Ben said, 'Does Mum not approve of Summer?'

He wouldn't let this go.

'She's surprised. Like you, but she doesn't disapprove. She seems happy I'm dating someone.'

'And was Dad?' Ben asked.

The air stilled at the mention of their father. The man who, more than anyone or anything, was the reason for the current coolness between them. As kids they couldn't have been closer, but as they grew older and it became clear that Will's future lay with the business and that Ben had other plans, the brothers' lives had diverged and they'd become increasingly distant. Did it really have to be like that?

They hadn't spent much time together around the funeral; Ben's visit had been short. He'd spent most of the visit with his mother making the funeral arrangements and Will had been working around the clock, attending to the business implications following their father's sudden passing.

'Dad never met her. You didn't have to have known Dad well to know that he wouldn't have approved.'

'Right,' Ben said, but he didn't sound convinced. He knew something was up.

Will had thought Diane would be the most difficult audience, but it was proving to be Ben. Ben who had barely spoken to him in a decade. Ben who still resented the fact that Will and their father had had a special bond. Ben who, even after all this, seemed to understand Will better than anyone in the world.

They'd grown up together, shared all their childhood secrets and despite a decade of separation it was harder to lie to Ben than anyone. For a crazy second, he contemplated telling Ben everything but stopped himself just in time.

Ben sipped his beer and winked at Will.

What the hell did he mean by that?

No. He had to keep this just between him and Summer. She was the only one he could trust to keep this secret. *Trust. Really? You've barely known her two weeks.* He felt himself slipping, letting down his guard. But he had to remain alert. He couldn't trust anyone, too much was at stake.

They all squished around a small table at lunch, Ben and Charlotte on one side and he and Summer sharing a small bench on the other. Summer's hip pressed happily and reassuringly, against his. The conversation was light, superficial. About the things they had seen, where they would go next. But when Summer got up to use the bathroom, Charlotte leant over the table and said, 'Okay, quick. Spill. How serious are you and Summer?'

Will nearly choked on his pad thai. 'What?' That was not a question he'd rehearsed an answer to.

'You'll have to excuse Charlotte. That was an impertinent question from someone you hardly know,' Ben said.

Will's heart rate began to return to normal, relieved he wasn't going to be forced to answer the question, but a grin grew over his brother's face and Ben continued, 'But a perfectly acceptable question for your brother to ask. How serious are you and Summer?'

Will knew his face was bright red and only partly due to the chili in his lunch. 'We're serious. We've been together for...'

'Yes, years. But you never introduced her before now,' Charlotte said.

First the doubt from Ben about his and Summer's relationship, and now from Charlotte too. Just when Will was beginning to think that the trip was going well. And to top it all off, Summer wasn't here. He couldn't just explain this question away with a kiss.

'I love her,' Will blurted, without thinking of the consequences. Or of how saying those words might make him feel.

I love her.

Something released in his chest as he spoke the words; he felt lighter, freer. Stronger, somehow. Of course he didn't love her. He liked her, very much, as a friend.

I love her.

Will didn't like to lie. He downright hated it. It usually made his heart race and his skin sweat, but once he saw the smile on Charlotte's face, the grin on Ben's and the glance they exchanged, his heart rate in fact, slowed considerably.

It was that easy.

'You'd better bring her to visit us in London then,' Ben said.

Will nodded. At this point it was preferable to go along with whatever they said and not risk anything else. 'That would be great.'

He expected his heart rate to increase, for the sweats to begin at his further lie, but neither thing happened.

'Yes, that would be fantastic. Ben has heaps of room at his place. Oh, you really should visit, Summer's never been.'

Will nodded again. Calmly. He was getting too good at this lying business. It was coming too naturally. Summer slid back into the seat next to him and his heart swelled. He moved closer to her. He'd missed her thigh pressing against his. Even in the heat, he wanted her touching him. That was so unlike him, but every moment she was next to him he felt content, less on edge.

'They were just asking when we're going to visit them in London.'

'Ahh. And what did you tell them, honey?'

The sound of that term of endearment felt just like that, sweet, syrupy sliding through his veins.

'Soon,' he replied.

'I'd love that.' She smiled at him now and he held her gaze, the pair of them understanding implicitly that the only way to save this situation was to focus on one another and forget that Ben and Charlotte and all of Ubud existed.

It was surprisingly easy to do.

Everything else around him fell away as he felt himself being drawn into Summer's sparkling green eyes. The world dropped away and he could almost imagine what it might be like to take Summer out in London.

Or Paris, or New York. Or even in Adelaide.

Summer was exhausted but strangely exhilarated as they got back onto the ferry. She'd had a fun day, and she'd been enjoying Charlotte and Ben's company so much there were times she'd forgotten why she was there. They were interested in many of the same things she was and it felt like she'd known them for ever and not just barely twenty-four hours.

Her feelings towards Will were more complex.

At times she felt close to him. Felt as though they were becoming friends. But then she had to remind herself that it wasn't real, none of it was. He was paying her to be there. She was no more than his employee. Any intimacy she might feel was simply due to the fact that she was pretending to be his girlfriend.

It was all in her own overactive imagination.

When they boarded the boat, Summer didn't take one of the narrow seats, instead she went to the bow of the boat, hoping a little bit of physical distance between them would help cool the confusing feelings she was having for Will.

Instead of taking a seat next to Ben and Charlotte, Will joined her at the bow of the boat and to her surprise, took her hand. He pulled her close, so close that she could feel the heat from his body and when he spoke into her ear to be heard over the loud hum of the engine, she felt his breath on her neck and a tingle slid down the side of her neck and into her chest.

'I think I may have messed up today with Ben,' he said.

'What do you mean?'

'He said he thought we made an odd couple, he's suspicious I didn't introduce you to my parents before this.'

'Oh, dear.'

Will's brother was right; they did make a very odd couple. This had been Summer's fear from the outset: that they were such an unlikely pairing no one could possibly believe they were together. He worked at the top of a high-rise; she worked on the street. He was driven by balance sheets and the bottom line; he craved order and certainty. She needed the more ephemeral things in life. Music, song, verse. Yet their bodies were inexplicably drawn together.

The salty ocean breeze rippled past them as the boat gently made its way across the narrow stretch of water between the islands.

Summer leant in to whisper into his ear. Would her breath feel the same on his neck as his had on hers, turning him into a quivering mess as his had done?

'It might be time to enact clause five point two,' she said.

When a confused look passed over his face, her heart dropped.

'Clause five point two?'

'The one about necessary physical affection to maintain the charade.'

'Ahh.' Understanding lit up his expression. His mouth was

mere inches from her ear. 'What do you think would be necessary?'

'Hand-holding is good. But we've done that, don't you think?'

He nodded slowly and let go of her hand, slipping it instead around her waist. She happily moved her body closer to his, pressed up against him. His body was hard, secure, and steady. She could stand like this all day.

'Like this?' she asked.

'Yes. Are they watching?' she asked as her back faced the rest of the boat.

'Furtively.'

'Perfect.' Summer slid her hand over Will's and up his bare arm. Feeling the firmness of it for the first time; it was warm and smooth and she felt his muscles tense beneath her touch.

'I like that,' Will said and for a second Summer let herself believe that he was referring to her touch and not her performance. But of course, he wasn't.

'It's a good start don't you think? But maybe something a little more. Did Ben sound very disbelieving?' she asked.

'He certainly sounded suspicious.'

His voice sent a wave rippling through her chest and into her belly.

'So maybe something a little more?' Summer shifted her body so that her right foot was between both of his, causing their bodies to be completely flush against the other's. Warm, firm and more excited than she'd felt in years.

Summer whispered into his ear, 'Are they still looking at us?'

'I don't know. If I looked at them, that would spoil everything. I'm supposed to be madly in love with you. I'm supposed to not be able to keep my eyes off you.'

'Good point,' she said.

She felt excited, on a precipice. But if she moved in and

kissed him, would it be too much? If she kissed him, would she be able to stop? Summer slid her hand up his arm to his shoulder. She stopped there and waited for a reaction from him, but he didn't move his eyes from hers. Summer slid her hand up the smooth skin of his neck and her fingers slipped into his hair. His eyelids lowered. Their breath mingled.

An actual kiss is just a formality now, she reasoned, and she lifted her lips the remaining millimetres to meet his.

Will's body was immobile against her. It was just a stage kiss. She'd done those before, where choreography required it, and that's all this would be. She moved her lips against his, chaste, tongueless, mouth closed. His arms tightened around her and her knees threatened to buckle.

This was good; this was fine. It was just an act.

Except that the kiss Will gave her back was not a stage kiss; his mouth opened, his tongue sought out hers. Sweeping, swooning, consuming, she opened her mouth to him and dipped her head back to allow Will to deepen the kiss even further. He tasted of the ocean air and escape and everything in her life seemed to click into perfect place. This was where she was meant to be. This was how she was meant to spend her life.

I want to be able to do this with him all the time.

With that thought, she pulled away. The fantasy had clearly overtaken her and was too much for her to handle.

This was *pretend.*

She caught her breath and waited for her heart rate to resume a beat that would allow her to look Will in the eye again.

Whoa.

She'd never in her life had a kiss like that.

If that was what he did when he was pretending, what would it feel like if he meant it?

Will coughed and looked down, also unable to meet her gaze.

Clause five point two.

Wow.

She was in big trouble if that was what clause five point two was going to involve.

Whoa.

Will pulled away from Summer, his head spinning, the floor unsteady beneath his feet. What had just happened?

Clause five point two. Whose idea had that been to agree to physical gestures in public necessary to maintain that charade? That's right. His.

Only the way he'd kissed Summer had gone far beyond what had been necessary. He'd fallen into the kiss; he'd been the one to open his mouth. He'd taken the kiss to another level. He'd been the one who had breached the contract. Summer looked down. Coughed to clear her throat. She clearly thought they'd gone too far as well.

He stepped away from her but instantly grabbed the railing at the edge of the boat, his knees unsteady, his hands shaking. They couldn't do that again. They had to do everything they could to convince his family they were madly in love without kissing, maybe without even touching. He didn't trust himself to even hold her hand without spinning her into his arms. He certainly didn't trust himself to hug her without sliding his hand around her waist and pulling her soft curves against him.

Most annoying of all when he finally did glance over to where his brother and Charlotte were sitting, they weren't even watching. He'd stepped over a line, risked everything, and for nothing. He had to regroup, get his head together, because right now his thoughts were a scattered mess.

'How about we have a night in? I mean, so we can have a break from pretending.'

He spoke quickly, the words came out in a rush, before he even knew what he was saying.

'I mean, so we can relax and not put on a show.'

Summer's shoulders relaxed. 'That would be great.'

'I can order dinner. If you like. Something local?'

'That sounds perfect,' Summer said, but she turned away from him and looked over the water, to where the ferry was slowly pulling into the pier on Nusa Lembongan. He might want to reach over and place his hand on her shoulder, but he couldn't. If that pretend kiss had proven anything it was just how dangerous kissing Summer for real would be.

CHAPTER SEVEN

SUMMER TRIED TO read the novel she'd brought with her for the trip, but the words bled together. Their kiss kept clawing its way back into her thoughts. And into her body. Was it any wonder? That kiss! Her body tightened just thinking about it, just remembering his arms around her, his hands sliding down her back, and up into her hair. His full lips brushing against hers, their pressure getting heavier and heavier, her being unable to stop her body collapsing against his. His hard and powerful, hers soft, pliant. Willing.

It wasn't just her imagination.

They both should've pulled away much sooner than they did. There was no doubt left in the mind of anyone on that boat that they were into one another.

Summer put the book down and stood. She was hot. Tropical heat plus an impossible attraction? She needed to cool her body down so she could think straight. The sparkling water of the pool beckoned.

She'd packed a sensible one-piece swimsuit—she was here on a professional basis after all. She retrieved it from her case and put in on with some sunscreen, and ventured cautiously out of her room, looking around for any signs of Will. After they had arrived back at the villa, they had both excused themselves. She'd told him she needed a rest and he hadn't argued. Both of them knew they were overdue for a timeout.

Seeing no sign of Will, Summer walked out to the pool.

She sat on the edge and lowered her feet in, the water temperature was just cooler than her body temperature. She slipped gratefully into and under the water, stretching her limbs out into some lazy laps. That was better. The water cooled her body until her brain was thinking straight again. *It's just an act, it's just pretend.* They may have got a little carried away, but they were both healthy, attractive thirty-somethings, was it any wonder? It might be an act, but did that also mean they couldn't enjoy themselves? Was there a rule that said they couldn't?

Oh, that's right there was. Clause six.

Did that mean they couldn't have sex or did it just mean sex wasn't part of the deal?

No, clause six meant No Sex. It was there to protect them both.

Summer looked up from the pool and there he was. Her core temperature spiked again. That wasn't entirely her fault. Will wasn't wearing very much; a pair of shorts, but nothing else apart from a grin. His shoulders were broad, swimmers' shoulders. Of course, since that was his preferred mode of exercise. His pecs were well defined, and his stomach flat and perfect. She turned her eyes away before she looked any lower.

'Hey,' she said, 'I was just getting out.'

'You don't have to. We have some time before dinner.'

'Great,' Summer said, but she scrambled out of the pool anyway.

Clause six. Clause six. She'd be in danger of breaching this contract if she stayed around him half-dressed for much longer. 'I was just going to have a quick shower.'

Summer went to her room and stepped in the shower, turning the water onto its coldest setting. After, she threw on a loose, casual dress, the least flattering item she could find in her suitcase and tried again to read her book while she listened out for the door and their dinner.

The food, a wonderful spread of satays, salads and rice, arrived and was laid out for them on the deck by the pool. She noticed a cold bottle of rosé was delivered with the meal.

Will got out of the water, dried himself off with a towel, then sat at the table as he was. Could he not put a shirt on?

Summer swallowed. Great. Will's beautiful torso was going to be her dining companion. He poured her a glass of wine and she sipped it, gratefully.

Focus on his face.

Unfortunately, looking at his beautiful eyes made her tummy flip. The sight of his lips just made her think of the kiss...

She focused on her meal. They ate the delicious meal in silence. When the silence changed from companionable to downright awkward, Summer asked, 'What's on tomorrow?'

'I'm not entirely sure, only that Mum told us not to make plans and to bring our party shoes.'

'What do they have planned, do you think?'

'Your guess is as good as mine.'

Summer sighed and looked out at the view. Anywhere but in Will's general direction.

'We've done fine so far,' he said. 'We've had a few bumps, a few close calls, but I think they are believing us. We haven't yet given them a reason not to.'

'Is this a midproject pep talk?'

'Something like that. You covered my not telling you about Georgia—thank you again—and we put on a sufficient show for Ben and Charlotte, that they don't suspect anything.'

'As long as we stay together, we should be able to deal with anything. Do you notice that things go wrong when we're separated?'

'That's true. We'll stick together.'

She made the mistake of turning her focus back from the ocean and he smiled at her. Everything inside her turned upside down.

Summer got up quickly from the table and started clearing the remains of their meal.

'Leave it. I'm not paying you to clean. Let's just sit over there and relax.'

Will refilled her glass and then disappeared to his room, returning moments later wearing a T-shirt.

Summer exhaled.

They sat on the daybeds by the pool and he asked her more about her grandfather and the guitar, and how she got into busking. Will sat forward, attentive as she told him all about how she'd always loved music as a child, how she'd been writing songs since as long as she could remember. He asked her about her writing process, what she loved about performing and despite her earlier resolutions to keep an emotional distance between her and Will, she found herself relaxing into the wine and conversation and the mood.

They finished the bottle and kept talking. When he suggested opening another, Summer was about to say yes, but a voice in the back of her head said, *Keep your distance. Stay professional.*

'I'm actually exhausted and might call it a night. I'm worried about what tomorrow will entail.'

'Yes, that's probably sensible.'

Summer stood and Will mirrored the move. They stood, facing one another, lit only by a table lamp from a room inside the villa and the moon.

'Thank you for a successful day,' he said.

'You're welcome. It was a pleasure.'

Pleasure? What was she saying. Parts of the day had been awkward, but there were no doubt parts, the part on the ferry in particular, that had definitely involved pleasure.

She stepped towards him, unsure why. 'Goodnight.' She contemplated giving him a quick kiss goodnight. On the cheek only. After the day they had shared it felt strange to part with only a nod. But she stopped herself just in time.

Will reached over and took a lock of her hair between his thumb and index finger. He twisted it through his index finger and studied it closely, as though weighing up two serious options.

Summer held her breath.

He was going to kiss her again.

But he didn't. He sighed and dropped her hair and stepped away.

'It's been a long day. You probably want some time to yourself.'

She did. And yet she didn't.

Summer wanted to see Will Watson lose some control. And then she realised she wanted to be the one to cause it.

And not just for show, but because they both wanted to. Because they both couldn't possibly do anything else.

Summer woke early, unable to settle her thoughts. Or the stirrings in her bones. There was no way she was getting back to sleep and she was hungry. She hovered outside Will's door. He was inside, probably still in bed.

Probably still naked.

Summer shook herself. Letting her thoughts drift in that general direction was the last thing she needed to do. Especially after yesterday's stage kiss that had quickly spiralled out of control.

It was still early. Diane's surprise event wasn't due to begin until lunchtime. Until then she was on her own. Except not exactly: she and Will had agreed to stick together all day, that way it was far less likely they would raise suspicions. They were stronger together.

But Will was asleep and she was jumpy.

And hungry.

Breakfast and coffee. That's what she needed and when she got back Will would hopefully be dressed. She put on a long skirt and a singlet and let herself quietly out of the villa.

Summer loved Bali. Even if it meant spending the week in a state of suspended sexual tension, she was visiting a beautiful place. She found a small cafe and ordered a coffee. She took out her notebook and opened a fresh page, feeling inspired.

But what to focus the song on? The tension? The longing? Or the beauty in this tropical paradise? The absolute impossibility of her and Will having anything resembling a real relationship. Because what they had, even the attraction, wasn't real. It was their minds playing tricks on their bodies.

That was all. It happened to actors all the time, as the gossip magazines showed. Every week a new pair of co-stars fell for one another, by the next week they had spilt.

Lost in these thoughts, Summer looked up and saw Charlotte. She waved.

Having breakfast with Charlotte was not in line with their new 'stick together' policy but it was unavoidable. It would look far worse if she didn't ask Charlotte to join her. Charlotte sat down gratefully.

They ordered their breakfast, a delicious chicken and rice for Summer and a sweet Indonesian porridge for Charlotte. As long as she kept the conversation to Charlotte, and not on her and Will, things would be just fine. But Summer had no such luck.

'I just don't know about Ben and Will,' Charlotte said.

'Their relationship, you mean?'

'Yes! What happened? I get the feeling the brothers used to be so close, but then their father was pretty awful to Ben and I think Will was forced to choose. What do you think?'

'I think… I think it's something Will is very touchy about.'

'Exactly! Ben too. But you must know something. What's he told you about his childhood?'

Oh, no…

Charlotte leant forward, eyes wide, obviously expecting a detailed description of the Watson brothers' childhood. She'd asked Will this, but his silly spreadsheet had failed to cover it. There was tension there, though she didn't really understand why. She did know that Will had admired his father very much, though strangely telling Charlotte all these things felt like breaking a confidence, even though it would prove she had a certain level of intimacy with Will.

'He doesn't like to talk much about it.' This was true.

'I know, same with Ben. And I know they both had very different relationships with their father, but they've let it come between them. Which is sad.'

Summer nodded.

'I know Will loved his father. Idolised him.'

'But they were good friends as kids, weren't they? What's he told you about when they were younger?'

Once Summer got out of there, she vowed not to let Will out of her sight until the end of the trip.

'Not a lot. He's really funny about it.'

'And you've been together what, two years?'

'About that. But…'

Charlotte's eyes widened and her jaw dropped hanging on whatever was going to come out of Summer's mouth after 'but'.

If only Summer knew.

'But I know he was happy as a kid. I think the problems with Ben started later, when they were older.'

Charlotte fell back in her seat.

'He does love Ben—I'm sure of it,' Summer added.

'What makes you say that?'

'He has one of Ben's paintings in his office. A huge one. Of the beach. Ben's really talented.'

Summer noticed Charlotte's cheeks redden and she began to wonder if Ben and Charlotte's relationship was really as platonic as Charlotte and Ben both claimed. Summer asked her more and Charlotte confessed that things between the two old friends were complicated, not least because Charlotte had once been engaged to a man who'd died tragically and Summer sensed this was maybe a big factor preventing Ben and Charlotte from being together romantically.

They ate and chatted until Charlotte said, 'Oh, here's Diane.'

'Just the two women I wanted to see. I need you both to come with me.'

Summer thought of Will. *Whatever happens, stick together.* 'I've got to get back to Will.'

'He'll understand. The bride always gets her way three days before the wedding. You leave him to me.'

With a ball of dread in her stomach, Summer followed Diane and Charlotte.

Just like their first night in Bali, Will had trouble drifting off to sleep. Auburn-haired beauties kept creeping back into his consciousness. One auburn-haired beauty in particular. The one who was only two sheets of artistically carved wood away from him in the second bedroom. It was late again by the time he fell asleep and later still when he woke.

It was unlike him to sleep in; usually he was up with the sun for a swim before getting to the office by seven thirty. In Bali his important mission, his one and only job, was Summer. And proving to their family that they were madly in love with one another. And yet he'd slept in.

He pulled on shorts and went looking for her.

He opened his bedroom door to find his mother sitting

on the couch, scrolling through her phone. She beamed and stood when he walked out.

'I'm sorry, sweetheart, but I've stolen Summer away.'

'What do you mean?' They were meant to stick together! That was the plan.

Diane laughed.

'Relax, I'll give her back. She's coming to my hen's afternoon. I want to spend some quality time with her. Get to know her.'

Hen's afternoon? Summer and Diane unsupervised. The lack of control over the situation increased his heart rate. They had agreed to stick together.

'Can I come too?'

'Can't stand to be away from her for a moment?' Diane grinned.

'No. I mean, yes.' Did that question even have a correct answer?

'Well, either way, it's too bad. You're going to Gus's thing. With Ben.'

Will knew he was beaten. He'd have to trust Summer to hold her own. And he could, couldn't he? Summer wasn't silly. He knew her well enough by now to know that she was clever. And wise. After a few near slip-ups, they'd shared more about themselves and were getting to know one another. Maybe not as well as a couple who had been together for two years, but they were more than strangers now—they were becoming friends. Summer would be fine.

He was the one who was going to have the bigger challenge, dealing with grumpy Ben. His brother was physically incapable of looking at Will without a scowl.

'But first, talk to me.' Diane patted the couch next to her.

Will sat down reluctantly. This wasn't going to be good.

'Sweetheart, Summer is lovely. I'm not sure why you kept her such a secret.'

'I…' He couldn't finish the sentence. He'd almost forgotten what lie they were meant to be telling around this.

'I'm so glad we have met her, however inadvertently. I hope it means that you'll spend more time with her,' Diane continued.

'What do you mean?'

'You've been using work as a distraction, as an excuse not to have a life. I hope that will end now that Summer has met your family. Now she can be much more a part of your life.'

Will's heart dropped. Meeting Summer, having her here for the wedding, wasn't the end game. As far as Diane was concerned, it was just the beginning.

'You seem happier.'

He did? He felt uptight. Anxious.

'You're more like you were when you were younger. Before you went into the business.'

Will wasn't sure what his mother was getting at.

'Did it change me that much?'

'It didn't change you exactly, but it brought out certain qualities. Ambition. Drive. All good qualities in moderation.'

What was wrong with being ambitious? It's what his father had always encouraged him to be.

'When you're with Summer, you seem more in tune with what's going on around you. Less like your father.'

His mother's words stung. 'What was wrong with Dad?'

Diane took his hand. 'You know I loved your father. Very much. But he didn't always know how to control his ambition. He didn't have a sense of balance in his life. And I see that with you as well. Ambition is fine, but you shouldn't let it control you. You need to make room for pleasure and kindness in your life too.'

Was she saying he was rude? He never wanted to be unkind. Just the opposite. He wanted to help! Why couldn't anyone see that?

'The business is important. The work is important. Keeping plastics out of the oceans is important—'

'Of course it is. But you know something, so are you. You're important. And you're important and special regardless of what happens to the business. And Summer, bless her, sees that in you.'

For a second his mother's words lit a light in his chest. Summer liked him.

Summer thinks you're special.

Then he remembered his mother only had part of the story. Summer was only *pretending* to like him.

His shoulders slumped and Diane squeezed his hand again.

'I'm sorry you didn't feel as though you could introduce her to us.'

Oh. That's what this was really about.

'I know you think your father wouldn't have understood, but I do, sweetheart. I think she's wonderful and exactly the person you need in your life.'

Will, sadly, was starting to think that too.

It was just his luck. The first person he was drawn to in years was exactly the one he'd agreed to keep his hands off.

Summer watched Charlotte leave the hen's afternoon. She'd been partying with Diane and her friends for the last six hours. They'd enjoyed a long, leisurely lunch at one of the island's upmarket beachfront bars, but Summer had been unable to fully relax, on alert for the constant queries from Diane, her friends and Charlotte about her and Will. Surely, she'd done enough? Served her time. She thought of Will, probably going out of his mind. He'd been peppering her with regular text messages asking how it was going and her answers of Fine, Great and Really, it's all fine hadn't seemed to allay his fears. He sent another saying, Let me know when you're leaving.

Instead of responding, she went over to Diane and told her that she'd be heading off shortly. 'To see Will,' she said. This had the dual effect of making Diane happy and telling Summer to leave.

Back at the villa, Summer was surprised to open the door and find Will, sitting on the couch, a glass of water in front of him, his phone in his hand and a worried expression on his face.

'Hi,' she said. 'I thought you'd still be at Gus's.'

'I thought we agreed to stick together,' he said.

'I know we did, but I could hardly say no to your mother. She made Charlotte and I go and help her set up for the lunch and then put gift bags together for everyone.'

Will rubbed his palm over the stubble on his chin and cheek and Summer wondered what it would feel like to do the same.

'How did it go?' he asked, standing. 'Do they suspect anything?'

Summer stepped towards him and rested her hand on his foreman. 'Relax, it was fine. I just told your mother I was leaving early to come and see you and I don't think I've seen her more excited.'

'There's a "but" isn't there?'

Summer contemplated not telling him about her conversation with Charlotte, but so much was riding on it for him and he could tell she was holding something back.

'I spent a lot of time with Charlotte.'

'Yes?'

'And she was quizzing me about your childhood and Ben's. She thinks there's a big rift between the pair of you and I couldn't answer her.'

Will stepped back and began pacing. 'What did you say?'

'I said you didn't like to talk about it. That I thought you were happy as kids but had drifted apart as you got older.'

'Do you think she believed it?'

'I don't know.'

'So now she'll wonder why I haven't ever talked to you about it.'

'Yes, but I didn't even have to lie. Any time I ask you about your brother, you get your back up.'

'So you think she suspects about us?'

'Look, I just don't know. I answered as best I could. But I do feel you're holding things back. I know we haven't known one another that long, but if this is going to work...'

'I've been sharing things with you.'

'Yes, but only the outline. I don't understand why you're finding it so hard to trust me. I want to help. I don't want to mess this up for you. I really don't.'

It was so strange to admit it, but it was the truth. She'd become so invested in this charade, in helping Will. And in protecting his family. It might have started as a type of job, a way of earning some quick cash, but it had become much more than that.

'This isn't going to work if you don't share more with me about you.'

'There's not much else to say. You've seen the spreadsheet.'

'All that tells me is that you like order. It doesn't tell me much else. I don't know why aquamarine is your favourite colour. You say chicken burgers are your favourite food yet I've never seen you order one. You don't make any sense.'

Will's shoulders dropped and for a moment she thought he was going to turn and walk into his room. But after a few deep breaths he looked her in the eyes and said, 'My favourite colour is aquamarine because it's the colour of the ocean. I don't eat chicken burgers, or any fast food, because my father died of a stroke aged sixty. And my favourite television show is *The Golden Girls* because I watched it with my grandmother. Are you happy now?'

Charlotte bit her lip to stop herself smiling. Her heart was melting and she wanted to hug him. But he wasn't done.

'And?'

Will looked skyward. 'And Ben and I used to be so close, but as we got older Dad hated the fact that Ben didn't want to join the business, he saw it as a type of rejection. Ben was hurt by his reaction and I was stuck in the middle. I should have made more of an effort to maintain my relationship with Ben, but I was a foolish young kid and I didn't and I regret it. And I'm not sure how to make it up.'

Summer walked up to him and kissed him on the lips.

She shocked even herself with her audacity and pulled back slightly. His eyes were wide, pupils dilated. Full of shock. She expected him to push her away. But he didn't. He wrapped his arms around her and pressed his mouth back on hers. Her lips parted, her body fell into his, remembering the kiss on the boat, needing him, wanting, with every cell in her body, to be wrapped up completely with him.

Their lips tugged and pushed, pressed, and teased. She felt his hands slide up her back, into her hair. She felt his body harden, the air in the room shifted.

Everything had changed.

CHAPTER EIGHT

IT WOULD'VE BEEN easier to fly under his own steam than tear himself away from Summer. Will needed her lips like he needed air. Surrounded by her touch, her scent, he didn't know which way was up.

But eventually the pounding in his veins, the throbbing of his body and the feeling that his legs might give way from the lack of air, made him pull back slightly.

And when he did, the spell was broken.

Panting, Summer stepped back and looked away.

That was amazing, he wanted to say. But good sense stopped him. It might have been amazing, but it wasn't part of their deal. He'd crossed a line and he wouldn't blame her for walking out right now.

She kissed you first, remember?

Yes, but the kiss Summer had given him had been a chaste peck compared with the full-body ravishing he'd just given her.

'I'm so sorry—I don't know what came over me,' he said.

'We just got confused. That's all. It's natural when you're playing a part, isn't it?' She was still catching her breath.

She was the performer, she would know.

'So, we should scratch it up to a blurring of our roles? Taking our act too seriously?' he asked. He wasn't an actor; he'd never even been comfortable stretching the truth. The kiss had felt real to him. As real as any other kiss he'd ever had, if not more so.

His body had taken over, his heart had expanded and rational thought was an afterthought. He didn't want to let her go, for a few moments he couldn't imagine breathing without her.

No, it wasn't real. A trick of his hormones. Or the tropical air.

It hadn't been real because who was he to be the judge of what was a real kiss or not? Georgia had told him she'd loved him and how had that turned out? He didn't know what was real. He didn't know the first thing about Summer's feelings, or even his own.

She was right: they had been pretending and had just been caught up in the act.

'It's been a fairly intense couple of days, don't you think?' she said.

'Definitely.'

'So, we just need to step back, take a break. Regroup?'

His thoughts exactly. 'Yes, I agree.' He could have hugged her for being so understanding. But that would have got him into deeper trouble. He wasn't sure he'd be able to let her go next time.

Summer continued, 'And just to be clear, we agree this is a business arrangement. It's not real.' She was running her hands through her hair, the straps on her dress were askew and all he wanted at that moment was to scoop her up, take her to his room and relieve her of her dress and its wayward straps.

Instead, he lied, 'Of course it's not real.'

'Of course not, because we have a deal.'

'Rest assured—I don't do relationships.' It was difficult to speak, he was still out of breath. It felt like something was pressing heavily on his chest.

'So, a break? Regroup later?'

He nodded and Summer turned and fled to her room.

He was in serious, serious trouble. He'd messed up.

He took a deep breath and the panic lifted somewhat. No,

it was okay. He just wouldn't do it again. He could control himself. Summer might be gorgeous and, yes, he admitted reluctantly, he was attracted to her. Very much.

But he could also stay professional.

He had to.

Will went to his own room and closed the door on the rest of the villa, and Summer. He just needed some time to himself. Time to breathe. He undressed and got into the shower, making the water as cold as he could get it. Which unfortunately, wasn't quite cold enough. His body still burned when he thought of kissing Summer. And as long as his body was this warm, he couldn't help but think of Summer.

He dressed in shorts and a T-shirt and lay on his bed with his phone. Summer had been right: he hadn't shared enough of himself with her. First, failing to tell her all about Georgia and now, not telling her much about Ben.

To be fair, he hardly spoke to anyone about Ben. That part of his life and those feelings had been tucked away somewhere. It was easier to just let them sit there and not deal with them. He was busy. He had important work to do and Ben didn't understand that.

But not only had he failed to share things with Summer, he hadn't got to know her as well as he should have. Ben and Gus had asked him questions today about Summer's music and he hadn't been able to answer them.

He looked up Summer on social media. It wasn't the first time; after making the deal with her he'd dutifully followed all her accounts. But this was the first time he'd actually thought to look up one of her songs. He realised his mistake. He should be familiar with her music; it was such a big part of *her* life.

Seeing Summer's beautiful face, he clicked on one of her videos. She was sitting in an armchair in a room, in front of a wall covered in photographs, guitar on her lap. She looked down at her guitar and not at the camera, strumming gently, her fingers moving hypnotically over the strings.

The song was happy, sweet. It had been uploaded a year ago. When she was still with that jerk Michael. Will's chest constricted.

He hated that she'd felt this way about someone who'd hurt her.

He hated that she'd felt that way about someone who wasn't him.

Which was ridiculous, because he didn't even know Summer a year ago.

The latest songs were also sad. But also, angry. Raw. As you would be if your lover had taken your car and your grandfather's guitar. You'd be upset if someone stole an important part of your livelihood as well as an item of immense sentimental value.

Will lay on his bed, watching song after song. Captivated. Utterly addicted. Letting her beautiful voice wash over him and the lyrics swell his heart.

Doing absolutely nothing to cool him down.

Summer knocked firmly on Will's door. If he really did sleep naked then she didn't want to go barging in.

Or maybe she did. Though that would be wrong. And definitely not part of the deal.

'Will, you need to get up.'

Summer too would have been happy to go back to bed. What she'd experienced last night in her bedroom could not have been called sleep. Every time she'd felt herself drifting off, her body would recall the kiss she and Will had shared and jolt her alert and awake.

She'd never experienced a kiss like it. The way the world shifted when his lips were on hers, the way her bones seemed to melt under his touch. The desire began to rise in her again now but she batted it away. Again.

She knocked on his door again. 'We're meeting your mother for breakfast and we want to get out of here before she arrives on our doorstep and sees we slept in two beds last night.'

The door flew open before Summer could step out of the way and she was suddenly nose to nose with Will.

Both jumped back as though they had been jolted by an electric shock.

They arrived at the cafe to find Diane and Gus leaning close, foreheads touching over a menu. Will looked at Summer and she nodded. No matter what had happened between them last night, they had a job to do. He picked up her hand. They strode in together, hands clasped.

Diane looked up and smiled broadly. She stood and pulled her son into a hug. Will closed his eyes as he hugged her and something snagged in Summer's chest. Will was about a foot taller than his mother and their hug was full of affection.

She didn't want Diane to find out that her son had lied; she wanted everything to be okay between them. She wanted Will to be happy.

They sat, ordered breakfast, and then Gus asked, 'What are you two lovebirds doing today?'

'I have some work to do,' Will said, colour rising in his cheeks.

The older couple frowned. 'You're meant to be on holiday, you do remember that don't you? We have people covering for you back home. They know to call you when it is absolutely something you need to do yourself,' Diane said. Then she turned to Summer. 'He's not a good delegator.'

Summer nodded. 'A bit of a control freak.'

Diane laughed. 'Isn't he just?'

Summer's chest warmed. She didn't always understand

him, but she was definitely getting to know him. Summer picked up Will's hand. He squeezed hers. An invisible force was pushing them together. Like an addiction. If her hand was not in his there was something missing.

Except that it's not real. It's only an act.

'You should go kayaking. Or surfing. Do you surf, Summer?' Gus asked.

'Not often,' Summer said.

'Really? Will loves to.'

'I know,' she said and leaned into him.

He smiled back at her. 'She prefers to watch me,' he said with a glint in his eye.

Summer laughed and her face went red. She'd never seen him surf, but suspected he was right; the view of Will on a surfboard would be something worth watching.

She leant over and kissed his cheek. It was daring, but felt right. It felt like something a flirty couple would do, and was that what they were meant to be? It was so easy to kiss him. And as long as they were physically affectionate with one another they were convincing as a couple.

'Oh, I know I've said it before, but it's so lovely to see you both together.' Diane's face was so earnest, Summer had to look away.

'Summer, I have a favour to ask. Will you help me get ready before my wedding? I won't keep you long from Will, but I need someone to pick up my flowers just before the ceremony and to zip me into my dress. And I'd love it if you would.'

Summer's stomach dropped. It was an honour…but…she looked up at Will. His face was frozen. She had to say yes, she couldn't not, but she could taste the bitterness of the lie on her tongue.

'I don't have a daughter and I'm not sure that Will or Ben want to help their mother into her dress.'

'I'd love to. It would be an honour.'

Diane exhaled. 'Thank you, the honour is all mine.'

Summer looked at Will and the pair exchanged forced smiles.

'So, surfing? Kayaking? What's it to be?' Gus said. 'Summer, you have to get this man to take a break.'

Summer was relieved to get back to the villa. This was their safe space, the place they could be themselves, with no need to pretend.

Will went to his room, no doubt to sneak in some work phone calls and Summer took her notebook out to the deck to work on some lyrics. She wrote down a few lines, even hummed a tune or two but longed for her guitar.

That's what this is all about, remember? In a few days you'll be home and you will have your guitar back. The thought sustained her, even as the only lyrics she could come up with were ones about first kisses. Longing. Forbidden desire.

She sighed.

'Hey,' Will said a while later, jolting her from her fantasy of kissing him in the pool. 'What are you up to?'

'Just making some notes. Thinking about a new song.'

'Great,' he said. 'Your songs are good.'

'How have you heard my songs?'

He held up his phone. 'Online. I looked you up.'

'Oh.'

'What kind of boyfriend would I be if I didn't know your songs?'

She nodded. She'd looked him up as well, but she still felt exposed that he'd listened to any of her old songs. Especially the ones about Michael, both the happy and the sad.

'They're really good. I didn't realise that you wrote that song for Ash Cooper.'

Cooper had been the biggest artist in the country a decade ago and the song she'd written had been one of his biggest hits.

'Yeah, well.' Summer pulled her knees up to her chest.

'That song was huge. You must still be earning royalties from it.'

She buried her face in her knees. She didn't want to hear this. Not from him, of all people. Not from Mr Carefully Drafted Contract. He'd know once and for all that she was a flake.

'What's the matter?' he asked.

'I signed away my rights to it.'

'What do you mean?'

'The copyright, all future royalties.'

'You got nothing?'

'They paid me one thousand dollars at the time. It was so much money and I didn't get anyone to look over the contract. I was so excited that he wanted to sing my song.'

'Oh, Summer.'

It was bad enough hearing the pity in his voice, she couldn't bear to see it on his handsome face as well. She pressed her face into her palms.

'Yes, I know, I should've been more careful. I should've got a lawyer. But I trusted him. I trusted them all. And I was so excited.'

Will didn't respond and she didn't look up, but eventually she felt the cushion next to her sag with his weight. He placed a hand gently on her shoulder. It didn't feel like pity, it felt like understanding.

'I'm so sorry.'

She lifted her head. 'I know—I don't even want to think about what might have been. How my life might have been different, so please don't try and tell me. I know it was a monumental mistake to not get someone to look carefully at the contract. Just like all the other mistakes I've made in my life.'

'We all make mistakes.'

'Yeah, I bet you never signed a contract so disadvantageous to you.'

He sighed. 'I've trusted the wrong people too.'

Georgia. He wasn't going to open her wound and she would do the same courtesy.

He'd trusted Georgia and been let down, just like she'd trusted Michael.

'It's a great song, Summer. And so are your others.'

Their gazes locked and her cheeks warmed. She was about to lean in and thought he was too.

Until now, *magnetism* has just been a word. But now she understood the cliché. When her hand wasn't on his arm, she was being pulled towards him, their bodies locked together.

No.

It was an act and it was confusing her.

The aim for this week was to convince Will's family they could be a couple, not to convince herself. The last thing she needed was to leave Bali with a crush on Will. That would be excess baggage she could not afford.

She got up. 'I just remembered I need to call my mum,' she said and went to her room.

Summer chatted with Penny for a while and then lay down. She read for a while but must have drifted off to sleep. When she woke, the sky was darkening and her stomach rumbled.

She opened her door and walked out onto the deck. Will was sitting on one of the daybeds, hunched over his phone.

'Are you still working?'

He turned to her and put his phone down, but not his tension. Will was coiled so tightly her own shoulders ached.

'Will, you seriously need to stop for a moment. Look at where you are.'

Will glanced towards the ocean then looked down again.

'Can you look me in the eyes and tell me you see a view as beautiful as this every day?'

Summer walked towards him and stood behind him. His square shoulders were magnificent but so tight. She reached down and lay her palms on them and squeezed. When he didn't react, she began to press and kneed, to search out the knots and massage them away. She wrapped her fingers around the front side of his shoulders, to the muscles below his collarbone and rubbed them as well, dragging her thumbs over the muscles in his back. He moaned and she froze. She should have asked first, shouldn't have just gone straight in, and started rubbing him.

He froze when she did.

'Sorry, that was presumptuous of me,' she said but didn't lift her hands.

'Don't stop. Unless you want to.'

She kept going. His flesh under hers felt so good, tight, but firm and strong. She could feel the tension ebbing away as she rubbed him.

'Summer, that feels so good.' His voice was almost a whimper. She wanted to lift his shirt and find the muscles lower down his back. Lower down his front. She settled with gently rubbing his neck, even going so far as to slip her fingertips into his hairline, touching his thick, soft hair.

Will turned and their gazes met, his eyelids heavy with want. He moved a hand up around her waist and pulled Summer onto his lap.

Every breath left her body and the air, already heavy with the afternoon humidity, weighed even heavier on them. It would be so simple to bridge those last inches to his lips, fall into this, let go once and for all. Will's arm slid up her back and into her hair too. She felt her body sway. She felt everything sway.

'At what point do we accept that there is something real here?' she asked.

'There can't be. I'm paying you.'

'I know. We agreed.'

Confusion creased his brow. 'We wouldn't be lying to them any more if this was real,' he reasoned.

She shook her head. No. That didn't make sense. They'd still be lying. Only the lie would be messier and harder to keep straight.

'We would. And it'd be harder to remember where the lie begins and where it ends.'

Will nodded; he leant forward but just rested his forehead on hers. He sighed.

'You and I…for real. It's impossible. We both know that,' she said.

'Why? Remind me again, because right now it feels so right.' He pulled back and smiled at her.

She smiled back.

'You're a billionaire, I'm a busker. You don't do relationships—you don't trust anyone. I just got my heart broken. Remember?'

He shook his head. 'Trivial details,' he said, but she knew he was joking.

With all her willpower, Summer pulled herself up and off his lap.

'Let's go out and get some dinner together. And then maybe watch a movie. Let's celebrate the fact that after today we only have two full days to get through.'

Will nodded. The wedding was the day after tomorrow and they were getting to the end of all the family obligations Will had. They couldn't relax, exactly, but there was every reason to think that they would successfully keep Will's lie a secret.

'It sounds like a plan, Summer Bright.'

* * *

At what point do we accept there's something real here?

Never, was his initial thought. Because there wasn't, there couldn't be. Yet she'd been sitting on his lap and he'd been seconds away from kissing her, hours after he'd sworn never to again.

They enjoyed a nice meal out and watched a movie together, talking for the third night in a row into the early hours. He enjoyed her company. They didn't have to spend so much time together when the others weren't around, but Will found himself enjoying the time he spent alone with Summer far more than the time he spent with his family. It wasn't just that the pressure to perform wasn't there, it was that Summer was becoming his friend. His confidant. She listened to him, without judgement and he was finding that it was natural to open up to her.

And he wanted to know all about her. Their lives were different, but that wasn't a barrier to friendship, he realised. She'd had so many experiences he couldn't have dreamt of: going on the road with the tribute shows, busking in central Adelaide, various odd jobs over the years, encounters with all sorts of people in the music industry. Her life had been fun, filled with laughter and happy applause from her audiences. He recalled from the night of the charity gala how much fun the audience had had. Summer brought joy to people's lives and he was in awe of that.

The next morning, as usual, Summer was up before him. She was sitting on the deck in a broad-brimmed hat and cute floral sundress.

I'm going to miss this.

He shook his head.

No, he wouldn't. It was going be a relief to get home and put this behind him. It would be a relief to stop lying.

She beamed when he sat down next to her.

'Morning. How did you sleep?'

'Like a log. You?' It was a white lie, like every other night they had been here he'd found it impossible to relax enough to sleep and thoughts of Summer kept sneaking back into his thoughts. And last night, into his dreams.

'Great. What's on the schedule today?'

'Nothing scheduled. I've told Mum I'll see her at some stage, but you don't have to come.'

'I'd be happy to. She might think it's strange if I'm not with you.'

He nodded. He had to focus on why she was here. Their charade had been working so far—it would be a shame to ruin it now.

Will checked his emails and Summer lay by the pool reading her book. He looked at her, jealously.

Working had never bothered him before. He'd enjoyed it; it gave him strength. It gave his life meaning.

You're on holiday.

Maybe his mother was right—he needed to remember he was on holiday. And maybe Summer was right as well. Did he use work as a distraction? Did he use work as an excuse not to have a life?

'Do you want to go surfing?'

Summer looked up from her book and her mouth dropped. 'Do you?'

'Yes, this is ridiculous—we've been here for four days and we haven't gone.'

'I haven't done it for ages.'

'You won't forget how.'

She laughed. 'Maybe not, but I'm not as young as I once was.'

Will looked at her. Summer had gorgeous curves, but her legs were lean and strong. 'You look pretty fit to me.'

Her face reddened. He'd meant to allay her fears, but

maybe he had crossed a line. But Summer was attractive. And fit and surely, she knew that? 'Let's go then. Now.' Suddenly there was nothing he wanted to do more. How long had it been? Ages. He'd been so caught up at work. He swam most mornings, but that was just in the pool at the bottom of his building and it had been too long since he'd felt the salt water of the ocean on his skin.

'Don't you have to work?'

'I am meant to be on holiday. I thought you'd think it was a good idea if I relaxed?'

She laughed. 'It would be. Let's do it.'

They passed Ben and Charlotte on their way to the beach.

'Hey, having a good day?' Summer asked them.

'Great,' Ben and Charlotte replied at once.

'We're just off to the beach. Do you want to join us?' Will asked. He didn't overthink it; his brother was here. Ben and Charlotte looked at one another and then nodded in unison. 'Yes,' they said.

'Great.' Will was with his brother for the first time in years; they should spend some time together, bridge the gulf between them. It wasn't too late.

Will was partly relieved, partly disappointed to see that Summer wore a long rashie over her swimsuit to protect her from the sun. It was probably sensible; her skin was pale and no doubt sensitive to too much sun. But it didn't stop him furtively admiring her curves and wishing for the hundredth time that day that they had met under different circumstances and he hadn't signed an ironclad agreement not to have a physical relationship with her. Or that he hadn't lied to his mother and his board about being in a relationship with her.

Yes, there were all kinds of reasons why they shouldn't have a physical relationship, but somehow, when he was around her, none of those reasons seemed to be very important.

They hired surfboards and Will made sure Summer remembered the basics.

When Ben and Charlotte arrived, Will and Ben took Summer out to the waves, the surf break being a decent paddle from the beach itself.

Ben hadn't been surfing for even longer than Will and the brothers naturally made fun of one another's rustiness, making Summer laugh. Ben also helped give Summer some pointers, and they all enjoyed the crystal-clear waters. The bobbing of the swell was calming and invigorating, Will scarcely wanted to get out of the ocean. This was such a good plan; they should have been doing this every afternoon.

Will, who hadn't been as sensible as Summer by wearing a rashie felt the skin on his shoulders start to tighten, a sure sign he needed to reapply sunscreen. He left Ben and Summer waiting for the next wave and paddled back into shore. After reapplying sun protection, he couldn't help himself but took his phone out to see how the markets had closed in Australia. Then, seeing that Ben and Summer were getting along so well he turned and made a quick phone call.

Will heard Charlotte gasp loudly. Then swear.

With his back to the ocean, he didn't see what she had seen, but when he swung back around all he could see was white foam and no sign of either Ben. Or Summer.

CHAPTER NINE

WILL DROPPED HIS phone and ran to the water. Lifeguards were also gathering and jet skis were being dragged to the water's edge. But there had been several dozen people out when the freak wave had hit. There were not many lifeguards.

Will strode into the water, but the swell was still too high, too choppy for him to be able to make out anything or anyone. Besides, the break was about fifty metres from the shore. Was he going to swim it? Or get his board?

He turned and went for his board, judging that he'd make up the time once he was back in the water. Once he had retrieved it and was heading back into the surf a lifeguard waved him back, but Will pretended not to understand, taking long strokes, and trying to battle his way toward the spot he'd last seen his brother and Summer.

A small dingy and some jet skis passed Will and he envied their speed as he headed slowly out towards the break, feeling sicker and sicker with each stroke.

Will soon realised how pointless it was, he couldn't see either Ben or Summer and the break was still so far away. How could he possibly find them?

Finally, one of the boats headed back, passed him and pointed to the beach. Will knew it was hopeless, with his chest burning he turned and swam back to the shore, panic rising even further with each stroke. By the time he reached the beach, exhausted and with his heart racing he was more terrified than he'd ever been in his life.

Please make her okay...please let her be fine.

He made so many deals with heaven he knew he'd never be able to repay all the promises he'd made to the universe at the moment. There was a lifeless body on the beach, the size and shape of Summer. He collapsed on the sand next to her, seeing for the first time that she was moving and coughing up water. He took her hand, not caring for a second what she was coughing up on him.

'It's going to be okay,' he whispered, as much to her as to himself.

When she had recovered enough to turn and focus on him, he pulled her into his arms and hugged her.

Summer hurt in about one million places. And a million more she didn't even know existed in her body. Her throat throbbed. Her eyes stung from all the salt water. Her leg hurt from where the surfboard had tugged and eventually broken free. And her right shoulder pounded for some reason she had absolutely no recollection of.

The whole incident was a blur. She remembered watching Ben, waiting for his next instruction, and then the sky had gone dark, like a cloud was passing across the sun. By the time she realised it was a wave, it was already on top of her, and there was barely enough time to take a breath, let alone brace herself.

The water had tossed her around and around until she didn't know which way was up. She'd scrambled in what she'd thought was the right direction, but couldn't reach air or even sand to be able to tell. Each time she thought she might be making progress the water would toss her in the other direction, and then nothing.

It was Will she saw first. She was on the beach, throat

stinging from coughing up half the ocean, her chest aching. She may have even vomited. Maybe even on Will. She wasn't sure. It was a while before she could open her eyes and actually focus and when she did, it was only one face she saw amongst all the others. He was sitting next to her, holding her hand. The second thing she noticed was the look in his eyes. It was terror.

For a second she thought, *Oh, my goodness, Ben. Something's happened to Ben.*

But then she realised Ben was also sitting next to her and watching with concern.

You. He's worried about you.

Summer was seen to by two paramedics who checked her over and asked her questions. Yes, she knew what year it was. It was a Friday. She was in Nusa Lembongan. And yes, she was okay, though when she tried to stand her knees gave way.

'I just want to rest. I'm fine,' she kept saying. And she felt that she was, just wiped out. Battered. But intact.

She lay back down on the sand, resting while everyone around her talked in various languages. She could just sleep there.

After a while, maybe minutes, maybe even seconds, Will shook her gently and said, 'We're going to take you to the medical centre to get you looked at. Can you sit? Do you think you can stand?'

At the clinic they gave her some paracetamol and anti-inflammatories and told Will to call immediately if her condition changed. Summer thought she understood everything well enough, but she felt that she could trust Will completely to remember all the instructions they gave him about medication and what to do. Summer let herself be led out of the medical centre and into a waiting taxi truck.

* * *

Diane was waiting for them back at the villa, pacing outside, but rushed over when she saw them. Will held one side of her and Diane took the other. Summer wanted to tell them both that she was fine and could walk by herself, but she let them lead her inside.

They sat her on the sofa, but what she really wanted to do was lie down.

At the medical centre, the nurse had helped her out of her swimming suit and into the sundress she'd worn over but she was suddenly conscious that she wasn't actually wearing any underwear under it.

'I'd like to get changed,' she said.

'Of course,' Diane said. 'Go help her,' she ordered Will.

Too exhausted to make an excuse for him, Summer let him lead her to her bedroom. The more time that passed, the easier it was to walk on her own, but she let herself be led into her room and to her bed.

Will closed her bedroom door and looked around. 'What do you want to wear?'

'PJs?'

'Good idea.'

He went to her suitcase, but she reached under her pillow to where she'd placed hers that morning and grinned at him.

'You can leave me, you know.'

Will grimaced, clearly torn. 'I can't really, you know. I need to keep an eye on you. I'll turn around.' Which he dutifully did.

'I'm not sure how that's helping,' she replied, but was also too sore to argue much. She tugged at her dress, but her shoulder snagged and she groaned. Will spun around and rushed to her. 'What is it?'

'It's just my shoulder. It hurts to lift my arm.'

She wanted to get out of the dress, it was damp and sandy

and itched her already aching body even more. If she was really being honest with herself, she really wanted a shower as well. She wanted a shower more than she wanted to hide her naked body from Will. 'I'll tell you what—if you promise to keep your eyes half-closed and instantly forget everything you see, you can help me.'

'I promise.'

'I think I want a shower though.'

'Okay, come with me.'

Summer almost laughed at Will's businesslike approach.

In the bathroom he started the shower then turned back to Summer. 'I'll close my eyes,' he promised.

'That could be worse—you'll have to feel your way.' She giggled.

He didn't laugh but his face reddened. He took the hem of her dress and then shut his eyes, keeping them closed as he lifted the dress over her head. It was loose, but she still felt a stab of pain as he pulled it over her head. She was grateful for the pain though as it stopped her from thinking about the fact that Will could at this very second be looking at her naked torso.

The shower was separated from the bathroom by a screen so she was out of his view, though he was still in the room. And she was glad of that. She didn't want to be alone. She let the warm water wash over her and through her hair, washing away the salt and whatever else the ordeal had left on her.

She turned off the water and reached for a towel, left in easy reach. She managed to dry herself effectively, even with her sore shoulder. The nurse had assured her it was probably just a soft tissue injury and would settle in a day or two. She wrapped the towel around herself and emerged.

'Okay?' Will asked.

'Yes. Much better.'

Back at her bed, she pulled her pyjama pants on under the

towel without too much trouble, but knew that getting the top over her head would be the challenge. She picked up the top and tried to lift it over her head.

Will pounced. 'Let me. I won't look.'

Summer didn't feel shy or even concerned that Will had any motive other than helping her. She trusted him. And she was totally comfortable. She stood.

He helped her manoeuvre her right arm into the armhole first and Summer managed the left. Then she let the towel drop and let Will help her get her head through the hole. The whole thing took less than ten seconds and when it was over, she felt like a new person, clean and mostly dry.

Her long thick hair was still wet and in the absence of drying it, she would usually pull it into a loose braid. She lifted her arm to do so, but again her shoulder snagged.

'What is it?'

'My hair.'

'What can I do?'

'You expect me to believe you're an expert in women's hairstyles?'

'I have many talents.' He smiled at her and something bloomed in her chest.

'Including hair?'

'No, not at all.' He smiled.

She laughed. 'Do you think you could help me with a basic braid, that will keep it out of my face?'

'I can try.'

She found her brush and a hair tie and sat with her back to Will. He was so gentle, so afraid of hurting her she had to reassure him that he could tug harder. As she sat there, with Will gently brushing and drying her hair she felt herself relax and all the worries of the past few hours began to slip away. After a while he presented her with a neat, perfectly suitable plait.

If he ever has daughters he will be able to take on hair duty, she thought. The image of a dark-haired little girl, with long curly locks and Will's beautiful eyes jumped into her mind. She squashed it away with a hint of pain. It wouldn't be her daughter whose hair he brushed and braided.

'You should lie down now. I'll get rid of Mum.'

Summer followed Will out of her room, doubtful Diane would leave without checking for herself that Summer was okay.

Seeing her freshly washed and ready for a rest, Diane moved in for a hug.

'I'm so glad you're fine. What a relief. Get some rest,' she said to Summer. She turned to Will, 'Look after her. Don't take your eyes off her.'

Diane kissed her lightly on the cheek and Summer went back to her bed.

'She's fine. I'll look after her,' she heard Will say.

'Of course. But let me know if there's anything I can do. Shall I come over with some dinner later?'

'Mum, it's the night before your wedding. You're meant to be having dinner with Gus's parent's, aren't you? We'll be fine.'

After seeing his mother off, Will came back to her room, but this time he waited at the door.

'You need to rest, but I don't want to leave you on your own.'

Summer imagined him stepping away from the door, going to his own room and didn't like the feeling that came over her. She patted the bed next to her.

'I could sit on the armchair.'

'I'd like you next to me.'

Will walked slowly into the room. 'Are you all right?'

'Yes, I'm fine. But I don't want to be alone.' The adrenaline and all the chemicals that had kept her going since the wave were wearing off; she was exhausted but also now left with the feeling of what a close shave she'd had. How lucky she'd been. But as long as Will was next to her she felt calmer. Secure. 'Can you stay here, please? Hold me?'

Without another word Will joined her on the bed. She lay on her side, facing away from him and he lay behind her, pulling her into a hug. She instantly felt better. Lying in Will's arms she knew everything would be okay.

Summer woke when the sun was low in the sky. She still ached, but her head was clear. She was in her bed, no longer being embraced, but could sense Will was still beside her.

She rolled over.

Will was next to her, propped up on some pillows and looking at his phone. He put it down when she turned.

'Hey, how are you feeling?'

Summer stretched, assessed her body. 'Not worse. My head feels better. I feel a bit fragile, but okay. Thanks for staying here with me.'

'Of course.'

'I don't know quite what came over me before.'

'Shock, probably.'

Yes, shock. That was it. Nothing more, or less. She'd needed his embrace.

She still needed it.

'I'm so sorry,' he said.

'What for?'

'I said I'd teach you.'

'And you did.'

'But I wasn't watching—I wasn't paying attention. I was working.'

'You went to get sunscreen!'

'But then I stayed and made a phone call. And that happened.'

Will blamed himself, but that was ridiculous.

'Ben was there.'

'I should have been there.'

Will's jaw was tight and his eyes hard. But she understood now that his aloofness, this barrier he kept against the world wasn't malicious, it was to protect him. She touched his arm gently. When he didn't flinch, she spread her fingers over his forearm and held it. 'I'm okay, everything's okay.'

Under her touch she felt his muscles soften. But just a little.

'I thought…for a moment… I thought you were dead.'

'But I'm not. I'm here.'

Hold me, she wanted to say again. *And never let me go.*

But Will seemed oblivious to her touch, still tortured by what had happened at the beach.

It was easier for her, in a way. She'd been knocked unconscious almost immediately and when she'd woken, she'd been on the beach, breathing. She thought of how she would have felt if their positions had been reversed. For Will, watching powerless from the beach, it would have been awful. Especially as control was something he clung to like a security blanket.

'You can't blame yourself—this sort of thing could have happened to anyone. It could have happened with you right there. You would've been wiped out too.'

'But I would've been watching.'

'Will, please, you've looked after me. You've been wonderful. Please stop worrying. I'm going to be okay.'

'Is there anything you need? Do you want to call your mother?'

Summer shook her head. 'No, I'll tell her all about it when I get back. For now, she'd only worry. What I do want though, is something to eat. I don't even remember if we had lunch.'

Thankfully Will smiled. This was something he could control. 'What do you feel like? Curry? Noodles? Or something entirely different? I'll get anything you want.'

Despite what Summer had said, it was his fault. He should have been in the water with her. Not checking his emails. If he'd been closer, if he'd been paying attention, then they all might have been prepared for the wave and managed to ride it out. He wasn't sure how. Ducking under. Bracing themselves better. But he'd have been there, closer. He couldn't shake the feeling that he should have done more.

Sitting next to him now, after dinner, she seemed fine. But Will wasn't sure if he was. They were sitting together on the couch, watching a movie, and resting. Summer was enjoying herself, laughing and sighing at the appropriate parts, but Will was having trouble following the plot.

It all turned out okay. Summer is fine, sitting here with you now.

But it almost hadn't. Summer was seconds, inches from being seriously hurt. Or worse. He knew, from watching his father pass away, that the difference between life and death was so fragile, so thin.

The thought of something happening to Summer made his gut tighten. Every time he thought of the white waves curdling the sea she and Ben had been stuck in he wanted to be sick.

His mother and brother had both called to check in on Summer and him, but otherwise they had had a quiet evening.

Summer yawned. 'I think I'm going to call it a night.'

'Good idea. Will you be okay?'

'I think so. But…'

Will froze. 'What?'

'But if you wanted to sit with me for a bit, that would be all right.'

'Are you sure you're all right?'

'For the hundredth time, yes. But it's been a big day and I don't want to be alone.'

'I don't want you to be alone. I'd feel better if I was with you.'

Summer reached over and squeezed his hand. 'I know that too.' And then she released it, but that touch alone reached something deep inside him he wasn't even sure he'd noticed before.

He'd come to care about her in the past few days. It wasn't part of the plan. It didn't even make sense, but there was no other way of explaining how shaken he'd been following the wave.

She's become your friend.

Yes, that was it. Friends.

As he stretched out on the bed next to her he felt himself relax. As long as he was here next to her everything was all right.

The last thing he wanted to do was undress her and kiss her all over. Part of him still wanted to do that, but the bigger part just wanted this. To lie next to her, to hear her breathing and to know that she was okay.

CHAPTER TEN

THE SUN STREAKING in at the edges of the closed blinds woke Summer gently. She lay there for a while, letting the events of the day before coming back to her gradually and taking in her current surroundings. She was in her room in a comfortable bed, but she wasn't alone.

Will lay next to her, facing her, his arm on her shoulder, but that was the only place they were touching. She could hear him breathing with the intensity of someone in a deep sleep. *I wonder if he's wearing anything*, she thought, and almost giggled, but didn't want to in case she woke him.

She was sore and stiff, but she wasn't in any pain, weirdly most of the soreness settled around her neck and shoulders, similar to a whiplash she'd once experienced after a rear-end collision. Her throat was a little scratchy, but all in all she thought she felt fine in herself.

Her last recollection from the night before was her lying on her bed and Will sitting up next to her reading to her. She'd insisted that she was fine and he'd insisted that he'd just stay until she was asleep. He must've fallen asleep himself.

Summer needed to use the bathroom and she was going to have to wake him eventually. She moved gently towards her side of the bed and his hand fell. She turned back to look at him sleeping.

How was this man so beautiful? And so full of surprises. A week ago, she could never have guessed that they would have spent the night sleeping next to one another, even platonically. She never would have guessed how peaceful Mr Excel Spreadsheet would look in his sleep. Will's eyelashes flickered and his eyes began to open. She knew she should leave and not be caught watching him, but she couldn't help it. She stared and waited for the moment his eyes began to focus, and then he would see her. Still drowsy from sleep, and totally unguarded. At that instant, he smiled and Summer's heart turned to a puddle.

'Hey, sleepyhead,' she said.

'Hey,' he answered.

'Despite the rumours, you do sleep in clothes. I have to say I'm a little disappointed.'

She knew she shouldn't flirt with him like this, but just as with everything else when it came to Will, she couldn't help herself.

'How are you feeling?' he rubbed his head and with his hair sticking up he looked even more adorable. She liked when he looked scruffy.

'I'm okay, really. A little stiff, but I think after a shower I'll be good.'

'You're taking it easy today.'

'It's the wedding! The whole reason I came.'

'Relax, we'll go to the wedding, but apart from that I think you should take it easy here.' Will stretched his arms high and closed his eyes as he did it, and she sneaked a further look at his T-shirt, riding up and exposing his taut, flat stomach.

Damn clause six.

'Hop in the shower,' he said. 'Breakfast should be here soon.'

'I'm supposed to go and help your mother get ready, remember?' Summer hadn't forgotten. Diane's comment that she didn't have a daughter stuck in Summer's gut and made her feel worse about the lie she and Will were telling. Diane had asked her to help her get ready for the wedding under false pretences. She wasn't Will's girlfriend, she wasn't about to be Diane's daughter-in-law, she had no business helping her get ready for her wedding.

'She'll understand. She'll want you to rest. Charlotte can help her.'

Summer didn't want to let Diane down, but was also grateful to have one less opportunity to slip up. 'Okay.'

'In fact, you should have a bath.'

Summer rarely had baths—there wasn't one in her apartment so they felt like such an extravagance.

A few hours later after a long bath, a leisurely breakfast, and a stretch by the pool, Summer went to put on the dress she was going to wear to the wedding.

It was another purchase from the op shop. One of the main advantages of working there, apart from the casual hours, was that she got first claim at new merchandise. She hadn't had a chance to wear this particular find, something originally from the nineteen-eighties, but by a well-known designer. It had likely been sitting at the back of a closet for thirty years by the time it made its way to the op shop in near perfect condition. A bluish-green colour that made her eyes look even more intense.

When she emerged from the bedroom and Will turned to look, he pulled a face.

'What's the matter? Is it not good enough?'

He shook his head. 'It's a beautiful dress. I've just never seen you in that colour. It looks amazing with your eyes.'

'Thank you.' Summer dropped her head and couldn't look at him. If he liked it, why had he frowned?

'You look beautiful, beautiful, Summer.'

Chairs were set out on the beach, decorated with green leaves and the bright orange and red of tropical blooms. A circle of flowers lay before the chairs, where the celebrant stood, waiting. Brightly coloured umbrellas stood around, providing partial shade. Some of the guests held pretty parasols to keep the sun away.

Will stood to the left of the celebrant, and next to Ben. He wore long pants and a white shirt, open at the collar and with the sleeves rolled up. Summer sat near the front and while she tried to focus on the happy couple and their vows her eyes kept darting back to Will.

As soon as the ceremony was over, Will was back by her side and holding her hand. It didn't feel like they were pretending any longer; it just felt right. Everyone was in a celebratory mood. Having had the chance to get to know one another over the past five or six days Summer felt like she'd come to know everyone so well. With a twinge she realised that this was nearly it, this was their last night and she'd say goodbye to everyone tonight or tomorrow.

She was having such a lovely time she'd begun to forget that she wasn't really a guest, wasn't a part of this family. And never would be. She and Will might have acknowledged that they were attracted to one another, but they had also spoken about why anything more than a flirtation would be impossible between them.

She didn't belong in his world and his made no sense to her. Here, away from real life, things were deceptively simple, but back in Adelaide, he'd be working away in his skyscraper and she'd be dragging her guitar over the city. She'd be scraping together each dollar she earned and he'd be putting together million-dollar deals, not even worrying if he could afford a cup of coffee.

It would be especially sad to say goodbye to Charlotte, which was silly as they hadn't even known one another a week, but she'd become such a part of Summer's life.

'I can't believe this is it!' Charlotte said, echoing Summer's thoughts. 'This is our last night,'

'Ours too,' Summer said.

'I'm so looking forward to you and Will coming to London.'

Summer smiled and let herself imagine for just a moment visiting London, a city she'd never been to, with Will. Seeing some sights, hanging out with Charlotte and Ben in some of the supercool places they no doubt frequented.

Just being anywhere with Will would be lovely...

No. She shook the fantasy away.

'I need photos,' Charlotte declared.

The women took some selfies together, then Charlotte said, 'And now some of you, you gorgeous pair.'

Summer and Will scooted closer and after a blink of approval from Summer, Will slid his arm around her waist and pulled her to him. Melting into Will's embrace it was easy to smile. Summer wasn't acting at all.

Charlotte gave a gooey smile. 'Look, see?' Charlotte held out the phone to them. 'You two are adorable.'

She looked at the photo, a close-up of their faces, their cheeks almost touching. She could still feel his body pressed against hers. Both pairs of eyes were smiling at the camera. His brilliant blue, hers deep, mossy green. Together they made aquamarine.

Will looked around the beach as the crowd thinned out. The day had gone well, mostly because Summer had been at his side almost all of the time. She was glowing in the fading light and her beautiful dress, so far from the barely breathing woman he'd sat with on the beach yesterday, but he still kept reaching over to take her hand, or touch her arm or to simply look at her, to reassure himself that everything was fine.

Before they'd left Adelaide, Will had offered to say some

words at the reception after the wedding. While Diane could speak for herself, and did, at length, Will felt that someone from her family should also say something. Her father had passed away, and then of course, her first husband.

Will had prepared some words a week ago but as he read them over now, he knew they were not quite right. He kept the shell of the speech, thanking everyone for coming, welcoming Gus to their family, but his first speech hadn't mentioned anything about what had brought Gus and his mother together in the first place.

It was a glaring omission. Just as important as all the other things.

'Mum, Gus, you two are an inspiration. You've reminded us about second chances and the power of love to heal. You've shown us that it is possible to love again after heartbreak.

'By taking these vows today, in front of all of us, you've shown how important love is. You both know what it is to lose love, and yet you love anyway. Bravely and with purpose.'

His eyes started to fill. This was love. He was witnessing it; unconventional, unexplainable. But unmistakable. His chest was full as he walked back to Summer. When she saw his glassy eyes, she smiled, slid her soft arms around his waist and pulled him close. His heart swelled even further; he thought it would burst.

'Thank you,' he whispered.

'What for?'

'For everything. For coming.'

'I'm glad I did.'

'Really? I've put you through hell. And I nearly got you killed.'

'It's been an adventure.'

He laughed. That's what he loved about Summer, her ability to put a positive spin on almost everything.

Love? No, it was what he admired about Summer. What he *liked* about Summer.

And he did like her, there was no point denying that. He liked her a lot.

The remarkable thing was that for most of the day he'd stopped worrying about the lies they were meant to be telling. He was with Summer. And he didn't care who believed it or not. They were friends, she was with him.

It stopped being an act and was simply fact. They might not have been an actual couple, together for two years, but they were a type of couple. Unconventional, to be sure, but that didn't mean they didn't have a bond, a common purpose.

He trusted her. They were a team.

After Diane and Gus had made their goodbyes, Will looked to Summer and she nodded. She'd had a long day and he wasn't going to make it any longer by lingering until every guest had left.

He went to order a taxi, but she waved him away.

'I'm fine to walk. It isn't far.'

They bid everyone else a goodnight and hugged them all. There were tentative plans for everyone to share a post-wedding breakfast before everyone flew home, but Will had the feeling that he and Summer had done what they needed to. It was over.

They walked slowly along the footpath the short distance to their villa. The sky was dark, but the air filled with the sound of singing cicadas. He wanted to stop right there and pull her into his arms. Feel her body against his, taste her lips on his.

You made a deal. You agreed that you wouldn't have a physical relationship. That was why Summer agreed to come here with you.

He couldn't renege on that arrangement now. That would mean going back on his word and he didn't do that, as a businessman or a man. If everyone went around backing out of deals, breaking promises, then no one could trust anyone.

But what if the deal was over? What if it was done? What then?

'We've got through the wedding, but what happens next? Back in Adelaide?' Will asked.

'We break up. Wasn't that the plan?'

'Yes, of course,' he said. He wasn't sure why he'd asked the question.

But was it the plan? What if the agreement was just to come with him to the wedding. Now the wedding was over, could he trust her with a new sort of deal? One that definitely did not involve a clause six.

Back at the villa, Summer flopped onto the couch by the pool and slipped off her shoes. She was exhausted, but also exhilarated. They'd done it. They'd made it through the wedding and no one had doubted—at least not seriously—that she and Will were a couple.

In about twenty-four hours they would be on a plane back home and it would all be over. Summer's phone pinged and she picked it up. Someone had paid seven thousand, seven hundred dollars into her account.

It could only be one person.

'You paid me. Already. Why?'

Will sat down next to her on the couch. 'The wedding's over. You've fulfilled your end of the bargain.'

'But we're not home yet.'

'I want it to be over.' Will's eyes were serious and his voice low.

'You want me to leave? Now?' Her heart cracked, but she went to stand.

He placed a hand gently on her arm. 'No, I want the deal to

be over. I don't want the money to be between us any more. I want to rip clause six to shreds.'

Understanding his meaning, and without saying anything further, Summer stood and went to her room. She reached into her bag and pulled out the contract.

'What are you doing?'

She picked up one of the lamps containing lit candles that adorned the deck, lifted the protective glass, and touched the paper to the flame.

They both watched, mesmerised as the flames licked the paper, curling gently around it, erasing the deal they had signed. But suddenly the flames took off, engulfing the pages and her fingertips. She cried, 'Blast!' and dropped the paper. 'It was supposed to be more elegant than that.'

Will stepped on the paper with his shoe, extinguishing the flames, a smile creeping over his face.

'I don't know, I thought it was pretty great.' Will stepped towards her and Summer held her breath. 'Just like you.'

He reached for her chin, held her face like it was the most precious thing in the world and tilted her mouth to his.

This kiss was like none of the others, there was nothing to hold them back, they were doing this simply because they wanted to, nothing more. Or less.

Gently at first, his lips teased hers with their softness. But Summer had waited too long. She opened her mouth, welcoming him, letting him know that she understood him and that she wanted this as much as he did. She threw her arms around him, wanting all of him and as soon as possible.

Tonight, they were equals, here because they both wanted to be. For tonight, at least, there was nothing between them. Except their clothes, which Summer started to deal with as quickly as possible. Her fingers deftly unbuttoned Will's shirt and, in a rush of relief she slid her hands into his shirt, over his bare chest and back. One of the many things she'd been dreaming of doing all week. Will's torso was simply spectacular, hard, smooth and the perfect fit for her hands to slide over.

She tugged his shirt off his shoulders and threw it on the floor. Then she was pressing herself against him, revelling in the way his skin felt against hers. Will's hand slid around her, cupping her breast and he kissed her, causing all kinds of turmoil inside her. Desire rose up in her like a flower opening.

As he was nearly a foot taller than her, she had to stand on her toes to meet his lips, but with each kiss, each caress, she swooned a little more, and the more blood rushed to the muscles between her legs, leaving less for her legs which were trying and failing to support her.

He slid his hands under her bottom and lifted her to him. Summer wrapped her legs around him, so they could hold one another tight, not breaking their bond. Groin to groin, he carried her to his room.

He laid her carefully on the bed, so carefully that Summer had to remind him, 'I'm fine, don't hold back.'

He regarded her from under heavy lids.

'I don't intend to,' she added.

His kisses scorched her skin, demolished her inhibitions. His lips teased down her dress, his hands explored under the hem and heaven help her when those same fingers found her underwear and began to stroke. Summer saw stars. And fireworks and any number of explosions.

She shifted away from under him, but only to shimmy out of her dress. Seeing this, Will kicked off his shoes and moved back to her.

Summer paused. His pants, his shorts. She'd dreamt of taking these off him. And now she was going to.

'I've wanted this for so long, you have no idea.' His voice was hoarse.

'I have some idea. I haven't exactly been keeping cool myself over here, you know?'

Summer unbuttoned his trousers and carefully eased them over his hips; she ran her palm over the front of his boxers, very much liking what she found there. He made a sound like a moan being stifled and her lips found his again. Kissing him was like magic. She loved the heavy look in his eyes, his lowered lids. He was unguarded, letting go. She was doing this to him.

How had she resisted so long? How had she ever thought this would be a mistake? It was glorious. She revelled in his touch, revelled in his reactions to her touch.

His lips traced a line of exquisite kisses from her earlobes to her nipples, sending her spiralling into an ever-increasing fever that would only be satisfied by one thing.

'Do you have protection?' she asked.

'Yes,' he mumbled, from his mouth's position between her breasts. 'But just a moment.'

How could he wait? She was ready to burst. Gorgeous, handsome Will, whose eyes made her muscles weaken and whose smile made them tighten again was laying kisses all over her body. She was helpless, hopeless, beneath him and at risk of falling completely apart. But with great effort, she held back. She wanted him, she wanted to join with him, to experience it with him. She could see the self-control etched across his face as they finally came together, loving her pleasure as much as his own.

Scrambling, scratching, climbing, chasing, until they reached the summit, one immediately behind the other. Looking into one another's eyes and understanding completely, they both let go.

What happens now?

Summer didn't voice the question aloud, but looked at Will the next morning, sprawled out on his bed next to her, messed up, crumpled. He'd never looked so gorgeous. He rolled over, smiled at her and her insides flipped again. God, he had an amazing smile. All the more precious because it still felt so rare. Will didn't smile easily, but when he did you knew he was sincerely happy.

As if he'd heard her unasked question, he said, 'So, you have a choice. You can leave on your flight tonight, as planned. But you could also stay.'

Stay? That wasn't part of any deal.

'The villa's booked for another night. But I don't have any meetings until the day after tomorrow. I could easily change our flights. See if we could get the villa for an extra night...' Will picked up her left hand and placed it between his. 'I'd like you to stay. With me.'

How often was she given the chance to spend two days in a tropical paradise with a gorgeous man? A gorgeous man she was beginning to have feelings for. Messy, complicated, impossible feelings. They may have shared an amazing night, but this moment was a crossroads. A point at which she should be sensible and go home as planned.

'We'd have two days. And then we'd go back to our own lives. Think of it as a stolen interlude before you start the rest of your life.'

Two days, no strings attached was the new deal he was offering. Which was good. It was all she could agree to. And she did want to stay. How could she possibly say no to forty-eight hours with Will?

Because every moment you stay, the more you're going to get used to this and the harder it is going to be to go back to the reality that is your life?

'It sounds lovely,' she heard her voice say.

'But?'

She shook her head. 'No buts. I'd love to stay.' *Love?* Why did she use that word? 'Just let me check on some things at home.'

'Of course.' He placed a tender kiss on her shoulder. 'And while you're doing that, I'm not going to let that pool go to waste.'

She watched him get out of bed, still gloriously naked, and walk out the doors that led to the deck and the pool, not bothering with swimmers. And why would he, looking like he did? Strong, hard, and totally edible. This man made her body swoon and her heart sing.

Another night or two in Bali with him couldn't hurt, could it? They had lost time to make up for. They could have been sharing a bed all week, instead of worrying about their deal and some silly promise they'd made before they even knew one another. Now their work was over and they were free to enjoy themselves. And one another.

Summer reached for her phone. Penny didn't pick up the first time Summer called. She waited a few minutes and then tried again, urging her heart not to race. She knew she shouldn't panic at this point, there were all sorts of reasons why her mother wouldn't pick up right away, most of them benign. Penny picked up the second time and apologised.

'Sorry sweetheart. I couldn't get to my phone fast enough.'

'How are you, Mum?'

'Fine, fine.'

One 'fine' seemed to cancel out the other.

'Really, how are you feeling?'

'I'm doing great. But more importantly, how are you? Are you still flying home this evening?'

'That's what I was calling about. Um, another opportunity has come up.'

'Then you must take it.'

Her mother had no idea what sort of opportunity Summer was talking about, but Summer didn't enlighten her. 'It would just be for another two days and then I'd be home. Would you be okay with that?'

'Of course, that's okay, I can survive without you, you know?'

'I know.'

'You're a grown woman, you don't have to ask my permission. Stay. Make the most of it. I'd feel guilty if you missed an opportunity because of me.'

Summer knew that even if Penny understood the real reason she wanted to stay was to sleep in the arms of a handsome billionaire, her mother would still urge her to stay.

'Thanks, Mum, I'll send you my new flight details when I have them.'

'Have fun, sweetheart. You're only young once.'

Summer ended the call. Her mother was right. She was only young once. She glanced to the pool where Will was doing slow, lazy laps. His broad shoulders and long arms making short work of its length. The villa was completely private, high hedges shielded the pool where the villa did not. They were perched on a twenty-foot cliff, there was no chance of anyone looking in. Summer threw off the sheet and walked straight out to the deck and the edge of the pool.

Will turned when he reached the end of the pool, but when he noticed Summer, he almost swallowed a mouthful of water. She was standing at the other end of the pool, gloriously naked. Her beautiful hair surrounded her face like a halo. Lit up with the morning sun it looked as though she was on fire. Just like he was. His eyes travelled from hers down her gorgeous nose, to over her chin, which was tilted slightly up, as if in a challenge, down over the dip in her collarbone to her voluptuous breasts. His gaze skimmed her waist, which was the perfect size for his hands. He felt himself becoming hard again. Will couldn't remember ever being this turned on by a woman in his life and not just once, but over and over. There was no limit to his desire for her.

He stood, transfixed, blood pumping so hard through him, watching, savouring as she walked down the steps and entered the water.

'Everything okay?'

Please be okay, please stay.

She nodded. 'Everything's fine.'

She moved slowly through the water towards him. Even though it had been mere minutes since he'd touched her last, his body ached for her. Every second it took her to reach him was an exquisite torture.

And finally, the water parted and there she was. He reached for her, pulling her against him, cherishing the way the water caused a different friction against their skin, loving the way she was almost weightless as he lifted her up and she wrapped her legs around his waist, bringing their mouths level.

This was heaven. He could quite happily stay here for ever.

He couldn't stay there for ever though.

A while later, after they had tried the pool and then her bed, Will's phone pinged with a message from his mother asking if they would be joining everyone else for a late brunch.

'We should go, you know,' Summer said.

'I don't want to share you.'

She laughed. 'I want to go.'

'Haven't you had enough of my family? They aren't your responsibility any more.'

'Not at all. And it'll be different today.'

Not completely different, because they still weren't a couple. Not really. But he knew what she meant. It would be nice to see his family and not feel like a total fraud.

'It could be the last time I see Ben in a while too,' Will agreed.

They were the last to arrive at the brunch, but the first to leave. The mood was happy, but subdued, with most of the guests departing on an afternoon ferry and evening flights.

The news that Will and Summer would be staying two extra nights was met with enthusiasm and envy.

When they finally hugged and kissed everyone goodbye, Will thought he saw Summer brush a tear from her cheek.

'What's up?'

'Nothing.' Summer shook her head and smiled. 'It's silly really. I won't see them again.'

'Ah.'

'And I know it wasn't real, I know that. But it's been fun. I've really liked getting to know them. You're very lucky, Will Watson.'

'I am,' he agreed, putting his arm around her, and pulling her closer. 'Don't think about that now. Let's enjoy this time.'

Maybe it was insensitive of him to dismiss her concern, but it was also the best thing to do. This was a brief moment they were carving out from the rest of their lives. Neither of them knew what would happen after and he didn't want to waste a minute of the next two days thinking about the future. For once he wanted to live in this exact moment. It was a new sensation for him. Not unpleasant, almost freeing.

For two days he'd forget his responsibilities—he'd forget he was Will Watson, Businessman. For two days he would just be one half of Will and Summer.

And he liked that idea very much.

CHAPTER ELEVEN

THE LAST TWENTY-FOUR hours had been amazing. They had moved between the bed and the pool and the shower…and the bed again. And then the daybed by the pool. It had been both exhausting and exhilarating, Summer had never felt so satiated. Or alive. When it came to Will her desire seemed to have no limits.

But in less than twenty-four hours she'd be back at home. In the real world. The idea of seeing her mother, pulling on a pair of white satin flares, and climbing on stage seemed so strange and far away from this.

What if this was your life?

It wouldn't be; it couldn't be. Even Will had to return to the real world, or his rarefied version of it anyway. He still had a job, shareholders, a board to answer to. He had an important business to keep afloat, and not just for the sake of his bank balance, but for the sake of the rivers and the oceans. His work was about more than just making money, as she'd once believed.

Lying on her bed, Will dozed next to her. Summer slid her hand up his bare arm and her fingers reached the edge of his T-shirt. They crept up, under and to his strong biceps. Oh. Her fingertips felt their way over the tight ridges of his muscles. Will opened his eyes and reached for her, Summer straddled him and he rose to meet her lips. They kissed, fast, wild. Desire bloomed inside her and spread instantly through her torso. She ached for him and pressed herself closer to him. She tugged at his T-shirt, lifting it over his head.

He looked up at her, and the sparkle in his eyes nearly brought her undone.

'What's the rush?' he asked, but let her lift the shirt over his head.

'A week of sexual tension?' Summer lifted her own dress over her head and was glad she hadn't bothered to put on her bra again.

'A week?'

'What? You didn't feel it?'

'Summer.' Will's eyes went dark and serious. 'I've wanted you since I first saw you on that stage.'

The mood shifted from a frenzied rush to something more serious. His kisses became slower, more deliberate, as though each one was laced with meaning. This wasn't just fooling around, not for him and certainly not for her. Not any longer anyway.

They didn't take their eyes from one another, she looked deep into his blue eyes as he moved inside her, feeling everything, noticing it all and committing all of it to memory. Wishing, foolishly, it could last for ever. Blocking out all the reasons why it couldn't and focusing on this moment alone, his touch, his smell, his breath on her neck, his fingers in her hair. Her body wanting to find its release, her heart wanting it to last for ever. Each stroke was more pleasurable than the last, each kiss more exquisite. His sighs reverberated inside her, her pleasure reflected in his eyes as they worked together, in unison to reach the climax.

After, they lay on her bed, her cheek resting on the magnificent work of art that was Will's chest and she absentmindedly played with the hair on his head.

'Would you like to see each other again? When we get home.' His voice wouldn't have drowned out a whisper.

Summer tried to open her mouth to respond, but her thoughts snagged. Was he suggesting a date? Or just a catch-up? Or something else? A relationship?

Given he was now naked and stroking her shoulder, she'd have to assume he meant the latter, but how could that be? Even if the contractual part of their relationship was over, he was still a billionaire and she was still a broke busker and unsuccessful songwriter.

Will pulled himself out from under her and his blue eyes met her green ones. 'You don't have to respond—you don't have to say anything now.'

She nodded. So he was talking about more than just a casual catch-up over coffee.

How would it work?

It was a little question, but with a huge answer.

And she had no idea where to begin.

Will loved the way Summer felt resting her head on his chest, her beautiful hair settled across his arms, his hand resting perfectly in the small of her back. His other hand held hers. The smell of the breeze, fresh off the ocean filled the room. The moment was perfect.

Except he'd gone and ruined it by asking her about the future. He'd asked on impulse, without thinking properly. The single thought he'd had at that moment had been, *I want to do this for ever.*

As soon as he'd asked if she'd like to see him again when they returned, he'd felt her body stiffen. And he'd remembered.

This was Summer. He cared about her too much for this to be just a fling, but did he really think that it could be anything else? The last time he'd fallen for someone he'd nearly lost everything. Summer wasn't Georgia, but there were still a million ways a relationship could go wrong.

This last week proved that; he'd told a lie and had come within a whisker of being found out. Wasn't it best that he gave relationships a wide berth?

No one is talking about a relationship though, he reminded himself. He was just talking about dating. Seeing one another. Being with one another.

'If, just say, if, we do see one another back in Adelaide, how would it work?' she asked.

Will wasn't sure what she was getting at. 'We'd go on dates,' he said.

'I can't afford the places you go to. I can't afford to go out much at all.'

This was the least of their obstacles. He had money. He had too much money. 'And if I said that I'd pay?'

'I'd say that's very generous of you, and kind, but I can't be beholden to you.'

'You wouldn't be.' He wasn't expecting anything from her. There would be no contract, just him and her, together because they wanted to be.

'Yes, I would. You'd hold all the power.'

'I wouldn't be like that.'

'Saying it won't make it not true.'

'You told me you didn't care about money, only music. That's what you told me.'

She looked blank.

'In the letter you wrote me.' The one I've kept with me every day since.

'I was wrong. About so many things.' Summer pulled away from him and his body was bereft.

Will sat, tried to figure out what to say next, but Summer grabbed a nearby robe and covered herself.

No!

He couldn't lose her. He'd pushed too fast, pressed too hard. He had to backtrack. He might not know what sort of future he wanted for them, but he knew one thing, he couldn't lose her. He'd had a glimpse of a world without Summer Bright in it two days ago and it had rocked him to his core.

They might not be able to have a serious relationship, but he wanted her in his life. In some wild, unpredictable way, he'd come to depend on her. Come to yearn for her. He liked the way he was when he was with her, he liked the way the world looked when he was with her. He might not know how to describe his feelings, but the one thing he was certain of was that he couldn't lose her.

'We don't need to decide anything now. We can just enjoy this time. I'm sorry I pressed. I know this is new. I just need you to know that I would like to see you again. I don't feel as though we're…finished.'

Summer pulled the robe tighter, but her gorgeous bottom landed back on the bed with a gentle thump.

She nodded and he breathed again.

'I don't feel as though we're finished either, but this does have an end date. We both know it.'

She clutched her hands together and twisted them in a way that made him want to grab them and soothe them and tell her everything would be okay.

But he wasn't sure if it would be.

Everything had an end date. Every contract, every deal, every relationship. He knew it as well as she did. The trick was always to find the right moment to exit. And he was no longer sure when that was. He had a feeling he was going to misjudge his next move and someone was going to get hurt.

'I shouldn't have brought it up. I'll only ruin what time we have left.' He needed to stop planning; he needed to be comfortable with not knowing his next move. Needing to predict and plan for the future had always been an essential skill to have in business. Not thinking about the future, even for a few moments was hard.

'The problem is, Will Watson, you've set such high expectations already.'

'What on earth do you mean?'

She threw her arms wide. 'I mean this! This place, this week. This afternoon. All of it. It's been wonderful.'

'And you don't think I can keep this kind of thing up?' he guessed.

'I'm sure neither of us can.'

'Could I at least try?'

He was serious, but she laughed.

'This is a holiday, for both of us. This isn't real. My life certainly doesn't consist of lying around an infinity pool in the tropical sun while I make love to a gorgeous and wonderful man.'

There was a message somewhere in her words but he only heard *gorgeous* and *wonderful*.

'And while I know your life has far more infinity pools and tropical sun than mine ever will, this isn't your real life either. Your real life is the office building I met you in. Where you look over the city and arrange business deals that effect everyone down below.'

Summer closed her eyes and paused, but he sensed she wasn't finished.

'I know that your role in the company isn't only important to everyone, it's important to you. And it's much more than just a job, it's your life.'

Was his life so incompatible with hers? She wouldn't be by his side at the charity events he attended, she'd be on the stage. Her financial position didn't bother him, but the difference between them clearly bothered her. For the first time he really saw it wasn't nothing. He imagined their situations reversed and felt cold. She was right. Here, in Bali, away from the real world, they could make things work. But back in Adelaide they wouldn't make sense.

He took a deep breath. He didn't like the conclusion he'd just reached, but that was too bad.

Live in the moment.

'So, we have one night left in Bali. Money is no object—I'm sorry to remind you, but it isn't—what would you like to do?'

'Now you're talking.'

'We could get someone in to make us an amazing dinner. Or we could go out to one of the restaurants. We could even get a boat over to the main island and explore some more.'

Summer pressed her lips together thoughtfully. If it was up to him, they'd spend every second they had left together in this villa, but he knew that Summer might never come back to Bali again. He also knew that if they did spend the next twenty-four hours wrapped in each other's bodies it was going to be even more difficult to untangle themselves when they arrived back home.

'Yes, that. I'd love to see some more.'

'Great,' he said, hoping he sounded sincere. 'I'll make a call or two.'

Will climbed out of bed, looking for his phone. He was still naked and noticed Summer watching him, colour high in her cheeks and a cheeky smile on her face. He wanted to burst. He also wanted to fall back onto the bed and pull her to him.

'We should get dressed,' he said before he was too tempted to do just that.

'Into what?'

'Something suitable for an amazing evening.'

Will made some calls and was assured that everything would be taken care of. He showered and dressed and tapped his fingers on his knee while he waited for her.

Live in the moment. Live in the moment.

Summer came out of her room and he was powerless to stop his jaw dropping.

'I got this in Ubud,' she said, doing a twirl. She wore a floor-length halter-neck dress, loose and flowing, just like her fiery hair around her shoulders.

She was amazing.

They shouldn't work, but they did.

No, he reminded himself. This wasn't real life.

Summer had no idea what Will had planned for them and he was keeping the plans close to his chest. And what a chest it was, covered now in a loose blue linen shirt, with the sleeves rolled up. She picked up his hand to stop herself from sliding her hand over his chest and through the opening where his top two buttons were undone to feel the firmness behind it. The man was edible and for a moment she regretted her decision for them to go out exploring the island. They should be back in the villa exploring one another's bodies.

They were picked up at the villa by a taxi and driven to the small port on the island.

'Where are we going?'

'It's a surprise,' he said.

But as soon as they were shown onto a private speedboat, their pilot asked, 'You're going to Nusa Dua?'

Will nodded.

Summer knew Nusa Dua was one of the most exclusive enclaves on the main island with luxury hotels and restaurants. Gus and Diane had contemplated having their wedding there but chose instead the more relaxed and casual atmosphere of Nusa Lembongan.

'I thought we could have an explore and then I've booked us dinner.'

'Wonderful.'

And it was.

The boat sped them across the bay and delivered them to Nusa Dua, its beautiful beaches, lined with palm trees and never-ending greenery. A car took them to a clifftop temple, where they got out to look more closely at the beautiful shrine. They were then delivered to a luxury restaurant overlooking the Indian Ocean and another magnificent Bali sunset. Pinks and oranges faded to purples and dark blues and finally the stars appeared. The open-air restaurant was lit with lanterns and candles.

Will couldn't have picked a more perfect destination if he'd tried. After a dinner that was probably one of the most delicious Summer had eaten in her life of lobster and barramundi and everything else besides, they watched a live show of Balinese dancers accompanied by a gamelan, an ensemble of Balinese instruments.

Though all of that was just window dressing. The most special part of the evening was simply being with Will. She kept wondering how easy it would be to let herself be swept along with the tide that was Will Watson. To let him take care of everything…

No, she reminded herself. *Because when you surrender yourself like that you risk everything.* And she wasn't going to end up like her mother. Or put herself in the position she'd let herself get into with Michael. She wouldn't let herself depend so much on another. Being with Will would mean doing that. He was so larger than life, his presence, his fortune so much, she felt in danger of forgetting who she was.

She wouldn't. Because by the time the sun set tomorrow, she would have said goodbye to Will for ever.

As the sun rose over their last morning in Bali and the room was gradually filled with a soft pink light, Will was still wide awake.

He hadn't slept a second. Hadn't lost consciousness for a moment. Every time he'd felt his mind drifting off, he'd been jolted awake again and felt Summer in his arms. Looked at her. Breathed in her scent.

He didn't want to miss a moment of it. Of her. Summer now lay curled around him and he watched her back rise and fall with each breath she took, his own in time with hers. Breathing in the same air, being in the same beautiful bubble.

If this was all the time they had, he was going to be there for every second. When the sun was higher in the sky and the light had brightened, Summer began to stir. Her glorious body moved against his and she lifted herself to look at him. She gave him an unfocused, drowsy smile and his heart twisted.

'Good morning, sweet pea,' he said.

'Good morning, honey.'

'Is it time?' she asked.

Not, what is the time? But is it time? Is it all over?

'Nearly. Breakfast will be here soon and we get picked up in about two hours.'

Summer rolled over and Will resisted the urge to pull her back. It was better this way.

'I'll just have a shower.'

'Good idea,' he said but his voice cracked.

It was a truly terrible idea. The only good idea was for her to lie back down with him and stay for ever. But that wasn't to be. She climbed out of bed and went to the bathroom, closing the door behind herself.

The breakfast was delivered while he was in the shower and he came out to find Summer dressed and finishing off hers.

She stood when he entered. 'I've had my breakfast. I'll go and finish packing.'

His heart fell. It was as though it was already over.

It is over, he reminded himself.

He shouldn't have let it go on this far because saying goodbye to Summer was going to be harder than he'd imagined.

But he'd have to. He didn't know how to convince her that they should see one another back home. Summer saw his fortune as a barrier. Not only his money, but his entire life. She wasn't expecting him to give anything up—and nor was he—but even he had to admit he didn't know how to make their lives fit together. He'd spent years negotiating all kinds of deals, solving all kinds of problems, but the one time he really needed to be persuasive all his powers failed him.

On the ferry across to the main island, they were both slightly subdued, which was to be expected due to their lack of sleep. Despite spending the majority of the past thirty-six hours in bed neither of them was well rested. Their conversation was stilted, about practical matters only. Will's emotions were churning inside him and he felt queasy.

It's just the ferry ride, he reasoned, even though he'd never had any kind of seasickness before in his life.

CHAPTER TWELVE

THE FLIGHT BACK was far more subdued than the trip over. They didn't quiz one another; they hardly talked. And Summer certainly wasn't filled with anticipation about what would happen when they landed.

Fed up with the silence, somewhere over the centre of Australia she turned to Will and said, 'Someone once told me that a debrief is an essential part of any project.'

'A post-mortem?'

'It didn't go that badly, did it?' She smiled, but didn't feel it. 'What does one talk about during a debrief?'

'Usually we would talk about what went well, what we learnt.'

'I think we convinced your family that we're a couple, so that went well.'

'A little too well,' he mumbled.

She knew what he meant. Diane, Gus, Ben and Charlotte had all liked her and embraced her into their family. She'd become close to them. Her chest ached at the thought she'd never see any of them again.

'What did you learn?' she asked. She wasn't ready to tell him that the main lesson she'd take away from this week was never get involved in a fake relationship with a gorgeous billionaire. Not that it was a life lesson that was going to be particularly useful in the future.

'Ah.' He rubbed his chin, still covered in a light stubble.

She liked it on him. It made him look softer, more relaxed. More approachable. Clean-shaven, Will was undoubtedly heart-stoppingly handsome, but with messy hair, a few days growth he was…hers.

She shook her head. He'd never be hers.

'I learnt that I can still be surprised by people.'

She couldn't help but smile. 'I did too.'

Will had surprised her, every day. She was right about many things, but so wrong about others as well. His tenderness, his ability to make her laugh. The way he seemed to genuinely care about her.

The way that despite their many differences, they still had so much to talk about.

The way he could do things to her in the bedroom that no one had ever been able to do. She'd thought that artists and musicians were her thing, but it turned out that business tycoons were also her kink.

'Anything else in a debrief?' Maybe he could tell her how to move on from this. How to say goodbye without it hurting so much.

'What we'd do better next time.'

'Next time?'

He reddened. They were back to this conversation. She wanted to see him again, but knew it was pointless. It would only hurt more to say goodbye to him in another week or two or however long it took to become glaringly apparent to him they would not work as a couple back in the real world.

'My mother's asked us around for dinner when they get back from their honeymoon. In about a month.'

'Oh.' What was he saying? He wasn't suggesting a date, or a catch-up. But to see his family.

They'd talked about this, hadn't they? No, they'd agreed to talk about it later, though Summer had said all she could say. She might want to see him again, but it was best for both of them in the long run if they didn't.

'That wasn't part of the deal,' she said.

'You set fire to that, remember?'

'The other deal we agreed to was forty-eight hours only. And you're threatening to break that one.'

'I'm a ruthless businessman, what can I say?' He held up his hands in surrender and grinned. She smiled too, even though her heart was breaking. How could that be?

'I don't think that dragging it on any longer than we have already is going to help either of us in the long run. We're too different.'

'Not really.'

'Our lives are too different. You run a billion-dollar business. I busk on the street. I have responsibilities.'

'Your mother.'

'Yes, and that's not nothing.'

'I didn't say it was. I just mean that we can overcome all those things.'

Will cupped her chin in his hands. She wanted to believe him. She wanted to rest her head on his shoulder, for everything to be okay, for everything to make sense.

'I don't belong in your world,' she said.

'How can you say that? I've been beside you all week, remember, watching you in my world as you call it. I've seen you with my mother, my family. Everyone. They adore you. You do belong in my life. As much as I do anyway.'

'What does that mean?'

'It means...' Will dragged his hand across his head. 'I don't always feel that I belong either. But with you, I do.'

'Because this is your world, Will, not mine. Mine is worrying about how I'm going to meet the rent, looking after my mother, hoping my next gig doesn't get cancelled.'

'If you were with me...'

'You can't support me, Will—that's what I'm trying to say. You can't support me and my mother. And if we were dating and you were paying for everything that's what it would feel like. It's okay for you to pay in Bali, but not back at home. It wouldn't feel right to me.'

'I…'

'Will, it's like I asked yesterday, how would it work? Going on a date every now and then? Or not going on dates, just hiding out in your apartment? Keeping our lives separate?'

'Yes, if that's what you want.'

But it wasn't what she wanted. She didn't want to simply see one another on the rare times their schedules allowed. She didn't want a fight every time about where they went and what they did and who paid. And she certainly didn't want to have a secret relationship, one where they never went out.

She wanted someone who was looking to the future with her. They didn't have to know everything, they didn't have to make lifelong promises, but they needed to be looking in the same direction. Most importantly of all, they needed to be able to share their lives together. Summer wanted a life partner. And she needed more than just an offer to go on a few dates.

She shook her head. 'I don't want a part-time boyfriend, Will.'

'That's not what I'm saying. I'm saying you can trust me.'

She was woken from the dream, confused, blinded by the clarity of what he'd just said. She'd be the one having to trust him, she had so much to lose, more than him.

Trust. It was a funny thing. 'Trust you? Will, we've been lying all along.'

'But not to one another. Of course you can trust me, I'm not going to steal from you, now am I?'

Summer's heart fell. Then rose again, but filled with hurt. And a bit of rage. She sat firmly back in her own seat.

'Meaning, what? I might steal from you?'

'I didn't say that and that's not what I meant. I trust you, Summer.'

She wanted to believe him, but to do so would be repeating the mistakes of the past. This was still the same Will Watson who was so terrified of trusting another person that he'd invented a fake girlfriend so his mother would stop setting him up with eligible women.

The same Will Watson who had been lying to his family and his shareholders ever since. The same Will Watson who had made her sign a four-page contract just for one week away together.

He would never trust a penniless singer like her.

'This is exactly what I meant last night. We're not equals.'

'Of course we're equals.'

'You own half of Adelaide. As of tomorrow, I'll have one old guitar to my name.'

'Summer, I trust you.'

She closed her eyes. She wanted to believe him. And she was convinced that he believed himself. But they both had to face the truth, it wouldn't work. Will was right, if it was simply the difference in their financial positions to overcome there might be a way through.

But it was more than that.

She would not let herself fall for him. She would not let herself rely on him. As soon as she fell for him, he'd have the power to break her.

It's too late though, isn't it?

She sat like that for a while, her eyes closed, unable to look at him. The significance of this realisation almost crushing her with its weight.

She loved him. He made her laugh, she loved his drive, she loved his smile. She loved his quirks. She absolutely adored him.

'Summer,' he said after a while. 'I don't know what to say. I don't know how to make this better.'

She picked up his hand. 'I know, Will, it's okay. I think we both need to accept this is our fate and move on. It'll be easiest in the long run.'

She couldn't love him. She wouldn't. Loving Will, giving herself to him would probably destroy her once and for all.

'Summer! Sweetheart!' Penny exclaimed when Summer pushed open the door and dragged in her bag. A suitcase which a week ago felt light and now weighted a ton. Just like her heart.

She looked around the unit; washing was piled in the sink and the place needed a tidy. She didn't blame her mother; she knew Penny had good days and bad days. Summer felt guilty for leaving her mother over what she now realised had been one of the bad weeks.

'You haven't been telling me the truth, have you, Mum?'

'I don't know what you mean,' Penny replied.

'Every day when I called, you said you were doing fine.'

'And I have been fine. I've been managing.'

Summer sighed. They had different definitions of *managing*.

'Well, I'm not going to go away again anytime soon.'

'It didn't go well? You said your performance was a success.'

'Oh, yes, it was.'

From the point of view of the deal it had been a raging success. From the point of view of her heart, it had been an abject failure. Summer started picking up glasses and mugs from the living room and carried them to the kitchen, where she started washing up.

'At least unpack first!' Penny called out, but Summer wanted to keep her hands busy and found the routine of cleaning soothing. She tidied the apartment, started a load of washing and then looked in the fridge to figure out what they would eat for dinner.

'Come and sit for a moment.' Penny pointed to the couch next to her.

Summer brought her mother a cup of tea and sat.

'I could say the same to you about not telling the truth.'

'What do you mean?'

Her mother gave her a knowing look.

'But I have,' she said.

Her mother eased an eyebrow and Summer's spine slumped.

'Okay, no. I may have left out a few details.'

It all came out. Meeting Will, the deal, meeting his family. How they'd grown closer. How he wasn't the uptight money-obsessed man she'd initially thought him to be. She told her about being swamped by the wave, leaving out some of the details. She told her about the wedding and how she and Will had decided to stay two extra days, leaving a few of those details out too.

Then she'd told her mother how when Will had asked to see her again, back in Adelaide, she'd said no.

'But why? You clearly care about him.'

Yes, she did. And that was the whole point. 'It could never work.'

'Why not?'

'Why not? Because he's a super successful businessman, Mum.'

'So? How is that a bad thing?'

'Because I'm me!'

'And what's wrong with you? Nothing.'

Spoken like a true mother.

'It's not that I don't feel worthy of him. I don't want to be dependent on him.'

'Why would you have to be? You're not talking about moving in together already, are you?'

Summer shook her head.

'I feel that he's so…successful, so much more than I am. His life is together and mine just isn't. I feel as though I might be in danger of being swept away and lost. Somehow.'

'Are you talking about money, or something else?'

'Money is important.'

'Heavens, I'm not saying it isn't. But are you using his money as an excuse?'

'No. But it isn't nothing.' Will had also suggested that his fortune wasn't a relevant consideration in any of this. But it was a huge barrier between them. An immovable elephant blocking the road forward.

'All of it. He's been hurt before, betrayed. He's got even less reason to trust me. And how can I trust him? How can I possibly believe that he won't get sick of me one day?'

Penny pulled a face. 'When did you get to be so cynical?'

'I'm not cynical. I'm realistic, Mum. You know as well as I do that relationships end. One person always ends up hurting the other. One person always ends up misjudging the other.'

Penny shook her head. 'I know I haven't been the best example, made the best choices. But I never said no to love. I never stopped believing in it. Not even now. Especially not now.'

Summer looked at her mother. She was bedridden some days; she found it hard to leave the flat. She still believed in love.

'He'll get sick of me one day.'

'Oh, Summer, I can't believe I'm hearing you speak this way. Do you honestly think that just because he's rich, that he thinks differently to you? That he sees you differently?'

'I *know* he thinks differently. I know his priorities are different to mine.'

'I've never heard you so down on yourself.'

'I'm not down on myself. That's *not* what it's about. It's just about the fact that we live in different worlds.'

'As far as I can see, you both live in this one. Not to mention the same city.'

'Mum, we met because I sang at a charity dinner he was at. He paid thousands of dollars to attend. I was paid four hundred. How is it supposed to work?'

'I thought you were more imaginative than this.'

'What's imagination got to do with it? How's that going to help with dealing with reality?' Summer's skin felt hot and she was suddenly aware that she'd worked her heart rate up to dangerous levels. She needed a break, she needed to take a moment to calm herself.

Penny looked at her with concern. 'You've had a long trip; you should have a rest.'

Summer nodded. She did need a rest. She needed to fall asleep and forget about Will for a few hours. And then tomorrow she needed to start forgetting him all over again.

The next day Summer woke before the sun rose, but rather than lie in bed and wait for sleep she knew wouldn't come, she got up and got to work. The first thing she needed to do was buy back her guitar and rig.

She arranged a time to meet Brayden then she got the bus to a cafe near his house. Brayden had the decency to look embarrassed by the situation, but she knew it wasn't his fault. It was Michael's. And he had been decent enough to hold on to the guitar while Summer gathered the money together.

'What's the best price you can offer me?' Summer asked, emboldened by the fact the guitar was sitting right there.

'I thought we agreed on seven-seven.'

'But what's the best you can do? You can't have paid Michael seven-seven.'

Brayden looked sheepish. Summer held her ground even as her insides were turning to mush. He could just pick up the things and leave.

But he didn't. 'Six thousand. I paid six thousand. I didn't know they were stolen.'

'How about I give you six-five. For your time. You still come out ahead.'

Brayden nodded and finally, finally, she held her guitar again.

And she hadn't rolled over. She'd argued for a better deal. She'd stood her ground and she felt like she could fly.

She now had enough change left over from Will's money to take her mother shopping for a new outfit and maybe some books she'd been wanting to read. Will's money was not going to be spent on bills; it was going to be spent on things that would make them happy.

Summer carried her guitar on her back and wheeled her rig home. One of the reasons for the high price tag of the rig was its light weight and portability. Even as she made her way back across town with it, it felt weightless. And she felt surprisingly light. The song she had started in Bali was coming to her now, also effortlessly, naturally.

It was unfortunate, she thought, that her best songs inevitably came to her when she was heartbroken.

There would be other heartbreaks and there would be joy again in her life, but after this song. She needed to get this song out of her and onto paper, into the air and out into the world. Once this one was finished and sung and out there then she could say goodbye to its subject once and for all.

It was a love letter to Will and a paean to heartbreak. It was about wanting something you knew you could never have.

CHAPTER THIRTEEN

'SUMMER WON'T BE COMING,' Will said.

Diane had returned from her honeymoon a few weeks ago and Will had been avoiding her, but she'd tracked him down in the one place he couldn't really avoid her: his office.

'Why not?' Diane asked.

Will had been dreading this moment since the airport. He'd been dreading a lot of things since he'd watched Summer wheel her small bag away from him at the Adelaide Airport without turning back. He dreaded facing each day without her; he dreaded going home from the office to his empty apartment. He dreaded spending the evenings alone. And most of all he found himself dreading waking up each morning and feeling the cold of the bed next to him.

But he'd also been dreading this moment and telling his mother the truth.

He knew he didn't have to tell her everything, but he also knew that if he didn't at least tell her, he'd still be lying in one way and he was tired. He was sick of pretending that everything was okay when it wasn't.

'We broke up,' he said. And it wasn't really a lie.

'Oh, darling.' Diane went to him and wrapped her arms around him. 'What happened? You both seemed so happy.'

'That's just the thing. We weren't.'

'Don't be silly. I saw the way you looked at one another.'

'Mum, there's something I have to tell you and I'm not

proud of it. I would like to tell you the truth and I know that you'll be upset. I am very sorry for it and I know you'll be disappointed, but please know I did it for you.'

Diane crossed her arms and narrowed her eyes.

'I made Summer up.'

Diane laughed. 'What do you mean you made her up?'

'When I told you I had a girlfriend and that her name was Summer, I made that up.'

'Summer isn't her name?'

'No, Summer is her name, but I invented a girlfriend called Summer Bright believing that no one in Adelaide would have such a name. But I should've checked because one does and we ran into her that night at the charity dinner.'

'I don't believe you,' Diane said. 'She is real. I found her. I booked her band for the gala.'

'I'm telling you the truth.'

Diane shook her head. 'No, that's too much of a coincidence, you must've met her before.'

'I hadn't met her. Our paths had never crossed.'

'Okay, so you made her up, but then you met, and she came to Bali. She came to my wedding.'

'Because I asked her to.' Will stopped, took a few deep breaths, but still sought to find the courage he needed to tell his mother the next part. 'We made a deal. She'd come to Bali and pretend to be my girlfriend for a week and I agreed to pay her almost eight thousand dollars.'

He couldn't read the look on his mother's face that moment. Incredulity? Amusement? Disgust? Maybe all three.

'I still don't believe you,' she said.

Will begin to pace. Why wouldn't she believe him?

'I'm honestly telling you the truth. I didn't have to, but I feel like I owe it to you to tell you.'

'So, you're saying you were pretending the whole time? I saw you hold hands. I saw you laugh together. I saw the way you looked at her. I saw how terrified you were when you returned from the medical centre. I've never seen you that shaken. Not even when your father died.'

'I felt responsible for that, it was my fault.'

Diane shook her head. 'Are you really saying it was all made up?'

'We did become close. We became friends.'

'Oh, there you go.' Diane put her palms on her knees and went to stand, as if that settled it.

'I wanted to see her again, I hoped we would, but we're just too different.'

'Nonsense. Everyone's different. Differences are what make couples work. Look at Gus and I.'

'It's not just that.'

Will looked down but felt his mother's gaze on him. 'I'm sorry for lying.'

Diane made a noise he couldn't interpret. 'Darling, I'm not entirely convinced that you did.'

Will said goodbye to his mother and tried to put the conversation out of his mind. He'd confessed, come clean and if she didn't believe him, well what was he supposed to do? Just get on with his life and try and forget the whole sorry business.

Two days later Will was turning his desk upside down to search for his phone charger. It wasn't plugged into the outlet where it usually was and he couldn't remember if he'd moved it or not.

Ever since Bali he'd been more disorganised than usual. Losing things. Almost forgetting appointments. It was just the break that had done it; his routine was out and it would come back soon.

As would his sleep.

And his appetite.

Since Bali he'd woken at 2:00 a.m. every morning, discombobulated, sweaty, almost panicky. Like he'd forgotten something important. He'd toss and turn for hours, only drifting off to sleep shortly before his alarm. The sleep deprivation was the likely cause of his forgetfulness during the day. And probably the loss of appetite as well. He didn't even feel like swimming any more, even though the days were hotter and the water was getting warmer.

He didn't feel like doing much at all.

Since Bali.

Since Summer.

It was silly; he and Summer didn't belong together so he shouldn't be so tied up about her. Logically they didn't have anything in common. On paper they didn't add up. He shouldn't feel like this. He should be able to sleep; he shouldn't feel like everything he ate tasted of cardboard.

He had enough self-awareness to realise that he wasn't doing great, but what else could he do? He couldn't call Summer; he certainly couldn't ask to see her. If he did, he'd be right back where he was a month ago. Not sleeping at all and yet still not wanting to get out of bed. He had to just let time work its special healing magic and keep putting one foot in front of the other until it did.

Starting with finding the damn phone charger.

He opened the bottom drawer of his desk, not really believing it would be in there. This drawer was simply full of bits and pieces he didn't really need but had never been bothered to throw out.

It wouldn't be in this drawer because he was sure he hadn't even opened this drawer since his desk was carried in here from his old office.

And sure enough, it wasn't. There was a phone charger, but belonging to a phone he hadn't owned in five years. There was a program from a conference he'd been to years ago and for some reason decided to keep, probably because it had sparked an idea that he hadn't pursued.

He pushed the program aside and froze. Beneath it was a business card. He reached for it, not sure what he was seeing, not sure if he was hallucinating, but then slowly, as if remembering a dream later in the day, he knew.

It was a simple business card, with a guitar, an email address, and a name. Summer Bright.

How did that get here? Even as he asked himself the question, he knew the answer. He'd picked it up, that's how. He'd seen a busker in the Bourke Street Mall one day and stopped. Partly because he'd been in a contemplative mood, partly because he'd really liked her sound, her singing. And her looks.

He'd tossed her twenty dollars and picked up one of her cards, intending to look her up and see if he could download her songs.

He'd chuckled when he'd seen her name, Summer Bright.

It suited her. And her songs, which were joyful and upbeat, but still clever and moving.

Yes, he'd vowed he'd try and find her songs because standing out there, in the sunshine, listening to her he'd felt happier and more fulfilled than he had in ages.

He'd practically skipped back upstairs, only to walk back into some crisis or another that had needed his immediate attention. The card had ended up in his bottom drawer and he hadn't thought of her again.

Except he had.

When his mother had asked the name of his fake girlfriend he'd said her name was Summer Bright.

And not because of the weather or the sun or anything else, but because her name was still lurking in his subconscious, waiting patiently for him to remember that she was there.

That she existed.

* * *

No matter how many times Summer looked down into her guitar case, she still couldn't believe it. It was filled with money. And not just loose silver change but notes. Of all colours. Not to mention all the people who had tapped on her QR code to give payments of five dollars. The code sat on the new stand, next to her business cards and next to a photo of Nina Sparrow, who last week had contacted her asking if Summer would help write her new album.

Nina Sparrow was probably the biggest pop star in the country right now. She'd recently broken through into the American market, increasing her fame to stratospheric levels.

A few weeks ago, Summer had uploaded one of her new songs to social media. The one she had written about Will. The exercise had really been one to prove to herself that she had her guitar back, but the song had managed to catch people's attention and once it caught on it was like a runaway truck. So many people had listened to it. Including Nina Sparrow.

Nina's unique blend of folk and pop was a perfect fit for Summer's style. She'd asked if she could record the song, and whether Summer would help her write a few more for her upcoming release.

Summer had given her a cautious yes.

After so many years of setbacks, disappointments and near misses, this was, she knew, it. She wouldn't make the same mistakes she'd made last time; she'd already engaged a lawyer to look over the contract Nina was offering.

She'd thought about contacting Will. The deal with Nina was noteworthy enough that she considered letting him know so she could thank him and let him know that if it were not for the money she'd made she wouldn't have done it.

But she'd never hit Send on the message. Because it wasn't

just the guitar that he'd contributed to her new success, it was the song itself.

The song she'd written about him.

Thanks for breaking my heart. I wrote a great song because of it.

No.

If he heard the song, maybe he'd think of her. Maybe he'd never even know that she wrote it and that was for the best. She didn't really want him knowing. She didn't want him to think that he had anything to feel sorry for.

The crowd before her wasn't moving. It was after five and people should be heading home. Or to the beach, to make the most of the warmer weather. But a patient and persistent group of people were waiting for her to sing The Song. The one she almost hadn't uploaded. The one that, against all expectations and odds had gone viral. The song that would signal the turning point in Summer's life.

The problem was she didn't yet trust herself to sing it without tearing up. It had been hard enough to sing it for the recording she'd posted. Yesterday, on this same spot, she'd pretty much fallen to pieces. But she had to try.

Besides, this was the song that would launch her career; she'd have to listen to Nina singing it and then hopefully, hear it being played on radio stations around the world. She had to make herself immune to the emotions and memories it evoked.

It was getting late and she needed to get home to her mother. It was now or never. She could sing it. She had to. She also had to live the rest of her live without Will—what was one silly song?

She drew a deep breath and said, 'I think this is the one you've all been waiting for.' And she strummed the opening.

You can do this. You can do this.

It was the mantra she told herself every morning when her alarm went off, always way too early.

You made the right decision.

Then she sang the opening words. *'It just wasn't meant to be...'*

Saying goodbye to Will had hurt more than the woman who had first sung to him dressed up as one quarter of ABBA could have ever imagined. More than the woman who had signed the contract across his back could ever have believed.

'It wasn't you...it wasn't me...'

Will had broken her heart, but he'd also given her so much. He'd inspired her hit song, but he'd given her the confidence and the nous to make sure that this time she wasn't cheated out of her rightful dues.

'I had to let you go...'

Summer reached the bridge and the key change and she saw him. Her voice cracked on the next note and she had to turn away. When she reached the end of the next chorus she looked back in his direction, hoping he'd be gone. Or maybe he hadn't been there at all. Just a figment of her emotions.

But he was still there and held her gaze with his.

He'd heard her song and no doubt knew it was about him. The lyrics *'We faked it until we made it'* alone would've given it away. She contemplated going over to him and telling him it was about another fake relationship she'd had recently, but that would be too ridiculous, even for her.

'Thank you all very much for listening, have a great night,' she said as soon as she'd strummed the final note.

There was applause and also a few calls for 'encore' but she shook her head and placed her guitar in its case. The crowd gradually dispersed, many of them tapping on her QR code as they went. She busied herself packing up, not daring to look in his direction, but conscious he was still standing there.

'Nice rig,' he said. 'The guitar sounds great.'

She forced herself to look at him and smile. She had to be brave. 'Thanks very much to you.'

'The song is great.'

'Thanks.'

Oh, no. He knew the song was about him and he was going to say something. Her heart wasn't just broken, it was ripped from her chest and smeared all over the song for all the world to see.

'No one knows the song is…that is.' She lowered her voice, 'It isn't *just* about you.'

Will's face reddened, but he stayed standing there, looking at her, shifting his weight from foot to foot.

She thought the worst thing had been walking away from him, but in terms of embarrassment and mortification, *this* was by far the worst. Standing before him right now, knowing that he knew how much he'd hurt her. And that the world knew too. He was wearing the full catastrophe, suit, business shirt and jacket, even in the heat. His outfit helped. A little. It put a bit of distance between them, this was business Will. Not shorts and T-shirt Will. Not naked by the pool Will.

That was the Will she missed most of all.

What was the etiquette in this situation? Hands-down there was not a greeting card that had a pre-prepared message for this moment. 'I'm sorry the song I wrote about our brief affair is now viral on social media. And I'm sorry it's going to be played everywhere in the world once Nina Sparrow, one of the biggest artists in the world, records her version.'

She had to leave, get home. Most of all, she had to leave Will behind, once and for all. But he wasn't moving. He was waiting for something.

'What are you doing here?' she asked.

He held up her business card. One of the ones that now sat on the stand next to her Square.

Summer Bright
Singer, songwriter, performer

There was an image of a guitar and her social media handle.
'You came to get one of my cards? You have my details.'
'No, I didn't just pick it up. I came to show it to you.'
'I don't understand. Where did you get it?'
'I found it in my desk drawer.'
'I didn't put it there.'
He smiled. 'No, you didn't. I did. Two years ago, when I first saw you busking on this corner. I've walked past you many times.'
'I still don't understand,' she said.
'I didn't make you up, Summer Bright. I *remembered* you. You were in my subconscious. Waiting there all along. When my mother asked who I was seeing, I didn't pull the name from nowhere, I was remembering you.'
'On purpose?' She still didn't understand what he was saying. Or even why he was here.
'No, because I was too silly. I saw you busking. I liked you. I picked up your card, so I could remember you, look up your songs. But I put it away and forgot about it. Except I didn't really.'
Summer let this all sink in. It was sweet. And bizarre. But it didn't change anything between them.
He worked in the sky; she worked on the ground.
'I know you have a lot to lose, but I do too. You have my heart, Summer Bright. I don't give that away easily, but you have mine and you'll have it for ever. Please be kind to it.'
'What about my heart?' Summer didn't know where those words had come from or how she'd let down her guard enough to say them.
'I will hold your heart, cherish it, protect it and love it, for ever.'

Relief, joy, rushed through her. Could it work? Could *they* work?

We'll fake it until we make it...

He'd collected her card years ago and held on to it. Because he'd wanted to know more about her. He hadn't chosen her name because he thought it was ridiculous, he'd plucked it from his subconscious because he'd remembered her. Remembered enough about her to wonder if she would be a good girlfriend for him.

He was right.

She was good for him.

She looked at him now more closely. Past the suit. His face was drawn, with dark circles growing under his eyes. He wasn't wearing a tie. His hair wasn't combed. He looked real.

And she wanted him. She'd always wanted him since she'd noticed him in the crowd that night from the stage.

He was beautiful. And he was hers.

She rushed to him, threw her arms around him and he caught her. Strong and sure. Her Will.

He pulled her tight and she pressed her face into his chest, breathing him in with deep breaths to catch her own breath but also to prove to herself that he was here, with her. Holding her. Loving her. She never wanted to let him go.

Will eased her face away and looked her in the eyes. 'I love you, Summer. I don't want to be apart from you again. I know there are things we need to figure out, I know—'

'I love you too.'

Will's expression broke into the most beautiful smile she'd ever seen, gooey and warm. And so Will.

He leant down again and pressed his lips tenderly to hers, sealing their declarations. But as soon as they both understood, she pulled him tighter, her insides curling with need and a months' worth of pent-up longing. Will pulled her tight and fell easily into the kiss. She was vaguely aware that they were standing on a busy street corner in peak hour but she didn't care. The only important thing in the world right now was Will.

A wolf whistle intruded into their bubble and they pulled back, panting.

Will said, 'I know there are things to work through, but I also know we can work things out.'

'Of course, you're an expert planner. But please, no spread-sheets this time.'

His brow furrowed, 'Really?' then his expression broke into a grin. 'If you insist.'

'I was scared,' she confessed.

'I was too. You need to know that I might be successful but I can still be stupid sometimes.'

'You weren't stupid. I just didn't see how someone like you could be with someone like me.'

Serious, Will held her back at a distance and said, 'I think you're perfect the way you are.'

'I think you're perfect too.'

The peak hour crowd swirled around them.

'I think it might be time to go somewhere a little more private.'

'I'd like that.'

Will helped her pack away her guitar and rig, but when his eyes landed on the photo of Nina Sparrow he asked, 'Why have you got this here?'

Summer told him about the song and the offer. 'And I've got someone to look over it this time.'

Will beamed. 'I'm so happy for you. Not for getting some-one to check the contract, but for the deal. It's so fantastic. I'm sorry I didn't know before this.' He looked down. 'Hon-estly, I've had to stop myself from checking what you've been up to.'

She picked up his hand. 'I understand. I've been doing

the same thing. But you should know, the song, I wrote it about you.'

'So, the world knows what a fool I am?'

Summer laughed. 'No, they know that we were both afraid, but...'

'Yes?'

'In the next song they'll know that we're madly in love.'

'And that we will figure out how to make our lives fit together.'

'And that we're learning how to be brave.'

He kissed her again.

EPILOGUE

'IT'S SO BIG,' Summer said as she threw her arms wide and looked around again at the magnificent room, all the more special for the view of the ocean it offered. 'Do we really need this much space?'

'I think we do.'

Summer had been spending most of her time at Will's spacious penthouse apartment, which was several orders of magnitude larger than her flat, but he was insisting they needed their own place.

It was true, she did still think of Will's apartment as his, even though she spent more nights there than not. It was nice that he wanted a place that was theirs.

Still. This place was massive.

'I think we do this,' he said. 'It's a good price, and a great spot.'

The beach was barely a minute away and that was good for Will. He loved surfing, loved being in the water and she loved joining him there. Anything that got Will out of his suit and into the fresh air was a plus as far as Summer was concerned.

But this place was more than she'd ever dreamt of.

The three-storey house had its original Victorian facade, and pretty balconies that took full advantage of the views across the beach and to the ocean. Behind the facade, it had been completely remodelled, though renovated sympathetic to the style, with high ceilings, classic mouldings. Traditional, but with modern touches, managing to be expansive, yet still homey and comfortable. The laundry was bigger than her old bedroom. It had more rooms than she could count.

I'm going to get lost, she thought.

'And those extra rooms in the garden, I thought that would be perfect for a recording studio.'

'What?'

'You heard me. A recording studio. For you. And, you know, in case Nina Sparrow drops by.'

Summer laughed. She'd gone to Melbourne twice to work with Nina in the past twelve months and Nina kept telling Summer she'd visit Adelaide soon. Summer had no doubt they would meet up, but have Nina visit her?

To a house like this, that would be an invitation Summer would be happy to extend.

'And now you're making so much money, it's a tax deduction.'

She smiled. He was still thinking about numbers, but that wasn't, she knew now, such a bad thing. He had helped her put aside and invest her earnings from her first contract with Nina and subsequent ones with two other artists. Summer was in demand as a songwriter, and for the first time in her life she had a steady stream of not insignificant income flowing in. The first thing on her list of things to buy was an apartment for her mother, but she wanted it to be close to wherever she and Will ended up.

'And just over the road, there's a new apartment complex.'

It was as though he'd read her mind.

'Most have sold, but there's a very nice, fully accessible one still for sale.'

'You don't think that's too close?'

'I've told you, I'd be happy for her to move in with us. It's you who has the issue with that.'

Summer loved her mother and did want to be close, but

even Penny thought that living with them was a step too far. But living up the street? That could be perfect.

'Yes, you've twisted my arm.'

'Oh, have I?' Will took her hand and then spun her, pulling her towards him and into his embrace. 'You think you can manage to live here?'

'You know I can—you know it's wonderful.'

'Summer, you need to realise you belong here. You belong with me. I can't live without you. I don't want to live without you and I want to live here with you.'

It wasn't just Nina Sparrow she would be able to welcome here, but her mother, Diane, and Gus and hopefully Ben and Charlotte.

And anyone else who happened to come into their lives. They would make this their home.

* * * * *

*If you missed the previous story in
the Invitation from Bali duet,
then check out*

Breaking the Best Friend Rule

*And if you enjoyed this story,
check out these other great reads
from Justine Lewis*

Beauty and the Playboy Prince
Back in the Greek Tycoon's World
Fiji Escape with Her Boss

All available now!

COMING SOON!

We really hope you enjoyed reading this book.
If you're looking for more romance
be sure to head to the shops when
new books are available on

Thursday 15th
August

To see which titles are coming soon, please visit
millsandboon.co.uk/nextmonth

MILLS & BOON

MILLS & BOON®

Coming next month

CINDERELLA'S ADVENTURE WITH THE CEO
Suzanne Merchant

The pressure of his hands on hers as they guided Sundance through the narrow channel between the headlands felt sure and solid.

She turned her head, looked up at him, and smiled, loving the way his eyes crinkled at the corners, the way the corners of his mouth lifted, as he smiled back.

The water in the cove was quiet and calm, the low sun sending golden shafts of light across the aquamarine sea. Jensen cut the engine so that the only sound was the lap of the ripples against the hull and then the splash of the anchor.

Beth didn't want to move. She wanted to hold onto this moment for as long as possible, the warmth of Jensen's body pressed against the length of her back and thighs, the feel of his steady breath brushing against her cheek. He lifted her hands from the wheel, folding them in his. Her breathing became shallow, her heartbeat loud in her ears.

Continue reading
CINDERELLA'S ADVENTURE WITH THE CEO
Suzanne Merchant

Available next month
millsandboon.co.uk

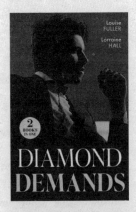

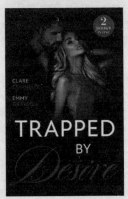

afterglow BOOKS

Afterglow Books is a trend-led, trope-filled list of books with diverse, authentic and relatable characters, a wide array of voices and representations, plus real world trials and tribulations. Featuring all the tropes you could possibly want (think small-town settings, fake relationships, grumpy vs sunshine, enemies to lovers) and all with a generous dose of spice in every story.

♪ @millsandboonuk
⊙ @millsandboonuk
afterglowbooks.co.uk

#AfterglowBooks

For all the latest book news, exclusive content and giveaways scan the QR code below to sign up to the Afterglow newsletter:

SCAN ME

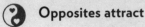

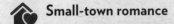
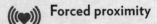
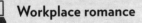

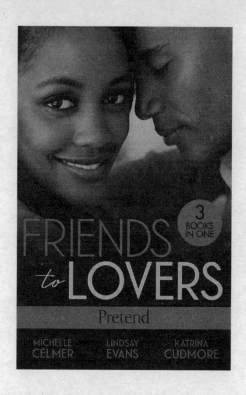